For
David Lynch —
With Esteem
And Personal Best Wishes —

[signature]

MANSE
One Man's War

MANSON SHERRILL JOLLY
Daguerreotype Circa 1863.
Restoration 1996 © Wilton Earle Hall

MANSE
One Man's War

A Novel
By
WILTON EARLE

Based On The Life And Legend
Of Manson Sherrill Jolly

ADEPT
Atlanta

MANSE
One Man's War
COPYRIGHT © 1996 BY WILTON EARLE HALL

ALL RIGHTS RESERVED
UNDER INTERNATIONAL AND PAN AMERICAN COPYRIGHT CONVENTIONS

NO PART OF THIS BOOK MAY BE USED OR REPRODUCED OR PUBLISHED IN ANY MANNER WHATSOEVER, OR TRANSMITTED, RECORDED OR STORED IN A RETRIEVAL SYSTEM IN ANY FORM, DIGITAL OR ANALOG BY ANY MEANS, MECHANICAL, ELECTRONIC, PHOTOCOPYING OR OTHERWISE, WITHOUT THE PRIOR WRITTEN PERMISSION OF THE COPYRIGHT OWNER:
WILTON EARLE HALL
P.O. BOX 176 STARR SC 29684, USA
TELEPHONE: (864) 352-2757   FAX: (864) 352-2643

LITERARY REPRESENTATION BY
ALBERT S. ZUCKERMAN, 21 WEST 26TH STREET, NEW YORK NY 10010
TELEPHONE (212) 685-2400. FAX (212) 685-2631

CERTAIN FICTIONAL CHARACTERS AND EVENTS DEPICTED IN "MANSE" PREVIOUSLY APPEARED IN "MANSE JOLLY" © 1973 BY 'GARET W. EARLE' A PSEUDONYM OF WILTON EARLE HALL DULY REGISTERED IN THE UNITED STATES COPYRIGHT OFFICE AND THE LIBRARY OF CONGRESS

LIBRARY OF CONGRESS CATALOG CARD NUMBER: 96-83128

ISBN 0-9632422-2-9

FOR INFORMATION ABOUT THIS AND OTHER BOOKS FROM ADEPT, CONTACT
ADEPT DISTRIBUTION CENTER
P.O. BOX 967 HARTWELL GA 30643
TELEPHONE (706) 376-5774.

MANUFACTURED IN THE UNITED STATES OF AMERICA

For Bill and Perry

- 1 -

Rain soaked his hair and beard and tunic – and slowly returned him to consciousness. And with awareness of the wet and cold came pain that throbbed from his head to his groin. His body was a single agony, as if everything inside had been torn loose and rearranged.

He searched for wounds and broken bones but found only bruises and scrapes – and a knot above his right temple – and blood on the tip of his finger when he probed his nostrils and ears.

He recognized the signs – artillery concussion.

Then suddenly the stench of rotting bodies overwhelmed him.

Struggling against both nausea and pain, Manse Jolly sat up and looked down the hill toward the river – and, after a few moments of uncertainty, recognized the terrain and began to remember how he got here.

His squad of scouts, assigned to The Army of Tennessee, had fought and secured this little piece of Southern Virginia at least six times, only to lose it yet again. But the Colonel had ordered them to try once more to find a fording point high enough in the mountains for the cavalry and its support infantry to cross undetected and attack the rear of the Union encampment six miles on the other side.

Manse and Tom – *where the hell was Tom?* – had scouted the area and found shallows at the base of this steep incline that ran down from a ridge trail to rocky shoals. The Colonel had approved, and they crossed at dawn. He and Tom took point. Four other scouts rode fifty yards behind them. The main force, one platoon of cavalry and a company of infantry, waited on the ridge a mile away for the signal to follow.

They had dismounted at the incline and led their horses.

He remembered the sound of small stones clicking beneath his horse's hooves.

Then there was only silence.

He should have sensed the enemy watching.

Artillery muzzle reports were his only warning, and their sound reached him too late. Explosions uprooted trees, lifted his horse, jerked the reins from his hand, and catapulted him through the air.

His head struck something, or something struck his head, and intense pain was followed by instant darkness.

He didn't know how long he had been lying there. His horse was only a few yards away, its entrails covered with green flies. From its bloat he guessed two days.

He tried to stand, slipped, steadied himself, stood, and looked around for Tom. They had maintained dual-point distance, about fifty yards apart. Tom's field of vision covered point-right; his, point-left. The incoming shell had exploded between them.

He saw Tom's mount – half-submerged in a shell crater – but Tom was not there.

The rain eased to a drizzle. March wind grew stronger; mountain air, colder. He returned to his horse and untied the blanket roll, supply bag and oilskin from behind the saddle. He put on the oilskin and shoved the blanket into the bag. His rifle was not in its sling, and he remembered that he had been carrying it, so it was probably buried in the mud. He looked down. His sidearms were holstered. And the broken saber he had honed to razor sharpness for close-quarters combat was still in its scabbard.

He found his cavalry hat five yards away.

He slung the supply bag over his shoulder and began the search for his squad.

In one spot he found the mangled flesh of two men and two horses, and one salvageable revolver. Nearby, he found the bodies of two others, their eyes staring, their sidearms and rifles intact. Their packs held the squad's extra ammunition. He put as many rounds as he could carry into his supply sack. One out of every three they had received during the past year was a misfire – problem was, you never knew which one.

He took their canteens. Scouts carried two – one filled with water, the other with clear corn whiskey. He uncapped a canteen of *white-water* – took a long drink and looked at the bodies. The thought of burying them crossed his mind and was dismissed.

During the first two years of The War, every company had a burial detail and a wagon of lumber to make coffins, and a preacher-soldier to read the Bible. By the beginning of the third year, they were stuffing more than one in a box. Soon after that they were dumping them in graves without boxes or sermons.

During the past few months they hadn't even attempted to bury the dead. Instead, they dispatched a rider to the nearest church, to report where the battle had been fought, and where the dead and wounded lay – with the hope that someone might come to tend and bury. But they didn't wait to find out – the risks of renewed battle, death or capture, were too great.

In the end there was only the Company Clerk's record of the dead, the wounded and the missing – nothing more.

He looked at their faces and said their names aloud. He was their sergeant, but repeating their names was all the burial ritual he could muster.

He pushed their images into that corner of his mind reserved for all the men he had known and cared about and watched die – and all the men he had killed just because they wore a different color uniform – and all the bits and pieces of bodies of men and women and children he had seen in towns blown apart by misdirected artillery barrages.

He compressed feelings in that already crowded recess, and resealed the opening.

Then he sensed the danger behind him.

His hand went to his sidearm as he turned.

"Leave them men alone," Tom Largent was leaning against a tree, his rifle at hip-level.

"Tom? God, man, I thought you were dead."

"Not yet, Manse – not yet – " Tom dropped the rifle, tried to hold onto the tree, and slid to the ground.

Manse ran to him, helped him sit up, gave him a swallow of whiskey, then looked at his right leg. It was crushed from knee to ankle, bone protruding, flesh and muscle exposed, black and green and rotting.

Manse reached inside his tunic and took out the gray scarf his mother had given him the last time he was home – the scarf Rebecca had sewed his initials on. He soaked it with whiskey and wrapped it around Tom's leg. He had protected that scarf through years of hell like it was some kind of religious relic, and now he knew that binding Tom's leg with it was the way his mama would want him to use it.

He could hear her voice in the wind, *Manson, you and Tom take care of each other, and both come home safe, you hear?*

He smiled. She was the only one other than Rebecca who called him *Manson*. That was his name, Manson Sherrill Jolly, but everyone, even his daddy and brothers and Tom, who was his best friend, called him *Manse*. But his mama insisted that a "manse" was a kind of house a preacher lived in, and her son's name was *Manson*. And he held tight to what his mama said, not because what she called him was all that important, but because her words reminded him that despite everything evil and godforsaken he had seen and felt and smelled in this war, he still had a family and a real life waiting for him.

He picked maggots from Tom's leg.

"Let 'em be, Manse. They only eat dead meat. That's how I can tell how far up the rot has come."

Manse looked at the wound and recalled the men he'd seen die from gangrene. He felt Tom's forehead. Infection's fever was high.

This time tomorrow, Tom would be dead.

"Got to get you to a doctor," Manse said, and handed Tom a canteen.

Tom took a long drink.

"Don't this beat all?" he said. "Yankee bullets miss me for might near four years, then my horse gets blowed down and smashes my leg against a rock. I reckon my daddy would call that a straight-up-pisser. Remember how him and your daddy always called bad luck a straight-up-pisser?"

"Yeah, I remember," Manse walked to the corpses of the scouts, removed their belts and braces, picked up two rifles, carried them to Tom, and splinted them to his leg.

"You rest here," Manse said. "I'm going up the trail and try to find us a horse or two."

"No horses there. I heard the battle. Went on for near two hours. That's why I dragged myself behind those trees and hid. I thought sure the Yankees would come here, but they didn't. Reckon they figured we'd all been blown to shit by the artillery, so there wouldn't be much here worth the picking. And there weren't much, were there?"

"Not much," Manse drank from his canteen. "How long ago was the battle?" he asked. "How long was I lying over there?"

"Nearabout two days," Tom said. "I thought you were dead. You didn't move. And I couldn't get to you. I kept passing out. And when I come-to this last time, I didn't expect to see you walking around. That's why I almost shot you – I thought you were a looter."

The intense throbbing in Manse's head made thinking difficult, but he knew he couldn't wait for the pain to pass.

"We've got to walk to that crossroads settlement and find somebody to take care of your leg," he said, and helped Tom to his feet.

"Chop it off is more like it," Tom said.

"That might be," Manse put his arm around Tom's waist to support him. "You just hold tight. We'll make it."

For an hour they hobbled and stumbled up the incline and along the ridge trail before they came to the spot where their unit had met the Union forces in a nameless skirmish. Manse counted sixteen Confederate corpses. Obviously most of his comrades had either fled or been captured. He mumbled a curse – Damned-Yankees. They always buried their dead, but stripped Confederate corpses of everything of value, then left them for the buzzards. None of the bodies wore boots. The Confederate Banner and Company Standard were gone, along with the tunic of the Company Commander.

Past sunset, into moonlight, they continued walking along the trail. Manse stopped repeatedly to listen for the sounds of men and horses, but heard none. The trek was hard, and the fatigue that wracked his body reminded him once again that, since he *had* to fight in this bloody war for four years, he was blessed to have done so on horseback rather than in the Infantry.

It was almost midnight when they came to a farmhouse.

Manse placated two dogs with his last strip of dried beef, then pounded on the backdoor until a farmer – lantern in one hand, pistol in the other – opened it.

"My friend needs a doctor bad," Manse said.

"No doctor around here," the farmer said. "If you live in these mountains, you do for yourself."

"Even amputating?" Manse's question was a plea.

The man hesitated. "I've done some in my years," he opened the door wider. "Bring your friend inside."

They lay Tom on the kitchen table. Manse plied him with whiskey while the farmer examined his leg. Then he left the room, and in a few minutes returned with his wife and two teen-age boys. Sleepily they followed their father's orders and produced two lengths of rope, a skinning knife, a rasp and a hatchet.

The woman tied her hair into a bun, then stirred coals in the stove and heated the knife blade and rasp until they glowed.

The boys bound Tom's arms, legs and torso to the table.

Manse held his head.

The farmer slipped the shorter rope around Tom's thigh and tightened it.

Then the knife sliced flesh.

Tom tried to say something - or scream – but passed out instead.

With the sure hand of a butcher, the farmer stripped meat from bone, laid aside the knife, raised the hatchet and severed the thighbone a few inches above the knee.

Tom's body jerked – his leg rolled off the table.

The farmer's wife used the white-hot rasp to cauterize the stump.

The kitchen filled with smells of frying flesh.

Manse picked up Tom's leg and walked outside. He removed the boot, used his saber-knife to scrape out bone and flesh, and threw the pieces to the dogs. Even a wooden leg needed a boot, and boots were the scarcest item in the Confederate Army.

He went back into the kitchen, put the boot in his supply sack, and thanked the two boys who stumbled sleepily back to bed.

The wife gave Manse a length of muslin, a bar of lye soap and a tin of liniment – "to keep the stump clean, and soft, so's it don't split while it's healing," she explained.

"You best go before first light," the farmer said. "Yankee patrols come by here most every day." He drank from a jug of whiskey, and passed it to Manse.

"Sorry I can't pay you. We got no money." Manse drank and felt the alcohol burn his stomach and ease his head.

"Didn't expect no pay. Didn't do it for pay," the farmer said as he wrapped Tom's stump. Then he took Manse's canteens and filled them from the whiskey jug while his wife went to the sideboard and removed tins and jars and put them in two feed sacks.

"Ain't much food," she said, "but we're pleased to share what we got."

"I thank you," Manse said. "But there is one thing more I need to ask – you got any idea where we can hide while Tom heals?"

The man thought, took another drink, then said, "There's a farm about six miles due west of here. It was burned out early in The War. The folks left. But there's ruins. And a good well. And woods. And a wide creek a bit farther on. You ought to be safe there – long as you keep on your guard."

Manse picked up one of the sacks, felt its weight, and, with effort, slung it over his shoulder, then reached for the other one.

"Hold on there," the farmer said. "You plain ain't got the strength to tote all that and your friend, too. When did you eat last, anyhow?"

Manse shook his head.

"I don't rightly remember," he said.

"Then you set down and eat something right now," the farmer's wife said, and opened the food-safe and took out bowls of left-overs and put them on the table.

"While you're eating," the farmer said, "I'll go hitch up the wagon. We got one mule – so spavined not even the Rebs or Yankees figured she was worth stealing. My older boy will drive you to that farm."

Manse was too tired to argue, but not too tired to eat cold squirrel, greens, yams and dark-bread.

After he ate, he thanked the farmer and his wife several more times, then picked up Tom and carried him to the wagon, laid him in the back, and climbed in beside him and cradled his head to lessen the jolts of the six mile trip.

The sun was rising when they arrived at the burned-out ruins of a large home.

Manse put Tom down behind some thick brush at the edge of the woods, then thanked the farmer's son again for getting out of bed and driving them here. The boy nodded sleepily and headed the mule toward home. Manse watched as the wagon moved out of sight. With a little luck, he thought, maybe The War would be over before that boy had to go get himself killed.

Manse chose a spot close to the creek and used the oilskins salvaged from his squad to make a lean-to, dug a fire-pit and hung supply sacks from a limb, then carried Tom to the shelter, laid him on a poncho and covered him with a blanket.

When Tom roused and tried to smile through pain, Manse gave him more whiskey, and he slept again.

Manse built a fire, and every few hours he washed Tom's stump and changed the muslin.

The well was their salvation. Tom sweated and drank a lot.

After three days, his fever broke.

When they had eaten all the food the farmer had given them, Manse set rabbit gums and coon snares – and laid fish lines made from muslin threads and split thorns, baited with pine-bark-worms – skills he had learned as a boy hunting, trapping and fishing with his brothers. He foraged, dug tubers and picked greens that he knew were edible – skills he had learned when he was older and needed them in order to survive four years of war.

Tom's leg healed slowly. Manse made a pair of crutches for him, then carved an oak limb into some semblance of a leg and foot, and polished it with rock and sand, nailed the boot to it, and fashioned belts and braces into a harness.

The first time Tom tried it on, he cried out in pain. The stump festered. They waited until it healed, then he tried again. And again it festered. But the scar tissue thickened with each wearing, and he could tolerate it a little longer.

During long days and longer nights, their conversations, as well as the silences between them, were as easy and natural as the shared friendship that had begun when they were small boys.

They had lived all their lives on adjoining farms in the Lebanon section of Anderson County, in northwest South Carolina, a few miles east of Georgia, a few miles south of North Carolina – in the Piedmont, where rolling hills climbed toward Blue Ridge mountain peaks. Growing up, they had spent a lot of time tracking and hunting with their fathers, and later with Manse's six brothers.

Tom Largent's daddy and Manse Jolly's daddy were best friends. Tom's mama had died when his younger sister, Rebecca, was born, and since then, which was almost as long as Manse could remember, their folks had lived more as if they were kin, instead of just neighbors.

Without question, Manse and Tom's families acknowledged their position in the social and economic structure of the South. The Jollys and Largents were *Small Planters* – several rungs below the *Southrons* who owned vast plantations and counted their acres and slaves by the hundreds and thousands – but their position was equally far above the *Crackers* who owned small patches of land and barely eked out an existence, but were still above the *Low-Downers* who owned nothing and worked as plantation overseers and paid hands, but even then remained a step above *White Trash*, who were above only the slaves.

Small Planters like the Jollys and Largents owned two to four hundred acres of land, had few if any slaves, lived well from their own toil, and shared with the Southrons strong belief in honor, loyalty, integrity – and other remnants of chivalry.

The only shedding of blood Manse or Tom had experienced before they went off to The War was the killing of deer and small game, and the butchering of livestock.

Then, in December of 1861, Manse's older brothers joined the Second SC Rifles. And Manse and Tom enlisted in the First SC Cavalry, where they were assigned to duty as scouts. For six months, they fought in small skirmishes in the southern sector of South Carolina.

Then the First SC Cavalry became an integral part of the Confederate push north that began with Stuart's Raids into Maryland and Pennsylvania in October 1862. For almost three years their unit fought back and forth, up and down and across Virginia – sometimes winning, sometimes losing. During 1864, mostly losing.

That year – last year – the Confederate cause had quickly gone from bad to worse to worst, beginning with General Hood's defeat and the death of seven thousand Southern soldiers at Franklin, Tennessee. Shortly afterwards, General Sheridan had driven the

Confederate forces out of the Shenandoah. And now Grant's Army, 125,000 strong, was laying siege to General Lee's battered 20,000 men at Petersburg.

The primary contingent of the First SC Cavalry had been ordered to the Carolinas to fight defensive actions. But Tom and Manse and their squad of scouts were attached to the decimated Volunteer Army of Tennessee and continued to fight in Virginia. Manse later learned that eventually his unit surrendered in North Carolina – but by then he and Tom had been left – presumed dead – in the Virginia mountains.

While Tom's leg healed, they talked a lot about family and friends and remember-whens but avoided discussing The War, even when one or the other of them awoke screaming in the night and had to be held until a nightmare passed.

On one such night, Tom asked Manse, "You think we're ever going to be able to forget all we been through?"

"I'm damn sure going to try," Manse said.

"You reckon we can take up where we left off before The War?"

"It won't be easy. And it'll take time. But I figure that somehow, we can," Manse said. "Getting things back to the way they use to be is something I spent a lot of time dreaming about during The War. Things like bringing in a new crop. Eating vegetables fresh from the garden. Sitting on the porch at dusk. Quiet, easy things." Manse rubbed his right temple and felt the throbbing ease. "I've had about all the excitement I ever want. Right now, peace and quiet sound real good to me."

"You leaving out something important," Tom smiled. "How about sitting on that porch with a pretty wife and some kids?"

"Some parts of my dreaming ain't no business of yours," Manse grinned.

"Well, if your dream includes my sister, Rebecca, you best remember that you got to ask my daddy's permission for her hand," Tom smiled. "And when I tell him what you're *really* like, you won't stand a chance of getting him to say yes."

Both men broke into laughter – laughter they hadn't shared for a long time.

And learning to laugh again made the days and nights easier.

Until they ran out of whiskey.

Manse decided that returning to the farmer's house to replenish their supply was worth the risk. Alone, on foot, he covered the distance in less than two hours. The farmer was more than generous, giving Manse six jugs thonged together so he could carry them across his shoulders. And giving him the latest reports on The War. The South was reeling, he said, but contingents of well-supplied infantry volunteers from Texas, supported by cavalry and artillery units – were rumored to be on their way to Georgia, Tennessee, and South Carolina. *If* the rumors were true, the tide of war might once again turn.

Manse carried the news and the jugs of whiskey back to Tom and their routine of waiting and surviving continued.

In mid-May, the rains of spring gave way to sun and warmth, and they decided they had spent too many months in the same clothes, with the same lice. They stripped and bathed in the creek, scrubbed themselves almost raw with lye soap, trimmed each other's hair, pounded clothes on rocks, and rubbed their bodies with lamp oil and liniment to kill anything left alive in hair or crevices.

And from beneath winter's dirt, two men emerged –

Thomas Jackson Largent. Lean and muscular. His hair sandy-brown, almost blonde. With his smooth skin and clear blue eyes, he looked younger than his twenty-nine years.

And Manson Sherrill Jolly. Thick-shouldered and tall. His face was an oval beneath hair that was auburn, like his mama's. He had an almost silky moustache and a thin beard that followed the contour of his jaw from temples to chin. His eyes were brown with flecks of green, set deep above high cheek bones and full lips. He looked older than his twenty-four years. Older even than Tom.

They lay naked beneath the healing sun on the bank of the creek until mid-afternoon while their clothes dried. Then they dressed.

Manse wrapped Tom's stump with muslin and helped him into the harness. It was time to check the fish lines and snares to see what was on their dinner menu.

They were within a few feet of the lean-to when they heard someone near the ruins of the house. The sound brought them down, flat on their bellies, and they crawled toward the voices.

A horse-and-buggy were at the well-trough. A young boy and an old woman were standing by it.

The boy was drawing water. The old woman was complaining about the heat and flies.

Manse and Tom stood and walked toward them.

The boy made a dash for the buggy and pulled a musket from beneath the seat.

"What you all want?" He pointed the weapon at them. It was almost as big as he was.

"Put that gun down, Addie. Can't you see they Rebs?"

The woman pushed the musket aside and nodded to Manse and Tom.

"Good afternoon, boys," she said.

"Afternoon, ma'am," Tom removed his cavalry hat.

"Excuse my grand-boy," she said. "We still tend to be a mite skittish."

"We surely understand," Tom said. "You're fortunate to have a fine lad like that so ready to protect you. We've been nervous ourselves, hiding here from Yankee patrols while waiting for my wounded leg to heal."

"No cause to hide no more," the woman said. "Ain't you heared? The War's been over more'n a month

Manse looked from the woman to Tom and back at the woman.

"It's over?" Manse said. "You sure about that? It's over?"

"That's right, young man. General Lee surrendered the Confederate Army at a place called Appomattox in Virginia."

Manse wasn't sure whether what he felt was joy or sadness or sickness.

They talked politely to the woman and boy, getting as much news as they could from them, then, when they had left, Manse and Tom began packing food and whiskey and bedrolls into supply sacks.

The next day, they started walking south – traveling as far as Tom could go in a day.

A week later they were lucky and got a ride to a rail-head on a wagon-load of scrap-cloth bales. Then they rode atop a freight car as far as the train went – tracks ripped up, un-repaired.

Then they walked again. Slowly south. Always South.

And as spring became summer, each day they drew a few miles closer to the world they had dreamed – and day-dreamed – about for four endless years.

A world they were not sure still existed.

***

The train hadn't been crowded when he boarded it in Washington, and so he had presumed that the coaches reserved for officers – even junior officers – would remain comfortable for the ride south. But at each stop, more spit and polish new second-lieutenants boarded, and by the time they reached Richmond the coach he was in was packed – and hot as hell.

He could hardly breathe. With each mile he became more pissed off – at himself and at the United States Army. He needed a drink. Badly. But he had finished off the bottle of whiskey he carried in his musette bag, and he wouldn't have a chance to buy another until the train stopped at Roanoke for evening mess call – at least five more hours.

He looked at his traveling companions, all going South as part of the Union Army Occupation Forces. Obviously none of them had been in service longer than their twenty-four weeks at Officers School.

Lt. Martin McCollum was the only *First Lieutenant* in the coach. And, by rights, based on his record, he should have been wearing Captain's bars – or a Major's leaf – and sitting in the comfort of the spacious Senior Officers' Coach, where the whiskey was plentiful and free. If his accomplishments had been on the field of battle, no one would have dared deny him the promotions that were his due.

He had been commissioned as a Second Lieutenant in Military Intelligence immediately upon graduation from City College of New York. At the time, he had accepted his commission as a compliment. In retrospect, he now knew that *that* was where his problems began.

He completed Intelligence School at the top of his class and was assigned to the Military Investigations Division of the New England Command in Boston. Within six months he had uncovered a ring of illegal profiteering in strategic materials. Seven Massachusetts political leaders, five supply officers, and eleven non-coms were convicted and sentenced to prison based on evidence he provided. He was promoted to First Lieutenant, received a commendation from Washington and was transferred to Military Intelligence Headquarters in the nation's capital.

Within another few months, he had amassed proof of a plot to assassinate two Cabinet Members – a conspiracy that led to a General and two Colonels who were in the pay of the Confederacy. Their civilian counterparts were arrested, tried and hanged. The General and Colonels were executed by firing squad.

And Martin McCollum expected a swift promotion to Captain.

But it did not come.

Instead, he found himself ostracized by his fellow officers. Word reached him that he was making some big mistakes – and some powerful enemies. He would be better off, he was told, if he took into consideration *whom* he was investigating, and made decisions based on what could be done for him if he cooperated with the political structure within the Army – and what might be done to him, if he failed to do so.

Born and raised in one of the poorest and toughest sections of New York City – having hoisted himself by his own balls and brain from a *cul-de-sac* future to a university scholarship and a position as an-officer-and-a-gentleman in the United States Army – Martin McCollum was damned determined to succeed on the merits of his accomplishments as an Intelligence Officer. He ignored the warnings and embarked on a one man crusade to prove his worth by sending corrupt US Army officers to prison as fast as he could gather evidence against them.

Because of his successful efforts to ferret out corruption and conspiracy within the Army, he was respected by the staffs of both the Secretary of The Army and the Union Army High Command – and resented by everyone in Military Intelligence, including his superior officers.

He had a chest full of commendations – but remained a First Lieutenant.

And drank alone, night after night. A pariah, still damn-determined to prove he was right.

He might have gotten through the remaining three-years of his Army service contract without inflicting further damage to himself, if he hadn't made the mistake of combining his hard-drinking with his hard cock.

When he wanted a woman, Martin McCollum, like his fellow junior officers, went to one of the better class whore-houses on Washington's west side, where the girls (most of them under fifteen) were fairly attractive and certified (as far as the Army doctors were able) to be free of disease.

By choice, he stayed away from wife-hunting at Washington Society dinner-dances – to which he was invited simply because his name was on the list of unmarried Intelligence Officers, all of whom were university graduates and most of whom – except for Martin – were from socially acceptable families.

Then one evening – an evening that would plague him as long as he was in the Army – for some reason he never fathomed, he decided that, by-god, if he was good enough to be invited to their soirees, he should, by-god, attend one of them and see what the hell it was like.

So he put on his dress-uniform, with its row of commendations (which no young Washington woman was likely to know represented Union Officers he had sent to the firing squad or prison, rather than battles fought against Confederate forces) and he went to a dinner dance where he recognized no one and no one, fortunately, recognized him.

And that was where he saw her.

She was beautiful, with a face – eyes and mouth, specifically – that aroused him as no woman ever had. She was not yet, of course, a *woman* – he knew that. She was perhaps sixteen, maybe seventeen. But it did not occur to him to be concerned about her age.

Quickly Martin downed three drinks at the gentlemen's bar, then walked to the ladies' wall, introduced himself, and asked her to dance. (He had taken lessons as part of his educational effort to convince himself that he *was* a gentleman.) Her name was Francine. They danced two turns, and his dark blue eyes seemed to entrap her. When he bowed and thanked her for the dance, she did not retire to the ladies' wall, but rather took his arm and stayed by his side – held onto him – all evening. He was as flattered by her as he was aroused. She asked him about his ribbons and, in response, he fabricated wilderness campaigns and major military battles. She asked about his family, and he fabricated a genealogy of professionally and socially prominent New York attorneys.

Before they parted, she gave him an address and invited him to call for her the following Saturday to accompany her horseback riding.

Martin presumed that implicit in her invitation were all of the rules of social propriety he had read and heard about. He was therefore more than a little confused when he arrived at the address to find himself at the exclusive Rock Creek Park Riding Academy, where she was waiting for him – with a liveried carriage driver – and no chaperone.

They exchanged pleasantries as the closed carriage followed a winding trail to a secluded part of the park where it stopped – and she kissed him – and he kissed her – and seduction began – and progressed apace. She bared her breasts and guided his face into her cleavage – and guided his hand through folds of crinoline to the unbuttoned crotch of her bloomers – and his finger entered her – or attempted to enter her – and he realized – naive as he was – that she was virgin – and warning flares of the ramifications of deflowered maiden heads came quickly to mind.

Martin withdrew his hand from her pubis, his mouth from her breasts, his head from her cleavage, and suggested they return to the stables – or that he have the driver take her home.

Francine exploded with anger at his *rejection* of her – then began to cry.

He consoled her as best he could and, by the time they arrived at the stable, she was calm. He kissed her gently on the lips and told her he would see her at the next dinner-dance, and, perhaps, afterwards he could call on her at her home, properly chaperoned.

He, of course, had no intention of going to the next dance, or calling on her – but he needed a fast exit, and these particular promises seemed the most expedient way out.

Martin spent the rest of that night with a girl the same age, but hardly virgin, at the best whore house he could afford, where he drank heavily and called her Francine each time he entered her – until he passed out.

His hangover was massive. He was thankful that the next day was devoted to solitary paperwork related to an investigation he had just completed.

As he prepared to leave headquarters at day's end, his commanding officer's attaché arrived with orders for Martin to report to the Colonel immediately.

"Just stay at tight attention, McCollum," the Colonel said when he returned Martin's salute. "I have waited a hell of a long time for a reason to ship your ass out of my sight – out of my command – out of Washington. And, now that the opportunity has presented itself, I intend to enjoy every goddamn second of it," he walked around the desk and stood with his face only inches from Martin's. "You've destroyed the careers of more good Army Officers than any man I know," his spittle sprayed Martin. "I am referring especially to my close friend, Colonel Hamilton Rabun. You remember him, don't you, Lieutenant? He's the innocent man you included in your so-called Cabinet-Assassination-Plot." He raised his voice. "He was in no way involved in that – "

"With all due respect, sir," Martin stared straight ahead. "The military tribunal convicted and executed Colonel Rabun – I only provided the evidence that – "

"Goddammit, don't interrupt me, Lieutenant! I didn't give you permission to speak!"

"Yes, sir," Martin flushed anger.

"You are damned good at what you do, McCollum – I'll give you that," the Colonel returned to his chair and sat. "In fact, you have such a damned fine record of destroying military careers, I have never been able to justify to Union Command changing your assignment, or transferring you. You've kept your ass clean and proper. Everything strictly by the book, Lieutenant – up until now," the Colonel smiled at Martin. "But now that ass of yours is mine, McCollum," he held up several pages of paper. "This is a formal complaint from General Matthews' office, charging that you lured the daughter of General Matthews' aide, Captain Frank Thomas – a young girl, Miss Francine Thomas – to Rock Creek Park stables and forced her to submit to aberrant carnal relations with you."

"Sir! I assure you, sir, I did not – " Martin blurted the words.

"You still don't have permission to speak, Lieutenant, so just keep quiet and listen." The Colonel's smile became a wide grin. "The young lady says you forced her to allow you to ejaculate in her mouth – an act that leaves no physical evidence – which I am sure is why you chose it rather than forcible rape."

"Sir – "

"For the last time, McCollum, shut your god-damned-mouth," the Colonel's smile disappeared." One more word and I promise you I will charge you with failure to obey a direct order, for which I can – and will – have you shot – is that clear?"

"Yes, sir," Martin was boiling inside.

The Colonel's grin returned.

"In a sense, Lieutenant, you might say this is your lucky day," he said. "I have decided not to prosecute you. With only the young woman's word against your word, you just might be acquitted, which would be a shame. So I have decided to use this occasion to rid Military Intelligence Headquarters – and myself in particular – of your presence in Washington. I wish I could simply force you to resign – but, as you know, all commissions in Military Intelligence have been extended indefinitely by the Secretary of The Army, because of the large number of investigations underway in the occupied territories of the South. Therefore, as an alternative, I have come up with a very special mission for you – "

The Colonel slammed an envelope on the desk. "These are your orders, Lieutenant. In my opinion, it's the perfect assignment for a man of your proven talents. You leave tomorrow morning by train for Greenville, South Carolina, which I understand is not, for a Southern town, a totally unpleasant place."

Martin McCollum did not relax.

The Colonel broadened his grin. "You will not, however, remain in that relative garden spot, Lieutenant," he said. "You will proceed to a hamlet some thirty miles from Greenville – the village of Anderson, South Carolina, which, to my knowledge, has *nothing* to recommend it." The Colonel picked up a sheet of paper.

"According to this summary, a company strength permanent garrison was established in Anderson at the end of the war by General George Stoneman, following a skirmish between a company under his command and a platoon of Confederate soldiers stationed at the Holding Bank located there. Seems that the general thought there was something strange going on in that little town. But then General Stoneman does have a history of making rather – shall we say *unorthodox* – field decisions," the Colonel put down the paper.

"Union Command has maintained that permanent garrison in Anderson – not out of respect for Stoneman's decision, but rather because the United States Army needed an out-of-the-way post where trouble-makers and incompetents could be assigned – officers and enlisted men who do not exactly fit the military mold, but who have not completed their tours of duty, so are not yet eligible for discharge. I think such an illustrious garrison deserves a Military Intelligence officer of your caliber, Lieutenant McCollum."

He handed the envelope to Martin. "You will conduct an independent investigation – for however long it takes – into those events that General Stoneman found *strange*." He handed Martin a second envelope. "The commander of the Anderson garrison – a Captain Phillips – will provide you with background information for your investigation. This is a directive which you are to deliver to him." The Colonel leaned back in his chair and laughed aloud. "You should fit in very well in Anderson, South Carolina."

Martin stiffened his back. "With the Colonel's permission, sir, I have one question – "

"Spit it out, Lieutenant. Just make it damned brief."

"Perhaps, sir, General Stoneman could provide me with some assistance. If it could be arranged for me to ask him – "

"Major-Generals in the United States Army are not required to answer questions posed by First Lieutenants, " the Colonel waved Martin away. "That's all, Lieutenant. You're dismissed. Forever!"

Martin McCollum cupped his chin in his hand and stared out the grimy window of the train. The pine trees and clay soil seemed to pass by endlessly, interrupted only occasionally when the train slowed to go through yet another small town. No one on the streets paid any attention to the coaches filled with passengers – perhaps because they had seen too many strangers – armies of strangers – passing through their towns during the last four years, and simply didn't want to look at any more.

With the luck he was having, Martin was sure that Anderson, South Carolina, would turn out to be smaller, hotter, dirtier and more hostile than any place this train passed through in Virginia or North Carolina. And god-alone-knew how long he would have to stay there.

Most assignments took a month or two. Considering that this mission had been created for him by superiors who never wanted him to return to Washington, he might just die of old age in Anderson, South Carolina.

Perhaps the pine trees and damn reddish clay soil did go on forever.

***

Where the road crossed a shallow creek, the rider reined in his white stallion and let him drink.

He opened his long duster, reached inside, removed a cigar case from the pocket of his black suit coat, took out a cigar, returned the case to his pocket, bit the end off the cigar, spat it on the ground, put the cigar in his mouth, twirled it in saliva, took out a box of matches, chose one, struck it with his thumbnail and lit the cigar.

When the tip glowed evenly, he drew in a mouthful of smoke, held it, then blew a soft cloud and watched it drift in the still air and dissipate.

Then he looked across the narrow stream, at the tip of a church steeple barely protruding above the tree-line – the only indication that there was a town nearby.

He leaned forward and patted the horse's neck.

"That's got to be it, old boy – " he said aloud.

"Anderson, South Carolina. Opportunity of a lifetime."

He laughed and nudged his mount forward.

-2-

Manse looked across red clay fields and pine forests, and smiled to himself.

Never in his wildest dreams had he ever imagined that he and Tom Largent would arrive in Greenville, South Carolina, riding atop a United States Army troop train. But on that humid August morning, 1865, that was exactly what was happening.

Manse's daddy always did say that Tom could talk the wool off a sheep's back. And if Tom hadn't demonstrated once again his ability to do exactly that, they would have most likely still been walking south – barely half way down the state of North Carolina from Virginia – instead of only thirty-five miles from home.

They had followed the rail lines, riding freight cars through Virginia. But when they crossed into North Carolina, things changed. All trains had been placed under the command of the Occupation Army. And General Sickles, now Military Governor of both Carolinas, had issued orders prohibiting anyone other than personnel with military passes, from riding any trains.

Of course, special-exception-tickets could be purchased at an exorbitant price – if payment was made in gold or yankee-dollars.

Since they had neither, Manse and Tom walked. But their three-mile-an-hour military pace was slowed by Tom's wooden leg to less than one-mile-per-hour. And they were further delayed by the need to forage, or offer their labor, in exchange for food.

It was at a water tower just south of Durham Station that their luck changed. They had taken shelter in the little cool that the tower's shadow offered, and were eating the last of their food – and talking about leaving the rail lines and heading south-westward toward the mountains where they might find a friendlier welcome than along this heavily traveled route – when a troop train arrived at the tower and two guards ordered them to leave the area "for security reasons."

Not anxious to argue with armed Yankees, Manse and Tom walked to the edge of the woods and sat under a tree and watched as two hundred Cavalry Troops double-timed out of coaches and slid open the doors of dozens of slatted box-cars, and led their horses out to be watered and fed, while cooks set up camp stoves and prepared afternoon mess.

While Manse and Tom chewed on hard bread and horse-jerky, they watched the Union Troops eat bowls of stew and fresh bread and baked apples.

"Smells almost good enough to make a man wish he'd fought on the winning side, don't it?" Tom forced a laugh.

"Does that," Manse said. "Specially that bread."

Then Tom stood and started walking toward the train.

"Where you going?" Manse got to his feet.

"To get us a ride home," Tom smiled at him.

Manse followed two paces behind as Tom limped to the serving tables and went directly to the four-striper in charge.

"Sorry, no hand-outs," the sergeant said before Tom got out a word. "We wouldn't have enough food for our own men if we fed Rebs at every stop."

"Not asking for a hand-out, Sergeant," Tom nodded politely. "Just wondered if you would kindly direct us to the man in charge of all those fine mounts."

"That would be Danny Ferguson – best Wrangler Sergeant in the US Cavalry. That's him standing next to the officers' coach, talking to the major."

"Thank you," Tom said and, without hesitating, hobbled into the midst of the eating troopers. Manse quickened his pace to stay beside him, and was surprised when the sea of Union uniforms divided to let them through.

When they were a few feet from Sgt. Ferguson and the major, Tom stopped, pulled himself to attention, snapped his hand to the brim of his gray Confederate cavalry hat, and saluted. Manse did the same. They held their salute until the major returned it.

"Begging your pardon, sir," Tom said, "but we would surely appreciate a few minutes of Sergeant Ferguson's time whenever he is free to speak with us. At the Major's pleasure, sir."

The major did not respond to Tom, but spoke instead to Ferguson.

"We will continue this at the next water stop, Sergeant," he said, and went inside the officers' coach.

Sgt. Ferguson walked to Tom and Manse. "Well, what the hell you want to see me about?" His tone was not friendly.

"We're Cavalrymen," Tom said. "Four years field experience. Scouts with – "

"You want to join the Union Army, I can't help you. You gotta get special goddamn papers. Washington has to make sure you shit the right color."

Tom smiled at Ferguson.

"We appreciate that information, Sergeant," he said, "but my comrade and I have seen all the uniforms we want to see for a while."

"Then what the hell do you want? We pull out in twenty minutes. I don't have time to swap war stories."

"I understand you're lead-wrangler, Sergeant. That's the most important job in any man's cavalry. But I'd venture a guess that after The War ended, your most seasoned troopers were mustered out pretty fast – "

"Mustered out, hell," Sgt. Ferguson interrupted. "When they heard The War was over, most of 'em just up and left and went home. And them that decided to stay, volunteered for the Western Command to go fight Indians."

"So what you're left with is a train-load of new recruits who don't know much about taking care of horses – except for some basic feeding and grooming," Tom said, and nodded an understanding smile.

"You'd be goddamn right about that," Ferguson said. " The major was just chewing on my ass because we've lost six mounts in the past two weeks. Killed by swamp fever, picked up on the Virginia coast. That means requisitioning replacements. Then training men to new mounts. We've got a good battalion vet-doctor. If he'd caught the symptoms early enough, he could've saved them all. But he can't examine every horse everyday. He has to rely on the troops to report when something's wrong. And these recruits are green as cow turds. They can't tell that their horse is ailing until it falls over – "

Sergeant Ferguson interrupted himself and stared at Tom, then at Manse. "Just what the hell you two got in mind, anyway?"

"Just this, Sergeant: For the last two years of The War, the Confederate Cavalry didn't have horse doctors anywhere but at command posts. Every man in the field had to learn to take care of his own. Not just spotting things that were wrong, but knowing what to do about them. We learned a lot – fast – because if we lost a mount, we all-of-a-sudden found ourselves in the Confederate *Infantry*. There just weren't any replacement horses."

"And so now you want to use your knowledge to help the Union Army take care of its mounts. That it?"

"I figure you know the honest answer to that, Sergeant. We got no love for the Union. But we *do* know horses, and we are willing to work hard. We'll check your mounts everyday – *all of them* – and report to you anything we think is wrong. If it's just a matter of routine care, we can show your troopers how to do. If it's urgent, you can let your horse doctor tend to it. Either way, you'll save mounts."

"And you'll do that in exchange for what?"

"Just let us ride the train south with you to Greenville, or as near there as you're going. Feed us when your troops get fed. And give us a place to sleep."

Sergeant Danny Ferguson took a bar of compressed tobacco from his pocket, bit off a piece, and chewed solemnly as he eyed Tom and Manse.

"We're part of a battalion ordered to Charlotte, to join up with others assigned to Greenville, Columbia, and Charleston. If you will do what you say, I'll ask the major to give you clearance to ride with us to Greenville. But there's one thing you can't do – "

He spat an arc of tobacco juice across both railway tracks.

"You *can't* ride in the troop coaches. Most of the non-coms like myself – and the officers, except for them gold-bar-virgins – saw plenty of combat. They wouldn't take too good to quartering with Johnny-Rebs. I wouldn't like it myself. I mean, it's all too goddamned fresh in my mind to say forgive-and-forget. I look at them muddy brown uniforms and gray hats you're wearing and all I can think about is a thousand of you bastards charging out of the sun at dawn, killing half the men I served with."

"Believe me, Sergeant, except for the color of the uniforms, our memories are the same. And just as fresh," Manse spoke for the first time. "We'll keep out of the way – wait until all your troops are fed before we go to the mess table – and keep our thoughts to ourselves, even if someone insults us. We're not looking to start any trouble. We just want to go home."

"Wait here," Sgt. Ferguson said and went inside the officers' coach. He returned in a few minutes with the major's permission.

During their time aboard the train, Manse managed to remain calm, though it was difficult to be so close to men who, only a few short months before, he wanted only to kill. When it was necessary that he and Tom talk to the Union Cavalrymen, they stuck to the subject – horses.

When the train was moving, Manse and Tom rode in the horse-feed freight car, resting on bales of fresh hay. When it was too hot inside, they rode atop the wood-car. At night, when the train stopped and the troops bivouacked, Manse and Tom took their bedrolls and walked outside the camp's perimeter to sleep.

Manse reckoned that walking all the way home from Virginia to South Carolina would have taken them five months. Walking only half-way, and riding the train the other half, had taken less than three.

Manse and Tom made no effort to contain their smiles when the train finally arrived in Greenville.

Their intention was to find Sgt. Ferguson and thank him – but that proved too difficult. The station platform and surrounding streets were a mass of cavalry and supply wagons – plus six companies of infantry – and more shiny new second lieutenants than Manse had ever seen in one place – all lining up in front of placards designating the destinations on their orders.

As they walked across the platform, Manse noticed a tall, beribboned, obviously intoxicated, First Lieutenant standing alone in front of the placard reading *Anderson*. If he and Tom had wanted to go to the town of Anderson, Manse might have suggested that Tom approach the Lieutenant and ask for a ride – but they had decided to make their way cross-country, following the less traveled rural roads that would take them north of Anderson – nearer the Lebanon community – and home. They stood a good chance of getting a ride with farmers or freight haulers headed toward Pendleton.

Their hunch proved right. Before they had walked a mile beyond the outskirts of Greenville, a wagon loaded with crates marked *"Furniture: S. Heaton"* stopped and the black driver offered them a tailgate seat. After a few of their questions received barely audible replies, Manse and Tom stopped trying to converse with the man, and instead spent their time looking for familiar landmarks along the route.

What they saw were deserted farms, fallow fields, and very little that was familiar except for a few weathered-wood houses, the rust-colored clay, and the deep ruts in the road. Things had definitely changed, Manse thought. Even the heat of August air and swirling red dust did not seem the same. But then, he and Tom were different, too – certainly not the same two men who had ridden this road four years before – going off to war.

At mid-day the wagon arrived at Clardy's Blacksmith Shop, midway between Rogers Crossroads and Powdersville. Alan Clardy was the best smithy in the area. At least that's what Manse's and Tom's daddies avowed, and they always sent broken equipment, including rolling stock, to Clardy for repairing, even though his shop was five miles farther from their Lebanon homes than the smithies in Anderson. Clardy's was where the freight hauler would turn south toward the old Dickerson Plantation – and Manse and Tom would continue on foot the few remaining miles home.

They got off the tailgate, thanked the driver for the ride, and walked to the entrance to the blacksmith's shed –

And Manse collided with a man who was coming out.

For a moment he stared at the man in disbelief.

Except for his clean shaven face, it was as if Manse were looking into a mirror.

"Manse – ?" The clean shaven reflection said.

"Larry – ?" Manse said. Then recognition replaced surprise, and Manse reached for his youngest brother, embraced him.

"Larry! Damn – damn – " Manse felt tears form.

"My god!" Larry said. "It's really you. Really you." He wrapped his arms around his older brother and hugged him. "Thank you, Jesus," he said softly.

The brothers continued to hold each other until Larry saw Tom. Then he released Manse, and embraced Tom – and reached again for Manse and held onto both of them. And they held onto him.

Until Larry stepped back, to get a good look at them, and said, "We all thought you were both dead. How'd you get here?"

Suddenly they were interrupted as an old mule and an old wagon came out of the smithy-shed – and the boy who was driving the mule and wagon let out a string of curses in an attempt to convince the old mule to stop.

Manse recognized the mule and wagon, looked at the boy, then at Larry.

"That's Johnny – Lewis and Bonnie's boy. He thinks being twelve makes him man enough to cuss," Larry said. "Watch your language, Johnny – and speak to your Uncle Manse and Tom Largent."

"They said you were *dead*," the boy looked down at them.

Manse laughed.

"Well, I reckon that proves you shouldn't believe everything *they* tell you," he said. "No matter who *they* are."

The boy looked confused, then grinned at Manse and Tom.

"I'm glad you're not dead," he said.

"So are we," Manse smiled. "Now tell me, how's your daddy?

Johnny's expression changed, as though a cloud suddenly crossed some inner sun.

"Papa's dead," he said. "The Yankees killed him."

Manse absorbed the words slowly – Lewis was dead. His oldest brother. The one who had taken over as head-of-the-family when their daddy died. Manse's sadness quickly became a pain shared with this young boy left without a father.

"I'm sorry, Johnny. I didn't know," was all he could say.

"Lewis was decorated for valor six times," Larry spoke fast, nervously. "He was home for three months on healing-leave after he got wounded the second time. Then he went back to the field and was killed inside a month. Bonnie was mighty proud of him."

"He was a man to be proud of," Tom said.

Manse looked up and said again, "I'm real sorry about your daddy, Johnny."

The boy wiped the back of his hand across his eyes, then sat on the wagon seat and stared straight ahead.

"Johnny and his mama and Melinda all live at home now. But you never saw Lewis and Bonnie's baby girl, Melinda, did you? She was born after you all left for The War." His words tried to cover the sadness in his voice.

Manse looked at Larry and said, as calmly as he could, "Mama wrote me about Sanford and Alex getting killed – but I didn't know about Lewis. We got no mail all of last year," Manse caught Larry's eyes and held them. "Just go ahead and tell me, Larry – who made it home?"

Larry looked down, kicked red dust, then looked back at Manse.

"You and me, Manse. We're the only ones who came home. And we're the only ones who are gonna be coming home. The rest of them are gone, Manse. They're all dead."

Manse stared at his younger brother, as if through sheer will he might change those words into some kind of nightmare he could wake-up from.

"*All* of them – Enos and Jesse, too?" he said at last. "All *five* of them?"

"All five, Manse."

Manse took a deep breath. His head pounded. A liquid chill rose from the base of his spine, filled him, and overflowed.

He had looked for them everywhere he went – had kept saying to Tom that, with six brothers in this goddamned war he was bound to see one of them sooner or later. And that was the hell of it – he probably had seen them – lying in some mud-hole, their guts torn open, screaming for somebody to shoot them and stop the pain.

They were *all* his brothers.

Tears froze in his throat and eyes.

He opened the cubicle where he stored war's emotions, pushed hard to force inside his feelings for five brothers – then he sealed it closed, and looked down the road toward the direction of *home* – and he asked in a low voice, almost fearfully –

"And Mama? How's Mama?"

"Barely holding up, Manse. All the dying has just about tore her apart. She spends most of her time up in her room. Or in her rocking chair on the porch. It's like all the wanting-to-live has been took out of her."

Then Larry looked at Manse, as if he had just thought of something.

"The Confederate War Secretary wrote Mama and Rebecca that you and Tom were missing and believed killed-in-action," he said. "Finding out you're *alive* is going to be the first *good news* she's heard in a long time," he grinned. "Yessir, having you home may be just what Mama needs to get her to smile. God knows, there's not been much around here to smile about."

Manse listened. Numbness persisted. He barely heard – did not feel.

The three men stood silent for a minute, then Tom shifted his weight and asked in a low voice, "What about *my* daddy, Larry?"

"Jesus, it just ain't right for you all to come home to this – " Larry wiped his hand across his mouth as if trying to stop what he had to say. But then he said it anyhow, because he had to. "Your daddy died about six months ago, Tom. It was a bad winter. He took sick and just couldn't make it through. He died the end of February."

Tom drew in a deep breath.

"And Rebecca? Don't tell me anything's happened to her."

"No. She's fine," Larry said. "She's living with us now. Moved in after your daddy died. She's grown up quite a bit since you left. But she's still Rebecca."

Manse and Tom put their belongings on the wagon, and sat in the back. Larry took the reins from Johnny.

The mule snorted and whinnied and broke wind and started down the road – and the wagon's wheel screeched loudly.

"Mister Clardy still can't get that wheel to quieten down," Larry's laugh was forced. "Remember how Daddy was always trying to get that wheel to hold grease, but it never would. Mister Clardy has tried to fix it at least twenty times that I know of. And he still tries every time I bring this old wagon to him. Today he was just supposed to mend broken trace chains, but he worked on that wheel, too."

The creaky wagon squeaked down the road.

Manse took a deep breath, exhaled, rubbed his right temple and tried to restore some semblance of normal feeling and thought. This was not the homecoming he had dreamed about, but he *was* coming home. Somehow he had to overcome what he felt – and overcome what he couldn't allow himself to feel – and accept the reality of whatever remained of the world he had left behind.

"How long you been back?" Manse spoke to Larry above the wheel's screech.

"Just over three months now. I joined up two years ago – soon as I turned seventeen. Didn't really want to leave Mama and Bonnie to manage alone, but I *had* to go. I recollect Mama said she wrote and told you."

"She did. So did Rebecca."

"I looked for you two when my company, or what was left of it, joined up with the First Cavalry in North Carolina, last January. But the clerk said most of your brigade's scouts had been ordered over to The Army of Tennessee."

"General Bonham needed scouts real bad," Tom said.

"Where were you two when The War ended?" Larry asked.

"Hiding out in the Virginia mountains. Artillery blew my horse down and smashed my leg on a rock. Had to have it took off." Tom knocked on the leg. "Almost good as a real one. Manse made it while I was healing." Tom paused. "Where were you when it ended?"

"With Johnson's Brigade. We surrendered to that son of a bitch, Sherman, on April the 26th," Larry spat over the side of the wagon. "A sad damn day for the South."

"There were a lot of sad days," Manse said in a voice too low to be heard.

"I figure we never did surrender," Tom said. "We didn't hear that The War was over until a month after it ended."

The mule picked up speed when it got within a half-mile of home. Just before they turned into the quarter-mile long driveway, Larry stopped the wagon.

"Johnny, you run on ahead and tell your grandmama that Manse and Tom have come home," he said. "That'll give her a little time to prepare herself for seeing them – so the shock won't be too much for her."

Johnny jumped down and ran towards the house. Larry flicked the reins, and the mule leaned into the harness and slowly the wagon moved up the drive.

The two-story house looked the same to Manse as when he'd left – but in need of paint, as were all the outbuildings – the barn, smokehouse, wagon shed, and cabins.

Manse watched as Johnny reached the front porch, climbed the steps, and walked to where a woman sat rocking.

The wagon reached the front of the house and stopped. The men got down.

Manse walked slowly up the steps to the porch, stopped at the top and said in a low voice, "Mama – Mama – it's me – Manse."

The figure in the rocking chair looked up at him.

"Manse –?" she said. "It *is* you. Really you." And the rocking stopped.

***

Captain Ralph Phillips leaned back in his chair and squinted through the cloud of smoke from his gnarled pipe.

"Just why the hell do you suppose those god-damn fools in Washington think we need a god-damn Intelligence Officer in this god-forsaken-damn place?"

Martin McCollum stood at attention and did not reply.

Whatever answer he gave to that question would probably be wrong.

The Captain picked up Martin's orders and read them again, then sighed apparent acceptance that he *had* to do something."

"You'll need a desk," he said.

"Yes, sir," Martin replied.

"And above all else, you will need an enemy," the Captain said. "Now that we have no war, you will definitely need an enemy to gather intelligence about. Right, Lieutenant?"

Martin looked at his new commanding officer. The man might be reasonably intelligent – but he was obviously crazy, like a lot of military officers Martin had met – especially ones who had commanded troops in battle. Apparently ordering soldiers to die did something to a man.

"Well, don't just stand there, Lieutenant – tell me – do you know who the enemy is? Or do you expect me to provide one for you? In the Western Command, I could do that. There is always one renegade tribe or another eager to take on the US Cavalry. I'm afraid, however, that in Anderson, South Carolina, finding a worthy adversary may not be so easy."

"Begging the Captain's pardon," Martin paused. "It is my understanding, sir, that you are to inform me of the details of my assignment here. I believe that information is in the second envelope I delivered to you, sir. The one you have not yet opened."

"Ah, yes, this one," Captain Phillips re-lit his pipe, picked up the envelope and looked at it. "Yes, it *is* addressed to me, isn't it?"

He tore it open and puffed while he read the pages.

"I'm sorry to have to tell you, Lieutenant, that this is not good."

"Not good, sir?" Martin felt concern grow.

"Definitely *not good* Lieutenant – because I have no goddamn idea what this directive is about!" The captain waved his pipe in the air. "It says I am to furnish you with background information on which you can base an investigation into the Confederate Holding Bank here in Anderson," Captain Phillips shook his head solemnly. "But in the two months I've been in command here, Lieutenant, I've heard of no such bank operating in this area."

"Begging the Captain's pardon again, sir – I think the Holding Bank was a part of the Confederate Army Military Command in Anderson. In which case it would have ceased operation at war's end."

"Very good, Lieutenant. No wonder you're an Intelligence Officer. Of course – yes, quite obviously – you are right. When the war ended, the Confederacy no longer existed – *ergo* there is no longer any Confederate Holding Bank in Anderson – *ergo, ergo* –

end of investigation!" Captain Phillips saluted. "Excellent work, Lieutenant. You went straight to the heart of the problem and solved it. You deserve a commendation. I will see that you get one when you return to Washington." He saluted again.

"Sir – " Martin returned the Captain's salute. "I believe, sir, that the information referred to in the directive – the background information you are to provide me – is for an investigation into questions raised by General George Stoneman about the Confederate Holding Bank in Anderson."

Captain Phillips became silent, then nodded slowly, seriously.

"I am damned glad you are here to explain this to me, Lieutenant Muck-Killin – "

"McCollum, sir – "

"McCollum – yes, that *is* your name. I see it here on your orders. And I repeat – I am damned glad you are here and know what this is all about, because it is obvious to me that your superiors in Washington are either a bunch of incompetents or idiots – possibly both. Nowhere in this directive do they mention General Stoneman's name. If they had done so, this entire matter would have been cleared up hours ago and we would not have been required to spend the entire day discussing it."

Martin blinked at the words but said nothing. He had been standing at attention in the Captain's Office in Union Army Headquarters in the Anderson, South Carolina, County Courthouse for less than ten minutes. Quite clearly, Ralph Phillips had his own system for measuring time.

The Captain put down his pipe.

"I assure you, Lieutenant," he said, "that if your superiors in Washington had simply *mentioned* General Stoneman's name in their directive, I would have immediately recalled that, when I assumed command here, I was required to sign for a rather voluminous file of information compiled by officers of General Stoneman's Brigade. Of course, I have no damned idea what is in that file because I have never read it. I wasn't ordered to read it – just sign for it. I can only presume that it contains the information you need."

"I am sure it does, sir." Martin needed a drink. Badly.

"Unfortunately, my aide, Lieutenant Pearson, is away – testifying in Greenville at the Court Martial Trial of two deserters – and he has the only key to the Restricted Files Storage Room so we can't get your file until he returns at the end of the week. Of course there *is* another key here somewhere, but Lieutenant Pearson is the only officer who would know where it is, so we still can't get the file until he returns."

"I understand, sir," Martin was anxious to get out of the office. "If the Captain will have someone direct me to my quarters, sir, I will await word from you when Lieutenant Pearson returns," he saluted. "Will that be all, sir?" He held the salute.

"Hell, no, that won't be all, Lieutenant. There are some other matters in this directive that we need to go over," Captain Phillips picked up and re-packed his pipe, then lit. "Put your hand down, Lieutenant. You look stupid like that. Consider your salute returned."

"Yes, sir," Martin dropped his hand.

The Captain blew three large billows of smoke, then tapped the page on his desk. "It says here you are to be given an office in my headquarters. Being an Intelligence officer, you're probably a keen observer and noticed when you came into this old courthouse that it's crowded as hell. The Army has taken half of the offices for Military Headquarters, and we still don't have enough space. But we can't take any more. The civilian administrators, tax collectors and elected officials need to have some place to work. Under these circumstances, the best I can do is give you a desk in the outer office – along with my aide, Lieutenant Pearson – and his aides – and their aides' aides," he stopped and read, puffed and looked up.

"It also says here you're to have your own personal billet – non-military. I suppose that is so you can conduct your Intelligence operations in secret." He wrote a note and handed it to Martin. "This will authorize a room for you at the Benson House – which, surprisingly, is a damned fine hotel. Give this to the clerk at the front desk."

The Captain took a final glance at Martin's orders. "And the last thing it says here is that you are not required to participate in the affairs of this garrison. As far as I am concerned, the less an Intelligence Officer participates – *meddles* is a better word – in the affairs of any garrison under my command, the happier I am. And the happier I am, the happier you will be. Is that understood, Lieutenant?"

"Yes, sir. Will that be all, sir?"

"It is already too much," the Captain said. "Go!"

"Yes, sir," Martin saluted, turned, and left the room, expecting to be followed by laughter, but was followed only by a cloud of smoke.

***

The boy held the reins of the big white stallion, and said, "I'll take good care of your horse, Mister," and held out his small hand.

The man dressed from hat to boots in black dropped a coin into the open palm, smiled at the boy, and patted him on the head.

"You do that, son," he said, "and I'll take real good care of you."

The boy nodded and led the horse away to the stables behind the hotel.

The man in black waited beside his saddlebags.

A black man in once-bright livery came out of the hotel door.

"What the hell took you so long, boy?" The tone of the man in black was harsh.

"I'm sorry, sir. I was carrying valises upstairs for one of the officers who just arrived."

The man in the black suit reached out and gripped the arm of the doorman.

"You best remember something –" his drawl was the lazy-tongue of the coast, "them Yankee officers and their soldier-boys will all be gone from here one of these days. And that'll leave just us white folks and you niggers to work things out between us. And us white folks got long memories – you hear me?"

"Yes sir, I won't forget," the doorman picked up the saddlebags and led the way into the Benson House hotel.

The man in black stopped and looked around.

"This is quite a place," he said.

"Yes, sir. Folks around here are mighty proud to have a hotel like this."

The man in black walked to the desk, smiled at the room clerk, and looked up the curved stairs toward the open gallery mezzanine.

"Yes, sir," he said, "this is the nicest hotel I've seen since Atlanta."

"Thank you, sir," the clerk said. "Forty rooms. Six suites. Excellent Gentlemen's Bar. Dining room on the mezzanine, overlooking the lobby – and the town square and courthouse – " he interrupted himself and frowned. "But I thought Atlanta was burned to the ground, sir."

"I was speaking of *before* The War," the man in black leaned across the desk and frowned. "Now let's me and you quit this here palavering – and get me a room."

"Actually, sir, we are quite crowded," the desk clerk said, then saw the threat in the man's eyes. "But we do have a few rooms that are usually reserved for officers. Perhaps I could arrange to get one of those for you," he said. "How long will you be staying with us?"

"That depends," the man in black said. "Yes, sir. That depends."

The clerk waited, then realized the man in black was not going to say anything else.

"Our rate is one dollar per day," he said, "including use of the bathing room," he hesitated. "The Benson House does, however, require payment upon registration – gold or US dollars," he smiled. "But we do have a weekly rate –five dollars – a substantial saving. That is why I asked how long you would be with us," he turned the large registration ledger around.

The man in black picked up a quill pen, dipped it in the glass ink bottle, shook it, and wrote in the big book, *Jefferson Brown*, and underlined his signature with a flourish.

Then he removed a small leather pouch from his waistcoat pocket, took out a five-dollar gold piece and put it on the ledger.

The clerk picked up the coin, unlocked a drawer and placed the coin inside, re-locked the drawer and turned the ledger around, picked up the pen, and recorded the payment beside the signature.

"If you'll follow me, Mister Brown," he said, "I'll show you to your room."

"Lead on, MacBeth" the man in black followed the clerk towards the great staircase.

"That's Shakespeare, you know?"

The clerk arched an eyebrow and looked back over his shoulder.

"Yes, sir," he said, "I know."

***

The hand that held his was thin and veined, and the face that looked up at him was drawn. But there was the beginning of a smile, and Manse leaned down and kissed his mother's cheek.

"I'm home, Mama," he said, and tears filled his eyes. "I'm home."

"Thank the good Lord, Manson," she said.

Her arms reached up and tightened around his neck and held onto him, and Maude Jolly pulled herself up from her rocking chair and stood facing her son. "Let me get a look at you," she pushed him to arms' length and her smile broadened, and she reached for Tom, and held onto them both and cried softly. "You're really here – both of you. " She stepped back and looked at them. "And you look middling fine – yes you do – excepting you're both too darn thin. We've got to get some weight on you –"

Her smile was joy.

Her hair was now more silver than auburn, and Manse had almost forgotten how tall she was. He always thought of her as small and frail, but knew that was because she was the smallest one in a very tall family – a tall husband and seven taller sons – and three tall daughters. All lean and tall and strong.

"Oh my God!" The front door flew open. "It's true what Johnny said," Manse's sister-in-law, Bonnie, threw her arms around his neck.

"Who's out there? What's going on? Bonnie, who is it?" A woman's voice came from inside the house."

"You won't believe it. It's Manse and Tom!" Bonnie shouted.

"Tom – ? Tom!" and the sound of someone running, then a young woman – her hair in a single long blonde braid down her back to her waist – her hands and arms covered with flour – rushed out the door, onto the porch, stopped, saw Manse, then Tom, and threw herself into Tom's arms, and buried her face in his neck.

Tom struggled for balance, found a porch post and held on with all his strength.

"Easy, Rebecca," Tom said." Easy – "

"You're *back*.." Rebecca said, and kissed her brother three or four times. "You're supposed to be dead, and you're not – "

"Only part of me – " Tom said.

Rebecca loosened her hold on her brother's neck and stepped back. "And just exactly what does *only part of me* mean?"

Rebecca's blue eyes did not leave Tom's – though they filled with tears as he told her about his wound and amputation– and pulled up his trousers leg to show her. Then he held her and assured her that now he was all right.

Only after she had wiped tears from her eyes, and flour from her cheeks, did she turn to face Manse.

"Welcome home, Manson," she said, and put her arms around his neck and pulled him to her and kissed him on the cheek, and tried to smile. "I hope you didn't lose any part of you."

Manse kissed her cheek.

"Far as I know," he said, "I've still got everything I left with – including the scarf you embroidered my initials on – though I'm afraid it got a mite stained wrapping Tom's leg – but I cleaned it up and it's good as new."

Rebecca laughed, and pulled away from his embrace.

"I'd forgotten all about that old scarf," she said. "But I'm glad you found a good use for it."

She walked back to Tom.

There was a moment of silence, then everyone turned to look at the small girl who was standing just inside the front door.

"You can come out, Melinda," Bonnie said. "It's all right. It's your Uncle Manse and Rebecca's brother, Tom," she took her little daughter's hand and led her onto the porch.

Melinda held onto the folds of her mother's dress, then looked up at Manse and said in a small voice, "Did you bring my Daddy home with you?"

Bonnie began to sob.

Manse did not know what to say.

"Please, don't let everybody start crying again, Uncle Manse," Melinda said. "I already cried lots for Daddy."

Manse leaned over and picked her up. Her arms squeezed his neck. Her tears ran down his cheek. He carried her down the steps of the front porch, down the drive, away from the others.

"Would you like to see my flower?" she asked. "I planted it for my Daddy, but he's not home yet."

"Yes, I would like very much to see your flower," Manse said.

"Then put me down, please," she said, and he put her down and she took his hand and led him to a small plot of dirt, in the middle of which lay a wilted weed.

"My flower's sick," Melinda knelt and tried to get the weed to stand.

"I think it needs water," Manse squatted down beside her.

"Mama said I should put water on it, but I forgot."

Through an icy blur Manse looked at the tiny child – and past her – to fields of parched red land.

There was no remedy for the past – the future was all they had.

"I tell you what let's do, Melindy – let's you and me plant lots of flowers – orange ones and red ones, and yellow ones – all along the drive and walkway – and all over the yard – clear to the road."

Melinda smiled and kissed his cheek.

"So many flowers, Uncle Manse?" she said.

Pain shot through his head, and he pressed his index fingers into his temples until it subsided. When his vision cleared, he said, in a low voice, "Yes, Melindy, so-many flowers. I have a feeling we're going to need lots of flowers real bad."

***

Martin McCollum had never been a guest at any of New York City's better hotels, but he had spent time *inside* some of those hotels, in various capacities – delivering ice, shoveling coal, and washing dishes while working his way through City College. And though he had doubted that any hotel in Anderson, South Carolina, was even inhabitable, by New York City standards, he had to admit that the Benson House was, as Captain Phillips had said, "surprisingly fine."

His room, number 39, was small, with a single bed, armoire, desk, and two chairs.

It was far from elegant, but Martin was grateful – and somewhat surprised – that he had not been given a cot in the crowded bunk room of the Junior Officers' Quarters – full of adolescent soldiers talking incessantly about what *they* would have done if The War had just lasted long enough for them to see action and show them stinking Rebs a thing or three.

In room 39, at least he had to listen to only his own lies.

Martin kicked his valise into the corner, and lay down on the bed.

Then immediately got back to his feet, checked his face in the mirror above the washstand, and left the room.

"Where is the bar in this hotel?" he asked at the front desk.

"Right through there, sir," the room clerk indicated swinging doors with etched glass windows.

Martin entered a large room filled with the smell of smoke and whiskey – truly the smell of men-only – men in uniforms like his own, and men in expensive suits, and some men, surprisingly, in homespun.

He moved to an empty spot at the end of the bar.

"Let me have a whiskey," he said to the bartender,

The man picked up a glass, set it on the bar in front of Martin, turned and took a bottle from the shelf behind the bar, and showed the label to Martin.

Martin nodded.

"Leave the bottle" he said.

"That will be one dollar twenty-five cents, sir," the bartender said.

"Put it on my account. Room 39."

The bartender pulled a ledger from beneath the bar, wrote into it, then closed it and put it back.

"Enjoy your drink, sir," he said, and moved away.

Martin filled his glass and drank.

With enough of this stuff, he thought to himself, he might actually survive duty in Anderson, South Carolina – and an insane commanding officer – and an impossible assignment.

He poured another drink.

**

At the other end of the bar, Jefferson Brown stood inside a circle of men for whom he had just bought a round of drinks.

"I would prefer you gentlemen just call me *Texas*," he said, and continued talking about his recent stay in Atlanta. "They're calling it *The New South* over there, and it's truly a city trying to live up to the name. Buildings going up every day. New railroad tracks like vines growing in all directions. And new streets – hell, they got so many named Peachtree-this and Peachtree-that, you can't tell where you're at half the time," he laughed and emptied his glass.

"I hear said there are niggers running for elective office over there," one of Texas Brown's listeners said. "Is *that* what they mean by *The New South*?"

"Well, sir," Texas Brown took out a cigar and took the time to light it. "It's like this – There are folks in Atlanta who say that the niggers are getting out of hand – thinking they're just as good as white people," he drew deeply on his cigar. "On the other hand, there are those who say the niggers *ought* to have a say in things – perhaps even ought to have the right to vote. And, yes, there some who go so far as to say niggers *are* just as good as a white folks."

"And where exactly do *you* stand on those matters, Mister Brown?"

Texas looked at the man who had turned away from another group in order to ask the question. He wore the uniform of a captain in the Union Army.

"Well, Colonel, I look at it this way. When it comes to some matters, a man needs to do a lot of thinking before he acts. And when it comes to other matters, it is best for a man to act quickly and not spend too much time thinking. And in matters such as we are discussing here, the best thing for a man to do is order another round of drinks," he laughed, and most of his listeners laughed with him.

"Barman," Texas said, "give these gentlemen another of whatever they're drinking."

Texas looked at the Captain and said, "Join us, Colonel."

"Captain."

"My apologies, sir. No offense intended, Captain. Please have a drink with us."

Captain Ralph Phillips shook his head.

"No, thank you," he said. "But I will take a match, if you have one to spare."

"Happy to oblige," Texas Brown took three matches from his waistcoat pocket. "Take them all," he said. "I always carry spares. Never can tell when I'll need to start a fire."

The Captain nodded thanks, put the matches in his pocket, turned and made his way toward the door.

Texas watched as Captain Phillips paused and spoke to a young lieutenant standing at the far end of the bar – then was gone.

"Know thine enemy," Texas said to himself.

-3-

Through the summer, their garden provided them abundant fresh vegetables for the table, as well as for preserving and pickling.

But meat was in short supply. The last hog had been butchered in early spring – only one cured ham remained in the smokehouse. The last few chickens strutted around the yard as if they knew that the eggs they laid protected them from being roasted for Sunday dinner.

Though they had little, the Jollys and the Largents knew they would not starve.

Now they put all their energy into returning the farm to full production.

Larry made two trips into Anderson to buy badly needed supplies with the few dollars Maude Jolly had put away. And with the supplies, he brought home local news:

Five-thousand men from the Anderson area had gone off to fight in The War. Less than two-thousand survived. And those that returned found themselves as poor as the Jolly family.

Political power was in the hands of the *carpetbaggers* – opportunists from the North who came south to take advantage of whatever they could take advantage of – and the *scalawags* – Southerners of similar persuasion and intent. Both were backed by the might of The United States Army. And to assure that things stayed as bad as they were, Provisional Governor Benjamin Perry, backed by radicals in Congress, had ordered the Army to occupy South Carolina indefinitely.

Larry reported all this at the dinner table.

Manse listened, but said little. When he did speak, it was about the work that needed doing. The farm was the center of his existence – what was happening in Anderson – or in the rest of the South, for that matter – was no part of his life, and he hoped it would stay that way.

That hope was shattered the first week of September.

Maude, Bonnie and Rebecca were in the kitchen. Johnny was off somewhere setting rabbit gums. Tom was mending harnesses. And Larry was on the top rung of a ladder, putting a new hinge on the barn door, while Manse braced the door in place.

"Now who the hell is *that*?" Larry said, and pointed toward the road where Manse looked and saw two riders followed by two wagons with soldiers on the seats. As they drew closer, he saw that one of the riders was a civilian, and, as they got even closer, that the civilian was fat and sweating, wearing a long coat and riding awkwardly.

"Looks to me like one fat civilian, one cavalry sergeant, and four bluebelly soldiers in two wagons," Manse said.

Larry laughed. "You recognize the man?" he asked.

Manse squinted. He thought maybe he did, but it had been a long time and he wasn't sure.

"I think his name is Headen – or some damn something like that," Manse said.

When they reached the drive, the sergeant raised his hand, and he and the wagons stopped, but the civilian continued until he was a few yards from where Manse stood.

He removed his hat and wiped his bald head with a large handkerchief, then stuffed it back into his pocket, cleared his throat, and said, "Hottest August we've ever had, don't you think?"

Manse felt no need to answer.

The man looked at Manse. "You're Manson Jolly – correct? I remember seeing you in Anderson with your brothers. A few years before The War. Am I right?"

"I'm Manse Jolly."

"I knew it. I never forget a face – or a name."

"I reckon having my name on that piece of paper you're holding helps," Manse spat in the dust.

"You got mighty sharp eyes, young man," he swung his leg over the horse's rump and lowered himself to the ground. "I'm Samuel Heaton," he said and held out his hand.

Manse made no move to shake it.

Heaton shrugged and let his hand fall to his side.

"I apologize for calling on you unannounced like this, Mister Jolly," he said, "but there is a certain matter which requires the rather prompt attention of you and your neighbor, Mister Thomas Largent. We rode by his place first, but no one was there."

"I'm Tom Largent," Tom walked out of the barn.

"Well now, this is a mighty good stroke of luck, finding both you gentlemen together like this," Heaton wiped his head again with the handkerchief. "So I reckon we should get straight to business – and the business is taxes," he chuckled. "One of the two things we must all face sooner or later – death and taxes."

"You find death funny, do you, Mr. Heaton?" Manse said in a low voice.

Heaton looked quickly over his shoulder as if to make sure the soldiers were still there, then he turned back to Manse.

"I don't mean to offend you, Mr. Jolly," he said. "But that's what the government has me doing these days – collecting taxes – and I realize that most folks aren't too happy to see tax collectors, so I try to inject a little humor in my visits when I can."

"You're a little late, Mister," Larry said, climbing down the ladder. "There was a squad of Union troops here collecting taxes right after I came home. They took might near all the corn we had."

Heaton cleared his throat. "I'm afraid that was a different matter entirely. They were requisitioning supplies for the troops garrisoned in Anderson. That was for the Army – what I'm talking about are State and District *property taxes* – a different matter entirely." He turned and reached into his saddlebag and took out a book, and said, "I brought along the Tax Ledger, just to be certain."

He hunted for the proper page, found it, held the book open and traced words with his index finger as he read – "Farm of Joseph Moorhead Jolly, deceased 1856. Location: Lebanon Community. Present Ownership: Widow Jolly, seven sons, three daughters. Total Acreage: two-hundred-forty acres." Heaton stopped reading and looked up at Manse. "That seem correct to you, Mr. Jolly?"

"Not quite," Manse said. "My sisters married and moved away even before Daddy died. And now there's only two – " The words brought a bitter taste to his mouth – "there's only two sons left – me and Larry here. The others were killed in The War."

Heaton looked down and slowly shook his head, then looked up at Manse.

"Now that you mention it, I do recall hearing about that. And I'll make a note to have the records changed," he said, and took a pencil from his pocket and wrote briefly in the book. "I am truly sorry about your brothers, Mr. Jolly. I fear that the late unpleasantness brought its share of grief to us all – "

Manse felt the pain in his head tightening. He wanted to end this conversation as quickly as he could.

"How much are the taxes?" he asked.

Heaton checked his book, and said, "Back taxes unpaid for three years, plus penalty and interest and reparations assessment – comes to one-hundred-forty-six dollars."

"A hundred-forty-six dollars?" Manse shook his head.

"That seems unreasonable, Mr. Heaton," Tom said.

"Well, I don't make the laws, Mr. Largent, I just – "

"Of course it's unreasonable, Tom. That's the whole point," Larry stepped between Manse and Heaton. "They make the taxes so damn high nobody can pay them. Then these blood-suckers foreclose and take the land for themselves."

"That simply is not true," said Heaton, stepping back. "Not true at all. The State and District require money in order to continue providing services – "

"Services, hell! Every damn cent is going straight into the pockets of you scalawags and the carpetbaggers – "

"Easy, Larry," Manse gripped his arm.

"But, damn it, Manse, it's true! They did it to old Colonel Ezekiel Dickerson. You remember him – the big planter down near Antreville. They taxed him and he paid. Then, a month later, they said he owed more – and he paid that. And they kept bringing him tax notices until finally he couldn't pay any more. Then they took everything he had – his house and his land." Larry turned back to Heaton. "And *you're* the one who stole the Dickerson place – aren't you, *Mister* Heaton? You kept the big house and the best land for yourself, and gave the rest to niggers!"

Heaton's handkerchief was out again, wiping his sweating face.

"I don't have to answer to you, young man," he said. "I bought the Dickerson property at foreclosure auction – all legal – nothing *sub-rosa.*," Heaton said, and glared at Larry. "And the correct word is *Freedmen* not *niggers*. You best learn that right quick."

Manse tightened his grip on Larry's arm, and looked at Heaton. "Is that true, Mr. Heaton? You took Colonel Dickerson's place, even after he paid his taxes?"

"This is all a matter of public record in the tax office, Mr. Jolly. Colonel Dickerson paid the local and state taxes he owed, but he did not pay the Special Reparations Tax levied by the federal government for damage done in the North during The War."

"How many damn taxes are there anyhow?" Manse asked.

"Only three, Mr. Jolly – thus far."

"But you're not collecting *any* taxes from them goddamn Yankee-loving bastards who live up in the Dark Corner, are you?" Larry spat at Heaton's feet.

Heaton took a quick step back. "The law states that certain loyal southerners who did not support the Confederate cause are exempted from taxation," he wiped his brow again.

"And them that are *exempted* include you, right?"

"I made no secret of my sentiments. I was against Secession, and for the Union. And I was persecuted by folks around here because I took that position."

"You should have been taken out and – "

Tom held up his hand.

Larry accepted the cavalry signal, and fell silent.

"What about my farm?" Tom asked. "Exactly how much do I owe, Mr. Heaton?"

"Well, let me see," the tax collector flipped a few pages in his book. "Including interest, ninety-two dollars," he said. "Your place is smaller than the Jolly farm – that's why the discrepancy. And I have included the interest owing. So the total amount is just ninety-two dollars, as I said."

"Ninety-two dollars. Might as well be ninety-two *thousand*," Tom's voice shook. "We came home from The War with nothing, Mister Heaton. It'll take a year to bring in a cash crop – "

"I sympathize with you and your problem, Mr. Largent, but I'm afraid neither you nor Mr. Jolly has a year. These taxes are due the fifteenth of October, in my office in the Anderson County Courthouse. Either they are paid, or your land will be foreclosed. These are your notices, gentlemen." He took two folded papers from his coat pocket and handed one to Manse and one to Tom, then turned, and with some effort, mounted his horse.

"Now I believe the sergeant here has some matters to discuss with you," he smiled. "So I'll just bid you good-day, gentlemen, and say that I look forward to seeing you in Anderson. By the fifteenth of October." He turned his horse and rode back to the wagons.

As he approached, the sergeant spoke to his men, and they drove the wagons into the farmyard.

"What do *you* want, Sergeant?" Manse asked.

"Supplies," the sergeant said.

Larry stepped forward. "The Army got supplies here last month."

"Supplies are requisitioned *every* month," the sergeant drew a notebook from his tunic and read, "Five bushels of corn, one barrel of flour, one side of pork – "

"Hold on," said Manse. "We don't have any of that."

"We can accept the same value in Union dollars or other valuables."

"Manse just told you – we've got nothing left," Tom said.

"I can't take your word for that, Mister. All you farmers say the same thing – " He nodded to his corporal. "Search the place."

The corporal and three soldiers jumped down from the wagons. Two of them started toward the barn.

Larry stepped in front of the first one. "Oh no you don't," he said. You're not taking any more of our food."

"Hold it!" The sergeant drew his pistol and aimed it at Larry. "Stand very still – all of you." He waved the pistol. "Search the barn and house," he said.

Two soldiers went into the barn. The corporal and the other soldier went to the house.

"This is no better than robbery," Manse clenched his fists at his side.

"Call it what you want, mister," the sergeant said. "I got orders to bring these wagons back full, and I follow orders."

Anger burned behind Manse's eyes. The throbbing in his head began again. But he said and did nothing.

Within a few minutes the soldiers came from inside the house carrying an old pistol and rifle – both weapons belonging to Manse's daddy, and neither of much value. "We found these and a little money, Sergeant," one said. A moment later the other two came out of the barn, each carrying a ham and a sack of corn. They put all the items on one of the wagons.

The sergeant looked down at Manse, Tom, and Larry, and flipped them a quick salute. "Until next month, gentlemen," he wheeled his horse and trotted down the drive to join Samuel Heaton. The wagons followed them out onto the road.

"Damned Yankees! Rotten scalawag!" Larry yelled after them, then he turned to Manse. "What are we supposed to do now? They didn't even leave us a gun to protect the women with."

Manse stood looking toward the settling dust of the blue-uniformed foragers. Then he drew a shivering breath, shook himself, and said, "I still got my pistols. They're hid in my blanket roll under the attic eaves."

The men walked slowly toward the house. The women stood on the porch. Maude Jolly sat and started rocking.

"That was the last ham," Bonnie said.

"And the last of our money," Maude Jolly said.

Tom lowered himself awkwardly onto the top step of the porch.

"Ninety-two dollars," he said, and shook his head. "Where in hell are we ever going to get ninety-two dollars – or anything that even comes close to that much money."

"I hid Papa's watch and Mama's rings," Rebecca said, reaching into the bodice of her dress and pulling out a battered watch in a silver case and two gold rings. "They must be worth something."

"We're not selling Mama and Papa's things to no damn scalawags," Tom said with anger.

"How are we going to raise ninety-two dollars if we don't sell the watch and rings?" Rebecca asked.

"Even if we sold them, it wouldn't be near what we need." Tom touched his sister's cheek gently. Then, in a soft voice, he said. "I'm afraid we'll just have to let the place go."

"Then what will happen to us?" Rebecca asked.

Manse answered, "You'll stay here, like you been doing. This is your home – yours and Tom's. We're your family."

"I thank you, Manse," Tom said.

And Rebecca kissed Manse on the cheek and said, "I thank you too, Manson."

Larry said, "We won't have *this* place – or *any* place – for any of us to live if we don't get hold of some money real fast."

"Manson," Maude Jolly's voice shook with tears. "Manson, tell me you won't let them take our home."

"I won't let them take our home, Mama, I promise," Manse walked to her, stood by her chair, took her hand and held it.

He looked at the discouragement in their faces and knew that they were all close to giving up. But he hadn't survived four years of war to sit on the porch and let some fat and sweating son of a bitch come and take their farm away.

And he wasn't going to let his family sit around and cry about it.

Manse smiled at Bonnie.

"Did those damn Yankees leave us enough food for noon-dinner?"

"Unless they fished the food right out of the boiling pots, we still got plenty," Bonnie returned his smile, then she and Rebecca went to the kitchen.

"Well, I guess we'd best go get cleaned-up," Manse said, and led the three men to the well-trough to wash away red dust and sweat, and cool down tempers.

"Any ideas what we can do, Manse?" Tom asked as he drew a bucket of water.

Manse shook his head. "Not yet."

"Damn 'em to hell," Larry said. "It's not enough we're flat on our backs, they got to kick us too."

Manse shrugged, and reached for a towel. "That's what usually happens to them that lose a war," he said.

***

Martin McCollum had to wait three weeks for Captain Ralph Phillips to deliver General George Stoneman's file to him.

When Captain Phillips' aide, Lieutenant Pearson, returned from Greenville, he could not locate his key to the Secured Documents

Storage Room. Then it took a week for him to find the back-up key to the room. And when the room was finally opened, the Stoneman File was not in it – so an additional week passed while records were traced – to determine that the file had not been stored in the Secure Documents Storage Room because Captain Phillips, when he assumed command, had decided that any file important enough to require his signature-of-receipt meant he would ultimately be responsible for its whereabouts, so he had it placed in his personal floor safe in the closet of his office – and he promptly forgot that it was there – until the Company Clerk located a record of the file and its whereabouts.

When, at last, the file was delivered to him, Martin began reading it at his desk in the outer office filled with the desks of aides, and aides to aides.

But General Stoneman's file quickly raised questions that Martin McCollum, as an Intelligence Officer with more than a dozen commendations for doing his job well – too goddamn well – took very seriously.

In order to analyze the reports and formulate an investigation strategy, Martin needed privacy and space. Room 39 at the Benson house wasn't exactly spacious, but it *was* private.

He informed Lt. Pearson he would be working away from his desk, and took the file to his room – along with a bottle of whiskey.

In Washington, he gauged the magnitude of a case by the degree to which it impinged upon his drinking. Most investigations didn't interfere with a drinking schedule that began each day at lunch. If the case developed intensity and interest, he found himself drinking only in the evenings – and even then, relatively little. He had decided that any investigation in Anderson, South Carolina, would probably permit cognac in his breakfast coffee – or round-the-clock binges.

But the case of the Confederate Holding Bank at Anderson was much more than he ever expected.

Confiscated minutes of final meetings of the Cabinet of the Confederate States of America included plans to transfer its treasury's remaining gold from seven Holding Banks to Mexico, where it was to fund a government in exile – the destination to which Confederate President Jefferson Davis was headed when he was captured and imprisoned in Georgia at the end The War.

The records showed that the gold stored in the Holding Bank in Anderson had been ordered sent by train to Charleston where it was to be loaded on a blockade runner destined for Vera Cruz.

Martin had seen similar reports in Secret Intelligence Files in Washington.

Washington had placed sufficient credence in those reports to order General Stoneman to send a company of his Cavalry to Anderson to capture the Holding Bank – and its gold – before it could be shipped.

But the gold had left Anderson by train less than three hours before Stoneman's forces arrived. Moving cross-country, the Company of Union Cavalry intercepted and stopped the train at the railway junction of Donalds, South Carolina. A bloody skirmish ensued between Union Cavalry hell-bent on capturing the gold, and a platoon of Confederate Guards determined to keep the gold out of the hands of the Union. The boxcar was locked, the guards were inside, the boxes containing the gold were nailed shut. In the end, most of the Confederates died rather than surrender. When the battle was over, the boxes were opened – but there was no gold inside. Only rocks.

General Stoneman was convinced that the gold existed, and most likely remained hidden somewhere in the Anderson area. He assigned a special Cadre to search the town of Anderson. But they found nothing. A report of the investigation was forwarded to Washington, and a copy of the file was retained at the permanent garrison established at Anderson by General Stoneman.

Military Intelligence in Washington concluded that it was more likely that whatever gold was in the Holding Bank had been shipped earlier – and was part of bullion captured at Charleston, Savannah and New Orleans.

But the evidence submitted by General Stoneman was sufficient to warrant a new, never-ending investigation – to be conducted by an Intelligence Officer named Martin McCollum whom Washington wanted to remand to the most godforsaken corner of the occupied South it could find.

But when he read, and reread, the Stoneman File, Martin's cynicism lessened.

He trusted his instincts, and his instincts told him that General Stoneman's instincts were right – something *strange* had happened to that gold – and whatever it was, it had happened *in* Anderson.

Martin capped the whiskey bottle. He needed a clear head to formulate his strategy.

And this time – when he successfully concluded *this* investigation – he wanted no goddamn commendation – and no goddamn promotion.

Just money.

***

The heat was stifling.

Texas Brown would have preferred being at the Benson House bar talking to the diverse mix of off-duty Army officers, local scalawags, newly-arrived carpetbaggers and local politicians who gathered there.

But drinking at the bar in the Benson House was only one part of his plan.

To find the men he needed, he had to ride the back roads, regardless of the heat.

Thunderclouds darkened the sky. Lightning flashed, followed by a crack of thunder, and Texas knew he would soon be very wet.

He spurred his horse *Blanco* – the same name as the white horse owned by his dead uncle who was the only member of his family who had ever actually been to the state of Texas – he spurred *Blanco* into a canter, and looked for signs of shelter.

But the only sign he saw was nailed to a cedar fence post.

It was old and tilted and painted long ago, and read *Whitfield*.

He rode onto a weed-grown wagon-road leading towards a ramshackle farmhouse.

"Might be all right, if the roof don't leak too bad," Texas brought the stallion to a halt at a hitching post, dismounted, tied the stallion loosely, looked once more at the blackening sky, and started up the steps.

"Hold it right there, mister."

Texas stopped, with one foot on the top step and one foot on the porch.

"Afternoon," Texas could not see who had spoken to him, but he presumed that whoever it was was armed. "Just looking for a dry spot till the storm passes," he said.

The screen door in front of Texas opened, and a woman's face peered out, followed by the rest of her – tall, blond, pretty once, but now lined and drawn.

Texas smiled and touched the brim of his hat, and said, "Howdy, Ma'am."

Now the rain was falling hard, and from the corner of his eye Texas saw a man at the edge of the porch holding a musket. "We ain't got nothing worth stealing," the man said as he moved up onto the porch.

Texas turned and smiled, "I'm not after anything except some shelter, friend."

The man's small, closely set eyes did not blink – nor did he lower the weapon.

"Then I reckon you can stay till the rain stops," he said. "After that, you best be on your way – "

"I'm obliged to you," Texas said, and was about to introduce himself when lightning flashed strong enough to feel, and thunder shook the house.

"Damn," Texas said. "I've got to get my horse out of that storm."

"Rain won't hurt him," the man said

"But lightning can," Texas said. "And if there's one thing I don't need right now, it's a horse struck dead."

"Cain't say I blame you," the man said. "I sure wouldn't want to lose a piece of horse-flesh that fine. He looks like the kind generals rode in The War." The man hesitated for a moment, then called toward the weathered barn, "Malachi!"

There was no answer, just the sound of increasing rain.

"Where the hell's that boy got to?" He put down the rifle and yelled through cupped hands. "Malachi – you hear me – you best git yourself here right now, boy!"

A frail figure came out of the barn and ran through the rain to the house, and up onto the porch, where he slipped and bumped into his father – who slapped him hard across the face – knocking him to his knees.

"You answer when I call you, boy! You hear me?"

"Yes, s-s-s-sir – I'm s-s-s-sorry," the boy raised his hands to protect his face from another blow.

"Quit your stammering and take this man's horse to the barn," he shoved his son off the porch.

The boy fell into a puddle, picked himself up, went to Blanco, untied him from the hitching post, and led him towards the barn.

"Damn kids these days just don't do nothing like they're supposed to," the man looked at Texas. "Do young'uns act like that where you come from, mister?"

"Seems things are pretty much the same everywhere since The War," Texas said. "I reckon it's because all the grown men went off to fight – leaving boys with nobody to teach'em what's right – and how to show proper respect."

"It's their mama's job to teach kids what's right," the woman said.

Texas felt surprise when she spoke. Then he smiled at her and said, "You're exactly right about that, ma'am. It's women-folk that *teach* children what's right – but it's the men-folks who need to *enforce respect* for what's right. Like the good-book says, *Spare the rod and spoil the child.* Without *the-rod*, young'uns get the notion they can do damn near anything they please – if you will pardon me using the word *damn* in your presence, ma'am."

The woman smiled and said, "I don't mind, mister. I heard it all before."

Texas turned to the man and held out his hand. "My name is Texas Brown," he said. "And I didn't get yours, sir – "

The man studied the offered hand, then shook it.

"Hezekiah Whitfield," he said. "Folks just call me *Whit..*"

"It's a pleasure to meet you, Whit," Texas smiled.

The smile was not returned.

"Just what is it you're doing out here, mister," Whit said.

"Please – call me Texas, Whit."

Whit thought for a moment.

"I can do that," he nodded. "So what the hell *are* you doing out here, *Texas*? Folks don't ride south of Twiggs for pleasure. They know better. Unlessen they got business here. You got business out here – *Texas*?"

"My business takes me *everywhere*, Whit."

"Exactly what business you in, Mister?" the woman asked.

Texas glanced at her, then back at Whit. "You might say I'm in the right-and-wrong business. I help people to do right and refrain from doing wrong."

Whit nodded again, and half-smiled.

"I kind of figured you for some kind of preacher," he said. "Wearing them black clothes and all?"

"Not exactly a preacher, Whit – though I reckon you could say I am on a kind of *mission*," Texas said. "Searching for some good and true men who are willing to fight alongside me against the *evil* that is trying to destroy all that is good and holy – right and honorable – in this great South of ours."

Texas took out two cigars and handed one to Whit.

"If I am any judge of men, Whit Whitfield," Texas stared at the man, "I would say I was *led* here today, through lightning and thunder, to find *you*."

Whit took the cigar, smelled it, then looked at the heavy rain for a few moments.

"No sense us standing out here on this leaky porch getting wet," he said and opened the door and turned to his wife. "Sarah Jane, go git us some of that honey Malachi brung home yesterday, and heat up some pone, and make us some coffee."

Then he nodded to Texas.

"Come on inside," he said. "Don't look like this rain's gonna let up anytime soon."

"Thank you, Whit, that's mighty kind of you," Texas said, and let the woman hold the screen door for him, and felt her breasts rub lightly across his arm as he passed by her.

***

Manse sat on the porch steps and stared into the quiet of evening. Larry sat on the swing. Tom was in a rocking chair, his leg propped on the porch railing. Johnny was lying on the steps near

Manse. The women had gone to bed, so custom permitted the men – Johnny excluded – to have a few drinks. It was the last of the corn whiskey Larry had found in the root cellar when he came home from The War.

"I've been thinking," Manse said –

"I know you have," Tom stopped rocking. "All through dinner you had that look you use to get during The War, when we were in a bad spot on patrol. And now you've got the look you use to get when you figured a way to get us out," Tom smiled and waited. "Well, you going to tell us – or make us guess – ?"

"I was just wondering," Manse said, "what happened to all the livestock from the plantations around here? On all the places we passed between Greenville and Anderson, there didn't seem to be many animals at all. Now I know that during The War the Confederate Army sent out Commissary Patrols to requisition damn near everything – and since The War, the Union army's done the same. But I just can't believe the big planters let the armies take *all* their livestock. Some of those plantations had thousands of cattle and pigs and sheep, not to mention horses and mules. I wager that some of them planters took a lot of their animals and drove them where no one would find them – "

"How could they possibly hide hundreds of head of livestock?" Larry asked.

Manse nodded toward the northwest, and said "By driving them up *there* – into the mountains – figuring to round them up when The War was over."

Larry was pensive for a minute, then became enthusiastic.

"I think maybe you've hit on something, Manse," he said.

"Like my Daddy use to say," – Tom interrupted – "I hate to piss on the fire just when everybody is getting warm, but don't you reckon that anybody that turned livestock loose in the mountains has already gone back and rounded them up by now?"

"That might be," Manse said, "except that there aren't many planters, big or small, who had even half their men come home from The War. That's not near enough men who know the mountains well enough to round up livestock that's turned wild. Remember what it's like up there, Tom? Hundreds of miles of nothing but ridges and valleys, and trees and rocks, and coves and hollows –

with no trails but game trails. I doubt the whole Union Army could search even a small part of it. But we've hunted those mountains all our lives. If there's any livestock up there, we'd be more likely to find it than anybody."

"Afraid I'm not up to mountain tracking," Tom said. "That takes two good legs."

"Larry and I can do the tracking. You and Johnny can take care of things here."

"But even if you're right, the Yankees will just *requisition* any livestock we bring here." The enthusiasm had left Larry's voice.

"Then we won't bring any here," Manse said. "We'll keep'em hid up in the mountains. Butcher them there, and bring the meat down."

"Right," Tom said. "We can hide it in the smokehouse behind false walls, like the ones the Confederate Army built to caché provisions in Virginia. Johnny and I can dismantle one of the cabins and use the lumber to build them, so nothing looks new."

"I think it's worth trying, Manse," Larry's enthusiasm warmed.

"Sure is a hell of a lot better than sitting around waiting for the scalawags to come and take everything from us," he said.

"It's decided then," Manse said. "We'll start first thing tomorrow." *And*, Manse thought to himself, *just maybe we're not licked yet – if there really is any livestock in those mountains.*

**

At dawn the next day, he and Larry set out. Each carried a bedroll, supply sack, oilskin, knives and ropes.

The morning was cool. The walking was easy. They followed roads north, then turned northwest onto paths that began to climb alongside streams – then became game trails leading through tangled undergrowth.

During the afternoon, foothills became steeper; valleys deeper.

By nightfall they reached the remote mountain area Manse had been heading for. They ate hardtack, drank water from a nearby spring, and slept on oilskins and blankets – CSA, faded and worn – not good for much longer.

The next morning they climbed to a ridge, walked it for several hours, then descended to a creek, followed it into a narrow gorge, and stopped at the sound of water falling.

"Remember that sound?" Manse moved faster – and a hundred feet farther on, he stopped – "Remember *that*?" he said, and pointed to a fifty foot waterfall.

"I was only here once," Larry laughed. "But I remember." He stripped off his pack and bedroll, then his shirt and his boots and pants and underwear – and ran and jumped into the pool at the base of the waterfall.

Manse laughed – and in his mind, in that instant the pool was full of splashing, ducking, laughing Jolly brothers – all seven of them, naked and freezing their asses off, and –

"Come on in, Manse," Larry yelled – and Manse stripped and followed.

"Damn – that's cold – " he shivered.

"What the hell did you expect?" Larry laughed and splashed his older brother with a cupped handful of icy water.

The urge to retaliate flashed, then faded.

"I'm too old for that shit," Manse said, but grinned to let Larry know it wasn't personal, then made his way back to the creek bank, and took a blanket from his bedroll and dried himself.

Larry followed him out – and dressed quickly without drying off.

"If you go over to that side of the falls –" Manse pointed and shouted over the noise of falling water – "if you go over to *that* side, you'll find the cave."

"I damn near forgot about the cave," Larry said, and moved to where Manse pointed, pulled away the brush, and uncovered an opening in the rock – a crevice large enough for a man to pass through.

Larry went in and disappeared.

Manse finished dressing, and followed him.

The cave behind the falls was one large room – dimly lit by shafts of light that filtered through crevices high above. The waterfall's noise was muffled, but the sound of water seeping through the rocks and dripping on the floor was clear.

"This place is plenty big enough to pen some small livestock," Larry said, "if we had any livestock to pen." He dropped his pack on the cave floor. "But it's damn cold in here."

"We can build a shack just inside the entrance," Manse said. "That way we can have a place to stay dry. We can have a fire and keep watch –"

"Right," Larry said. "To guard all the livestock we *don't* have."

"We hardly started looking yet," Manse said. "Don't give up."

They made their way back out of the cave into the gorge, and climbed again to the ridge, and renewed their search.

They found signs of deer and smaller animals, but no cows or pigs or horses – until late in the day, when they worked their way down from the ridge, into a deep ravine that led into a small cove filled with a thick stand of laurel – which was where they found the pigs – a boar, two sows and five piglets.

Manse and Larry grinned at each other.

It took them the rest of the afternoon to herd the pigs to the cave.

They were exhausted by the time they finished building a pen with branches – and began eating another meal of hardtack.

Larry built a fire to stave off the cave's damp chill.

Manse laid his poncho as close to the flames as he dared, and pulled his blanket over his head.

"We got to build that shack soon as we can, so we don't freeze to death," he said, and closed his eyes – and drifted off to sleep.

Which lasted until morning when the smell of fresh blood clogged his breathing, and his scream echoed off stone walls.

"Manse – " Larry shook him. "Wake up, dammit – "

Sweat chilled Manse.

"You all right?" Larry had a knife in his hand. The fire had been rekindled and was roaring, and on a rock was the carcass of a piglet he had just butchered.

"Yeah, I'm all right now," Manse nodded, and rubbed his temples to relieve the pain that tried to split his head apart. "Just a bad dream," and he got to his feet and went out of the cave and knelt down and washed his face in the cold mountain water.

By the time he walked into the woods and relieved himself, and returned to the cave, the piglet was almost cooked.

"That sure smells good," Manse skewered a piece of pork on his short-sword, and bit off a piece that burned his tongue. "Sure beats hell out of hardtack," he smiled at Larry, who returned the smile through grease-covered lips.

They ate the entire piglet before they left the cave.

At mid-morning they stood on a steep slope and looked down into an oval cove. Its only access was a pass sealed by a fence of boulders. Grazing beside a spring were a rust-colored stallion, four mares, two colts, a bull, three cows, and six heifers.

"I'd say we're looking at somebody's idea of a corral," Larry started down, then stopped, picked up something from the ground, brushed it off, and turned back to Manse. "Cavalry bridle," he said, and held it out.

Manse took it, and saw the barely visible *CSA* stamped into the leather.

"Any sign of a brand on any of 'em?" he asked.

Larry made his way closer to the horses maintaining enough distance so they wouldn't bolt and run, then said, "None that I can see."

Manse took his time going down, looking for signs that anyone had been here recently.

"Some son of a bitch from our own Commissary Service probably brought these animals up here and hid them, planning to come back later and get them and sell them," Manse said. "The fact they're still here means he never made it back."

"May as well find out if these horses are broke-in," Larry said. "No sense in walking if we can ride."

Larry chose a black mare, and Manse the rust stallion. They fashioned rope halters, bits, and reins, slipped them on, and mounted bareback. The horses bucked and reared a few times, but soon gave in and settled down.

"Well," Larry said when the horses were standing quietly, "we found what we came for – now we can spend the rest of the day trying to herd 'em back to the cave?"

Manse rubbed his face in thought, then said, " Let's just take the horses, and leave the cattle. We can come here to butcher them. No sign anybody's been around lately."

Larry agreed, then added, "we could use a mule or two to carry out the meat."

"Then let's go find us a mule or two," Manse said.

They blocked the entrance again, and rode their new mounts slowly up to the ridge and headed toward the next valley.

Their luck held. Within a week they had found four mules, and an assortment of livestock – including a young bull with a full set of horns that almost castrated Larry when he dismounted and came too close in an attempt to rope it.

They built a stout fence of rocks across the narrowest point of the gorge beside the waterfall, to pen animals there rather than keep them inside the cave where manure and dampness had quickly created an overwhelming stench.

Then Larry used his infantry-issue hatchet to cut down small pines, and Manse used his close-quarters-saber to trim the branches, and they built a notched log shack just inside the cave's entrance.

They decided that one of them should remain at the cave to protect their livestock from theft – and search for more.

Larry volunteered.

They butchered three steers and two hogs, tied the sides of beef and pork on the mules, and Manse mounted the rust stallion.

"You take care of yourself up here, you hear?" he said.

Larry said he would, but he hoped Manse would hurry back soon with a jug or two of whiskey, to help stave off mountain night-chills."

Manse laughed and promised he would do just that, and he started the trek home.

Hiding livestock in the mountains to be butchered and sold in secret wasn't exactly what he'd dreamed about when he was in the army – but if that was what it took to bring peace to his family and to his life, he could make that adjustment, just like he had made others when it was necessary. His only prayer was that, from now on, his dreams might be peaceful – not violent.

***

***

Martin McCollum's first decision was to visit the Banking & Arms Building on University Hill.

It had been Confederate Army Headquarters in Anderson, and also housed the Confederate Holding Bank. All of the records so meticulously kept by Confederate Army Company Clerks stationed in Anderson during the five years of the Confederacy had been seized, and classified, and filed by equally meticulous Union Army Company Clerks.

Inventory records showed that gold ingots had indeed been stored there as of March 1865, when the Confederate Cabinet, meeting in Abbeville, South Carolina, ordered all remaining assets of the Holding Bank be crated and shipped by special train to Charleston – corroborating information Martin already possessed.

He also located a Military Log Book with a list of the names of all visitors to Confederate Army Headquarters during the six months prior to its surrender. He decided that was as good a place to start as any. As it turned out, most of the names were Confederate enlisted men home on recuperative leave, reporting for reassignment. He talked to the few he could locate, who had survived The War, and from them, he learned nothing.

In order to question returning Confederate Officers whose names appeared in the Log, Martin needed a directive from the Greenville District Commandant, which required a requisition from Captain Ralph Phillips.

"You're farting in the wind, Lieutenant," the Captain said. "These Rebel Officers have a code of honor. They won't tell you anything about any gold, even if they know anything about any gold –which they probably don't."

"If you don't mind, sir, I would still like to request the directives so I can question these gentlemen," Martin was standing, but not at rigid attention.

"Very well, Lieutenant, I'll put in the request, but I think you'd be better off – " Captain Phillips interrupted himself and exhaled a spiral of smoke. "Never mind what I think. *You* are the Intelligence Officer."

"Begging the Captain's pardon, sir – " Martin said. "I am open to any suggestions you may have, sir."

"Then – instead of expecting some ex-Rebel-Officers to talk – if I were you, I would question employees of the Peoples Bank of Anderson, where the civilians do their banking. Bankers always know more about the money in a town than anybody else – even if it's in another bank – even a military holding bank."

"Thank you for that suggestion, sir," Martin brought his heels together and saluted. "I will follow up on it."

Martin smiled to himself. He had been right. Captain Phillips *was* intelligent – which did not, of course, alter the fact that the captain was also crazy as hell.

"Hold your *cojones*, Lieutenant," Captain Phillips put his pipe down. "Does that mean you *do* want the directives – or you *don't*?"

"I will appreciate your requisitioning them for me, sir, while I pursue the other avenues of investigation you have suggested."

"Save the horse shit for the stables, Lieutenant. I hoped you would save me a lot of paper work and forget the requisitions. But my ploy didn't work, dammit, so you're dismissed," Captain Phillips returned the salute.

Martin went directly to the Peoples Bank of Anderson where he was met with degrees of non-cooperation ranging from complete ignorance to absolute evasion. No one presently employed by the bank had been working there six months before. The bank was now owned by two men from Ohio. Martin began to re-evaluate (again) his opinion of Captain Phillips.

In the end, the bank's newly appointed president – a cousin of Samuel Heaton – did give him a list of names of Andersonians who had been associated with the bank during the war. Four of the names on the list refused to see him. Two agreed to talk to him, but didn't tell him anything.

The seventh name was an elderly lady he found sitting on the front porch of her home on West Market Street – fanning herself in the early October afternoon.

" I am most certainly willing to tell you what happened to all that gold, young man," she said. "Your army took it – stole it – along with everything else."

"By *my* army – you mean the *Union Army*?"

"That's precisely what I mean, young man – *your* army."

Martin sighed, and had to admit to himself that there was a possibility he had been ordered by his unfriendly superiors to find gold that was already locked in a vault in Washington.

"Pardon me, ma'am, but would you mind telling me precisely how you know that *my* army took the gold?"

"I know because I *saw* the men who took it," she said.

"You *saw* the men?" Martin tried to conceal his disbelief. "Would you be good enough to tell me everything you remember?"

"Well, first of all, it was last spring. A beautiful spring until *your army* came and ruined everything."

"Excuse me, ma'am, but do you recall what *units* – what *men* of *my army* you saw?"

"Of course, young man. It was General Stoneforth's men."

"General Stone*man*'s Brigade?"

"Yes. That's right – Stone*man*. General Stoneman's men."

"Please go on."

"They rode into Anderson shooting and yelling and carrying on. It was a disgrace. Then they started stealing things from the stores – and forced their way into the Confederate Holding Bank up on University Hill – looking for gold, they said."

"And did they find gold there?"

"My understanding is that the vault was empty, and even under brutal torture, the four brave Confederate soldiers guarding the Bank revealed only that everything had been shipped away earlier. Well, sir, from what I heard, that sure made General Stoneman's men very angry. So they proceeded to the People's Bank of Anderson and forced the president and manager to open the vault there. And when they found that it, too, was empty, your General Stoneman's brigands went berserk. They tortured bank officials – and when they didn't find what they wanted – they hanged two of them in the town square – and threatened to hang more men unless someone showed them where the gold was."

Martin was suspicious. "How is it that you know all these details, ma'am?" he asked.

The old lady stopped fanning long enough to look at him.

"Because my brother was the president of the People's Bank of Anderson," she said. "And he was one of the men your General Stoneman's men hanged. That is how I know, young man."

Martin could say only, "I deeply regret that, ma'am."

The lady closed her fan, raised it, and pointed it at him.

"Young man, don't offer me any of your apologies or condolences," she said. "They are of little value to me. Instead, explain to me, if you can, *why* your General Stoneman allowed his men to act in such a barbaric manner?"

Martin did not answer her.

She wouldn't have believed him anyhow, if he told her that the General had issued specific orders prohibiting looting, theft of property, or physical injury to the civilian population of Anderson – or any community occupied by his Brigade in its lightning sweep through the Carolinas.

So, rather than an answer, Martin asked her another question.

"Ma'am, can you remember the exact date General Stoneman came to Anderson?"

"Clearly. It was late afternoon – on March the twenty-third."

"Do you recall seeing any of the insignia on the uniforms – or hearing any of the officers called by name?"

"Now how would I be able to do that, young man? Those soldiers wore all sorts of things. Some even wore ladies' plumes in their hats. Their attire was as outrageous as their conduct."

"Did you actually see General Stoneman or any of his staff?"

"Not that night – no. My sister and I stayed inside and closed the shutters, so we didn't see much until the next morning when a group of Union officers rode in."

"That was the following morning?" Martin asked.

"That's what I said – the next morning."

"Was there any sign of the soldiers who caused the trouble the night before?"

The old lady thought for a moment, then shook her head.

"No – come to think of it," she said, "I don't recall seeing a single one of those horrid men. I presumed that sometime during the night they had found the gold they sought, and delivered it to General Stoneman."

"It sounds like renegades," Martin said, more to himself than to her.

"Renegades, Lieutenant?"

Martin decided to try to explain, despite the secrecy of the file.

"Yes, ma'am," he said. "Some soldiers who were under orders to find food and supplies for the Union Army, found it more profitable to do whatever pleased them, including stealing and pillaging. I assure you that if General Stoneman had caught these renegades, he would have hanged them."

"He did hang *two* men while he was here. One was my brother," the lady said.

"Yes, ma'am – you told me that," Martin paused. "Is there anything else you remember, Ma'am?"

"Only that about ten o'clock my sister remarked that it had become very quiet outside, so we risked a peek, and didn't see any of your soldiers – just the flames of a house they burned – and those two poor men hanging from a tree."

She was silent for a minute, then said, "You may wonder why I am telling you all of this, Lieutenant – you being an enemy officer. My reason is simple – I want everyone to know what went on here. I want everyone to know how you yankee soldiers killed my brother."

***

Texas Brown reached inside his coat, took out his cigar case, removed his last cigar.

"Running low. Got to buy a new box," he said aloud to no one except his horse,

But he knew he didn't have the money to buy a box of cigars. His cash reserve was as low as his supply of smokes.

He smiled and bit off the tip of the remaining cigar and spat it into the dust. The men who bankrolled him in Atlanta had been generous – in most matters. They had underwritten the cost of this fine stallion, the tooled saddle and bridle and saddle bags – had bought him two pairs of the finest western-style boots, and had ordered hand-tailored for him two suits and two waistcoats – and even bought him two hats.

But they had limited the amount of cash allotted to him from their Treasury. In its place, they had granted him exclusive territorial rights to the Piedmont District of South Carolina – all income from dues, sales, and grants in that entire area – less, of course, a percentage to be remitted to Atlanta.

By giving him less money, they said, they were providing him with increased incentive – as if he needed more incentive to do what he was doing.

Thus far his territory had brought him practically no income.

But if tonight was any indicator – and if he was any judge of men – he would soon have all the money he needed – perhaps, eventually, all the money he wanted.

Tonight he had recruited fourteen men, good and true –

Well – to be honest with himself – they were actually fourteen men who might be worth a shit in a bucket.

But it was a start.

And it was ample evidence to him that coming from Atlanta to Anderson had been the right move.

Now the only thing he had to do was choose the right target for his initial action.

It was late in the evening. Texas looked forward to a nightcap at the Benson House bar.

Building an empire – especially an invisible one – was damned thirsty work.

-4-

The argument between Rebecca and Tom erupted after breakfast the Monday following Manse's return from the mountains.

It wasn't that Manse eavesdropped – it was impossible *not* to hear every word.

The beginning was innocent enough. Manse and Tom, with Johnny's help, had loaded the wagon with meat to take to Anderson to sell, and Tom had gone to the door of the bedroom Rebecca shared with Bonnie and Melinda, to ask his sister for the list of things that she and the other women-folk wanted him to buy in town.

Rebecca, wearing her best Sunday dress, was seated before the mirror combing out her long blond hair, which she usually wore in a single braid.

"I thought you only did that before you went to bed – or if you were expecting a gentleman caller," Tom said, as Rebecca counted the strokes.

She pretended to throw the brush at him.

"I'm going to Anderson with you and Manse," she said.

"Oh no you're not. You can't," Tom said. "We have business to take care of. Selling meat. Paying taxes."

"Please, Tom," Rebecca stood. "You've just got to let me go with you. I'm so tired of looking at the same old front yard, and fields, and kitchen and stove and all," she paused. "I promise you I won't get in the way. I'll shop for what's on Mama Jolly's list – and Bonnie's list – and my list – while you and Manse do what you've got to do."

She walked past her brother and started down the stairs.

"We aren't at all sure we'll get enough money from the meat to pay the taxes," Tom hobbled after her, "much less do any shopping. Besides, I don't think Anderson is a good place for you to wander around shopping all by yourself."

"Now how would you know that, Tom Largent?" Rebecca turned around at the bottom of the stairs and faced him. "You haven't been to Anderson since before The War – and I was there just last year, when Lewis was home with Bonnie. It seemed safe enough then."

She walked into the kitchen. Tom followed.

"Things have changed, Rebecca. Changed a lot since we lost The War and the Yankees took over everything –" Tom looked around the room for help. "You tell her, Manse. Maybe she'll listen to you."

Manse stared at Tom, then at Rebecca, but he couldn't find words for what he wanted to say, because what he felt had nothing to do with Rebecca going to Anderson. What he really wanted to do was tell her how much it meant to him that she lived at the Jolly farm and he got to see her everyday, and how beautiful her hair and eyes were –

When he said nothing, Maude Jolly took over the conversation.

"To my mind, you're being plain unreasonable, Tom Largent," she said. "Seems to me Rebecca would be perfectly safe going anywhere with two big strapping men like you and Manse. And she surely knows a lot more than either one of you about buying cloth and threads and things like that – things we sorely need if there's enough money to buy them. And if there's not, well then she will at least have had a pleasant ride into Anderson –which is something she hasn't done for more than a year. So I see no reason why she shouldn't go."

With that, Tom's argument was lost.

***

Manse drove the wagon. Rebecca sat on the seat between him and Tom. Hidden beneath a stack of oilskins, loose boards and pine branches, was the load of meat that Manse and Tom planned to take to Gerald McClure, who ran a general goods store. On the ride into town, they talked mostly about what they would and would not tell Mr. McClure about the source of their beef and pork, and they speculated on how much money they might get for it.

Rebecca wondered who they might meet up with that she knew,

and who they might meet up with that she *didn't* know, and – as they came into town, she wondered aloud, "Did you ever see so many bluebelly soldiers in one place at one time in your whole life?"

Manse and Tom laughed and assured her that, yes, they had.

Anderson had changed little during the four years since Manse was last here. It was made up of seven blocks of streets and buildings oriented around a Town Square, the center of which was the County Courthouse. But, while the town itself had remained much the same, the makeup of the population on its streets was radically different.

Gone were the expensively dressed Southron ladies from the large plantations, walking with their parasols and maid-servant slaves. They had been replaced by women in dresses four years old and older, worn and sewn and re-sewn – women who had come to town from farms and small plantations to buy or trade for enough staples and goods to keep their families through the coming winter.

And there were new classes of women.

There were well-dressed wives of scalawags who had been able to turn a dollar throughout the war years selling goods that had run the blockade, and after The War, joined by northern carpetbaggers, supplying the needs of the occupying Union troops.

And there were the brilliantly clothed fancy whores who worked in the houses of pleasure by night, and by day paraded – and spent their money – on Main Street.

And there were the women of color – freed by law and taking full advantage of their right to dress and walk as they pleased and not have to step down in the gutter whenever a white man or woman passed by.

All of them mingled on the sidewalks where the only mediating element was the ever-present military blue of Union uniforms – worn by men who were seen by most Andersonians as their enemies. Not former enemies, but enemies still.

Even the whores, if they were Southern, showed hatred through their eyes even as their bodies faked surrender.

In the midst of the town's crowded streets, Manse began breathing fast and sweating. He guided the mules into the alley behind McClure's General Store, got down from the wagon, and wiped his face with his handkerchief.

"You all right?" Tom asked.

"Yeah, I'm fine," Manse took a deep breath, then knocked on the store's back door.

He heard the sound of bolts being pulled, and the door opened and out stepped a large man wrapped in a white apron over an immense belly.

"Well I'll be damned and gone below – it's good to see you, Manse," the big man enfolded him in a bear hug, then released Manse and reached up and grabbed Tom's hand and shook it so hard he almost pulled him off the wagon. "I saw young Larry a few weeks back and he told me you boys were home. Welcome back, Tom." Then he looked at Rebecca. "And I would recognize that sister of yours anywhere – though I must say you've grown even more beautiful in the year since last I saw you." He reached up and helped her down from the wagon.

When her feet touched the ground, she smiled up at him.

"Morning, Mr. McClure," she said.

"Sure and that smile has made my morning," McClure laughed. "Now tell me, what can I do for you folks today?"

Manse reached into the wagon and lifted an oilskin.

Gerald McClure stood on a wheel-hub, whistled softly, and nodded a butcher's solemn appreciation of what he saw. "Fine quality beef and pork. Been killed how long?"

"Six days," Manse said. "Five hung in the smokehouse."

"Well, it's rich men you'll be if you've got much of this hidden away. I've a contract with the Yankee army for all the fresh meat I can lay my hands on – and believe me, these days the price is high."

"We've got six sides of beef and four of pork here," Manse said. "What do you reckon it's worth?"

"Depending on how it weighs out. I would guess somewhere between three-hundred and three-hundred fifty dollars – if that sounds fair to you?"

"Your word has always been bond to us and ours, Mr. McClure," Tom climbed down off the wagon.

"I thank you for those kind words," Gerald McClure shook Tom's hand again.

"We are talking about Yankee dollars?" Manse said.

"There ain't no other kind anymore, Manse. Whether we like it or not, our Confederate States are gone and won't be back. I figure, one way or another, we're all Yankees now."

Pain flashed through Manse's head, then dulled and dissipated through his temples.

"I'll have my boy come out and take this load inside to weigh it," Gerald McClure said. "Then we can settle up."

"We'd be much obliged to you, Mr. McClure," Manse said, "if you could you go ahead and advance us two-hundred-fifty dollars. We've got taxes to pay."

"You're going to see Samuel Heaton – " McClure turned his head and spat the bad taste from his mouth.

Tom and Manse nodded.

"Son of a bitch," McClure muttered, then said, "Sorry, Miss Rebecca."

Rebecca half-smiled but did not enter the conversation.

"His office is in the Courthouse –" McClure continued "– right next door to Bluebelly Army Headquarters. But you'll find him most often sitting at the big corner table in the Benson House bar."

"The notice he gave us says we're to pay at the Courthouse," Manse said, "so I reckon that's where we'll go."

"You boys hold on a minute and I'll get your money," Gerald McClure went into the store – returned in a few minutes – and counted out the money in twenty-dollar, and ten-dollar green paper bills, with some five-dollar and one-dollar gold coins – and handed it to Manse. "I hate to see you give good money to that snake Heaton, but I guess there's no alternative to taxes."

"There is *one* –" Manse stopped his words when Tom's eye caught his.

They walked away from the wagon. Manse counted out one hundred dollars and handed it to Tom, then gave twenty dollars to Rebecca.

"Will that be enough for your shopping?"

"Now how would I know how much things cost?" Rebecca asked. "I haven't been in town for a year. And I didn't buy anything then. So you'll just have to come with me and tell me what we can afford to buy and what we can't."

"Why don't you go on into McClure's Store and look around," Tom said. "Manse and I will be back as quick as we can," "No sense in you trailing after us. We may have to go to the Benson House bar and they don't allow women – or girls – in there."

Rebecca stuck out her tongue at her older brother, turned the two men around, and placed herself between them, linked her arms with theirs, smiled and said, "I'd rather be escorted by two handsome gentlemen down Main Street than poke around some dusty old store."

She tugged hard and the three of them moved out of the alley onto the wooden sidewalk toward the Courthouse.

***

When not engaged in an investigation that held his interest, Martin McCollum spent a lot of time drinking –and an equal amount of time observing the inner-workings of the military establishment that, for the time-being, owned him – and studying the volumes of rules that governed it. As a result, he had decided that US Army regulations were not designed to stand up for long under the stress of peacetime reality. Rather they were promulgated to provide young men of limited capabilities with limited responsibilities – under the command of older men of equally limited competence.

Given enough time, and a sufficient number of those younger men to die as the result of their elders' tactical mistakes, the older men could actually develop a degree of efficiency and win wars.

But, Martin found that, when the warfare ended, the Army rapidly returned to its pre-war level of complacent inefficiency and general stupidity.

The placement of his *desk* proved that point.

As a lieutenant in Army Intelligence, he was supposed to work as unobtrusively as possible. In fact, in those instances when he conducted his investigations in secret, he had his highest rate of success.

In Anderson, South Carolina, however, he was required to wear his uniform at all times – as were all Army personnel occupying the South. Worse than that, his desk, with his name and rank and the words *Army Intelligence* engraved in large letters on a brass plaque, was placed directly in front of one of the street-level windows of the Anderson County Courthouse – a window broad enough to ensure that passersby could see not only the desk, but the idiot lieutenant who sat there day after day sorting papers that everyone in Anderson knew concerned the town's biggest joke – *the missing Confederate gold.*

Martin sifted through another stack of meaningless reports, then stretched, and dared a glance out of the window.

He usually avoided looking outside. The eyes of passersby made him uneasy. And all too often, he became the target of schoolboys who found his face behind the window's glass a perfect target for balls of horse shit.

But this day, he leaned back in his chair, yawned and, against his better judgment, looked out the window – and saw no eyes full of hate or balls of manure. This time he saw, coming across the Square, two men. One had a straggly beard. The other had a severe limp. And between the two men was a girl. But she was more than just a girl. She was a young woman with cascading hair that shone like gold in the sun. And a special tilt to her head.

And she and the two men were walking toward the Courthouse.

Martin's masculinity awoke from months of abstinence, and he found himself moving to the door as though some great magnet were pulling him to her.

They collided – Martin McCollum exiting the Courthouse – the two men and the girl entering. In the confusion, he looked into her eyes and saw there no hatred – only bright blue reflections of the Army Lieutenant the young woman was looking at.

Then one of the men asked Martin a question, and he pointed to the office of the Collector of Taxes, stepped back out of their way, and watched as they walked down the hall and knocked on the door.

Martin hurried back into the office he shared with military aides, and their aides, and stood by his desk.

"Any of you men know those three people who just came in the Courthouse?" he asked the two sergeants and four corporals who were present.

As the senior officer in the room at the moment, he rated five *"No, sir's."*

"You mean the two men and the young woman, sir," asked the sergeant whose desk was nearest the door to the captain's office, and whose desk-plaque read *Sgt. Alexander Jerlier Commissary Requisitions.*

"Yes, Sergeant Jerlier, that's exactly who I mean. Do you know who they are?"

"The bearded man's name is Jolly. The other man, and the woman are Largents. Brother and sister. They live with the Jolly family."

"And do you know where they live?"

"Area called the Lebanon Community, Sir. A good ways out of town. I can show you on the map."

"Not necessary, Sergeant. But thank you."

"You're welcome, sir," Sgt. Jerlier said, and smiled, making Martin feel as though the man was reading his thoughts about the young woman. He definitely should keep his eye on this Sgt. Jerlier.

Then the name clicked in his memory – *Jolly.*

Martin thumbed through a stack of papers on his desk. There it was – *Jolly, Lewis* – on the log of visitors to the Confederate Holding Bank. In fact, it was on there a number of times. Because of that, Martin had inquired about the man –and decided that questioning his family would be just another waste of time.

But *now* – perhaps *now* he should re-open this area of investigation. Yes, he definitely should question all the Jolly family. And anyone else who lived at the Jolly home.

He held onto his page of notes and walked out into the hallway and waited. Within a minute the door to the Tax Collector's Office opened and the two men and the girl headed toward him.

Martin pulled down his tunic, stood tall and stepped in front of the trio.

"Excuse me, Gentlemen, Miss," he bowed slightly and dared another fleeting look in her eyes – a look she did not return. "One of the sergeants in my office informs that you are Mr. Jolly and Mr. Largent. I am Lt. Martin McCollum, US Army Intelligence – " Martin held out his hand. Neither Manse nor Tom shook it. He paused to gauge their reaction. They did not appear impressed.

"I need to speak with you," Martin said.

Manse glared at him, "How much do you want?"

"I assure you that all I want is information, Mr. Jolly," Martin's tone was intentionally less than friendly. "I understand that you returned home only recently, but that your youngest brother – Lawrence, I believe his name is – was at home until two years ago, and that another brother was home on extended leave twice, recuperating from wounds. Is that correct?"

"Yes. That was my brother Lewis. But why are you so interested in my family?"

Martin ignored Manse's question. "And his widow still resides at your home, along with your mother – and Mr. Largent's sister, – who, I presume, is *you*," Martin let his eyes lock onto hers.

Rebecca met his look, then nodded *yes* and very quickly looked away.

Tom stepped in front of Rebecca, blocking Martin's view.

Martin looked at Manse.

"I would like to come to your house and ask your mother and Miss Largent some questions."

"Not unless you tell us what this is all about," Manse frowned.

He found the Lieutenant's interest disturbing –

His thought was interrupted – an interruption that was sudden, not loud. The door at which they stood was pushed open and two soldiers entered, holding the arms of a tall black man who was manacled and shackled.

"Mister Tom? And Mister Manse? It's sure nice to see you all home safe," the man said.

"Robespierre – What the hell have they got you all chained-up for?"

"They won't tell me, Mister Tom. They just come to the station and got me and brunged me here."

A lieutenant who appeared to Manse to be too young and too small to be in any *real* Army, walked into the hallway.

"Did he give you any trouble, Corporal?" the lieutenant asked.

"No, sir. He just asked why we were arresting him, and I told him he would find out soon enough, and he came along peacefully."

"Take him to the stockade," the lieutenant said. "I'll question him there."

"Yes, sir," the two soldiers saluted, then turned to Robespierre.

"Okay you, let's go," The corporal said, and they led the black man away.

"Just what is Robespierre accused of?" Tom asked Martin.

"To be honest, I don't know," Martin said. "This is Lieutenant Francis Marion Pearson. He is Captain Phillips' aide. I'm sure he can tell you – if he will."

Martin looked at the lieutenant."

Lt. Pearson flashed hostility, then said to Tom, "he killed a girl."

"I don't believe that," Tom said. "Robespierre has been free more than twenty years. Been working around the train station long as I can remember. He wouldn't kill anybody."

"I'm really not interested in *your* opinion. Three witnesses say he did it, and that is sufficient for me," Lt. Pearson did an abrupt about-face and walked away.

"Free for twenty years? That's unusual, isn't it?" Martin was intrigued.

Manse looked at Tom. Tom nodded, and answered.

"Yeah, I reckon it is kind-of unusual," he said. "Robespierre was Old Mister Tobias McGukin's slave. And about twenty years ago there was a fire at the McGukin house, and Mister McGukin was trapped inside, and Robespierre went in and got him out. Saved his life. So Mister McGukin set him free. Even gave him his last name, because most slaves didn't have one – and got him a job working at the train station." Tom stopped talking and shrugged. "That's about it. The whole story, I mean."

"Very interesting." Martin mentally filed the information. "Now, gentlemen, back to my question. When may I call at your home?"

"I'm not sure we want – "

Martin abruptly interrupted. "This is not a matter of what you *want*, Mr. Jolly. If you prefer, I can send a squad of Cavalry to your home and have them escort you and your family here under a legal summons to answer my questions."

His eyes locked on Manse's. Neither man blinked.

"The decision is yours, Mr. Jolly. But I would prefer to keep this as cordial as possible – so please tell me when I may call?"

Manse turned to Tom. Again they exchanged nods.

"Any evening after supper, Lieutenant," Tom said, "And before eight o'clock. That's about the only free time we have."

"Very good. I'll be out to see you in a couple of weeks."

Tom nor Manse nor Rebecca replied. They simply walked past the lieutenant and left the Courthouse.

Martin took out his watch, flipped open its case – *quarter of twelve* –exactly enough time for a whiskey or two before lunch – after which he could return to the arduous task of sorting papers in an investigation whose status had gradually regressed from *exciting* to *less-than-interesting* to *dull* – to *futile*.

***

Manse and Tom insisted that Rebecca wait in the Benson House lobby while they paid the taxes, which, to their surprise, she agreed to do –whispering in Tom's ear that she needed to go to the ladies lounge anyhow, because she had suddenly been overtaken by her female time. With that, she left them.

The lobby was two stories high, with great wooden columns supporting the mezzanine and floors above. It was filled with military personnel, salesmen, and others of less obvious occupations, sitting and reading newspapers, or just watching.

Before The War this had been the meeting place of the wealthy and powerful, which included both Southrons and small planters. Those two groups never entertained each other in their homes, nor ate together in the Benson House dining room, but there was an unspoken understanding that allowed them to cross social lines and discuss agricultural matters, politics, gossip – and even exchange contrary opinions – so long as they did it in the Benson House bar.

"Do you recollect when we use to come here with our daddies, when we were little boys?" Tom asked.

"Sure I remember," Manse said. "We'd sit under the table and try to stay out of the way. And your daddy would make us sandwiches from that free-lunch table. And we'd eat and listen to the grown-ups."

"I reckon that was one of the ways we learned some of the things a man needs to know," Tom said.

"The hell we did," Manse said. "About all I learned under those tables was that horse shit smells the same on a Southron's boots as it does on a small planter's."

They laughed together.

Then they nodded solemn, silent assurance to each other – as they had done a hundred times during the last four years – just prior to engaging the enemy.

"Might as well get this over with," Manse said.

They pushed open the swinging doors and walked into the bar.

The room was designed for men and occupied by men. But no longer was it the domain of Southrons and small planters. Now all power lay with the United States Army, and the talk was between officers, and the subject was usually paperwork or home.

The civilians who were in the room seemed comfortable around the uniforms, suggesting they all had dealings with the military.

It was easy to find Samuel Heaton. He was at the large round table in the corner – the table formerly reserved for plantation owners and powerful politicians.

Across from him sat a man dressed all in black.

Heaton looked up and motioned Manse and Tom to his table.

"Good day to you, Mr. Jolly. Mr. Largent. How you all been?" His smile was broad. "Take a chair," he said. "Have a drink. But first, let me introduce you to – "

"I came to pay my taxes – not socialize with you," Manse took money from his pocket and counted out one-hundred-forty-six dollars onto the table, and said, "I'll take a receipt."

Conversation in the bar stopped.

Heaton looked at the money, then raised his eyebrows, gathered the bills in a neat pile, shuffled some papers, wrote a receipt, and handed it to Manse, then turned to Tom.

"And how about your taxes, Mr. Largent?" he said.

Tom glared at him and dropped a crumpled wad of bills and coins on the table.

Samuel Heaton carefully straightened out the bills as he counted them, then stacked the coins on top and wrote Tom a receipt and gave it to him.

"Don't know how you boys raised that much money, but I'm pleased to receive it – on behalf of your state and county governments, of course," he smiled.

Laughter rippled through the room.

Manse's eyes narrowed and his temples pounded, and he made a move toward Samuel Heaton, but stopped when Tom touched his arm and said, "It's done, Manse – let's go."

They turned and left the bar.

**

Martin McCollum had walked across the Square to the Benson House, into the lobby, and was heading to the bar for his mid-day drinks when he saw her standing beside one of the six columns that surrounded the lobby and supported the mezzanine.

Then the door to the bar swung open and the two men she had been with came out. The face of the one named Jolly was tense, and flushed with anger. The other one – her brother – appeared calm. She went to him. He put his arm around her and showed her a piece of paper, and talked to her, and she started crying.

Then they began to argue.

They were out of earshot so Martin couldn't hear her words – until her voice rose when she said, "To hell with them, Tom," and she snatched the paper out of his hand, and pushed past him – headed into the bar.

But the bearded man – Jolly – caught her arm and stopped her. He said something to her, and took the paper away from her. She protested. Then Tom joined the discussion and the two men escorted her to a chair where she sat and stared at the wall.

Then Manse and Tom looked at each other, nodded solemnly, said nothing, and walked back into the Benson House bar.

In a few minutes, the door swung open once again, and they came out.

Her brother, Tom, had money in his hand, and he gave it to her.

She stood and smiled and kissed his cheek, then she kissed the cheek of the man named Jolly.

Then the three of them headed across the lobby, straight for him.

For the second time in twenty-five minutes, Martin McCollum was confronted with a Jolly, two Largents, and one large door.

But this time he was prepared. He lunged and held the door open for them just as they reached it.

One of the men said, "Thank you, Lieutenant."

And the young woman blinked the most beautiful blue eyes he had ever seen, and looked at him and smiled slightly and said, "Yes, Lieutenant – thank you."

Then they were gone.

And Martin knew it would now take at least three whiskeys to get him through lunch, so he could sit at his desk all afternoon and think of those eyes and that hair – and imagine what lay beneath that dress.

He paid little attention to the man dressed in black who came out of the bar, passed him, and followed them out the front door of the hotel.

***

Manse had fought hard to control his temper. All he wanted to do, once they paid the taxes, was get the hell away from bluebellies, scalawags and carpetbaggers – get the hell out of Anderson and back to the farm where he could work off his rage.

The last person he expected to create yet another problem was Rebecca.

When they came out of the bar, she was still seated. Still staring at the wall. And when Tom told her the taxes were paid and they could now go shopping, she said that she had been thinking and it made her mad that they had to pay to keep a farm that was already theirs –

And Tom said he didn't like the idea any more than she did, but he didn't want to lose their land –

Then Rebecca stood up and said that giving all their money to a man like Heaton was just plain wrong. Larry was right, Heaton would just keep coming back again and again for more and more until they couldn't pay anymore and then he would take their land anyhow. Then he would have their money *and* their land – while they had nothing.

The more she talked, the angrier Rebecca became. It just wasn't fair, she said, that she was getting ready to go shopping for cloth to mend dresses and shirts and trousers and underwear yet again – and she and Bonnie and Mama Jolly and Melinda and Tom and Larry and Manse couldn't even afford shoes and boots – while white trash scalawags were wearing new clothes and driving new buggies drawn by fine horses.

By that point Rebecca had begun crying – and she grabbed the tax receipt and said, "to hell with them, Tom, I'm going in there and get our money back," and she started toward the door to the bar – until Manse stopped her.

That was when Manse told Tom that actually he thought that what Rebecca was saying about Heaton and the taxes made a lot of sense. The Jolly farm was as much land as they could possibly work. And they stood a better chance of paying taxes on just one farm – and keeping it and making a living from it.

Tom looked sad, but then he and Manse exchanged nods, and without any further words, it was agreed.

Rebecca gave the tax receipt to Tom, and the two men went back into the bar.

When they walked directly to Samuel Heaton's table, the room became quiet.

"Back so soon, gentlemen?" Heaton laughed. "What do you want now – to prepay the new Reparations Tax? Actually it won't be due until the first of next year, but I could give you a substantial discount for early payment."

"Tom wants his tax money back," Manse said, and took the receipt from Tom and put it on the table in front of Heaton.

"That right, Mr. Largent? You want your ninety-two dollars back?"

"Yeah," Tom said. "I want my ninety-two dollars back."

"If I refund your payment, Mr. Largent, you understand that your farm will be foreclosed within the month – "

"Yeah, goddammit, I understand!" Tom said. "But I'd rather see that happen, than put all my money in your pocket – "

"If you're sure that's what you want, then here's your refund," Samuel Heaton counted out the money. "That's a nice little place you've got out there. Of course, I already own a plantation, so I'm not interested in it for myself, but I know some freedmen who are looking for a small farm. I'll let them know it's coming up for auction. They'll make mighty fine neighbors for you and the Jolly family."

He smiled from Tom to Manse.

"You Yankee-sucking son of a bitch, I ought to –" Tom shouted at him.

Manse grabbed Tom's arm with both hands and said, "Let's go."

The man in black had not said a word – but his expression said he missed nothing.

Samuel Heaton's face was scarlet as he half-rose from his chair and shook his finger at Tom.

"You had best be careful, Largent," he said. "There are laws against intimidating public officials. I can have you arrested – "

"You don't need to warn Tom and me, Mister Heaton," Manse said. "We know who won The War," his voice was calm. "But I tell you this, if the Union keeps passing laws telling us southerners everything we're allowed to say and do and think, then one day there's going to be a whole mess of trouble."

An officer standing at the bar turned to face Manse.

"Is that a threat, Mr. Jolly?"

"No threat, Captain," Manse said, holding up one hand as though to appease the man. "Just an observation."

Manse's grip on Tom's arm tightened, and he started them toward the door.

Then, from somewhere in the room came a voice:

"Them two Rebs look like they'd like to take on the whole damn Army Of Occupation single-handed."

Manse and Tom walked out of the bar, followed by laughter.

In the lobby, Tom handed the tax money to Rebecca.

"You're angry with me," she said.

"No – I'm really not," Tom said. "I didn't think it was the right thing to do, until I did it. Now I *know* it was right. We're going to do whatever it takes to hold the Jollys and the Largents together. And I don't mean just surviving. We deserve more, and I aim to see we have it."

"Agreed," Manse said, and found a smile for Rebecca. "Now let's get you started shopping, while Tom and I get the supplies."

Rebecca kissed Tom's cheek, then turned and kissed Manse's.

That same Lieutenant was coming into the Benson House, or going out, and held the door open for them.

They walked along Main Street and left Rebecca at a dress shop with instructions to buy something for all the ladies at the Jolly farm – and a doll for Melinda.

Then Manse and Tom headed back towards Gerald McClure's Store – walking slowly – walking off anger and tension.

Tom stopped them beneath a tree on the Square, and took a deep breath.

"We both got to stay calm, Manse. I remember how we use to be in battle," he said. "When I think back on it, I still can't believe some of the things we did. What we both need to do now is keep reminding each other that The War is over – and that we can't let them damn Yankee soldiers and shit-eating scalawags get the best of us. I mean, if we was to end up in jail, what would happen to our folks? We got to think of them."

Manse nodded understanding.

They walked around The Square and north on Main Street. Soon the sight of people walking and talking, carriages and wagons stirring up red dust, dogs barking, children running in a hurry to get someplace, penetrated their hostility.

Manse changed the subject. "You kind of like Bonnie, don't you?"

"Sure I do," Tom said. "I like all your family."

"Don't give me that I-like-all-your-family-shit," he said. "We been together too long. I see the way you look at her – and she looks at you."

"Come on, Manse. Just because – "

"You don't have to explain anything to me, Tom," Manse smiled. "If you and Bonnie were to take a liking to each other, nothing would please me more. She's a fine woman. And fine-looking, too."

"She is that." Tom smiled.

They reached the wagon in the alley behind McClure's Store.

They walked in the back door, into a storage room lined with shelves.

Gerald McClure, sleeves rolled, was cutting beef.

"And what can I do for you boys now?"

"Tom has a list of the supplies we need," Manse said. "And I want to talk to you about something."

"The wife is at the front of the store. She'll be happy to help you, Tom."

Tom left and Gerald McClure said, "There's no one around, Manse. You have my word on that. So feel free to speak your piece."

"Do you know where I can buy a rifle, Mr. McClure?"

"Depends on what kind you got in mind, Manse."

"A Henry forty-four. The kind a man can load on Sunday and shoot all week."

"It's not legal for anybody but the military to own a Henry." Gerald McClure paused. "But I might be of some assistance. Wait here a minute." He unlocked a door, went down stairs to the cellar, and returned with two Henry Rifles wrapped in oil-skin.

"They're not new, of course. I bought them from a Yankee officer."

"How much, Mr. McClure?"

"For which one?"

"Both."

"That 'd be quite a bit of money, Manse."

"Could you take a little out of what you owe us every time we deliver meat, until they're paid for?"

"I could – but I tell you what – I'll make you an even better deal. I'll give you the rifles if you promise to deliver meat to me every week – and not sell to anyone else."

"I couldn't promise delivery more than once every two weeks –"

"Every two weeks, then."

"But I still ought to pay you something for the rifles."

"Don't you worry about that. I'll just raise my prices to the Officers Mess enough to cover the cost of the rifles. That way, you can consider them gifts from the Yankees," he grinned. "But I will sell you the cartridges."

He opened a cabinet and took out two boxes. "Two-fifty a box," he said. "More expensive than caps and balls, but you load twelve, fire twelve and reload faster than you could load and get off one shot with an Enfield three-band, or a Springfield – or even a Remington Zouave. The same is true with pistols, too. No more nibbing, balling and bear greasing six chambers to reload a percussion revolver. You can load six cartridges in half a minute or less."

"But I can't afford new pistols."

"You don't need new ones. Convert what you've got."

"Much trouble?"

"Not for a man who knows weapons. I've got a couple of conversion kits you can have."

"I can't afford anything else."

"I told you not to worry about money. Take them."

Manse thanked him again, re-wrapped the rifles, carried them to the wagon and put them under the seat, then went into the General Store to help Tom with the supplies.

***

Tax collectors – and what they knew – and what they did – and who they did it to – provided Texas Brown with valuable information. For that reason, he had cultivated Samuel Heaton – in order to sit with that fat-assed scalawag at the large round table in the corner of the Benson House bar – to watch and listen.

So today he had had the best seat in the house when those two farmers came in with their anger and pride in evidence.

Heaton had tried to calm them even before they reached his table.

"Well, well, well, if it isn't Mr. Jolly and Mr. Largent," he said. "It's a pleasure to see you again. What can I do for – "

"We're here to pay taxes," the one called Jolly said, and the other one said nothing.

"Taxes. Of course, gentlemen. After all, that's the business I am in – "

But Jolly had stopped Heaton short by counting aloud onto the table seven twenty-dollar bills, one five dollar gold piece and a one dollar gold piece, then saying, "There's your goddamn taxes, Heaton. Now I want a signed receipt."

"And you shall have one. That's only proper business." Samuel Heaton had then opened the large book beside him, stopped at a page, made notes on it, written out a receipt, signed it, and handed it to Jolly.

Then he turned to the other man.

"How about you, Mr. Largent?"

Largent had stood for a moment, looking down at the bills he held in his hand, then he seemed to give in to what he knew he must do, and he put four twenties, one ten, and two one-dollar gold coins on the table.

Heaton went through the same procedure to record and receipt the payment.

Then Heaton had looked up at them, and said loudly enough for everyone to hear, "I don't quite know how you boys raised that money – but you've saved those farms of yours, and, with a little luck, you'll be able to do the same the next time around. Meantime, I thank you on behalf of the state and county governments for your prompt payment. I will see that the money is put to good use."

Someone over by the bar snickered, and a few men laughed.

Jolly and Largent turned and walked out of the room.

A voice beside the bar said, "Samuel, how'd you get so good at squeezing blood out of turnips?"

There was more laughter.

"Just a natural talent, gentlemen," Heaton said.

Then the door to the bar opened and the two men, Jolly and Largent, were back, walking straight to Heaton's table again.

"I want Tom's tax money back," Jolly said, threw the receipt on the table. "Ninety-two dollars."

Heaton silently counted out the money.

"If you change your mind again," he said, "you have a week to pay the taxes. If not, you understand that your land will be foreclosed next month."

"Yeah, goddammit, I understand," Largent said.

They turned and stalked out of the bar again.

Some of the patrons snorted, but no one laughed.

Texas Brown leaned close to Heaton.

"Excuse me, Samuel," he asked in a low voice, "but just who the hell was that?"

Heaton mumbled something.

"Sorry, Samuel, I couldn't hear you."

"Jolly – " Samuel Heaton spat out the word. "Troublemakers. Named Jolly and Largent."

"Thank you," Texas said, and got up, excused himself, and walked toward the door, almost bumping into a first lieutenant coming the other way.

"Beg pardon," Texas said, but the lieutenant went on into the bar without a word.

Texas smiled recognition of the officer who was the butt of local jokes – the one who sat by the courthouse window at the desk with the big plaque that read *Army Intelligence* – the officer who had asked practically everybody in town if they had knew of anybody who had stolen and hidden away any Confederate treasury gold.

Texas wished he had time to get a message to Sergeant Jerlier who worked in that same office. The Commissary Requisition sergeant knew more about the people in the Anderson District than damn near anyone else – and was willing to share information gathered on his monthly visits and searches – for a price.

Texas wanted to know more about those two men, Jolly and Largent. But he didn't have time to get word to Sgt. Jerlier to meet him outside of town, to tell him what he knew. And Texas made it a point never to go inside Union Army Headquarters – or to be seen talking to Jerlier.

He would have to approach these two men using only his well-honed instincts.

***

An hour later, Rebecca had finished her shopping, Tom and Manse had loaded the wagon, and they were on the road home.

For what seemed at interminable time, the two men listened to Rebecca's detailed description of every gift she had chosen for the women in the Jolly household, and her reason for the choice.

When finally she paused to catch her breath, Manse gave the mule its head and unwrapped one of the Henry rifles, held it, weighed its balance, sighted the barrel's length, and handed the weapon to Tom.

Tom held it, sighted it, and said, "No damn wonder the Yankees won The War."

"It's a hell of a weapon all right – " Manse interrupted himself at the sound of hoof beats on the road behind them.

Tom put the rifle under the seat.

Manse stopped the wagon, and they waited.

A white stallion moving at a gallop overtook them, and Manse recognized the rider as the man who had been sitting with Samuel Heaton in the Benson House bar. He wore a broad brimmed black hat, a black suit and brocade waist-coat, and black western-heeled boots. Twin pearl handle revolvers rested in holsters hanging from a gun belt tooled to match his saddle. He reined in a few yards from the wagon.

"Mind if I ride a ways with you, Mr. Jolly? Mr. Largent?"

Manse recognized the man's drawl. It was Carolina coastal. Low-country.

"Depends on what you want," Tom said.

"Just a little palaver, Mr. Largent."

"Let's get one thing straight," Tom said. "We got nothing to say to any friend of Samuel Heaton."

"Hell, I'm no friend of Heaton's."

"You were sitting and drinking with him," Manse said.

"I sit and drink with lots of men."

"We still got nothing to say to you, Mister – "

" – Brown. Jefferson Brown. But most folks call me *Texas*," he smiled. "It's a pleasure to make your acquaintance, gentlemen." He tipped his hat to Rebecca. "And you, too, Miss."

Manse touched Rebecca's arm. His eyes asked her to keep quiet. She complied.

"I still don't reckon we got anything to say to you, Mr. Brown," Manse said.

"Fine – but I got something to say that might interest you, if you'll let me ride along," he said. "Just let me palaver – then make up your mind."

"Suit yourself. The road's free. Least it's supposed to be," Manse picked up the reins and the wagon rolled.

Tom turned on the seat, in order to keep an eye on the man – and shifted his position to make picking up the Henry rifle easier – if need be.

"I liked the way you two told off Heaton. That took a lot of guts with a yankee captain standing right there. I've seen men thrown in the stockade for less," Texas Brown looked from Tom to Manse. "And you're mighty right, Mr. Jolly – there *is* going to be trouble if them Carpetbaggers and Scalawags and Freedmen keep doing like they're doing now – and the Army keeps on backing them up."

"I understand there'll be an election next month," Tom said, as though talking to himself, not the horseman. "After that, maybe the Yankee troops will leave."

"Yeah – and maybe one day the sky will rain money, but don't count on it," Texas raised his voice above the wagon's squeaking wheel. "Grant you, there'll be an election all right, and the Yankees will see to it that some fine-Southerner gets elected Governor. But with South Carolina's new yankee-writ state constitution, the governor don't have any power. The Radicals in Congress and the Carpetbaggers know they got a good thing going, and they're out to make it even better – for themselves."

"But I heard that President Johnson is going to – "

"Johnson ain't ever going to be strong enough to piss up-wind – excuse me for the language, ma'am – " Texas tipped his hat to Rebecca. "With Lincoln dead, Congress is going to flat *give* the South to the niggers. They're already promising niggers white-women, if they vote right – no offense, ma'am –" He tipped his hat to Rebecca again. "You just mark my words, gentlemen. There's gonna be a nigger legislature running this whole state before long."

Manse listened, absorbed, doubted, and said nothing.

"But Freedmen don't have the right to vote," Tom argued.

"They will. Congress and the scalawags and carpetbaggers have got to give niggers the vote. They want to own everything of value that everybody in the South has. And they know the fastest and easiest way to steal it is by giving the niggers the vote, then making sure the niggers vote the way they want them to. I see it coming, sure as day following night. I just left Atlanta. Been there two months. And I tell you, things are getting worse all over the South. I know. It's my business."

"Just what *is* your business, Mr. Brown?"

"Something you may not have heard about yet, but before we get to that, let me set one thing right – I'm not a damn scalawag. I fought under the Stars And Bars, just like you did." Texas Brown reached inside his coat and took out a cigar case. "And I'd be honored if you gentlemen would allow me to offer you a good smoke – one Confederate to another," he said.

Tom and Manse exchanged looks. Nodded and accepted. Stopped and lit.

"That's the best cigar I've had in a lot of years," Tom said.

"Damn fine," Manse blew a cloud of smoke. "My thanks to you for sharing," he started them moving again. "If you can afford cigars like this, your business must be profitable."

"It can be," Texas exhaled a long stream of smoke. "I'm taking a chance talking about my work to anybody I don't know – but I've got a sense of Confederate trust about you two gentlemen – and the lady," he tipped his hat yet again to Rebecca, who avoided meeting his eyes.

"So, because I trust you, I'm going to put my cards on the table face-up–" Texas said. "I'm here in South Carolina to organize the Piedmont Klavern of the Ku Klux Klan."

"The who?" Tom said.

"Of the what – " Manse said.

"The Ku Klux Klan. Right-thinking-men who want to protect the South, particularly our womenfolk, from niggers and scalawags and yankees." Texas paused, inhaled the cigar, and exhaled a cloud of smoke.

"Surely you've heard of Nathan Bedford Forest," he said. "Without a doubt he was the smartest and bravest general in the whole Confederate Cavalry. Truly one hell of a man. Well, sirs, General Forest is the leader of the Ku Klux Klan."

Texas paused again, awaiting a reaction.

"We've heard of General Nathan Bedford Forest all right," Manse said. "Every man who rode Cavalry Gray heard of him. But I never heard of this KuxKlan you're talking about."

"Ku. Klux. Klan." Texas Brown said again, slowly. "General Forest got the idea when he read that over in Scotland there once was a group of men who rode around putting true religion into

Catholics by scaring hell out of them. He figured the same thing would work on niggers and yankees – and it does!"

"Just exactly what does this Klan do?" Tom asked.

"A kind of missionary work – to put the fear of God in black souls. We wear robes and hoods so nobody knows who we are. Hell, just the sight of a fifty white-robed men on horseback scares the pants off niggers. Off the bucks, anyhow. I never knowed a wench to wear pants." He tipped his hat again to Rebecca, then laughed.

"Of course, occasionally some nigger don't scare easy – or sometimes there's a Scalawag or Carpetbagger who's done something real hurtful to a Southerner. On them we occasionally have to use a horse whip. Or fire. Or a rope."

Manse drew deeply on his cigar.

"That still don't exactly explain you and Samuel Heaton drinking together," he said.

"It's this way, Mr. Jolly. When I came to Anderson, I didn't know anybody. And I had to be damn careful who I trusted. So I got to know Heaton. He does his business in The Benson House bar. I sit and listen to what folks say when they come in to pay taxes. And if I like what I hear – if they show some guts, like you two gentlemen did today – then I go talk to them – like I'm talking to you now."

Tom smiled and looked at Manse. "Makes more sense now, don't it?"

"Yeah. Does." Manse leaned out of the wagon. "Pleased to know you, Texas Brown," he shook Texas' hand.

Then Tom and Texas shook hands.

"Think you two might be interested in joining the Klan?" Texas asked.

"We're mighty interested in knowing about what you're doing," Tom said, "but I doubt we can join up. Me and Manse are staying busy trying to get our lives going again."

"Besides," Manse said, "we got women-folks to look after, and your Ku Klux Klanning sounds risky. But you're sure welcome to come out and visit us. We'd be proud to have you for supper sometime."

Texas shook his head. "I plain don't understand you two," he said. "I guess you just don't hate bluebellies and Scalawags as much as I do."

"Truth is," Manse said, "I found out in The War that the hate in me runs real deep – and I'm not looking to stir it up."

"Well I'm not giving up on getting you two to join the Klan. We need men like you. And sooner or later, you're going to need the Klan. So I'll take you up on that supper-invite, and we'll talk about it some more then," Texas Brown tipped his hat.

"Be seeing you all again soon – I promise," he said, and wheeled his horse around and galloped toward Anderson.

For a minute the wagon squeaked on, and they were silent.

"Seems like a nice enough fellow," Tom finally said.

"Smokes fine cigars," Manse nodded.

"I wouldn't trust that man as far as I could throw him – or that big white horse of his," Rebecca said. "You two be careful around him, you hear?"

-5-

Larry came down from the mountains two weeks later, leading four mules laden with sides of beef and pork. The next day, he and Manse packed the meat in the wagon to take to Gerald McClure.

Rebecca asked to go along, but Tom insisted that she was needed at home to help with preserving their store of vegetables, fruit and meat for the coming winter.

Manse nodded his agreement – and welcomed the prospect of spending some time alone with Larry.

For a while the two brothers rode in silence – except for the squeaking wheel.

Manse finally spoke.

"You doing all right in the mountains by yourself?" he asked.

"Yeah. Fact is, I kind of like it," Larry said. "When I was in the army, everywhere was so crowded all the time, I wished I could just go off somewhere and be real quiet," he laughed. "Guess I'm getting my wish."

"I remember feeling the same way," Manse said. "I could hardly wait for the day to come when I could get home to the farm and just go from one sun-up to the next without worrying about somebody shooting at me. And me having to shoot back."

"Yeah – " Larry paused. "Except I got to admit I get awful riled-up at times – like when I see what them damn scalawags like Samuel Heaton are doing to folks around here," Larry spat from the wagon to the dust. "Don't they make you mad as hell, too?"

"Yeah – they do," Manse said. "I could've real easy killed all them sons-of-bitches in the Benson House bar when me and Tom went in to pay taxes. But then later, sitting on the front porch, giving it quiet thought, I told Tom I had to laugh, because the way I see it, Heaton and them Yankee soldiers that came to the house with him did us a pretty big favor – "

"Favor? How the hell you figure that?"

"Think about it. Because we had to pay taxes, we came up with the idea of going up in the mountains to find livestock to butcher and sell to Mister McClure – so he can turn around and sell it to the Yankee army," Manse half-smiled. "If Heaton hadn't demanded tax money – and threatened to foreclose the farm – and all them Yankee soldiers didn't need meat to eat – we wouldn't have enough money now even for food, much less the supplies we need for planting and fixing up the place." Manse's smile became a grin. "As it is, thanks to the tax collector and the bluebellies, we've got enough money for you to go shopping for yourself today, if you want to."

"I see what you mean," Larry smiled. "Maybe I will get me a new pair of boots," he said. "These Confederate infantry issue are about to fall apart."

"Get yourself two pairs," Manse said. "One for work – and a dress pair for church and special occasions. Like weddings."

"Who's getting married?" Larry said. "You and Rebecca?

"Hold your horses –" Manse felt flushed. "I'm not talking about me. I'm talking about Tom and Bonnie. Mind you, Tom hasn't said anything direct to me – but I been noticing things – looks between him and Bonnie – and him going with her to collect eggs – to have an excuse for them to get away from everybody."

"You reckon they're talking about marrying?"

"I'd be willing to wager my gold watch –" Manse said. "If I had a gold watch –"

They laughed together, and Manse felt as close to happy as he could remember being since before The War. The warmth they shared on that ride to Anderson was a memory he would carry with him for the rest of his life.

After they delivered the meat and bought supplies, they walked three blocks from McClure's Store to Otter's Leather Shop, where Larry bought two pairs of boots.

And as they were walking back to the wagon, they ran into Texas Brown. He and Manse shook hands, then Manse introduced him to Larry.

"It's always a honor to meet another man who served under the Stars And Bars," Texas clasped Larry's hand and slapped him on the shoulder.

"Likewise," Larry said. "Manse and Tom told me about meeting you – and a little about your *work*. It sounds interesting."

"Did Manse also tell you that him and Tom invited me to your house for supper *sometime* – " Texas laughed.

"Yeah, Manse told me we were expecting you to come eat with us one evening real soon," Larry said.

"Well now then, I reckon this is as good a evening as any to take you folks up on that invite," Texas said.

Larry looked at Manse.

Manse hesitated, then nodded.

"Seems we did invite Texas to come for supper *sometime*, and I reckons this is as good a supper-time as any," Manse said, then turned to Texas. "Why don't you just ride along with us back to the farm."

"It won't be nothing but country cooking," Larry said. "Ham and biscuits with red-eye gravy, and garden greens, and sorghum."

"Hell-fire, Larry," Texas said, "where I was raised, that was a real special Sunday dinner."

***

What Texas Brown called his "flash" had begun early in life.

It was a sudden brightness that lit up inside his head, just behind his eyes.

And it happened every time he met anyone for the first time.

Sometimes it was just a quick flicker, but at other times it was so bright it seemed to illuminate the whole interior of his skull with a painful light.

When he was a small boy, the sensation frightened him.

Unable to talk to his father about it – or anything else – and unable to believe anything his mother told him – he asked his favorite uncle what the light was – and his uncle told him that such flashes were what Indians called *the gift of lightning* – an omen of the importance of the role that man, or woman, he was meeting would play in his future.

Texas trusted his uncle – so he trusted his uncle's interpretation of the flashes. And all his adult life, he used those illuminations to judge men – and women.

The flashes – and the judgments – became so much a part of him that he relied on them without question to determine the amount of time and effort he devoted to cultivating a person's friendship and trust.

The illumination that Texas Brown experienced when he saw Manse Jolly in the Benson House bar was the strongest gift-of-lightning he had ever felt. He knew, without doubt, that the auburn-bearded man with the strange eyes was going to play a very important part in his life. So strong was the feeling that he had no choice but to find out as much as he could about Manse Jolly as quickly as possible.

But what he had learned in the few weeks since their meeting was neither impressive nor enlightening. Before The War, Manse Jolly had been a small planter. Now he was no more than a poor dirt farmer. It didn't make sense to Texas how such a *nobody* could conceivably be destined to have a major influence on Texas Brown's life.

But there was no getting around the fact that the *flash* had definitely been there when they met, and it persisted every time he saw Manse. Therefore, Texas did not question it – and was quick to manipulate an invitation to accompany Manse and Larry home for supper.

He was anxious to get to know the people around Manse, in an effort to better understand the man, and, hopefully, uncover the reason the flash entwined their lives.

After supper, with a fire going to take the chill off, Texas sat in the parlor and drank coffee with the Jollys and the Largents. According to Bonnie Jolly, who was a right pleasing looking lady, but never said much, it was the first *real* coffee that had been served in the Jolly home since before The War.

Mealtime conversation had been pleasant, but Manse had said little. Even when Texas asked him direct questions, his responses were short. Not impolite – just short. He was, Texas decided, a man who had an awful lot of anger packed tight inside him. It was going to be interesting to find out what it would take to manipulate him – to make him explode.

Tom Largent, on the other hand, was easy to talk to. Sincere – and damned persuasive. He wouldn't be an easy man to sway.

Texas needed to find out what moved Tom – other than Bonnie Jolly. Those two didn't take their eyes off each other all evening.

Texas knew that Larry Jolly was going to be the easiest one to influence. He was young, outspoken, and full of anti-Yankee, anti-nigger hate. He could use the Klan for an outlet – and he was the kind of man that Texas – and the Klan – could use.

The one person, however, that Texas could not help staring at every chance he got was Rebecca Largent. *That* was a piece near worth dying for. But he would have to move softly to get to her. She didn't like him – didn't trust him – and he could feel it. He needed to work on her slowly, carefully – like he had worked on other young women, in other places, at other times. In the end, he was sure she would be worth the effort.

The boy, Johnny, and the little girl, Melinda, would be easy to own.

Texas Brown decided that he needed to use this, his first night in the Jolly home, to play good-old-boy – to convince them that Texas Brown was a truly *nice man*. The best way to accomplish that, he knew, was to dominate the conversation –

"And so, even though I never been west of Georgia, I always dreamed of going to Texas. I had an uncle who lived there most of his growed-up life. He come back home when I was still kind of young. Died of consumption right before The War started. He told me lots of stories about Texas. Fact is, he was the one that started calling me *Texas*. I never cared much for my real name – Jefferson Washington Brown. Rather be called Texas. But I couldn't ever get my Daddy or Mama to call me that. I was raised on the Georgia Coast south of Savannah. Ever hear of the Sea Islands? Sapelo and Cumberland are the big ones, but there are lots more little ones. Escaped slaves hid there, and we use to go hunt them. Got twenty-five dollars a piece for ever one we caught and brought back alive. That was my favorite sport when I was growing up – tracking down and catching runaway niggers."

"Another slice of cake, Mr. Brown?" Maude Jolly took advantage of his pause.

"No thanks, ma'am. It's mighty good, but I reckon three pieces is plenty, even for a growing boy like me." He laughed and took out his cigar case. "Mind if we smoke in your parlor, Mrs. Jolly?"

"Not at all, Mr. Brown."

Texas passed cigars around, then he, Tom, Larry and Manse bit, spit and lit.

"You planning to go to Texas to live one day?" Larry asked.

"Sure hope to. Mind you, I tried hard all through The War to wrangle a way to get to Texas to join up with Captain John Gray Smith's brigade. *Lightning Jack* they called him. Real hero of the Confederacy. I been told he was born right here in Anderson District, and moved out to Texas about twenty five years ago, and became a big rancher. Mighty fine man, from all I've heard," Texas exhaled a cloud of smoke. "Anyhow, I was conscripted into the Infantry, and got wounded at Pittsburgh Landing. Not wounded bad, mind you, just a bayonet in the thigh. And when I got out of the hospital, the Army sent me to Andersonville Prison to be a guard. You better believe we gave those Yankees what was coming to them there. Anyhow, I worked with guards there from Texas and I heard a lot of interesting things from them. They told me –"

"Hold on a minute, please," Manse held up his hand to interrupt. "There's a rider coming up the drive."

"I'll go look," Johnny ran to the front door. "It's a yankee soldier, Uncle Manse. "

"Probably that Lieutenant who talked to us in town," Manse said.

"I'll go see." Tom stood and limped to the porch.

They listened.

"Evening, Mr. Largent," they heard a Yankee voice say.

"Evening, Lieutenant McCollum," Tom said.

Then came the sounds of a man dismounting and walking up the steps to the porch.

"I trust this is not an inconvenient time to come to call, Mr. Largent."

"No more than any other time. Guess you might as well come on inside."

They entered the parlor, and everyone in the room stared.

Texas smiled to himself – watched and waited.

***

***

Martin McCollum saw so much unadulterated hatred in their eyes, he was tempted to do an abrupt about-face and leave.

But then he looked at Rebecca, and all the emotions that had brought him to the Jolly farm overpowered him.

Every day for more than two weeks, he had looked out the window, hoping she might reappear. Then, today, he had seen Manse Jolly in the company of a younger man, who, from his looks, had to be his brother. They were talking to the civilian, Texas Brown, who Martin saw often in the Benson House bar – and about whom he had heard interesting rumors – but knew few facts.

"My apologies for calling this late, Mr. Jolly," Martin abided by the rules of Southern politeness and spoke first to the head of the household.

Manse hesitated, then stood – but did not extend his hand.

"This is my mother, Lieutenant. Mama this is Lieutenant – I'm sorry, I don't rightly recollect your name –" Manse said.

"My name is McCollum. Lieutenant Martin McCollum, Military Intelligence," Martin said. "It's a pleasure to meet you, Mrs. Jolly."

Maude Jolly did not acknowledge his presence.

"And this is my sister-in-law, Mrs. Bonnie Jolly," Manse said. "And Tom's sister, Miss Rebecca Largent – "

"Yes, I recall seeing Miss Largent with you and Mr. Largent in Anderson," Martin looked at Rebecca, hoping for a glimmer of recognition, but received no more response from her than from the others.

"And this is my brother, Larry. And my nephew Johnny."

Martin McCollum nodded to each.

"And I reckon you know Texas Brown – " Manse said.

"We've never been formally introduced, but I've seen Mister Brown often in Anderson."

"And I see the Lieutenant every day when I walk past the courthouse window," Texas smiled, and the meaning of the remark and the smile were not lost on Martin.

Bonnie Jolly stood. "Excuse me, gentlemen," she said, "but I have to put Melinda to bed."

"My bedtime, too," Maude said, and got up from her rocking chair.

"And mine," Rebecca said.

"Please, Mama, Bonnie, Rebecca, " Manse said. "The reason the lieutenant is here is because he wants to ask you all some questions about something."

"I got no answers for the lieutenant, Manson," Maude said.

Martin felt tension increase, and knew it was time to display understanding and charm.

"Please, Mrs. Jolly," he said. "I know how you must feel, having a Union Army Officer in your home. And I do apologize for the intrusion. But I promise that my questions will be brief."

Maude sat down. Bonnie and Rebecca stood on either side of her chair.

Martin was uncomfortable with the hardness of their stares. He cleared his throat.

"Perhaps I should start by giving you a little background, so you will better understand the need for my questions," Martin directed his words to everyone in the room, but his eyes rested on Rebecca.

"During The War," he said, "there was a platoon of Confederate troops stationed in Anderson, entrusted, along with its regular garrison duties, with protection of the Confederate Trust Bank where gold, and jewelry donated to the Confederate cause, were stored." He paused. "When Jeff – President Davis – and his cabinet met for the final time, thirty miles from here at Abbeville they ordered the treasury of the Anderson Trust Bank to be sent by train to Charleston, and from there to – "

Texas Brown's laugh exploded.

"Sorry, Lieutenant," he said, "but I just can't help myself." He laughed again. "I reckon everything folks in Anderson are saying about you is *true* – you are *seriously* looking for *Confederate gold*."

"You find that amusing, Mister Brown?"

"I find it more than amusing, Lieutenant. I find it down-right ridiculous. Don't you Yankees know the South didn't have nothing left when The War ended? That's how come we lost."

Every one in the room now joined the laughter – embarrassing and infuriating Martin. This was not what he had planned.

Then he caught Rebecca watching him. Her eyes studied him – seeming to sense his discomfort – and take pleasure in it. He fought for composure. Now was his chance to show *her* that he was a man of importance and responsibility – on a mission of consequence. He would not be intimidated or ridiculed. He allowed his eyes to smile at her, then he turned his head to glare at Texas Brown – and put on his most polite tone.

"Of course, Mister Brown, Army Intelligence is quite aware that most of the Confederate Treasury had been depleted prior to Appomattox. But several of the Trust Banks captured by Union forces at the end of The War each yielded more than a million dollars in gold."

" Didn't they capture the one in Anderson?" Tom asked.

"Yes. But by the time General Stoneman's Brigade arrived, the gold had already been shipped by train – just hours before – to Charleston. The General sent cavalry cross-country, and they intercepted the train near the town of Donalds, but the crates that were supposed to contain gold bars were full of rocks."

"That's a powerful good story, Lieutenant," Texas shook his head. "Probably never was any gold on that train – or in that bank neither."

"The facts disagree with you, Mr. Brown. A number of Confederate soldiers died defending what they believed was a shipment of gold. And we know, from the Confederate Trust Bank inventory, that there *was* gold there. General Stoneman's Brigade captured records indicating that a substantial number of bars of bullion had been packed in small wooden crates and taken to the train station. Since they were not in those crates when the train was intercepted and captured, Army Intelligence concludes that the gold is still somewhere in or near Anderson – " Martin moved his gaze back to Rebecca. "And Intelligence Headquarters in Washington has sent me here for the express purpose of investigating the gold's disappearance – and finding it."

"Having any luck?" Texas smiled.

"My investigation is on-going, so I am not at liberty to discuss details," he said. "But I am making a modicum of progress. I am presently questioning anyone with even the remotest connection to the Trust Bank. That is why I'm here this evening." He looked at

Bonnie. "It is my understanding, Mrs. Jolly," he said, "that, during the three-months that your husband, Sergeant Lewis Jolly, was home on recuperation leave, he made a number of visits to the Trust Bank. His name appears several times in the Log Book signed by all personnel entering or leaving the Banking And Arms Building on University Hill – "

"That wasn't just the Trust Bank, Lieutenant," Larry Jolly interrupted him. "That was Confederate Army Headquarters for Anderson District. Anytime any of us was home on leave, we reported there."

"I am quite aware of that," Martin's tone was sharp. "My question was addressed to Mrs. Jolly"

He turned again to Bonnie.

"Did your husband ever tell you the purpose of his visits there, or divulge to you any information about the Bank?" he asked.

"That was quite a while ago, Lieutenant," Bonnie's voice trembled. "As well as I can remember, Lewis went there a few times to get his leave-pay, and later, when he healed, to find out where his Brigade was – so he could rejoin them."

Martin nodded understanding to Bonnie, glanced at Rebecca, to make sure she was still looking at him – which she was – then he looked at Maude. "And, if you don't mind, Mrs. Jolly, is there anything you know, or may have heard, about the bank or the gold?"

"I'm not very familiar with much that goes on in Anderson, Lieutenant. But I did hear about your General Stoneman's visit. As I understand it, he killed four prominent businessmen – had them shot by a firing squad – or hanged – I'm not sure which – and tortured several others – " Maude Jolly stood. "Sorry, but I don't think I can help you find the gold you're looking for. Nor would I if I could – even if you tortured me. Now, with or without your permission, I am going to bed."

Texas stood. "Goodnight, Mrs. Jolly. I sure enjoyed that meal."

"Thank you, Mr. Brown. Please, come again."

Bonnie picked up Melinda, and, without a word, she and Johnny followed Maude from the room. Rebecca hesitated then, with a quick glance at Martin, she said, "Goodnight Mister Brown – Lieutenant – " and she was gone.

"I seem to have upset your mother, Mr. Jolly." Martin said. "I apologize."

"Mama just plain don't like yankees, Lieutenant," Manse stood with his back to the fire. "She lost five sons in The War —"

"And me and Manse don't like damn-yankees either, Lieutenant," Larry said. "We lost five brothers."

"And Bonnie don't like yankees, she lost her husband," Tom said.

"And the young'uns lost their daddy," Manse added.

Martin felt the tension in the room heightening.

"So, if you got no more questions, Lieutenant," Manse said, "why don't you just get the hell out of our house."

Martin looked from Manse to Tom to Larry. This was not, he decided, a good time to attempt further conversation.

He put his hat, nodded, and said, "good night, gentlemen," turned and walked to the door.

"If you'll hold on a minute, Lieutenant, I'll ride along with you," Texas Brown said. "After dark it's good to have company on these country roads."

"Fine, Mr. Brown. I'll wait for you outside," Martin walked out onto the porch and waited while Texas went to the hall-tree and put on his gunbelt.

"I surely thank you folks for the nice evening," Texas said. "And I know I'll be seeing y'all again real soon."

***

Manse tried unsuccessfully to push away his headache.

The parlor was quiet until hoof beats faded.

"Hope that yankee bastard never finds that gold," Larry said.

"If there is any gold," Tom smiled. "You want a drink, Manse?"

"I could use one," he said.

"I'll get the jug," Larry said, and went to the kitchen.

"What do you think about the Lieutenant, Manse?" Tom asked.

"Just another yankee, far as I could see," Manse spat in the fire. "Sure wish he hadn't come here and upset Mama like he did. We were having a real nice evening till he showed up."

"Mama Jolly sure seemed to enjoy Texas Brown, didn't she?" Tom smiled. "I haven't heard her laugh so much in a long time."

"Yeah," Manse said. "He's quite a word spinner, all right – and one hell of a big man, too. Didn't realize how tall he was. Course I hadn't seen him except sitting with Heaton and on his horse. Them heeled boots add two, maybe three inches, but he's got to be six-four barefoot."

"At least that," Tom said. "And he seems a nice enough fellow. But I figure he's out to take care of Texas Brown first, and nobody else matters much."

Larry returned with a jug and three glasses.

"One thing sure," Manse said. "He's hell-bent on this Klan stuff," he finished his cigar and threw the stub into the fire.

Larry passed the glasses around, then poured and said, "While Manse was settling accounts with Mister McClure, and I was loading supplies, I saw Elk Marett and Whit Whitfield. They said they rode over to Georgia with Texas last week. They're real high on him and the Klan. They say it's doing lots of good over there, and it will over here, too."

"I got my doubts that Texas Brown only wants to do good," Tom said.

"You'd be right about that," Larry said. "Whit told me that when the Klan goes after some new-rich nigger or scalawag and burns his house, they loot it first. That's how the Klan gets its money."

Tom shook his head and frowned. "But that's just as bad as – "

"No, it's not, Tom," Larry interrupted and raised his voice. "Them damn niggers and scalawags are stealing everything in sight. Robbing everybody. I don't see nothing wrong with taking some of it back." He lifted his glass. "Here's to the Klan," he said.

Manse knew the argument would soon get out of hand.

"Here's to *us*," he said, and drank – and grimaced. "God-a-mighty that's bad whiskey McClure sells. Tastes like a polecat crawled in the mash and died."

"Too bad we're not rich enough to buy yankee-bottled," Tom said.

"Next trip down from the cave, I'll go by Drubber Pickens and get some of his home-stilled corn like Daddy used to buy. It's still the smoothest around," Larry said. "And I reckon we can afford that."

"You doing okay up in them mountains by yourself?" Tom refilled their glasses.

"Yeah, like I told Manse today, everything is fine. But I'm sure hoping we can work it out for y'all to spell me time-to-time." He smiled. "I reckon sooner or later I'm going to need to see something female other than ewes and sows." He finished his drink and walked to the stairs. "It's been a long day. I'm turning in. See y'all at breakfast."

Tom and Manse said good-night, then silently watched the fire.

"Frankly, I'm glad Larry is staying at the cave," Tom said. "If he spent much time around Anderson, I reckon he'd be right slap in the middle of Texas Brown's Klan."

"I think you're right about that," Manse felt the whiskey and the fire warm him – and he remembered this room filled with Jolly brothers laughing and arguing – and teasing *little brother Larry* about being too young to drink with them.

"The War sure changed him," Manse said. "Remember how timid he used to be?"

"Yeah, I remember," Tom smiled. "But then I reckon The War changed everybody – and everything –"

"It surely did that," Manse stood.

"I've got to make a run outside," he said. "Then I reckon I'll turn in, too."

He finished his drink.

"Think I'll have one more," Tom refilled his glass.

***

Manse walked out the back door. His need to relieve himself was not as pressing as his need to be alone – to inhale cool autumn air – to try to sort out why he had felt so much anger toward that Lieutenant McCollum. It wasn't just because he was a yankee – or even because he had intruded into their home, spoiling their evening. It was something else. Something in his attitude – and the way he looked at Rebecca. Even though the yankee officer didn't actually question her about anything, he never took his eyes off her.

For that matter – now that Manse thought about it – the same thing was true of Texas Brown. Every time Manse noticed Texas's eyes, they were on Rebecca.

Or maybe it was just his imagination, fired by some kind of jealousy.

Though Manse could never seem to find the words to talk to Rebecca about his feelings for her, he resented any other man's attention to her.

One thing was sure in his mind – what he felt for her was more than some school-boy emotion. And soon he would *have* to talk to her – or perhaps lose forever the chance of finding out if she shared his feelings.

***

Tom sat and took off his boot, then stood again and loosened his belt, unbuttoned his trousers, slid them down around his ankles, sat again and took them off. Then he loosened the leather harness that held his wooden leg in place, and twisted it loose from the stump.

It was a relief to free his thigh from the straps – to let it breathe. At the same time, a pain akin to amputation itself returned every time he removed it – or put it on again.

He took a jar of liniment from the low-shelf by the chimney, and opened it.

Then he heard her behind him.

Bonnie carried a glass. Her flannel gown hung loosely, neck to ankles.

"Melinda wanted some water," she said and put the glass down and crossed the room to him, knelt in front of his chair, took the jar from him, and began rubbing the liniment into his stump.

Slowly she massaged scar tissue, and Tom felt the strange sensation that she was rubbing the bottom of his foot and his toes.

They were silent until she finished, then she wiped her hands on her gown, and recapped the jar.

"Have you talked to Manse yet, about us?" she asked.

"No, not yet."

"Something is bothering you, Tom. I can tell. What is it?"

Tom hesitated. He didn't really want to ask her – but questions plagued him.

"Are you real sure, Bonnie?"

"Yes, I'm real sure."

Tom took her hand.

"It's not just so Melindy and Johnny will have a Daddy?" he asked.

"It most certainly is *not*," Bonnie's tone bordered anger. "I wouldn't ever marry a man I didn't love – not for any reason. No matter what," she touched his cheek. "When Lewis was killed, I thought my life was over. But I kept on going, just for the sake of Johnny and Melinda. I was sure that I would be alone for the rest of my life – that there could never be another man for me. Then I opened my eyes one day and saw you – really *saw* you for the first time – and my heart filled with more love than I had ever felt – "

Tom interrupted her: "You're sure it's not *pity* you feel – for this part-of-a-man that came home from The War?"

"You are the most complete man – the most gentle, sweet, complete-man I've ever known – " Bonnie lowered herself onto his lap and pressed herself close to him – warming through flannel the stump of his leg.

Tom's arms slid around her – held her tightly, as if afraid ever to release her.

"I love you, Tom," she said, and kissed him.

***

Martin McCollum was quietly replaying the evening in his mind, wishing he had been able to think of at least a few questions to ask Rebecca Largent – just to hear her voice and command her attention. But all he could do was look at her while rambling and posturing. He was sure that the story of this evening – of the Yankee Lieutenant's continuing idiotic pursuit of non-existent gold – would be met with gales of laughter when told at the Benson House bar in Anderson – most likely by Texas Brown.

Martin looked at the figure in black who rode beside him.

He was hard to see, even in bright moonlight.

But his voice boomed in the night above eight hoof beats.

"I was in Atlanta for a while before I came here," Texas said. Not much like it used to be. And talk about soldiers – seems all I ever saw there was blue coats and black faces," he laughed loudly, then decided to ride for a while in silence. He was still trying to figure out the meaning of the powerful flash he had experienced when McCollum entered the Jolly home. Why the hell should he feel that a damned yankee soldier was going to be important in his life. It made no more sense than the flash he received when he met Manse Jolly – and Tom Largent – and Larry – and Rebecca.

Now he had no choice but to pursue them all, to find the answers.

And he decided that the best approach to Martin McCollum was through conversation on a personal level.

"What's the matter, Lieutenant?" Texas asked. "You're awful quiet. You upset about something?"

Martin hesitated, then decided that this was an excellent opportunity to interrogate this enigmatic man whom, intuitively, he neither trusted nor liked. Perhaps the best way to proceed was to take Texas Brown into his personal *confidence* – or at least make him think that was what he was doing.

"Frankly, Mister Brown," Martin said, "I was just wishing I didn't have to make visits like tonight. I always feel very uncomfortable in the homes of Confederates. And I'm sure I make them feel equally uncomfortable."

"Don't fret about it, Lieutenant. It could've been a whole lot worse. They could've shot you," Texas laughed again.

Martin did not smile.

"I don't understand you, Mister Brown," he said. "I see you most often in town drinking with Unionists. Then I find you at the Jolly home, acting as if they were your closest friends." He paused. "You aren't by chance courting Miss Largent, are you?"

"Me? No. But I sure noticed the way you kept looking at her. Don't tell me you're interested in that little rebel piece?"

"I merely asked if you were courting her, Mister Brown. I had no ulterior motive. It was just a question," Martin felt uncomfortable – again. "Though I admit she *is* quite an attractive young woman," he said.

"Forget her, Lieutenant. You can be damned sure she don't like yankees any more than the rest of them folks do. And even if she did, them boys would blast your ass off if they ever caught you sniffing around her."

"I imagine you're right – but you didn't answer my question, Mister Brown. What *were* you doing at the Jolly home?"

"Visiting, Lieutenant. It's an old Southern custom. Calling on folks. Getting to know'em. Making friends. Having a little supper. Setting a spell. Talking. Like I said – *visiting*."

"Are you sure that was all?"

"Now just what the hell's that supposed to mean, Lieutenant?"

"I merely wondered if you might have been there to conduct some *business*."

"Business? No – I got no business, Lieutenant."

"Haven't you, Mr. Brown."

"Nope – I don't – And why don't you call me *Texas* like everybody else does."

"Fine – Texas it is. And you might as well call me Martin, since that is my name," he smiled to himself. He *was* making headway – but he would be damned glad when this evening was over and he could get back to the Benson House bar. He needed a drink.

"I'd be pleased to call you *Martin*, Martin," Texas smiled to himself. He *was* making headway. "So tell me, whereabouts up-North you from, Martin?"

"New York."

"You one of them fine rich New York gentlemen I've heard about?"

"I'm afraid not. I grew up dirt-poor in a place I hope never to see again. I had to work like hell to get a scholarship to City College. It took an Act of Congress to make me an officer-and-a-gentleman."

"Well at least we've got one thing in common," Texas laughed and trotted his horse. "Nobody ever accused me of being a gentleman either."

Martin kept pace beside him.

"Tell me, Martin, you really think that gold you were talking about is hid somewhere around here?"

"I'm convinced it is."

"In that case, if you'd like, I'll see what I can find out for you. Folks hereabouts are bound to talk more easy to Texas Brown than to that uniform you're wearing."

"I'm sure that's true," Martin smiled to himself. "And I assure you that Army Intelligence will greatly appreciate any assistance you could render in this matter."

"To be honest with you, Martin, as far as I'm concerned, the god-damned US Army and all it's *intelligence* can go straight to hell. This-matter is gonna be just between us two not-so-gentlemanly-gentlemen."

-6-

Texas Brown warmed himself by the newly kindled fire and watched Whit Whitfield supervise the three men who were erecting two wooden crosses.

The first week of November had brought an ice storm. Freezing wind blew across the Savannah River, chilling this thick stand of pines and hardwoods that Whit had selected as "the perfectest place for the Klan to meet."

Texas took the cup of coffee Whit handed him, and smiled to himself.

Everything he had predicted would happen, was happening:

South Carolina had held its election on November first, and elected James L. Orr, an Andersonian, as Governor. He had distinguished himself as a colonel in the Confederate Army, and when Congress permitted him to take office immediately, Southern hopes ran high.

Then the new Governor pushed through passage of The Black Code – laws that severely restricted the rights of freed slaves, prevented their filing suits in state courts, refused them work in most occupations, and gave white employers virtually absolute power over any blacks they hired.

White Carolinians were jubilant.

But the US Congress screamed its objections! The Union had won The War, they said, but now South Carolina was trying to reinstate slavery. The Black Code could not be tolerated. Obviously the South had not yet learned its lesson, therefore Southern states would not be permitted Federal representation. The Senate and House refused to validate the state's newly elected Congressional delegation.

On orders from Washington, the Freedman's Bureau did not acknowledge The Black Code. The Army backed them, and South Carolina's Governor and State Legislature were rendered impotent.

President Johnson and Congress continued their tug-of-war, and the South remained occupied territory.

Texas Brown had built his Klavern of The Invisible Empire in anticipation of just these events. Now he spread the word that a new order was rising from Confederate ashes – to restore Southern honor and protect Southern women. The men who heeded his message and joined the Klan became his apostles.

And he had anointed, as his strong right arm, Whit Whitfield.

Texas had known, when the lightning flashes led him to Whit's house that first afternoon, that they were cut from the same cloth.

Whit provided Texas with information about residents of the Anderson District who shared his vision of what the South could again become, once the niggers and scalawags and bluebellies had been put in their proper places.

Before The War, Whit had worked as an overseer on one of the Southron plantations south of the community of Twiggs. It had been his job to get maximum production from the slaves in the fields. In exchange for loyal service, the plantation owner had given him twenty-five-acres of bottom land near the Smith-McGee Crossing on the Savannah. There, not far from his work, he built a small house.

It was, he later told Texas, a goddamned good-enough life for a man who knew he "wouldn't never be no rich Southron, and really didn't give a shit about ever being one of them anyhow." He had a good wife, Sara Jane, who cooked and washed and took care of their kids and did as she was told – *whatever* he told her to do, which is what a wife was supposed to do. And he had good friends to talk to, and to drink and hunt with –

But then The War had come, and Whit had enlisted to fight in the infantry. And he had seen most of his closest friends die from yankee bullets and cannon fire during those four years.

And afterwards, he had come home to find nothing left of the South he had known.

Uppity niggers and thieving carpetbaggers and scalawags now had the upper hand. Backed by bluebelly rifles and bayonets, they could do anything they wanted.

Whit figured they would have tried to steal his farm, if it hadn't been so small, and in such an out of the way place. If they ever tried, he told Texas, they would have a hell of a fight on their hands.

He would carry a whole bunch of bluebelly-bastards to hell with him.

Texas finished his coffee and looked past the fire now blazing against a sky of early night, and watched Whit greeting early arrivals for the meeting. The number of dues-paid Klan members had passed thirty, and tonight each of them was expected to bring one or two recruits.

Texas nodded to himself. Whit Whitfield was the perfect man to serve as the Klavern's recruiter – and enforcer.

And Whit had brought to Texas a man to help him enlist new Klansmen and require compliance with their code of loyalty, obedience and silence – a tall, skeletally thin man with sunken eyes and blackened teeth – Etheridge LaVerne "Elk" Marett.

Whit told Texas that before The War, Elk Marett had been the best tracker of runaway slaves in the Anderson District – maybe in the whole state of South Carolina. And he had his own ways of dealing with runaways when he found them – ways of breaking bones and cutting off pieces of their bodies, to make sure they didn't run a second time.

In those good-old-days, Whit said, Elk Marett's name conjured fear in every slave who ever heard it.

But that had changed, too.

When Elk came home from The War, the profession of slave-tracker no longer existed.

For Texas Brown, Elk and Whit were perfect disciples. They follow his orders, without question, and gladly accepted whatever share of Klan-generated revenue he offered them.

And above all, they enjoyed their work.

***

The first Monday evening in December, Bonnie and Tom announced their plan to marry on Christmas Day. The practicality of celebrating two major events on one date, Tom said with pride, was Bonnie's idea.

After dinner, Manse opened a bottle of elderberry wine that Larry had bought from Drubber Pickens, and they sat in the parlor, each adult sipping the one glass allotted by Maude Jolly.

As they laughed and kidded Tom and Bonnie, Melinda quietly crawled into Manse's lap. "Uncle Manse," she said, "when Mama marries Uncle Tom, you'll still love me, won't you?"

"Yes, Melindy," he said, "I'll always love you." Manse hugged her and kissed her cheek. His assurance seemed enough for her. She jumped down and went to Tom, who picked her up and held her on his lap until Bonnie announced it was bed-time.

When Melinda and Bonnie and Tom had gone upstairs, and Manse was alone in the parlor, he considered finishing the bottle of wine, but it was too sweet for his taste, so he corked it and carried it to the kitchen.

He had presumed that everyone had gone to bed, so was surprised to find Rebecca in the kitchen drying glasses. He walked past her, into the pantry, put away the wine bottle, brought out a jug of whiskey, and poured himself a drink.

"You're not going to pour me one?" Rebecca said.

"I didn't know you liked corn whiskey," Manse wasn't sure she was serious.

"I'm not sure whether I do or I don't," she smiled. "Nobody ever offered me any."

"Well, please – allow me," he poured a drink and handed it to her. "You may want to water it down a little," he said.

"I'll try it the way you and Tom and Larry drink it," Rebecca said, and tilted the glass and swallowed its contents in one gulp.

Then she choked, began to cough, and dropped the glass. It shattered.

"Burns," was the only word that came out as she reached for her throat.

And she could not stop coughing.

Manse pulled her to him, put his arms around her, and began to pat her on the back. Slowly her coughing eased. But he kept his arms around her. She pressed her head against his chest. He moved his right hand from her back, slid it under her chin, raised her lips to him and kissed her.

"No, Manson. Please, no – " Rebecca gently pulled her self free of his embrace, but remained close to him.

"I'm sorry," he said.

"Don't be sorry," she said, and blushed. "I guess I reacted like that just because I was surprised – "

"But I do apologize," Manse said. "I should have first asked your permission, and expressed my feelings and intentions – done things the proper way" he paused, then words came out in a torrent: "But somehow I figured you knew what I felt – what I've felt for a long time. What I hoped you felt, too – " Manse held her at arms' length. Held her eyes with his own.

Rebecca's tears trickled slowly.

"Oh, Manson," she put her arms around his neck, kissed his cheek, then released him and stepped back. "Manson – how can I say this? Your words are – are even more a surprise than your kiss."

"But I thought surely you knew – "

"I guess I've always felt like I was your little sister, Manson. Like I was the luckiest girl in the world because I had *eight* tall, strong, big-brothers – one Tom and seven Jollys – And all of them loved me and watched over me and wouldn't ever let any harm come to me."

Manse felt her words burn.

"What you're saying is that you love me *like a brother* – " he said. "And that is all that can ever be between us."

"No – I'm not saying that at all, Manson. What I am trying to say, is that I'm *confused*. This is all happening too fast. I know that I've always felt very close to you. And I've come to have even stronger feelings for you since you and Tom came home from The War. But I've never allowed myself to feel anything more *special* than that."

"Does that mean that maybe there is a chance – ?" Manse fell silent.

"Yes – I think that's exactly what I mean, Manson – that there is a chance for us. Just, please, give me time. Time to think. Time to know my feelings," Rebecca tip-toed and kissed his lips. "Goodnight, Manson. And – thank you for being the special man you are."

Manse wasn't sure how long he stood there after she left the kitchen. Finally he picked up the jug and his glass and walked back into the parlor where he poured a drink, drank, stirred the fire, sat, poured another drink, and stared into the fire.

Before The War, things had been steadier. A man could deal with emotions like love.

But now so much scar tissue clogged his heart and brain with pain and anger that the strongest feeling he could identify within himself was a cold and empty numbness.

***

Martin McCollum finished his second whiskey-and-coffee, signaled for a refill and studied in the mirror the scene of citizens and officers who were also having mid-morning drinks at the Benson House bar. He was aware that he was spending more and more time here because he was making less and less progress with his investigation – and because he had seen not one trace of Rebecca Largent since his embarrassing visit to the Jolly farm.

Then the doors to the bar swung open, and Martin shifted his stare in the mirror to the reflection of Captain Ralph Phillips who was as early an imbiber as Martin. But rather than merely nodding to Martin then moving past him to the opposite end of the bar, as he usually did, the captain stopped beside him.

"Buy me a coffee and brandy, Lieutenant, and I'll provide you with some *intelligence* you don't know. How about it?"

"I'll buy you a drink, Captain," Martin's tone was surly and sarcastic, "But I doubt that I would be interested in any intelligence *you* could furnish me – Sir."

"Not even information about that pretty Missy Largent that you've been asking Commissary Sergeant Jerlier to find out more about – such as who her current gentlemen callers are – and who her amorous liaisons were before The War – and things like that – ?"

Martin wasn't sure what to say. Every time he thought he had his crazy commandant figured out, the bastard let him know that *he* knew as much as Martin did about what was going on – within his command – and in the environs of Anderson.

Martin swigged down the balance of the cup of hot coffee and tried to keep his tone cool.

"You know something about Miss Largent, Sir?"

"I know she's standing on the corner in front of McClure's Store, with a rather nice looking brunette woman – "

"Now – Sir? She's standing out there *now*?" Martin straightened up from his bar-slouch, tugged his tunic down, and picked up his hat.

"I thought you would be interested, Lieutenant. I just didn't know *how* interested," he smiled. " I'll have this brandy – and my next one –on you."

"Have as many as you want, Captain," Martin returned the smile, turned and walked from the bar, across the lobby, out onto the sidewalk, put on his hat, and looked across the plaza, past the courthouse – and saw her.

She was holding a cloth dress-bag and a wicker hat-box. With her was Bonnie Jolly, who also held several packages.

As he walked across the plaza toward them, his mind rehearsed words for this chance encounter. *So-nice-to-see-you-again. What-a-pleasant-surprise.*

This time he would communicate, not try to conquer.

Then he saw Manse Jolly and Tom Largent come out of McClure's General Store and walk to the two women.

Martin stopped, adjusted his tunic and hat again – and continued toward them. He would not be denied this opportunity.

Martin reached them, and said, "Good morning, Mister Jolly. Mister Largent. Mrs. Jolly, Miss Largent. What a pleasant surprise to see all of you here."

They each nodded to him, but only Manse's eyes met his.

"Morning, Lieutenant," was all he said.

"My congratulations to you, Mr. Largent, on your forthcoming nuptials. And my very best wishes to you, Mrs. Jolly."

Manse glared at Martin McCollum. More than ever he didn't like the fact that this man knew so damned much about his family.

"And just how did you hear about the wedding, Lieutenant?" Manse asked.

"I hear lots of local *news*, Mr. Jolly," Martin said. "One of the duties of an Intelligence Officer is to gather as much *information* as possible about the community and its residents."

Tom Largent sensed the anger in Manse, and moved to curb it.

"It will be just a simple home wedding, Lieutenant," he said. "Nice as we can make it, times being what they are."

An unpleasant silence followed.

Martin tried to break it.

"I was just saying to some local gentlemen that I had no idea it ever got this cold in South Carolina," he held his smile.

"January is sometimes even colder," Rebecca said, and met Martin's smile for the first time, only to have it erased by Tom's frown.

"Did you get everything you needed to buy, Bonnie?" Tom said.

"I think so," Bonnie said. "My goodness but prices are high. I haven't been shopping in such a long time."

"Then, if you've got everything on your list, I guess we are ready to go," Tom took Bonnie's dress cover and hat box.

"You need any help with your packages?" Manse asked Rebecca.

"No, I can manage," she smiled at Manse, then at Martin.

Manse glared at Martin.

"By your leave, Lieutenant," Manse said.

"Of course," Martin said. "It's been a pleasure seeing all of you again. I hope you have a Merry Christmas. And a very happy wedding."

As they walked away, McCollum touched Manse's arm.

"May I have a private word with you, Mr. Jolly?" he said.

Manse held back while the others walked on towards the wagon.

"What is it, Lieutenant?" he asked.

"I know this is somewhat out of the ordinary. Perhaps I should be asking Mr. Largent, but since you are the head of the house – "

"Ask me what?" Manse's tone was sharply impatient.

"Mr. Jolly, may I have your permission to visit your home?"

"Visit? – What for?"

"To call on Miss Largent."

"To call on Rebecca?" Manse felt fire inside. "The answer to that, Lieutenant, is – *hell no*, you certainly may *not*!"

"May I ask why-not?" Martin persisted.

"I'll tell you why-not," Manse glared at him. "We get enough visits from Union soldiers. They come every month to rob us. I'm sure as hell not having one of you in my house by choice."

Manse did an abrupt about-face –muttered *Goddamn-Yankee* – and walked away.

Martin McCollum stared after him – muttered *Damn Stupid Shit-Kicker*, and shrugged his shoulders. He had asked permission, and, as expected, he had been rejected.

He would simply have to find another way to get to Rebecca Largent.

Right now, he needed a drink. Or two. Or three. Before lunch.

He crossed the Square to the Benson House.

Texas Brown entered the bar just after Martin walked in.

"Buy you a drink, Lieutenant?" he said.

"Yes. Thanks."

"Two sour mash," Texas ordered.

"You're looking kind of low, Martin," Texas smiled. "What's ailing you? You not having any luck with your treasure hunt?"

Martin shook his head.

"It's not that," he said. "Something else is on my mind today." Martin downed his drink and ordered another. "But as long as you've brought up the subject of *our* investigation, tell me – have you found out anything?"

Texas lowered his voice

"Why don't we talk about this upstairs in your room."

Martin nodded, finished his second drink and walked from the bar, through the lobby and up the stairs. When he entered his room, he left the door ajar, opened a bottle and poured two drinks.

Texas came in, and they sat at the small table by the window.

"Here's to Christmas," Texas said, and raised his glass.

"What have you learned?"

"Don't be in such an all fired hurry, Martin. First let's have a little drink to Christmas," Texas sipped. "Damn good whiskey," he drained his glass. "Now, Martin," he said, "I'm ready to talk. But first, there's a couple of things I need to know."

"What kind of things?"

Texas bit the end off a cigar and spat it on the floor. "Just exactly what are you planning to do with all that gold, if you find it?" He struck a match and lit.

"It is my duty to deliver it to the United States Army."

Texas eyes narrowed.

"Don't spoon-feed me none of that *duty* horse-shit, bluebelly," he said, and stood. "I can see right off that you and me ain't gonna get any business done here this morning."

He adjusted his hat, and started for the door.

"Hold on a minute," Martin said "Sit down."

Texas smiled and returned to his seat, and waited.

Martin poured him another drink.

"Well?" Texas said, "Are we going to talk like two *men*, or are we going to act like two goddamn preachers spouting on about *duty*?" He spat the word.

"All right," Martin poured himself another drink. "I will admit, I have thought about keeping a small percentage of the gold – when and if I ever find it – as a kind-of reward for myself."

"That's better," Texas smiled. "My old daddy use to say that speaking truth always makes a man feel better," he exhaled smoke. "Now tell me, Martin, if I found the gold for you, would you be willing to *split* that reward with me?"

"Have you found it?" Martin half rose from his chair.

"Now don't go getting yourself all worked up," Texas said. "If I had found the gold, would I be sitting here palavering with you about splitting anything? Hell, no! I would've been long gone with it."

Martin sat back down.

"But you've found out something – haven't you?" he asked.

"I got nothing to say to you until you tell me exactly what our deal is," Texas said.

Martin hesitated, then said, "All right. We split it even – half and half."

Texas persisted. "Half and half of what?"

Martin smiled. "Half and half of whatever we can get away with," he said. "Is *that* good enough for you?"

"Yeah, I reckon as how *that* is good enough," Texas laughed.

"Very well," Martin grinned. "Now that *that* is settled, tell me *everything* you have found out."

"You take me for a damn fool? If I tell you everything I know, you won't need me anymore."

Martin aimed his darkest stare at Texas.

"I strongly advise you to tell me what I want to know."

"That sounds like a threat to me," Texas said. "And I goddamned sure don't like being threatened by no man — specially a bluebelly lieutenant who's got nothing to back it up with."

"I don't particularly care what you like or don't like," Martin finished his drink and poured another. "As for *backing up* my words, perhaps I should remind you that I am an Intelligence Officer. The citizens of this area may not readily volunteer information to me, but they can often be coerced into divulging quite a lot in exchange for exclusion from requisitions — or similar favorable treatment which I can arrange. And while I may not have learned a hell of a lot about the gold, I have learned quite a lot about *you*. And your activities organizing a Klavern of the Ku Klux Klan in this district."

Texas did not blink. He pulled for control, and made a mental note to do no further business with Commissary Sergeant Alex Jerlier.

Then he forced a laugh.

"Somebody has sure been feeding you a righteous load of horse shit if they been saying things like that about me, Martin."

"Do not make the mistake of underestimating me, Texas," Martin did not lower his eyes. "That could prove fatal. I didn't get my medals for killing men on the battle-field. Mine were awarded for standing men up in front of firing squads," Martin eased back in the chair but continued his stare. "If I take that information to Captain Phillips, he'll have you in the stockade by sundown — and you'll stay there a long time."

Texas took a deep puff on his cigar. Now he understood the meaning of the flashes he saw whenever he was around Martin McCollum — warning flashes of distrust.

He smiled at Martin through a haze of smoke.

"I pride myself that I don't often misjudge men," Texas said. "but I reckon I might've put you one or two notches too low."

Martin started to say something, then changed his mind.

"Do you have another one of those fine cigars?" he asked.

Texas took out his cigar case and extended it.

Martin selected one, and Texas returned the case to his pocket.

Martin knew that this was the closest they would ever come to shaking hands.

Texas struck a match and they lit.

"Seems we both know I can't allow myself to get arrested," Texas admitted. "But likewise you can't afford to have me arrested because your chances of finding that gold are a damn zero without me. So I reckon what we've got here is a what they call a Mexican stand-off."

"That certainly appears to accurately describe our situation," Martin said. "So I think we should set aside all this posturing and return to our original idea of working together – whether we like it or not."

"I like those words," Texas smiled.

"You said you needed my help with something," Martin said.

"Yeah. I did," Texas said. "There's a nigger in the stockade by the name of Robespierre McGukin."

"I remember the name. A Freedman. What about him?"

"Get him turned loose."

"But he's being held for murder – "

"Martin, because you're an Intelligence Officer, Captain Phillips thinks you know things his other officers don't. So just tell him that the witnesses who say they saw Robespierre kill a girl are lying – which is true. All them just-freed-niggers flat hate Robespierre because he was free all those years while they were still slaves."

"And if I succeed in getting him set free, what then?"

"You just make sure Robespierre knows that *Mister Texas Brown* is the man who got him out of the stockade."

Martin thought a moment.

"And I presume," he said, "that, no matter what I say, you won't tell me any more than that?"

"I figure that's all you need to know for now, Martin. But later I promise I'll tell you everything," Texas smiled.

"Very well, I will accept your word – for now," Martin finished his drink. "I will try to get McGukin freed before Christmas," he said. "Which reminds me – since you and I both find ourselves alone for the holidays in this godforsaken town of Anderson, South Carolina, perhaps we can have Christmas dinner together."

"Let's just make it a Christmas *drink*, Martin," Texas stood, walked to the door. "I don't mind drinking with scalawags and carpetbaggers – and even a bluebelly, now and again – for business reasons – but I make it a rule never to break bread with them."

He stopped and turned.

"To be real honest with you, Martin," he said, "I'd just as soon eat with niggers."

He left the room.

***

Not since before The War had Manse felt the warmth of family that he felt on Christmas Day when he walked into the parlor for Tom and Bonnie's wedding.

The room was brightened by the colors of the women's new dresses – dark green for Maude, turquoise for Rebecca, peach for the bride, and violet for Melinda. (A slight clash of color was created by Melinda's insistence on wearing the bright red shawl she had received for Christmas.)

The men wore their new suits and boots, and stood around a little awkwardly until the service was completed, and the women went to the kitchen to put the finishing touches on dinner while the men went outside to enjoy a drink of Dubber Pickens' best whiskey. Even the Rev. Zachariah Eskew, a close friend of Tom's and Manse's daddies who came out of retirement just to officiate at this occasion – even the good reverend did not refuse a glass or two.

Christmas dinner was baked hen and dressing, peas, corn, pickled beets, biscuits and cornbread, cake with hard-sauce, pecan pie, and coffee.

Afterwards, Manse asked Rebecca to walk outside with him. And on the back porch, in the cold air of Christmas night, he gave her a gold heart-shaped locket with the initials "M" and "R" engraved inside.

"Thank you, Manson, it's beautiful," she said, and kissed him softly on the lips. "But I didn't get you anything. We all said that the new clothes and everything we got for the wedding were all the Christmas presents we were going to give this year."

"This isn't a Christmas present," Manse tried to pull out the right words. "It's something I want you to wear next to your heart while you're thinking about the future – and about *us*."

Manse held her close for a silent moment, then they went back into the house and joined the others.

Everyone agreed it was the happiest day they'd had since before The War.

There was no way Manse Jolly could know that Christmas 1865 was the last Christmas his family would share.

***

During the time he spent working with the Klan in Georgia, Texas had learned well the fear that they instilled in every man or woman who ever heard the muffled beat of four-hundred hooves padded by croker sacks – then saw a sea of white robes floating through the night beneath torches held high.

In January, he officially designated Whit Whitfield and Elk Marett as his Exalted Cleagles, seconds in command to the Klavern's Grand Dragon. It was their responsibility to communicate to members the times and places for meeting – and to sell robes and collect dues – and the Piedmont Klavern of the South Carolina Ku Klux Klan began its terror.

Texas chose their victims carefully. He preferred successful men. They made the Klan's efforts more profitable.

But he often picked carpetbaggers, scalawags, or freedmen who were less well-off, because they stirred the greatest hatred in his followers.

And it was, Texas knew, men's hate and fears that created men's prejudices – the foundation on which the Klan was built.

***

In late January, Captain Ralph Phillips entered the Benson House lobby flanked by his aides, two first lieutenants, who were flanked by their aides, two second lieutenants, who were followed by one Army Intelligence Officer who resented like hell being ordered to accompany a line officer anywhere.

As commandant of the Union Army forces garrisoned in Anderson (one company of cavalry and one platoon of infantry) Captain Phillips' responsibilities had, until recently, consisted primarily of requisitioning sufficient supplies for his troops, occasionally jailing ex-Confederates who threatened local officials with bodily harm, and keeping the streets relatively free of drunks.

But now – quite suddenly – the Ku Klux Klan had emerged from the shadows, and, by-god, there was some excitement in this sleepy quagmire of Anderson, South Carolina.

At last Captain Phillips felt like he was in charge of a real military command, not a small town police force.

Of course the Klan was hardly a worthy adversary for the US Army, and Anderson would never provide the stimulation that accompanied fighting Indians in the Western Command – and it probably wouldn't take long to bring a few dirt-farmer Klansmen under control – but for as long as it took to track down and hang these night riders, Captain Ralph Phillips intended to enjoy himself.

He nodded to faces he recognized among the crowd of men in the Benson House lobby. He stopped and shook hands with Samuel Heaton who was standing next to that tall southerner who always wore black.

Then the captain led his aides, and their aides, and *his* Intelligence Officer to the mezzanine stairs where they turned and faced the crowd.

When Ralph Phillips began to speak, the lobby became quiet.

"This area is currently besieged by a group of robed and masked men who call themselves the Ku-Klux-Klan," he said. "They are, in fact, no more than a bunch of cowards who are afraid to show their faces, or to meet their adversaries on a field of combat."

There was a low murmur of agreement.

"Within four short weeks, the Klan has been responsible for six incidents of looting and burning, four brutal floggings of freedmen, three equally brutal floggings of whites, and three murders of freedmen by hanging."

Captain Phillips paused.

Texas noticed that Martin was looking at him.

"Last night," the captain continued, "Morris Berne, the attorney who came here two months ago from Ohio to serve as Director of Allotment of Seized Lands for the Freedmen Bureau, was brutally murdered. Night-riders burned his house. We presume they looted it first. That is their pattern. Then they took him and a young

Freedman who lived at his home, into the barn and hung them naked by their ankles and flogged them with horse-whips and chains. Mr. Berne died from the flogging. The Freedman is still alive – but barely."

Captain Phillips paused to let his words sink in.

Texas returned Martin's stare – and added a half-smile.

"What does the Army intend to do about this?" Samuel Heaton took advantage of the captain's moment of silence. "Surely you can protect the law-abiding citizens of Anderson from this bunch of renegade night-riders."

"I intend to do just that, Mister Heaton," Captain Ralph Phillips felt warmed by the fear in the room. "I want everyone here to spread the word that today I am declaring war on the Ku Klux Klan. I am invoking Military Procedure Laws, giving the troops under my command full discretionary power to dispense with legal formalities in matters of search and seizure. I am doubling night patrols in this district. And I solicit any information you can furnish me to help identify the men responsible for these acts."

***

Just after sundown, Texas reined his horse into the stand of pines where Whit Whitfield and Elk Marett waited.

"A Yankee Patrol arrested the Pinson boys last night," Texas said. "Stopped them on the Powdersville Road. Found robes in their saddle bags. And a watch from that lawyer's house," Texas covered his concern with anger. "I thought our men understood the rules."

"We've told'em all, over and over again, Texas, that they wasn't never to take their robes with them," Elk said.

"They know they're supposed to turn them in to me and Elk after meetings and ridings," Whit said. "Just like they know we'll bust their asses if we find out they've held back any loot for theyselves."

"That goddamn Captain Phillips has charged them with murder. I reckon they'll be tried in Circuit Court when the judge gets here in March," Texas said, then glared at Whit. "You sure them two won't talk to save their hides?"

"They won't talk, Texas. You can count on it."

"Whit's right," Elk Marett said. "They're damned honorable men."

"You'd better be right," Texas reached inside his coat and took out two envelopes and handed them to Whit.

"Take this money to their folks," he said, "and get word to the Pinson boys that the Klan will see to it that their families have everything they need."

Texas paused.

"And while you're at it," he said, "you can let them know that if they should decide to do any talking to the Yankees about the Klan, things could just as easy go real bad for their families."

"We'll tell'em, Texas," Whit said. "But I can vouch for them Pinsons. They'll stay quiet, no matter what."

Whit put the envelopes in his pocket.

"Anything else?" he asked.

"Damn right there's something else," Texas said. "We've got to show them bluebellies that arresting two of our men won't stop the Klan."

Texas handed each of the men a cigar.

"Tell me – who's the richest freed-nigger in the whole Anderson District?" he asked.

"That would be old man Dickerson's house nigger," Elk said. "They gave him some kind of big-shit job at The Freed-Man's Bureau cause he can read and write."

Texas struck a match, and leaned from his saddle to light their cigars.

"The men in the Klan hold some real hate for him, do they?" he asked.

"That they do," Whit said.

"He's the one what stole the Sutherland farm at one of them scalawag tax auctions," Elk said.

"They purely do hate him," Whit said, and sucked smoke.

"And rightfully so. He's one more uppity nigger," Elk said.

"Thinks he's good as white folks," Whit added.

"Then I reckon he's the one we ought to go visit tonight," Texas said. "You two get the word to the men that we ride at midnight."

The skin on Elk Marett's skull tightened, and his black-toothed smile broadened.

"We gonna burn the nigger out?" he asked.

"Yeah – we sure as hell are," Texas spat.

"I figure it'll be a good night's work," he said, "to let this uppity-nigger watch his house burn down while we hang him slow – real slow."

-7-

Ralph Phillips waited until his aide, Lt. Francis Marion Pearson, had left the office and closed the door behind him, then the captain opened a desk drawer and took out a bottle of whiskey – changed his mind, put it back, opened another drawer, and took out the quart of sipping-bourbon he had been saving for a special occasion.

Occasions, he decided, were never likely to be more special than today.

Hanging two men, side by side, on the same gallows, had indeed been a glorious way to greet the dawn.

He opened the bottle and, rather than sipping, took a long swig.

These damned southerners did not know how to do many things very well, but they did know how to make good sour mash. He set the bottle down, reached in the drawer, took out a glass, filled it, put his feet on his desk, lit a cigar, and decided to spend the rest of this spring morning relaxing, sipping and smoking. He deserved a few hours just to savor his situation.

In the wake of initial acts of violence by the Ku Klux Klan in January, Capt. Phillips had altered the pattern of Army patrols. Or, rather, he had done away with any pattern, ordering random routes, at random times. And during the very first week of Savannah River night patrols, his men had stopped two riders and found in their saddle bags Klan robes and hoods and a watch taken from the attorney who had been killed by the Klan.

It was pure luck, he knew, but luck was as good as strategy if it brought the desired results.

He had put the Klansmen – two brothers named Pinson – in the stockade and charged them with murder, and set a trial date before a military tribunal.

But then the civilian authorities – the sheriff and magistrate and prosecutor – filed protests with the state courts, contending that the Military had no jurisdiction over the murder of civilians when the defendants charged with the crime were also civilians. The Pinson brothers, they argued, should be tried in the next session of Circuit Court, scheduled for March.

Captain Phillips argued that, since the Army had made the arrest, the Army should try the Pinson brothers. In fact, he wanted very badly to go ahead and try the two men, and hang them, without any further delay – but then he decided it might be prudent to be judicious, so he appealed to General Sickles, Military Commander of the Occupied Territories of North and South Carolina, for determination of jurisdiction. General Sickles forwarded the matter to Washington, and subsequently advised Captain Phillips that a decision would be made before the March Session of Circuit Court opened in Anderson.

Two weeks ago Washington had ruled that, under Military Occupation And Reparation Laws enacted by Congress and signed into law by the president, local Army commanders could legally arrest anyone suspected of commiting a felony, and subject them to trial before an Army Tribunal. If found guilty, they were to be sentenced and punished by the Army, under the Uniform Code of Military Justice.

Only arrests made by civilian authorities were to be tried in State or District Circuit Court. And there weren't such arrests because Anderson had only one sheriff and three deputies.

Washington's grant to the Military of the right of arrest, trial and punishment of civilians was a victory that consolidated the Army's – and Captain Phillips' – power.

But during the two months that the Army was awaiting that jurisdictional decision from Washington, all hell had broken loose in Anderson.

Civilian crime increased. Bushwhacking, robbery, theft, murder and rape, committed by freedman, scalawags, carpetbaggers, and some Union Soldiers who had turned renegade, had become almost commonplace.

Civilians were afraid to venture out of their homes after dark.

All of which suited Captain Ralph Phillips just fine.

In the name of Law and Order, he assumed even more power.

As quickly as possible after Washington approved military trial of the Pinsons, Captain Phillips convened a six-officer Tribunal, and personally presided over the proceedings that convicted them.

Despite the fact that standing orders specifically stated that all executions be carried out on the gallows at the Greenville District Command Garrison, Captain Phillips had received special permission to hang the Pinson brothers "from horseback in the Anderson stockade because of the substantial risk that Klansmen may attack any military escort transporting the prisoners to Greenville, and in such event, the Army may sustain significant loss of men."

Capt. Phillips was still smiling, and pouring himself another congratulatory drink, when Lt. Pearson knocked on the door and said that Lt. McCollum wanted to see him.

"Show him in," Ralph Phillips sighed.

When Martin entered, the captain returned his salute without bothering to look up.

"Well, what is it?" he said.

"I need to discuss two matters with you, sir," Martin remained at attention, but his eyes were on the captain's bottle of whiskey.

"Before you begin, Lieutenant, I have a question for you: Did you *enjoy* the hangings this morning?" He smiled. "I thought that witnessing a double execution might be of particular interest to you since, from your records, I understand you have been responsible for the execution of quite a few men," Capt. Phillips emptied his glass, then refilled it. "Of course you always had your fellow soldiers executed by firing squad. Isn't that correct, Lieutenant?"

Martin's gut tightened with anger, but he remained calm.

"It is my duty as an Intelligence Officer, sir –" he spoke louder than necessary – "to gather evidence and present it to military tribunals. Verdicts are rendered – and punishment is meted out – by others."

"Of course, Lieutenant. All of us are just doing-our-duty, aren't we? And I certainly wouldn't want you to feel defensive about the fact that during The War you were responsible for the deaths of more Union soldiers than Confederates," he relit his cigar. "We should all enjoy what we do, Lieutenant. I enjoyed watching those two cowards get jerked off their horses this morning – and strangle to death at the end of a rope. Much more fitting than a broken neck on a scaffold. The Klan likes to make its victims suffer. I think we did well to return the favor, don't you?"

"To be quite candid, sir, I don't particularly enjoy watching men die. Quickly or slowly." Martin remained at attention, hoping that at any moment the captain would order him at-ease, ask him to sit, and offer him a drink – but that did not happen.

"From your answer, Lieutenant, it's quite obvious that you were never in combat," Captain Phillips said. "If you had been, you would know that watching the enemy die can be quite a pleasant experience. And that there are a hell of a lot worse ways to die than the rope or the firing squad," he exhaled a billow of smoke. "But enough of this pleasant chit-chat, Lieutenant – please, go ahead and tell me – what are these two-things you feel are so important that you had to interrupt my morning?"

Martin did not hesitate.

"First of all, sir," he said, "I think you should know that there is a lot of anger in the district over this morning's hangings – "

"Jesus Christ, is that a fact?" Ralph Phillips laughed aloud. "I would never have guessed that folks around here might get upset because we hung two of their local boys." He glared at Martin. "If this is the *intelligence* you came here to provide me, Lieutenant, then I certainly understand why you are generally considered an idiot – and your work here a joke."

Martin's face flushed. He strained to control his temper.

"With all due respect, sir. If the captain will allow me to complete my statement – "

"By all-damn-means, Lieutenant McCollum, complete it. Then get the hell out of my office and let me get on with what was the beginning of an enjoyable day until you arrived – "

"The local citizens are not upset just by the hangings," Martin spoke very slowly now – deliberately intent on antagonizing Ralph Phillips. "They are angry that no members of the Pinson family were allowed to visit the condemned men, to say good-bye – nor were any civilian authorities present to witness the execution, to determine that it was carried out in a proper and humane manner, as prescribed by law – "

"You can stop right there, Lieutenant," Captain Phillips slapped his palm down on the desk. "The Pinson brothers were Klansmen, and their execution was carried out by me in the manner that I deemed proper. I am not required to submit to civilian authority. I presume you read the legal opinion from Washington."

"Yes, sir, I did indeed read it. And I wrote quite a substantive endorsement of your decision to carry out the executions here rather than transporting the defendants to Greenville – "

"And I appreciated that support, Lieutenant. It is what I expect from officers under my command," Ralph Phillips picked up the bottle and drank. "Frankly, McCollum, I don't understand what the hell it is that you are trying to say to me. If something else is bothering you, then spit it out. I don't have all day."

"The most disturbing fact, sir, is your order refusing to allow the bodies of the two men to be given to their families for burial."

"I decided, Lieutenant, to have their bodies buried in unmarked graves within the stockade," the captain said.

"I know that, sir, and I respectfully request that you reconsider that decision. If you give the bodies to the family, the people here will have one less grievance against the Army. And such a gesture will take some of the venom out of the Klan's angry rhetoric. My sources inform me that we can expect violent retaliation."

"Request denied, Lieutenant. I want the Klan to get angry. I want them to retaliate. And when they do, I will meet them with increased military force. And every Klansmen we capture, I will hang," Captain Phillips said, and glared at Martin. "In fact, Lieutenant, I plan to make future hangings public – in the Courthouse Square – from horseback – with the cowards wearing their damnable robes."

"But, sir –"

"No further discussion, Lieutenant," Captain Phillips said. "Unless there is another subject on your mind, you are dismissed."

"There is one other thing, sir."

"Then goddammit, man, tell me what it is and get the hell out of my sight!"

"It concerns the freedman, Robespierre McGukin, sir," Martin's tone became more polite. "As you may recall, in December I provided you with information that the men who say they saw McGukin kill a young woman, are themselves the killers. They have, in the meantime left this area, making it impossible to arrest them."

"Yes, and I recall also that you asked me to free McGukin from the stockade – which I could not do as long as the matter of my jurisdiction was awaiting decision from Washington."

"Right, sir. And now that you have been successful in having your judicial position affirmed, I wish to renew my request."

"And just precisely what would McGukin's freedom mean to *you*, Lieutenant? Surely your interest is more than merely seeing-justice-done."

"Very astute, sir," Martin smiled and bit his tongue. "The release of McGukin would help establish my credibility among the community of freedmen. They tend to trust no one. But the freedmen who worked as servants in the homes of wealthy and influential Anderson residents know virtually everything that went on here during The War," Martin swallowed to wet his parched throat. "By helping McGukin, I hope to find out, from him and other freedmen what happened to the gold from the Confederate Holding Bank."

Captain Ralph Phillips again slapped his palm on the desk and laughed aloud.

"Lieutenant McCollum, if there is *anything* I can do to help you find that non-existent gold, I will be happy to oblige." He picked up the quill pen from his desk, dipped it in ink, and scribbled a note on a sheet of paper. "Give this to Lieutenant Pearson. He will arrange a release for McGukin – and withdrawal of all charges against him."

He handed the paper to Martin.

"Thank you, sir," Martin said, and this time his smile was genuine.

***

Texas Brown rode fast toward the Jolly farm.

During January and February, he had taken advantage of every invitation to visit there – for lunch or dinner or supper or just for a drink and conversation.

In March he had begun showing up without an invitation. And to assure his welcome, he always brought small gifts for the women and children, and slipped a bottle of good whiskey, and a supply of cigars, into his saddle bags for the men.

But today he was not going visiting for pleasure. He had a problem:

Robespierre McGukin had been released from the stockade at two o'clock this afternoon.

And, Martin told Texas, "I let McGukin know that the man he could thank for his release was Mister Texas Brown."

Thus the hard part – getting Robespierre out of the stockade – had been accomplished.

And the rest should have been easy.

But – within an hour after his release – Robespierre disappeared.

The two Klansmen Texas had ordered to follow him, reported that "that big nigger just disappeared into thin air."

He worked at the train depot, but he wasn't there, and no one seemed to know where lived.

At least no one who knew, was telling.

And neither Texas nor Martin could search for him without drawing unwanted attention to themselves.

Then one of Martin's sources told him that before The War, Robespierre spent a lot of time out at the Largent farm.

So it was logical to assume that Tom Largent or Manse Jolly just might know where Robespierre lived.

It was late afternoon when Texas rode up the drive to the Jolly house.

Manse was sitting on the front porch steps with Melinda.

Texas walked his horse the last few yards to keep from stirring up dust.

"Howdy, Manse. Melindy." Texas swung his leg over his horse's rump, dropped to the ground, removed his long-coat, and laid it across the saddle.

"How's my best girl?" he said, and picked up Melinda and kissed her cheek.

"Can I wear your hat, Uncle Texas?" she asked.

"Sure you can, Melindy," he put his large black hat on the small girl's head, then gently put her down on the porch.

Manse stood, they shook hands, then sat on the steps.

It was best, Texas decided, not to push the conversation.

"Anything happening worth talking about?" he asked.

"Just spring plowing and planting," Manse said. "Tom and I were saying just last night that we reckoned you must be staying busy. You haven't been out for a while."

"Truth is, I been going at it day and night," Texas said. "But before I start talking about all *that*, tell me about the family. Seems awful quiet out here. Where is everybody?"

"Tom took Mama and Rebecca and Johnny to revival services over at Old Stone Church," Manse said. "Bonnie's upstairs resting. Guess you haven't heard – she and Tom are expecting a baby."

"Now that's mighty fine news," Texas slapped Manse on the back. "Wish Tom was here so I could give him a good cigar to celebrate," he pulled out his case. "But that don't stop me and you from having one." He emptied the case into Manse's hand. "Here – give all these to Tom with my congratulations." He took out a match, struck it, lit his cigar, held the match for Manse – and decided he still needed to do a little more *visiting* before getting down to his reason for being here.

"And how's Larry?" Texas asked. "I haven't seen him in Anderson but one time since Christmas."

"He's fine. Wishes he could spend more time here at home, and Lord knows, we could sure use his help with the planting – but he keeps finding more and more livestock up in the mountains – and between searching and finding and butchering and hauling it down here, he's as busy as we are."

Manse watched the way Texas nervously rolled the cigar between his forefinger and thumb, and he knew this was more than just a *visit*.

"So, go on now," Manse said. "Tell me the news with you."

Texas proceeded slowly. "Reckon you know that the Army finally went ahead and hung the Pinson brothers."

"Yeah, we heard," Manse said.

"They were good men," Texas said. "Dumb as owl shit, but damned loyal. Didn't tell the Army anything."

Manse listened, smoked, waited.

"I tell you, Manse, that bluebelly Captain Phillips has got so many problems he's about to go crazier than folks say he already is," Texas grinned. "And it's not just problems with the Klan. Some of his own soldiers have turned renegade – bushwhacking and stealing. Reckon they see the scalawags and freedmen getting away with it, so they figure they can, too. And all Phillips knows to do is send out more patrols."

"Yeah, there was one by here a week ago. That Commissary Sergeant and his squad of cavalry. But they weren't requisitioning. Just poking around. Asked a lot of questions. Searched the place, but didn't find anything. The rifles and pistols, and what little money we've got, are hid in the smokehouse walls with the meat."

Manse stubbed out his cigar.

"That reminds me," he said. "I've just finished converting my revolvers to cartridge. Like to show them to you, if you got the time."

"Afraid I can't today, Manse," Texas said. "To be real honest, I rode out here just to ask you one question that I need answering real bad – then I got to be getting back to town."

Manse waited.

"It's about that big free-nigger they call Robespierre McGukin," Texas said. "You know much about that boy?"

"Known him most all my life," Manse said. "Last time I saw him, the Army had him shackled and was taking him to the stockade. Said he murdered somebody." Manse frowned, and rubbed his forehead. "But I'd swear on the Bible, Texas, old Robespierre never killed anybody in his whole life."

Texas smiled. This was the moment. He had the words ready.

"Seems you're right about that, Manse," he said. "The Army let Robespierre out of the stockade this afternoon. Said there wasn't no real evidence against him."

Manse nodded silent approval. And waited, again.

Texas chose words carefully. He did not want to make Manse suspicious

"Some of my boys told me that Robespierre worked at the train depot before the Army put him in the stockade, but nobody's seen him around there since he got out today," Texas said, and paused. "And, to be honest with you, Manse, I kind-of need to talk to that boy – but nobody seems to know where he lives. Not even Whit and Elk – and they usually know most everything. But then Whit said he did remember hearing, a long time ago, that Robespierre used to be out at the Largent farm a lots before The War. So I rode out here to see if maybe you and Tom know where he lives."

"I reckon we might," Manse felt suspicions rise, and decided to talk a lot without saying too much.

"Before The War," he began, "Tom's daddy had two slaves – Janie and Matthew. They had been reared on the McGukin place. That's where Tom's daddy bought them. Anyhow, Matthew and Robespierre was kin, I think. Or maybe they just grew up together. Anyhow, after Robespierre was freed, he'd sometimes see Tom's daddy in town with Matthew and ask to ride out to their farm on the wagon and visit for a day or two. I recollect that Tom's daddy use to laugh and say that was just fine with him because Robespierre always helped Matthew with chores and did extra work around the place while he was out there." Manse paused. "I remember Matthew telling me and Tom that nobody but him knew where Robespierre lived."

Manse hesitated again, then took a long draw on his cigar and exhaled before continuing.

"You have to understand, Texas," Manse said, "that Robespierre was always afraid that a slave-tracker like Elk Marett might catch and chain him and sell him to a trader who would take him somewhere far off, where nobody knew him, and sell him as a slave. Never mind he was free. Freed-slaves didn't have any rights to speak of – so they had to be extra careful."

"What you're really telling me, Manse, is that nobody knows where Robespierre lives, except this nigger, Matthew," Texas exhaled a sigh of frustration. "You know where I can find *him*?"

"I'm afraid Matthew can't help you," Manse said. "Tom's daddy freed him and Janie just before The War started. They went to work as house niggers for the Arlington Orr's – Governor Orr he is now. Matthew use to drive the Massa-carriage," Manse watched Texas's eyes. "Matthew and Janie both died of the diphtheria-pox in the epidemic-plague of fifty-nine."

Texas slowly shook his head.

"I guess that means that only Robespierre, hisself, knows where he lives."

"Well, I didn't say nobody knows." Manse said. "When me and Tom was boys, we pestered old Matthew so much about where

Robespierre lived, that he finally told us. But we never told anybody, because we never figured anybody but us really cared where one freed-nigger lived. And up to now, nobody has."

Texas drew deeply on his cigar, then tapped it out on the step and tossed the stub into the weeds.

He knew that Manse hadn't yet decided whether to tell him what he wanted to know.

Silently. Patiently. He waited.

Manse nodded his head slowly as he rubbed the back of his neck and waited for the throbbing to subside.

"What do you really want with Robespierre?" Manse looked Texas straight in the eyes. "When the leader of the Klan goes looking for a nigger, it's not usually just to talk."

"I can't argue with that, Manse. You're right, the Klan don't usually ever talk to niggers. But this here ain't Klan business. This is personal – just between me and Robespierre. I badly need to know what he might have heard during The War about some of them Unionists who live up in the Dark Corner. I figure a freed nigger would've heard lots in them days. And if he can tell me what I need to know, I can sell the information. So I'm willing to pay Robespierre for what he knows. If I can ever find him." Texas spat and stared at the ground.

When he raised his eyes, Manse's were still locked onto his.

Neither man spoke or blinked.

Then Manse broke the silence.

"I'm going to trust you, Texas – that you're telling me the truth about just wanting to *talk* to Robespierre. But I got to give you warning – if anything happens to him because of what I tell you, I would be forced to do-something about that."

"Nothing will happen to him, Manse. I promise. I'll see to it that the Klan don't never bother him. You got my word."

"And you've got my-word," Manse's tone carried his meaning.

He paused.

"Unless Robespierre has moved," Manse said, "I reckon he still lives right there at the train depot where he works."

"In the depot?" Texas looked at him in disbelief. "How the hell could he live in the depot and nobody see him there?"

"Not *in* the depot, Texas – " Manse half-smiled. "Robespierre lives *under* it. To start out, he moved some foundation stones and crawled under the depot and dug him out a place to sleep. And over the years he made it into a room big enough for him to stand up in. But Matthew said he never goes in or comes out except at night."

"Well I'll be damned," Texas laughed. "Under the depot!"

"Unless he's gone somewhere else," Manse said. "Lots has changed since The War."

Texas smiled to himself, then to Manse, and turned to Melinda.

"Can I have my hat back now, Little Darlin' ?" he said.

She put it on his head and kissed him on the cheek.

He stood, shook hands with Manse, stretched, then walked to his horse, put on his long-coat, mounted, patted the horse's neck, and said, "You don't know how much I appreciate what you just told me, Manse. I truly do," he smiled. "You give my best to the family, you hear? But most of all to Bonnie and that new baby."

He smiled, tipped his hat, turned the horse in its length, and rode off.

***

Texas would not have heard the sound of stone sliding on stone if he hadn't been standing less than ten feet from it – waiting for it.

He stepped back against the depot wall, into the darkness of shadows.

Then he heard the sound of stone on stone again, and the figure of Robespierre McGukin rose and stood for a moment in the moonlight. He bent down and picked up a bucket, walked to the tracks, stepped between them, and moved toward the water tower.

He came within three feet of where Texas stood, passed without seeing him, then stopped at the feel of a pistol barrel against his neck.

"Not a sound, nigger," Texas' voice was a deep and threatening whisper.

"Yes, suh," Robespierre said.

"Good," Texas said. "Now you keep walking to the tower. You and me are going to have us a little talk."

"Please, don't kill me, mister," Robespierre said. "I ain't done nothing I should get killed for."

" I told you to be quiet, nigger. Just keep walking." And the two men – one big and black, the other big and white and dressed in black – moved silently until they were beneath the tower where they stopped.

"My name is Texas Brown," Texas said. "You've heard of me?"

"Yes, suh. I heared it was you what got me out of that stockade. That's what I heared. And I surely thank you for that. But didn't nobody tell me why you done it."

"I'll tell you *why*," Texas said. "But first, turn around."

When Robespierre turned and was facing him, Texas made a show of holstering his pistol.

"You must be hungry," he said. "You been down in that hidey-hole of yours for three days now."

"I had me some beans. The rest of my food spoilt while I was in that stockade."

"I figured you'd be hungry, so I brought you some supper." Texas handed Robespierre a basket. "Help yourself."

Robespierre opened the basket. The smell of cold fried chicken brought a smile. He picked up a drumstick and took a bite.

"You had a right to wonder why I helped get you out of the stockade," Texas said while Robespierre chewed. "And the answer is real simple: There's some questions I need to get answered, and I think you're the only one who can answer them for me."

Robespierre stopped chewing.

"What questions are them, Mister Brown?"

"Questions about some small crates – and some big men – Robespierre," Texas said, and chuckled at his own clever words. "Yes, sir – small crates and big men."

Robespierre chewed again, more slowly than before.

"You've been living in that hole under the depot for quite a few years – right?"

"Yes, suh."

"And you were living under there during all of The War – "

Robespierre nodded, his mouth now full of cold cornbread.

"And you were there that night towards the end of The War when soldiers brought some crates down to the depot."

Robespierre continued chewing.

"Those crates were supposed to be put on a special train. That right?"

Robespierre hesitated, then nodded.

"There were about twenty or more soldiers guarding those crates. But then someone came and talked those soldiers into leaving the depot – leaving those crates, unguarded. Is that right?"

Robespierre was silent.

"God-dammit, boy, you answer me, you hear?"

"Yes, suh. You right. A man come down and told the soldiers that there was all kinds of food for them up at the Whitner Cafe, and he told the soldiers to go there and eat," Robespierre said.

"And that man was a real important man who all the soldiers knew and believed, so they did what he said. Right?"

"Yes, suh. They all knowed who he was."

"And when that important man told the soldiers he would watch the crates while the soldiers went to eat, they all went to eat – and when they came back, the crates were all still here."

Robespierre would not meet Texas eye-to-eye. He stared at the ground, and pushed cinders with his toe.

"But the crates that were there when the soldiers got back, weren't really the same crates that were there when they left? Ain't that right, Robespierre? They just *looked* like the same crates."

Robespierre did not answer.

"I'm talking to you, nigger," Texas raised his voice. "I'm asking you if the crates the soldiers loaded on that train when it got here were the same crates the soldiers had brought from the bank – and, goddammit, I want you to answer me, you hear?"

"Yes, suh."

"Yes, sir *what*? Yes, they were the *same* crates – or yes, they were *different* crates –?" Texas' voice became a low growl. "And you damn well better not lie to me – or I'll have your black heart cut out."

"They was different crates," Robespierre said quickly. "They looked the same – but they was different crates."

"You sure about that?"

"Yes, suh. I'm real sure."

"Tell me how-come you're so real-sure?"

"Cause I toted all the ones that had come from the bank and been stacked on the platform, down to my room when the soldiers went to eat. Then I took them ones that looked the same, but wasn't the same, out of a wagon and stacked 'em on the platform just like that first bunch of crates had been stacked. It was the ones from that wagon that the soldiers loaded on the train."

Texas grinned.

And Robespierre asked if he could get a drink of water.

Texas said all right, and Robespierre opened a small cock in the side of the water tower pipe, bent and put his mouth beneath the flow of water, and once again felt Texas' pistol against his neck.

He swallowed – from thirst and fear.

"I got just two more questions, Robespierre," Texas said, and cocked the pistol. "I figure the man who sent the soldiers away, and got you to substitute the crates, came back later and took the crates away from your room under the station. Is that right? I mean, they're not still down there, are they?"

"No, suh. Yes, suh. I mean, no, suh, they ain't still in my room. And yes, suh, they *did* come back a few days later, and I toted them crates out of my room and loaded them in a wagon, and they hauled them away."

"You said *they*. How many men were there?"

Robespierre did not answer.

Texas pressed the barrel of his pistol harder against his neck.

"Answer me, boy," he said.

"Three," Robspeierre's voice was a whisper.

Texas backed-off and let Robespierre straighten up.

"There were three men?"

"Yes, suh. There was three," Robespierre answered.

"Who were they?"

Robespierre shoulders slumped, as though he had known all along they would get to this question. And there was no answer which would not condemn him.

"I can't rightly tell you that, Mr. Brown."

"Oh, yes you can, Robespierre. I went to all the trouble to get you out of that stockade, because I want the names of those men – and you *are* going to tell me."

Robespierre began to tremble.

"I cain't tell you," he said. "If'en I do, they'll kill me for sure."

Robespierre fell to his knees.

"Please, Mister Brown, don't make me tell you."

Texas decided it was time for his own threat.

"Robespierre," he said, "have you ever heard of the Ku Klux Klan?"

The question did not seem to surprise Robespierre.

"Yes, suh," he said. "I've heared of them." "Then you know what the Klan does to some niggers –?"

"Yes, suh. I knows."

"Well here is something you *don't* know, Robespierre – " Texas paused. "I am the leader of the Ku Klux Klan in these parts," he said. "I am what they call the Grand Dragon."

"Yes, suh, I knows that, too," Robespierre said.

And he knew he could die for saying that – but he reckoned that he was already a dead man.

So he lowered his head and said, "Go ahead and do what you gonna do, Mister Brown, but please do it quick."

"I'm not going to shoot you, Robespierre. One shot would bring the whole damned Union Army garrison down here to investigate. And I'm not interested in spending all day tomorrow answering questions about why I shot a nigger."

Robespierre sighed relief.

"Besides," Texas said, "the way things are around here now, the damn Army might even hang me for it," he grinned at Robespierre.

Robespierre did not smile.

"The fact that you already know I'm the leader of the Klan may be all for the good," Texas said. "At least you know that whatever I tell the Klan to do they'll do. So if I tell them to come for you and cut your balls off and make you eat them, that's what they'll do."

Robespierre nodded.

"So here's the way I see it, Robespierre – if you want to save your worthless black skin, you had better to tell me the names of the three men who stole those crates."

"I done already told you, Mr. Brown, I cain't tell you that. Them men will kill me if I do."

"Robespierre, I reckon those men figure you're too dumb to know what was going on. If they thought you knew what was in those crates, they would have killed you that night."

Robespierre was quiet for a moment.

"I ain't thought about it like that before, Mister Brown," he said. But I reckon as how you just might be right.".

"I know I'm right, Robespierre," Texas smiled. "You and me both know that the biggest mistake lots of white folks make is thinking all niggers are dumb as mule shit," he snorted a laugh. "And while that's mostly true, every once in a while, one of you black bastards turns out to have more than ape brains – and it's them smart ones I watch out for – and kill before they can turn on me," Texas uncocked and holstered his pistol.

"So you can just take my word for it, Robespierre – you've got nothing to fear from the men who stole those crates. Nothing at all."

Texas leaned over. His whisper was a loud hiss.

"But you *do* need to be afraid of what the Klan and I will do to you if you don't tell me who those three men were."

There was a minue of cold silence between the two men.

Then Robespierre spoke, barely audibly.

"One was that colonel what had come home a while before The War was over – " Robespierre said. "He was the one that got me to move them crates. And he – "

Texas lit a cigar and listened.

When Robespierre finished reciting all the details of the theft, he looked up at Texas.

"Please promise you won't let them Klan-men do nothing to me, Mr. Brown," he said.

"Robespierre, as long as I'm Grand Dragon of the Klan, you're safe – so get the hell off your knees."

Robespierre stood up.

"I did you a favor and got you out of the stockade," Texas said and dropped his cigar stub into the dirt and stepped on it..

"And now you've told me what I need to know, Robespierre, so you and I are even," Texas smiled broadly. "Take your basket of food and go –"

***

***

The sun was just above the horizon when Robespierre McGukin crawled under the depot and pulled the foundation stones back into place.

A few minutes later, Texas Brown walked across the Square, toward the Benson House.

His smile had become a grin.

And he said, half-aloud –

"You're a free man, Robespierre McGukin – and I'm goddamn close to being a very rich one."

-8-

Manse and Larry finished loading the meat from the smokehouse while Tom hitched the mule to the wagon.

"You got the list of supplies?" Tom asked.

"Right here, Tom," Larry tapped his pocket. "Your list. And the one Manse gave me. And Bonnie's." Larry climbed up on the wagon. "I sure will be glad to get to town," he said. "I been up in them mountains so long, I've nearly forgot how to talk – and do some other things," he grinned at his brother.

"You stay away from that fancy new Anderson whorehouse, you hear me?" Manse returned the smile. "You just might not ever come home."

"From what I hear, that place is mainly for scalawags and yankees," Larry picked up the reins. "And I damn sure wouldn't go near any woman *they* had touched," he spoke above the squeaky wheel as the wagon moved down the drive. "So don't worry. I'll be home before supper."

Manse and Tom stood by the smokehouse and watched until the wagon was on the road.

"You gave him a pistol, didn't you?" Tom asked.

"Gave him one of the Henry's," Manse said.

"That's even better," Tom nodded and smiled but his expression was serious. "Things seem to be getting worse every day," he said, "what with bushwhackers and renegades and all."

They turned and walked to the barn. When they went in, Manse suddenly raised his hand. They stopped, but neither man spoke.

Manse picked up a pitchfork, walked to a stall filled with hay, and prodded the outline of a man's leg.

"Come out from under there or I'll run you through."

A large section of hay moved, and Robespierre McGukin stood.

"What the hell are you doing under there?" Manse's voice was stern.

"Sleeping, Mister Manse. Just sleeping. I don't mean no harm. I just ain't got nowheres to go where I can be safe."

"I thought you had a good place to live underneath the train station," Tom said.

"Seems like all of a sudden too many people knows about that, Mister Tom, so I cain't stay there no more. But then I recollected how I used to see Matthew and Janie out at your daddy's farm, so I went there, but there ain't nobody living there now. So I come here to ask Mister Manse if maybe I could stay here."

"You haven't gotten yourself in more trouble, have you, Robespierre?" Manse asked.

Robespierre opened his mouth to answer, then closed it, and shook his head.

"Speak up," Manse asked.

"No, suh, I'm not in no trouble like I was when they put me in that stockade-jail. But I'm powerful scared," Robespierre's voice shook. "Scared of them soldiers. And them Ku-Klanners," he looked from Manse to Tom. "Cain't I, please, stay here and work for my keep. I works real good. Real hard. You knows that."

Manse looked at Tom.

"We could sure use an extra hand," Tom said.

Manse turned back to Robespierre.

"You go on up to the house and ask Mrs. Largent to give you some breakfast," he said.

"Thank you, suh," Robespierre's fearful expression turned into a wide grin, and he left the barn.

"He can fix up that old cabin back of the smokehouse, and live there – " Tom said, then interrupted himself. "Didn't you tell me that last time Texas was here, he asked a lot of questions about Robespierre?"

"Yeah, he did," Manse said.

"You don't reckon Texas set the Klan onto him, do you?"

"I doubt that," Manse said. "I made it real clear that nothing bad better ever happen to Robespierre."

***

Texas Brown didn't like to be seen talking to Martin McCollum too often, or for too long a time. Doing so might arouse suspicion among Anderson scalawags, carpetbaggers, and certain military personnel.

Martin agreed.

So today they exchanged words quickly in the alley behind McClure's General Store.

"I got the information we need," Texas said. "I'll come to your room later on and we – "

"Texas – " Larry Jolly shouted as he came out the back door of McClure's Store.

Then he saw Martin, and his voice cooled.

"Afternoon, Lieutenant," he said.

"Afternoon, Mister Jolly."

"So they finally let you come into town," Texas laughed.

"If you gentlemen will excuse me," Martin said, "I have to get back to my office." He turned and walked away.

"Just as well," Texas said when Martin was out of ear shot. "We don't want to drink with no bluebelly, and we've got some drinking to do. Come on. I'm buying."

Texas started them walking towards the Benson House.

"I was hoping I'd run into you," Larry said. "I only got time for one drink. I've already bought the farm supplies. But I still need to pick up a few things for Bonnie and Mama before I head home. "

"Just one drink. I promise," Texas laughed as they entered the bar. "Two sour-mash," he ordered.

They took their drinks to a table.

"How's Tom? I missed you and him both the last time I was out to your place."

" He's holding up pretty good, considering he's gonna be a daddy," Larry laughed and drank. "Manse told me you came out a while back, but said you didn't stay long. Said you been real busy."

"Yeah, it's hunting-season, you-know?" Texas lowered his voice. "I keep hoping you might find the time to do a little *hunting* with me sometime soon."

"I'm aiming to do just that, Texas, just soon as I can," Larry said. "I been talking to Manse and Tom about Johnny spelling me sometimes. They agree with me he's getting big enough to stay up in the mountains by himself. Now all we got to do is convince Bonnie. Soon as we do that, I'll be able to join you."

"I'm looking forward to that day, Larry. I truly am. We need men like you," Texas said, and lifted his glass and drained it.

***

They sat at the table by the window in Martin's room, and Texas told Martin *almost* everything that he had found out about the gold.

"So all the time that General Stoneman's men were searching high and low, the gold was hid under the train depot, and they was walking around right on top of it," Texas laughed.

"And you know who stole it? And where it is now?"

"I only got ideas about where it's hid, but I know for damn sure who stole it. Three of 'em. Two Colonels – Orr and Brown. Big heroes in The War. Both come back home to Anderson a while before Appomattox – one wounded, the other with swamp fever caught during the Low-State Campaign. They were in on it with a judge named Fant. I figure the last thing they ever want is for folks around here to find out they stole gold from The Confederacy. They would probably be lynched before the Army could arrest them," Texas smiled again. "The way I figure it, them three men being such big heroes is just going to make it that much easier for *you* to carry out *my* plan."

"And just precisely what is *your* plan?"

"It's real simple, Martin. You go visit Judge Fant and show him your Military Intelligence identification and tell him that you need to see him and Orr and Brown together – that you need their help with a high-secret investigation you're conducting. But you don't say any more than that to him."

"But what if – ?"

"Goddammit, Martin, don't start to *what-if* me. Just do what I say – and say what I tell you to say – and I promise you that them three fine southern gentlemen will do anything you tell them to do."

***

***

At dusk Larry Jolly was halfway home. Shadows of pines latticed Lebanon Road. He cursed the mule's slowness, then cursed himself for staying so long at the Benson House bar. But Texas Brown was such a hell of a nice fellow, and Larry had been having such a good time it had been hard to leave even when he finally did.

Besides, he hadn't figured it would take almost an hour to get the things on Bonnie's list. Why was it that the things women put on lists were never in one place, like farm supplies were. He had gone to three different stores, just to find the items. Then he had had to wait at every store while ladies who were ahead of him made up their minds about the colors of buttons, or high-top-laces, or yarns.

Now it would be after dark when he got home – which didn't bother him – but he knew it would upset his mama. She always fretted when anybody was late for supper.

Larry thought about his conversation with Texas.

They had talked a lot about The War – something Manse and Tom never did. And Larry had been surprised when Texas said that there were things about the military that he missed – and Larry realized that he missed them, too. Things like the closeness of comrades – and the excitement of combat – and the chance to test courage.

He knew that Tom and Manse had seen a lot more action than he had, and he wondered how the hell they had been able to settle back so easily into the boredom and routine of farming after what they had been through.

Life without comrades and action and purpose wasn't to Larry's liking. That was why he felt drawn to Texas Brown and the Klan. They offered all three.

Larry laid the rifle across his lap and lit one of Texas' cigars.

He had decided that he needed to talk to Manse and Tom as soon as he got home. Somehow he had to make them understand that Larry Jolly wasn't still the baby-brother of the Jolly boys. He had come to manhood on battle fields, just as they had, and his opinions and feelings about The War and the Klan were just as valid as theirs.

If he wanted to ride with Texas Brown, then that was his right – and he would do it, whether they liked it or not.

Soon he would start alternating weeks in the mountains with Johnny, and that would give him the chance –

Then it happened – quickly –

Two men stepped out of the woods.

One grabbed the mule's halter, the other pointed a pistol at Larry.

The wagon stopped.

Larry dropped the reins, grabbed the rifle and stood.

"Get away from the mule or I'll shoot," he aimed the rifle at the man with the pistol.

Larry did not see the two men who came out of the woods behind him – did not see the one who raised his rifle and fired – but he did feel searing pain when the bullet bored a hole between his shoulder blades.

Larry Jolly pulled the rifle's trigger as he fell from the wagon to the road.

He heard the wheel squeak as the wagon rolled forward, but he didn't have the strength to crawl out of the way.

The front wheel crossed his back, and he screamed.

The rear wheel followed, but he felt no more pain.

He tried to move, but could not.

He could hear their voices echo as if from a distance, though he knew they were near.

"Get the mule."
"Whoa."
"How's Eddy?"
"Deader'n hell."
"Get that rifle."
"I will, soon as I get his boots off."
"Is he dead?"
"Not yet."
"See what's in his pockets."
"Goddamn, look at all this money."
"Come on! Let's get the hell out of here."

Their voices faded, leaving only the quiet of woods, like the quiet of his mountains.

A shadow descended and covered his legs, then flowed slowly up his back.

And though the shadow could be neither seen nor felt, Larry Jolly knew it was there – just as he knew every detail of what was happening to his body.

One of his lungs filled and stopped.

Then the other.

And the shadow drowned him.

***

"Maybe he had trouble with the wagon, or just decided to stay in town," Tom said.

"I'm going to find out." Manse finished his breakfast and stood.

Hoof beats sounded on the drive.

Manse, Tom, Bonnie, Rebecca and Maude got to the front porch just as Texas Brown and Martin McCollum dismounted.

"Larry?" Manse asked, and knew the answer even before they spoke.

"Afraid so," Texas nodded. "Patrol found him last night on the Lebanon Road. About halfway here. Shot. And his back broke."

"Oh, Lord God, no," Maude Jolly held onto Bonnie and Rebecca, and sank into her rocking chair.

Manse's throat tightened. Pressure behind his eyes increased and surged with the familiar mixture of fear and rage that sent blood-red streaks flashing as precursors to battle.

"Who did it?" Manse's voice was calm.

"No way of knowing. It was a bushwhacking, plain and sure. His boots were gone. And his rifle. And the mule and wagon and everything in it. And there wasn't no money on him. But Larry put up a fight – there was a dead nigger close by."

"There will be a full investigation, Mr. Jolly. I assure you of that," Martin spoke to Manse but looked at Rebecca whose eyes did not meet his. "Please accept my sincerest condolences – "

"We don't need sympathy from the likes of you," Manse said. "Smartest thing you can do right now, Lieutenant, is get on your horse and ride the hell away from here."

Martin wanted to say something, but decided that silence was prudent. He looked at Rebecca again, and her eyes met his for a moment, then she turned her back on him.

Martin mounted his horse and rode away.

"Larry is at the undertaker parlor in Anderson," Texas said. "You want me to have him brought here?"

Manse did not reply. Instead he sank to his knees beside Maude Jolly's rocking chair – and put his head in his Mama's lap – and felt her thin fingers caress his face, and wipe his tears.

Melinda snuggled close to him. He felt Rebecca's hand touch his cheek.

Manse could not move – could not speak.

Tom answered Texas.

"Take Larry to Lebanon Church," he said. "That's where the family burying plot is."

***

Preacher Zachariah Eskew led the cortege.

Texas and Johnny and Robespierre carried the pine coffin from the church to the grave Robespierre had dug.

Maude leaned on Manse.

Tom walked between Bonnie and Rebecca, and carried Melinda, who hugged her doll.

The casket was set down near a large stone marker bearing the single chiseled word – Jolly.

Preacher Eskew opened the Bible.

"I am the resurrection, the truth and the light," he read. "Whosoever believeth in me shall never die." He paused. "Let not your heart be troubled; I go to prepare a place for you. Fret not because of evil-doers. Love your enemies. Bless them that curse you. Do good unto those that hate you." He closed the Bible.

"I know that it is painfully difficult to turn the other cheek, especially at a time like this," he said. "But the Bible teaches that we are to accept everything as part of His great and divine plan. And we must accept it with abiding faith. In the name of the Father, the Son and the Holy Ghost. Amen."

Tom stood by the coffin, his head bowed, then he looked up.

"Lord, Larry was a good man," Tom said. "And too many of his short years were spent fighting a war that took five of his brothers from us. We don't question Your ways, Lord, but if you will, please try to help us understand your reasons for all this. And if you won't do that, then, Lord, please, give us the peace that passes understanding. Amen."

There was silence except for wind blowing across the hillside.

"If anybody else wants to say some words, go ahead," Tom said.

Texas Brown shifted his weight, looked at their sad faces and tears – felt oppressive silence reassert itself, and decided somebody had to say something else.

When he spoke, his voice was a soft drawl.

"I didn't know Larry the way you all did," he said. "But I reckon I was the last one to see and talk to him. We visited together while he was in Anderson. And I tell you, I never enjoyed a talk with anybody any more than I did the talk we had. He was a mighty fine and mighty smart young fellow. And like his brothers, he was brave – fighting in The War for all the good and Christian and moral things that the honor of the South has always stood for. And he was caring and loving about his family. And, in the end, *honor* and *bravery* and *courage* and *caring* are the onliest important things to a *real man*. And I reckon that, now that he's gone, I'm gonna miss Larry nearabout as much as you all do."

Tom waited through a few moments of silence, then said, *Amen* again.

Manse and Texas slid ropes under the ends of the coffin and lowered it.

Maude Jolly sank to her knees by the open grave. Her lips moved silently in prayer.

When she had finished, Tom and Rebecca helped her stand and walk back to the church. Bonnie, Johnny and Melinda followed.

"Let's go," Texas touched Manse's arm.

"You go ahead," Manse said. "I want to cover him."

"Sure," Texas nodded understanding, and walked away.

Manse took the shovel from Robespierre.

"I want to do this alone," he said. "You ride home with Mister Tom."

Robespierre ran to catch up with Tom – giving Texas Brown wide berth.

Manse took off his church-going coat and shirt, and laid them on the ground.

Then he began to shovel red clay.

Each clod resounded on the wooden coffin like the report of distant cannon, until the box was covered by a layer of earth, and soil fell quietly onto soil.

Sweat and tears mingled and rolled down Manse's face.

When Larry's grave was filled, he put aside the shovel and knelt and smoothed the mound of earth with his hands.

And he thought of that rainy March day, ten years before, when he and his brothers had come here to bury their father. There had been unbeatable family strength then. Now only he remained.

Manse shivered as he stared at the line of family crosses:

Joseph Moorhead Jolly. *Beloved Father And Husband.* 1802-1856.

Margaret Jolly. *Infant Angel* . 1823-1824.

And five crosses, each with the words –

Not The Body – Only The Spirit.

Joseph Lewis Jolly. CSA. 1827-1864.

James Sanford Jolly. CSA. 1832-1863.

John Alexander Jolly. CSA. 1836-1862.

Jesse Alford Jolly. CSA. 1838-1864.

William Enos Jolly. CSA. 1843-1864.

And now there would be another –

Lawrence Freeman Jolly. CSA. 1846-1866.

Manse tried to stand, slipped and fell, and lay unmoving on the mound and sobbed.

"You've forgot us, God," he said. "You turned your back on us. You don't care that my six brothers are dead. You didn't even let Larry die in battle, defending the honor of the good. I don't know why You don't give a damn, God, but I do give a damn."

He lay on the cool ground for a few minutes, wiped his tears with the back of his hand, stood, picked up his shirt and his coat, and walked slowly, alone, the six miles home.

***

***

"Bonnie finally got Melinda to sleep," Tom said, and poured drinks for Manse and Texas. "Everyone is in bed but us. You're welcome to stay the night here, Texas."

"I reckon I'll be safe enough on the road," Texas said.

"If you want me to, I'll ride along with you," Manse's speech was whiskey-slurred. "And I just hope some bushwhackers try something so we can blow them to hell."

He finished his drink, added wood to the fire, and saw his brothers' faces in the flames.

"I appreciate the offer, Manse," Texas smiled. "But I reckon you ought to do yourself a favor and get a good night's sleep. It's been a long day."

"Yeah, guess I could use some sleep at that," Manse yawned and stretched in the fire's warmth. "But I'll be coming into Anderson tomorrow morning to start looking for the bastards that killed Larry."

"And just what are you aiming to do if you find them?" Tom directed his words to Manse, but looked at Texas.

"I'm going to kill them – that's what," Manse said.

"I reckon the Union Army will likely get more than a mite upset if you do that, Manse," Texas said. "They got their own way of investigating killings. By-the-book, they call it. And they don't specially like it when anybody does things different."

"Don't tell me you believe for a minute that them goddamn yankees are really going to try to find out who killed Larry?" Manse's reddened eyes flashed anger. "You know as well as I do that they don't give a shit. To them, Larry is just one more dead rebel."

"All I know for sure, Manse, is that if you go around asking questions about what happened to Larry – the Army is gonna start watching *you*. And if you find Larry's killers – and you kill them – the bluebellies will be pleased to hang you for your trouble. They call it due-process-of-the-law."

"To hell with their dewprocess – "

"Wait a minute," Tom interrupted. "Dammit, Manse, listen to what Texas is saying. And remember what you and me already talked about – it won't help our folks, or anybody, if you and me wind up rotting in a yankee prison – or hanging from an Army scaffold." Tom's eyes met Manse's and would not let go.

"Your Mama needs you more than ever now, Manse," Tom said. "You're the only son she's got left. And Bonnie needs me, especially with our baby coming. So no matter how we feel, we can't go out and start killing yankees or renegades or scalawags or carpetbaggers or anybody."

Tom put his arm around Manse's shoulder.

"Please, Manse," he said. "Listen to Texas. He has ways of finding out things without stirring up the Army."

Manse looked at Texas.

"You think you can find out who killed Larry?" he asked.

"Given a little time, I know I can," Texas said.

"And when you find out who did it, then what happens? Do you and the Klan kill 'em? Or can I?"

"Once we're sure who did it," Texas said, "then I think the three of us –you and me and Tom – ought to capture the bastards and take them to the Army with proof that they're the ones – and let the Army hang 'em while we watch."

Manse poured drinks and raised his glass.

"Now that's what I call damn good thinking, Texas," he smiled. "Yes, sir, I like that. We'll let the yankees do our killing for us."

-9-

Martin McCollum handed the envelope to Texas Brown.

"Judge Fant has arranged the meeting for early this evening at Orr's home," he said. "If I don't return by midnight, make sure Captain Phillips gets this. It identifies the conspirators, but it doesn't mention your role in my investigation. You may read it. It's not sealed."

"You'll be back," Texas took the envelope and slipped it into his coat pocket. He would read it later. No sense making Martin think he didn't trust him.

"I'll come by your room later tonight," Texas said. "I'm not sure exactly what time. I've got some information that just might lead to Larry Jolly's killers, but I have to go see for myself if what I've been told is real. If it's just another rumor, I'll be back early. If it turns out to be true, I'll need to go see Tom and Manse. In that case, it could be real late before I'm back. But soon as I can, I'll be here – right anxious to hear how your meeting went."

***

Martin mounted his horse at the cavalry stable, and rode onto Main Street. Two passers-by nodded to him, and he felt the hatred behind their manners. He touched the brim of his hat, to return their politeness – and their sentiments. Along with their dislike of all yankees, he knew they joked specifically about the dumb-ass Intelligence Officer who was looking for lost Confederate gold.

But more importantly, Martin knew they feared him. He had been in Anderson more than a year, during which he had questioned citizens from all social strata, and his investigation had provided him with more private information about Andersonians than any man had a right to know – especially a yankee.

In addition to hearing family secrets, real and rumored, Martin had determined what actually happened in Anderson during the final days of The War.

In the spring of 1865, just before Lee surrendered, renegade Union Army deserters rode into Anderson and terrorized the town for one day. In the Confederate Trust Bank they found no gold, but looted anything else they could find. Several citizens were tortured to find out where they kept their valuables, and one lawyer was killed. A store of liquor was found in Gerald McClure's cellar –but plans for a drunken orgy were abruptly halted by word that Stoneman's Brigade was headed to Anderson. The deserters knew the General would hang them on the spot. They scattered as Union cavalry entered the town.

Stoneman ordered a systematic search of Anderson, without looting or torture, but no gold was found. When his brigade rode out, he left a contingent of men to occupy the town, and Union forces had been here ever since.

In the minds of most Andersonians, however, Stoneman's Brigade of US Army Cavalry – and the renegade Union army deserters – were one and the same.

The War may have ended, but its wounds would never heal.

Martin rode east from The Courthouse Square, along shady streets to the edge of town, and turned onto the carriage drive of an ante-bellum home that reflected the splendor of the Old South.

Few families had come through The War with sufficient wealth to maintain such mansions.

Martin dismounted, hitched his horse, walked up the steps and across the verandah. A liveried black man opened the door.

"Can I help you, sir?"

"Yes. I am Lieutenant McCollum," Martin nodded politely to the servant. "Governor Orr, Judge Fant, and Colonel Brown are expecting me."

The door opened wider and Martin entered a circular foyer with a winding staircase at the far end, and double doors on the right and left.

"This way, sir."

Martin followed the man through the doorway on the right, into a library.

Behind an ornately inlaid mahogany desk sat Governor Orr, almost bald, his face puffy and flushed from excess of both rich food and good liquor.

Beside the desk stood Judge Fant, through whom Martin had arranged the meeting. He was lean, darkly handsome, and looked much younger than his years.

Colonel Brown, tall and thin, with penetrating gray eyes, was at the fireplace, his elbow resting on the mantle.

"We are all here, Lieutenant," Governor Orr said without rising. "And, to get straight to the point, we are most interested to learn why you have requested this meeting."

Martin did not approach the three men, nor offer to shake hands. He waited till the servant slid closed the doors behind him, then he spoke.

"I am First Lieutenant Martin McCollum, United States Army Intelligence," he said.

Colonel Orr waved his hand as though brushing away time-wasting words.

"We are well aware of who you are," he said.

"Then I presume you are also aware that I have been assigned to investigate the disappearance of a considerable amount of gold from the Anderson Confederate Trust Bank," Martin said.

Colonel Brown looked down at him.

"Are you making any progress?" he asked.

"A modicum, I think," Martin allowed his smile to break. "For example, I have managed to learn when the gold was stolen – how the gold was stolen – and who stole it."

Martin sensed their fear. It chilled the room.

"That is quite interesting, Lieutenant," Governor Orr said. "But what has that to do with us?"

"It has everything to do with you, gentlemen – because I have incontrovertible evidence it was you who stole the gold."

Fear turned to heated anger.

"Just who the hell do you think you are, Lieutenant?" Judge Fant glared at him. "How dare you so brazenly walk in here and accuse three of the leading citizens of this community of larceny. Your accusation is insulting!"

Martin smiled and said nothing. Causing three men of wealth and power to squirm was not an opportunity he often had.

Colonel Brown's eyes were the color of steel.

"I find myself admiring both your imagination and boldness, Lieutenant – concocting such a charge as this – then bringing it here to use as an instrument of extortion. I assume that extortion is your intention – is it not?"

"I prefer to think of this meeting as the formation of partnership, Colonel," Martin said. "I am certain that the three of you have already divided the gold. What I propose is a redistribution of shares, to include one more partner – me."

"The man has balls," Colonel Brown said.

"More balls than brains," added Judge Fant.

"You really expect us to take you seriously, Lieutenant?" Governor Orr broke a laugh.

"I suggest you take me damned seriously," Martin said. "I know how you substituted crates of rocks for the crates carrying gold from the Confederate Trust Bank, and I know that the gold was hidden for a while in a room beneath the depot – the room of a freedman named Robespierre McGukin – until you later had it moved."

"I told you that nigger was smarter than you gave him credit for," Colonel Brown said.

"Shut up, before you say too much," Judge Fant snapped at Brown, then cleared his throat and turned to Martin.

"Let us say, for the sake of argument, Lieutenant, that the theory you are advancing here may perhaps be partially-correct," the judge said. "Let us hypothesize that we did, in fact, find a way to salvage a shipment of gold which was being sent to underwrite a doomed venture –"

"Oh for the love of Christ, Fant," Governor Orr interrupted. "Get to the damn point."

"All right. All right," Judge Fant glared at the governor. "My point is simply this, Lieutenant: It is quite one thing for you to allege that we stole the gold – but it is quite another to prove it."

"Spoken like a true lawyer," Martin said. "But in this instance, Judge Fant, I don't have to prove anything. Under Military Law, all I have to do is file charges against you, and on my authority as an Intelligence Officer, the Commander of Union Forces in Anderson

District – Captain Ralph Phillips – will arrest the three of you. And eventually he will find the gold, wherever you have hidden it. And when he does, the US Army of Occupation will confiscate not only the gold, but everything that you gentlemen own."

"And what will happen to you, Lieutenant, when we tell your superiors that you offered to exchange your silence for a share?"

" I will deny it, and they will believe me – not you," Martin said.

"Not believe us," Governor Orr stood. "Young man, the word of three honorable men is – "

"Honorable? Don't talk to me about honor, Governor Orr. You have none," Martin raised his voice. "You are a trio of vultures – richer today than you were before The War because you stripped the carcass of the Confederacy as it lay dying. There may be some semblance of honor among thieves, but there is none among raptors."

"Now see here – "

"No, you see here," Martin shouted. "When I have you arrested – and your fine southern friends and neighbors find out what you have done – it will take the entire Union Army to prevent them from lynching you Honorable-Gentlemen as traitors to the Confederate cause."

Colonel Brown reached behind a vase on the mantle, picked up a pistol, and studied it a moment.

"You weren't foolish enough to come here alone, were you, Lieutenant?" he asked.

"I came alone, but not unprotected, Colonel," Martin replied. "I have arranged for a full report of my investigation to be delivered to Captain Ralph Phillips if I do not return to my office by nine o'clock this evening."

Colonel Brown returned the pistol to the mantle.

It seemed to Martin that each of the men was waiting for one of the others to solve their problem with the right words.

But all three remained silent.

Until, finally, Colonel Brown stepped away from the fireplace.

"Gentlemen," he said, "I suggest we cease this futile parrying and discuss business."

He sat in a leather chair, motioning Martin to sit in the chair opposite him.

"As an attorney," Judge Fant said, "perhaps I should remind you of something, Lieutenant McCollum: By demanding a share of our spoils, you implicate yourself in our conspiracy, and, to use your choice of words, you likewise become a traitor – in your case, a traitor to the United States of America."

"I readily admit that my actions here today constitute betrayal of my uniform and my country, Judge Fant," Martin met the Judge's eyes.

"A candid man. I like that," Colonel Brown said, and smiled. "Very well then, if traitors we are, then let us deal like four traitors. Or, traders, if you prefer."

He looked at his friends.

"I think we should offer the lieutenant ten percent," he said.

"I'm not interested." Martin shook his head.

"What did you have in mind?"

"Forty percent."

"Since you have elected to become our partner, Lieutenant, you should expect no more than your fair share," Governor Orr said. "Including you, there are four of us, therefore you may rightfully claim no more than twenty-five percent."

"And if I refuse?"

"You won't refuse," Colonel Brown said.

Martin half-smiled.

"You're right, I won't refuse," he said. "I accept your offer."

"We are in accord, then," Judge Fant said. "There are sixteen boxes, Lieutenant. All safely hidden. Each is heavy but not large. Such is the nature of gold."

"There were twenty boxes – not sixteen." Martin's tone was suddenly not friendly.

"True, there *were* twenty," Judge Fant said, "but one contained jewelry donated to the Confederate cause by the women of South Carolina. The items in that crate could be readily identified, therefore we decided to bury it. We cannot afford to take chances."

"And the other three?"

"We each took one for our personal use – to underwrite the rebuilding of our lives following The War," Judge Fant said. "What is spent, is spent, Lieutenant. You may have one-fourth of what remains. That is our offer. I hope you find it, and our logic, acceptable."

Victory assured, Martin said, "I accept both."

"Well, then," Colonel Brown said. "Perhaps you can give us an idea of when you want to take delivery of your share."

Martin hesitated, then decided to disclose a portion of truth.

"Quite frankly, Gentlemen," he said, "I have a few months to serve before I can resign my commission. And since I am assured by you that my share is safe, I will not ask for delivery until I resign and prepare to leave the South."

Martin stood and put on his hat.

"If my plans change, I will notify you," he said. "And I will expect to hear from you if you encounter any problems. Otherwise, I suggest we not contact each other."

"Before you leave, I do have one question, Lieutenant," Judge Fant said. "I am curious. How did you find out? We were, we thought, very careful."

Martin was prepared for the question.

His fabricated answer flowed smoothly.

"It was your Southron attitude that led me to you," he said. "There were quite a few freedmen who knew what you had done – but you discounted them as unimportant simply because of their color."

Martin enjoyed being the center of their uneasy attention – and the continued cause of their uneasiness.

"I made it a point to question every Freedman who had been a slave in the home of a Southron," Martin said. "House-niggers, I think you call them. And I offered them money for information about their former *masters*. Those who were too loyal to sell me information, I intimidated. With the knowledge they provided, I compiled dossiers on every Southron in the district. And during my investigation, I heard about Robespierre McGukin and his room beneath the train depot – and I began to develop a theory of how the theft was accomplished."

"And Robespierre confirmed your theory?"

"No – I wish it had been that simple, Judge, but it wasn't," Martin continued the lie.

"I questioned Robespierre, among others," he said, "but he was much too frightened to tell me anything of value. So, in the end, I was forced to rely on my training and logic. And logic dictated that only someone trusted and respected could have learned the time of the planned shipment – the kind of crates and their markings – and all the myriad details necessary to execute the theft."

Martin paused and smiled.

"It wasn't difficult then to narrow the dossiers of Southrons down to you three gentlemen. You were heroes of the Confederacy – above reproach – and you were in Anderson prior to the end of The War. You had the opportunity and the means, therefore you became my obvious suspects."

"And what happens if another Intelligence Officer reads the file of your investigation and uses the same logic to reach the same conclusion?" Orr voiced their concern.

"Don't fret, Gentlemen," Martin said. "In return for a partner's share in this venture, I feel an obligation to protect all four of us."

His smile broadened.

"In order to insure that no one follows my path to you," he said, "I will send a report to Military Intelligence in Washington, stating that I have conclusive evidence that three months before The War ended, all gold from the Confederate Trust Bank in Anderson was secretly transported to Charleston, and from Charleston, by blockade runners, to a rendezvous with a contingent of Confederate forces at Brownsville, Texas, and from there to Vera Cruz, Mexico – all on direct orders of President Jefferson Davis who, as you well know, is currently imprisoned in Georgia."

Martin paused to savor their reactions to his story.

"I understand that your President Davis and his Cabinet Members are proving very uncooperative in providing information to the US Army, so it is unlikely that he will confirm or deny the information that I furnish my superiors in Washington. And based on my report, I will recommend that the investigation be closed. My resignation from the service will also be attached to it. And I am confident that Military Intelligence in Washington will accept my report and my recommendation – and my resignation – with equal measures of pleasure."

Though Martin knew that the three men couldn't possibly comprehend the significance of everything he said, their nods and smiles told him that they had accepted his words.

This meeting had definitely been a success.

Martin tipped the brim of his hat, turned and walked from the library.

***

"Evening Manse," Texas said, then he dismounted, tied reins to the hitching post, and removed his long-coat.

"Evening, Texas," Manse waited on the porch.

"Where's Tom?"

"In the mountains," Manse said. "It's real hard taking care of things up there – and here on the farm, too – with Larry gone –"

Something in Texas' manner stopped Manse in mid-sentence.

"You've found Larry's killers – " he said.

"I sure as hell have," Texas walked up on the porch.

"Well go on, tell me. Who are they? Where can we find them?"

"Hold your horses, Manse," Texas raised his voice. "Settle down and I'll tell you everything – " he handed Manse a cigar.

They lit.

"I got hold of a copy of the Army report," Texas said, "and found out that the nigger Larry killed was named Emry. So I got Whit and Elk to find out everything they could about him. And the two of them found out from Klan-members Emry lived with a Low Downer name of Red Tompins out near Neals Creek. The two of 'em – a nigger and a white man – lived in the same house together. Can you believe that? Story is they even shared women. Anyhow, Whit and Elk are pretty sure that this nigger Emry, who Larry killed, and this Red Tompins, and a couple of renegade bluebellies, are the ones that killed Larry. Story going around is that they've been doing a lot of bushwhacking hold-ups at night on roads in Anderson District – and what they rob from people, they sell to that smart-ass nigger, Sed Jacobs, who has a place out on Green Pond Road."

"You sure they're the ones, Texas?"

"When I first heard it, I wasn't real sure – but I am now," Texas relit his cigar. "Whit and Elk told me that Red Tompins and his two yankee soldier buddies always go out to Sed Jacobs' place on Fridays and drink and eat supper and play cards. Then about midnight they go to that fancy new whorehouse south of town. They say that lately Red and them soldier-boys have had plenty of money for whores and gambling. So – late this afternoon, I rode out to Sed Jacobs and snuck through the woods to less than a hundred yards from his house – and sure enough, Manse, I saw your wagon and mule there. And if that weren't enough, while I was watching, Red Tompins and Sed Jacobs and two soldiers come outside to take a piss, and I got a good look at Red – and damned if he wasn't wearing them boots that Larry bought for Tom's wedding."

"That's all I needed to hear," Manse said. "Let's go get the sons-of-bitches."

Manse stood.

"Whoa there," Texas said. "Remember what we decided – that we wouldn't do anything crazy. We need to take our time and do this thing right. Tomorrow evening I'll get Whit and Elk, and we'll meet you and Tom, and we'll capture them damned bushwhackers when they least expect it – when they're on their way from their card game to the whore house. Then we'll take them – and the boots and the mule and wagon – to the Army. That'll be more than enough proof so that the Army won't have any choice but to hang 'em."

"I don't want to wait," Manse said. "Let's you and me go do it right now."

"I can't go with you tonight, Manse. I got a real important meeting with somebody. Besides, it's too late to get Whit and Elk, and we might need them. Let's wait and do it like we promised Tom."

Manse nodded reluctantly. "All right then," he said. "But we're damn sure going to do it tomorrow night."

***

***

Manse ate little and said less at dinner. When the family was in bed and the house was quiet, he went to the pantry and took out a jug of Drubber Pickens' corn whiskey, and sat in the rocker on the porch, and drank and rocked. And the more he rocked, and the more he drank, the more he wished he had insisted that Texas go with him to get Larry's killers *tonight*.

During The War, he had learned the hard way that once you scout a situation and know the enemy's location and strength, you should immediately devise a plan, and take action. Things can change fast. A chance missed might not come again.

The three men who killed Larry were at Sed Jacobs *now*. They would be riding together to the whore house about midnight. Three men on a desolate road were easy to capture – especially if the last thing they expected was to be stopped, disarmed, tied up, turned over to the army, and charged with murder.

That was something else he had learned in The War – that the element of surprise is more valuable than a whole squad of men.

He could do it alone.

He would do it alone.

Manse took a long drink, cobbed the jug, and tiptoed upstairs. Everyone was asleep. He shook Johnny and whispered that he was going into town and would be back by dawn, then he went to the smoke-house, got his pistols, and went to the barn and saddled his horse.

The sound of hoofbeats awakened Johnny. He turned over in bed and mumbled, "I'm coming with you, Uncle Manse," then he went back to sleep.

***

Manse moved as near to Sed Jacobs' house as he dared.

A full moon lit the night. Three horses were at the hitching rail. The wagon was nearby.

Voices came from inside the house.

There was no reason to risk closer inspection.

Manse returned to the woods. Watched and waited.

Two hours passed, then a young black man and woman came outside. They carried lanterns, and lighted the way for two soldiers and a civilian who followed them out. The group exchanged goodnights.

Manse hurried back to his horse, mounted and galloped a quarter of a mile down the road until he reached a spot that his experience told him was right.

He tied his horse in the woods, then moved to the ditch beside the road, and waited.

He heard them before he saw them. They were riding slowly and talking loudly, and paying no attention to the dark shadows.

Manse drew his revolvers and held his breath. Horses and men came closer.

Manse stood.

"Stop right there," he stepped into the road.

"What the hell is this?"

"Just don't move," Manse said. "I got two guns on you."

"If you planning on robbing us," one of the soldiers laughed, "you're too late. We just been plucked clean in a card game."

"Shut up and get off your horses, one at a time," Manse said. "You first – "

The civilian dismounted. Then one of the soldiers.

"Now you," Manse ordered the other soldier.

"Get him!" the civilian shouted.

Both soldiers and the civilian drew pistols and fired.

Manse dived into the underbrush. Bullets whined and ricocheted.

The mounted soldier wheeled his horse around. Manse fired at the silhouetted target. The rider dropped from the saddle.

The other soldier and the civilian threw themselves into the ditch on the other side of the road.

Firing ceased.

Manse lay on his stomach, searching shadows for movement.

His head throbbed.

His guts tightened.

His throat dried and constricted.

He was in battle again. Listening. Waiting. Senses heightened.

Suddenly, from across the road, volleys of rapid-fire chipped tree limbs above his head.

Manse knew the tactic. He looked to his left, then his right, and, as expected, saw the soldier crossing the road to out-flank him.

Manse aimed and fired and his target fell.

The road was silent.

Then Manse shouted, "ten seconds, is all you've got. Stand up and raise your hands or I'm coming after you."

Now the throbbing pounded in his eyes.

"One. Two –"

"Don't shoot, I'm coming out." The civilian rose from the ditch, walked to the middle of the road, dropped his pistol, and raised his hands above his head.

Manse stood and walked to the man.

"You robbed a young man driving a wagon on Lebanon Road a few weeks ago – "

"Who says?" the man replied.

Manse stepped closer and aimed at the man's head.

"Your name is Red Tompins – " he said.

The man hesitated. Manse shoved the pistols close to his face.

"All right – all right – " the man said. "Yeah, I'm Red Tompins. So what?"

"It was you that robbed and killed my brother on Lebanon Road," Manse said.

"We weren't aiming to kill nobody, Mister," Red Tompins said. "The fellow that was driving that wagon pulled a Henry on us and shot my friend Emry dead. When he done that, we didn't have no choice but to defend ourselves."

Manse glanced down, and in the moonlight he saw the boots Red Tompins was wearing.

In an effort to control his rage, Manse bit his lip so hard it bled –

Then he pointed his pistols at the man's stomach – and his index fingers squeezed – and the pistols fired –

And two holes opened in the man's gut – one just above his belt buckle – and one just below.

Red Tompins' eyes bulged. He grabbed his abdomen and dropped to the ground, doubled up, moaned and sobbed.

"Goddamn you," he said. "You've done gone and killed me."

Manse holstered his pistols, and spoke through clenched teeth.

"When you get to hell," he said, "tell them friends of yours that Manse Jolly killed you for murdering his brother."

Manse stared at the dying man.

Then he heard hoof-beats galloping toward him.

Manse ran into the woods and mounted.

And hesitated – unsure which way to go.

He had struggled for a year to live peacefully, but now he knew that there would be no peace for him.

He nodded solemnly, turned his horse, and rode north – toward the mountains – the cave.

Tom was there.

Together they could decide what Manse should do now.

-10-

Texas Brown had never before ventured into US Army Headquarters. In fact, he had studiously avoided going inside the Anderson Courthouse – even to district offices – except when he visited Samuel Heaton in order to gain access to the rolls of delinquent taxpayers and pending tax auctions – fertile ground for Klan recruitment.

But just before dawn this morning, he had answered a loud knock on his hotel room door, and found a corporal who said that Mister Brown was to proceed immediately to the office of Lieutenant Martin McCollum, Army Intelligence Officer.

Now Texas entered a large room filled with desks at which commissioned and non-commissioned officers shuffled papers with an air of urgency and tension that he could smell and taste.

Texas and Martin had been together most of the night, discussing and toasting Martin's successful meeting with the two colonels and the judge, so Texas was more than a little concerned that Martin would send for him this morning – officially and openly.

Texas walked to Martin's desk.

"What's so goddamned important it couldn't wait until a decent time of day?" he asked in a voice kept low, calm, and controlled.

"I thought you should be informed right away –" Martin said – "since you are so close to the Jolly family – that Manse Jolly killed two soldiers and a civilian last night."

"You sure?" Texas strained to control nerves.

"I'm positive," Martin said.

Texas sat down in the chair beside Martin's desk and said, in an even lower voice, "I got just two questions: What makes you so sure it was Manse?" He glared at Martin. "And just why the hell did you bring me here to tell me this in a room full of soldier-boys?"

"I'll answer your first question first," Martin said. "According to the report, last night a Freedman named Sed Jacobs played cards at his house with two soldiers and a civilian named Red Tompins.

According to Jacobs, the three men left his house just before midnight. A few minutes later, Jacobs heard shots. When he went to investigate, he found the two soldiers dead, and Tompins shot in the stomach but still alive. Jacobs brought him into town, where he lived long enough to tell the Duty Officer that they had been waylaid by a man who identified himself as Manse Jolly – and said that he was killing them to avenge the murder of his brother."

Texas shook his head in disbelief.

Then he nodded belief.

"I sent for you," Martin said, "because Captain Phillips has ordered that all known associates of Jolly be brought in for questioning – including you."

Martin bit his lip and looked around.

"I told the captain that I wanted to question you personally because you are one of my confidential-sources-of-information – a man I would vouch for, and a man Samuel Heaton would likewise vouch for. And, because of your importance to me in my intelligence work, I didn't want you questioned by anyone other than me."

"That was mighty nice of you, Lieutenant," Texas smiled.

Martin returned the smile.

"The less the Army knows about you, the better for us both," he said.

They were interrupted.

"Lieutenant McCollum!" Captain Ralph Phillips shouted as he came from his office.

"Yes, sir," Martin stood and faced his superior.

"I want you to take command of the squad I am sending to the farm of this man Jolly – in case he is stupid enough to return home."

"But, sir, I am not a line officer," Martin protested. "My assignment here is – "

"I don't give a good piss in a thunderstorm what your assignment is, Lieutenant. This garrison is badly under-manned. I am placing Sergeant Jerlier's squad under your command. You will remain on duty at the Jolly home indefinitely. And in addition to this assignment, Sergeant Jerlier will continue his requisition schedule – and you, your regular intelligence-work – whatever the hell that is," Captain Phillips looked from Martin to Texas.

"But, sir, " Martin said. "That constitutes double-duty which may not be ordered except in war-time – "

"This *is* war-time, Lieutenant McCollum," the captain raised his voice for all to hear.

"And double-duty is precisely what you and Jerlier and every man under my command will pull until such time as I direct otherwise. And any soldier who fails to follow my orders will face charges of insubordination – and a firing squad. Is that clear?" he shouted, and without awaiting a reply, turned and went back into his office.

Texas looked at Martin.

"Appears like you ain't got much choice, Lieutenant," he said. "Mind if I ride with you?"

"I was just about to ask you to accompany me," Martin said, adjusting his sidearm. "I know damn well the Jollys won't welcome the sight of me, but maybe they'll be reasonable to deal with when they see you."

***

At the Jolly farm, Martin gave Sgt. Jerlier instructions for the deployment of troops, then he and Texas walked to the house.

Bonnie, Johnny and Rebecca stood on the porch, despair in their faces.

"Morning," Texas said, and stopped at the foot of the porch steps.

"You riding with bluebelly bastards now, Texas?" Johnny said.

"Just take it slow and easy there, Johnny, " Texas said. "No call for that kind of talk in front of your mama," Texas tipped his hat to Bonnie. "Lieutenant McCollum is here because he was ordered to be here. He's just doing his duty, like a soldier has to do, no matter what army he's in."

"Just what exactly is your duty, Lieutenant? – To hang my brother-in-law?" Bonnie's lips tightened.

"Well I'm sorry to disappoint you," she said, "but he's not here. And neither is my husband. He's gone to Pickens. To see someone about borrowing some more money. And we've already been searched this morning. Twice. So there's not really anything left for you to find."

"I have orders to remain here in case Mr. Jolly returns, Mrs. Largent," Martin said.

"I suppose you'll take over the house and force us to sleep out in the barn," Rebecca glared at him. "Or do you have some other indignities in mind for us, since our men folks aren't here to protect us?"

"Why no, Miss Largent. Nothing of the kind," Martin felt off-balance. Why was it that her eyes always seemed to be saying more than her words. "My men and I will quarter in the barn," he said. "If that is all right – "

"It most certainly is not all right –" Rebecca turned to Texas. "Do we have to put up with these – these yankees?"

"I'm afraid so, Miss Rebecca," Texas struggled to hold his laugh inside. "But Lieutenant McCollum seems a reasonable man. I'm sure he'll intrude on you folks as little as possible – and try to act like a gentleman" Texas said – and thought to himself that Rebecca Largent wasn't just beautiful. Part of her was tough as chap-leather.

Texas would have sworn that Martin McCollum couldn't be embarrassed, much less cowered, by any woman.

But Rebecca Largent had just done both.

"If you'll excuse me, I'll see to my men," Martin said and walked away.

Rebecca's eyes followed him.

Texas' eyes were on her.

Real soon, he thought, he needed to find a way to get her alone, so he could have her on his terms.

Right now, however, there were other things to deal with.

"Have you seen Manse?" Texas asked Bonnie.

She shook her head.

"Then I reckon he must have ridden on up to the mountains, where Tom is."

Bonnie and Rebecca exchanged glances.

Texas smiled.

"Look, ladies," he said, "I know Tom's not in Pickens borrowing money. Him and Manse trust me. They told me all about the cave – everything except exactly where it is."

He looked at them.

"Do either one of you know how to get there?" he asked.

"We don't," Bonnie said, and looked at her son. "But Johnny does."

"How do I get there, Johnny?" Texas asked in a low voice.

"I'll go with you and show you the way."

Texas shook his head.

"You can't do that," he said. "Lieutenant McCollum has orders not to let anybody leave here. Besides, it's up to you to protect your Mama and Rebecca and Melindy when Tom's away."

"All right, I'll draw you a map," Johnny said, and came off the porch, picked up a stick, knelt and drew in the dirt.

"Head north. Ride the main road towards Pickens till you get a mile past Old Rock Fork, then take the trail that leads toward Walhalla Ridge. But leave it at the white rock ledge, and head north-northwest. You'll know you're going right when you cross three creeks and see the two peaks on your right. Then, about half-way between Tamassee and Jocassee – "

"Whoa. Slow down there, boy," Texas said, and took a small notebook and pencil from his pocket, licked the pencil's lead, and said, "Now let's start again. Real slow, so's I can make my notes. I'm not the world's fastest writer-downer."

***

Following Johnny's directions, Texas rode until roads became narrow trails across valleys, over passes, into coves and along ridges.

Finally the trails all but disappeared, and he was forced to dismount in order to lead his horse through woods dense with spring laurel growth.

Eventually, at the edge of a ravine, he looked down and saw Tom's horse.

"Tom! It's Texas!" he shouted, then started down the steep path into the ravine.

"Right behind you, Texas," a voice said, and Texas spun around to face Manse and Tom – both with rifles cocked, but pointed at the ground.

"Damn, you scared the piss out of me," Texas said and smiled, but was careful to keep his hand away from his holster.

"How'd you find us?" Tom asked.

"Johnny," Texas said. "Johnny gave me directions. Damn good directions, too."

"Why'd you come?" Manse asked – his voice slightly slurred.

"I figured you'd want to know what's happening at your place," Texas said. "I never figured you might shoot my ass off for trying to help."

"Just making sure," Manse said.

"A good idea," Texas said. "Now I wonder if you two have got a cup of something warm for a man who's come all the way up here to try to show his friendship."

The three men walked down to the waterfall, and behind it, into the shack just inside the cave's entrance.

Tom poured coffee.

Manse laced it with whiskey.

Texas offered cigars.

They sat, spat. Lit and drank.

Then they spoke of what had happened last night.

"Good thing you rode up here instead of going home, Manse," Texas said. "They got soldiers all over your place."

"They better not be bothering Bonnie – and Mama Jolly – and Rebecca," Tom's tone was part threat, part fear.

"Don't worry," Texas said. "I went by there. Your folks are all right. That Lieutenant McCollum is in charge of the soldiers there, so I don't reckon they'll bother your family."

"How did the Army find out it was Manse?" Tom asked.

"Red Tompins lived long enough to tell them who done it," Texas said, and finished his coffee, put down his cup, then turned to Manse. "I thought that me and you and Tom agreed we were going to capture those three bastards and let the Army hang 'em. That way you wouldn't have got yourself into all this trouble."

Manse shook his head, as though trying to clear it enough to make sense of what had happened.

"I swear to you, Texas," he said, "I was going to wait for you and Tom, so's we could do it together, like we planned, but then I got this feeling that them murdering bastards might run, and we might never find them. So I decided to take 'em by surprise and get their guns and tie 'em up and take 'em to the Army, all by myself. I figured it would be easy. Tom can vouch that I captured three prisoners at a time more than once during The War, right, Tom?"

"Yeah. More than once, for certain," Tom said.

"And I had everything under control," Manse said, "until one of them drew down on me when he was dismounting. Then they all started shooting – and all hell broke loose. That's when I shot the two soldiers."

Manse paused and took a drink.

"The one named Red surrendered to me – and I was figuring to tie him up and take him to the Army in Anderson," Manse said, "but when I saw that he was wearing Larry's boots, something took hold of me and I couldn't stop myself from pulling both triggers."

Manse paused and stared at the fire.

"I'm not really sorry it happened the way it did," Manse said. "To be real honest with you, Texas, the only regret I got is that I couldn't get that son-of-a-bitch Sed Jacobs, too."

"You leave that nigger to me and the Klan, Manse," Texas said. "Right now all you need to think about is not letting the Army catch you. Captain Phillips is damned upset about you killing two of his soldier boys. So for the time being I think the best thing you can do is stay up here in the mountains."

"I reckon the Yankees are mighty suspicious that I'm not at home," Tom said.

"They were at first," Texas said. "Then Bonnie and Rebecca and Miss Maude and Johnny – and even Melindy – all swore you had gone to Pickens, to try to borrow money to pay more taxes –"

Tom smiled.

"That's what they're all supposed to tell anybody who asks for me any time I'm away from the farm," he said.

"I backed them up," Texas said. "Told Lieutenant McCollum that I knew for sure that you was in Pickens, and I was going to ride there to find you and tell you what had happened."

Texas stood.

"So I reckon them soldier boys will be expecting you to come back with me," he said.

"Then I guess we ought to head on home," Tom's look was a question directed at Manse.

"Yeah, you go on with Texas," Manse said. " I'll be just fine."

"There's plenty of food and whiskey here for a week or so," Tom said.

"I'll leave you the cigars I've got with me," Texas said. "And just as soon as things settle down, I'll be back with more of everything."

***

Martin McCollum had ordered two men to stand guard on the walkway between the drive and the porch of the Jolly home, and one to watch the rear of the house, and ordered Sergeant Jerlier's squad set up a mess tent near the barn entrance, quarter their horses in stalls, and themselves in the hayloft.

To Martin, everything seemed in logical order.

When Captain Ralph Phillips arrived in late-afternoon with the headquarters platoon of cavalry from Anderson, he immediately made it clear that he did not agree with Martin's logic.

"This is the most stupid deployment I have ever seen," he said. "I want two-man pickets, and their shelters, spaced at twenty-yard intervals in the woods along the road. Set up the mess tent in those pines across from the pickets. Put your command tent ten yards farther down the road. It can double as quarters for you and Sergeant Jerlier. Readiness will be four-on-four-off at night. Sergeant Jerlier will receive the necessary manpower to make his rounds for requisitions every day. That will mean daylight readiness of eight-on, four-off."

"Every day, sir?" Martin asked.

"Damned right, Lieutenant. Every. Day," Phillips said.

And while Sgt. Jerlier implemented the new deployment, Captain Phillips accompanied Martin to the front porch, and told Johnny Jolly to ask the ladies of the house to come outside so he could speak to them.

As they were coming out onto the porch, Tom and Texas arrived and dismounted.

Bonnie rushed from the house to Tom.

Rebecca and Johnny helped Maude Jolly to her rocking chair. The look in her eyes suggested that her mind and heart were someplace else.

"This is Mister Largent, Captain," Martin said when Tom and Bonnie reached the porch steps. "He was not here when we arrived this morning."

Captain Phillips looked down from the porch.

"Where have you been, Mr. Largent?" he asked.

Tom did not reply.

Instead, he limped up the steps, brushed past Ralph Phillips, and went to where Maude Jolly sat. He leaned down and kissed her cheek, and whispered something to her that caused a fleeting smile to cross her face. Then he straightened up and, for the first time, looked directly at the captain.

"I went to Pickens yesterday on business," he said. "I spent the night there with friends."

Texas Brown walked up on the porch and stood between Tom and the officer.

"I can vouch for that, Captain," he said. "With Lieutenant McCollum's permission, I rode to Pickens this morning to tell Mr. Largent what had happened here, and I found him right where his family said he was."

Captain Phillips cut his eyes from Tom to Texas, then back to Tom. He wasn't sure which of these two men he distrusted more.

The captain stared at Tom.

"When was the last time you saw Manson Jolly, Mr. Largent?" he asked.

"Yesterday. Right before I left here," Tom said.

"Did he tell you what his plans were for last night?"

"Only that he was still looking for his brother's killers," Tom half-smiled at Phillips. "And from what Texas Brown tells me, I reckon he found them."

"Perhaps he found one of them," Captain Phillips said, and did not return Tom's half-smile. "We have reason to believe that the civilian – his name was Tompins – *was* involved in the death of Lawrence Jolly, but there is absolutely no evidence that the two soldiers killed by Manson Jolly had any part in the murder of his brother – or in any other crime."

"If Manse killed them, then you can be sure they were the ones who murdered Larry."

"If you are so sure of that, Mr. Largent," Captain Phillips said, "then perhaps you will help us – and Mister Jolly – by asking him to surrender and tell his story in a court of law."

"At what kind of trial, Captain – civilian or military?"

"Military law prevails in this District," Ralph Phillips said.

"With you as judge – and jury?"

"As senior officer, I would preside, yes."

"Then even if I knew where Manse was, I wouldn't ask him to surrender. You would hang him no matter what."

"He killed two United States Army soldiers," Ralph Phillips raised his voice. "For that, he deserves to hang."

Unconsciously Tom's hand moved to his belt and the pistol he had once carried there.

Texas touched Tom's arm, and looked at the Union officer.

"I'm sure you can understand, Captain Phillips," he said, "that Mr. Largent and his family are kind of upset right now," he looked to Martin for support. "So, if you got no more questions – sir – I think these folks need some supper and some time together."

"It *is* their dinner-time," Martin added rather feebly, and held open the front door, half-blocking the entry so Rebecca would have to walk close to him.

"Close the door, Lieutenant McCollum," Captain Phillips barked the order. "I haven't said yet what I came here to say."

Martin closed the door, and when he looked at her, he caught a hint of laughter in her eyes.

"I regret any inconvenience that the presence of my men may cause," Captain Philips said, "but I intend to do everything possible to capture Manson Jolly. As of today, I have authorized a reward of three hundred dollars for information leading to his arrest. Posters to that effect will be circulated. It seems, however, that my aide, Lieutenant Pearson, has been unable to locate a likeness of Mister Jolly. He informs me that when he was here this morning, you ladies told him that you have neither a photo nor daguerreotype of the man. If that is true, then Manson Jolly was surely the only soldier in the Army – Confederate or Union – who did not send at least one tintype of himself home after he enlisted."

The Captain turned to Martin.

"Have your men search the house again," he ordered. "Every closet. Every cabinet. Every drawer. Until you find a likeness of Jolly."

"Wait – " Maude Jolly's voice came from the rocking chair, and it was weak.

"You all have already done enough damage to my house today," she said, and struggled to stand.

Holding onto Tom's arm, she reached inside the shawl wrapped around her shoulders, and took out an oil-skin pouch, from which she unwrapped a tintype of her only living son. She held it up to the light so she could see it clearly, then drew it to her breast for a brief moment before handing it to Captain Phillips.

***

Manse paced the cave as if it were his cage.

Tension drew his nerves taut, and the ache in his head made decisions hard to come by.

He ate little, smoked and drank instead.

His thoughts were of life before The War – smiling faces of brothers and friends.

He slept only when alcohol numbed him, and then his thoughts dissolved into dreams of the violent frenzy of close-quarter-killing – an orgy of carnage he had not previously allowed himself to remember.

And at the climax of each nightmare's horror, came the orgasmic release of the saber's thrust that he had felt in every battle.

Nights blended into dawns into days into dusks into darkness.

Isolation drove him deeper into himself. Nights and days passed, but time lost all meaning.

He slept on his stomach, his face buried in crossed arms, a pistol in each hand.

***

A week later, he was sitting in darkness, in the deepest recesses of the cave, when he heard Texas call his name.

Manse walked to the entrance and stepped past the waterfall, into sunlight.

Texas led his horse into the ravine. The saddlebags were full, and two supply sacks were tied across its rump.

"This is near about everything I could think of that you might need," Texas handed Manse two sacks and he carried the saddlebags. Once inside the shack, they unpacked food, cigars, and whiskey.

"All you need now," Texas said, "is a willing woman."

Manse did not smile.

They sat near the fire. Manse removed the coffee pot, filled two cups, and added whiskey.

They lit cigars.

Manse stared into the fire, smoked, drank, and said nothing.

Texas tolerated the silence as long as he could.

"You decided what you're going to do yet?" he asked.

"Been giving it thought," Manse said, then fell silent again.

"How about heading out west? To Texas. It's a mighty big state. And no way all the bluebellies in the whole damned US Army could find one man out there – if he didn't want to be found."

"I thought about that," Manse poured another drink. "But I reckon it's just not in me to leave."

"Well, in that case, I guess you could stay up here for as long as you want. This cave is surely well hid," Texas reached inside his coat and took out a rolled piece of paper and handed it to Manse.

"Of course, it won't be exactly like you're free," Texas said. "The Army wants you pretty bad."

Manse unrolled the poster, and held it up:

WANTED FOR MURDER MANSON S. JOLLY REWARD $300

"They got those up all over," Texas said.

Manse studied his likeness above the words.

"I sent that tintype to Mama two months after I enlisted," he said. "I thought maybe she'd want it if I got killed."

"I reckon most of us did the same during The War," Texas said.

"I sure didn't figure Mama would ever see it on a wanted poster," Manse said.

Silence thickened, and the two men drank.

"Texas – " Manse said finally, but fell silent yet again.

"If you got something to say, Manse, then go ahead and spit it out," Texas said.

Manse rubbed his mouth, as though that might help release the words.

"Being up here all alone and all, I been thinking a lot," he said, "and what I've been thinking may likely sound crazy as hell – so, if I tell you, you got to promise you'll try to understand."

"I'll try hard," Texas said, and watched Manse take another swallow of whiskey, and wondered if he drank as much when he was alone as when they were together.

"Texas – " Manse began slowly – "When I found them three that killed Larry, I felt like I used to feel in The War – just before a battle. My head started pounding like it always did when killing and dying were coming close." He paused. "It was like I wanted The

War against the yankees to start all over again." He paused again. "Does what I'm saying make any sense to you?"

"I'm not real sure yet," Texas said, "but you keep talking, and I'll do my best to keep up."

"I reckon what it comes down to is this, Texas. I honest-to-god think that what the yankees are doing to the South right now is worse than what they did during The War. At least in The War they were fighting battles against our army, but now they're just using Union soldiers to back-up killing and raping and robbing folks who've got no way to fight back. And what's worst of all, they're taking away the only thing us Southerners have got left – our honor." Manse drained his cup. "I figure, Texas, it's time somebody started fighting back."

"Sounds to me like you're aiming to be that *somebody*."

"Might as well be me," Manse said, and held up the poster.

"The yankees are looking to kill me – shoot me or hang me –" he said. "But they can only kill me once. So I might as well take as many of them with me as I can."

Manse smiled. Then grinned broadly. Then laughed – and looked at the poster and laughed again.

Then he let out a yell that became a scream and echoed until it filled the cave.

Then silence reasserted itself, heavier and thicker than before.

Texas struggled to dredge words from the emotional mire.

"I got to admit," he finally said, "that I do appreciate what you're saying," Texas took a drink straight from the jug. "And I want you to know that you're welcome to ride with me and the Klan anytime you want to. That's exactly what we're trying to do – restore Southern honor. Protect Southern women. Make the South what it use to be. And me and my men would be proud to have you join us."

"No offense, Texas," Manse said, "but my daddy always taught me to do whatever I thought was right – then own up to whatever I did – which don't exactly fit in with wearing a hood over my face."

Manse paused, awaiting an argument, but there was none.

Instead, Texas nodded, and smiled.

"I understand," he said. "Just you remember this, Manse Jolly – I'm your friend. Whatever you decide to do, I'm ready and willing to help you any way I can. I'll tell my boys that if you ever ask any of them for anything, they're to oblige you. After all, we're all of a like mind. The Klan don't never kill nobody but niggers and scalawags, and Manse Jolly don't kill nobody but yankees."

***

Every time Rebecca Largent closed her eyes she saw Manse's face.

After an hour of trying to sleep, she gave up, got out of bed as quietly as she could – to avoid waking Bonnie and Melinda – and put on her robe and slippers and went downstairs to the kitchen.

Tom was sitting at the kitchen table, reading by the light of a single candle.

"I see you couldn't sleep either," he said.

"Too blamed hot," Rebecca said and drank a dipper of water, then wet a cloth and wiped her face.

"I wanted to take a walk," Tom put aside his reading, "but the soldiers won't let me go outside. Said we are all confined-to-quarters after dark."

"I don't see how they can rightfully do what they're doing to us, Tom."

"I don't either. I told Sergeant Jerlier I wanted to see Lieutenant McCollum to ask him just how-long they plan to keep us from going anywhere. But the lieutenant is in town, and not expected back until later this evening," Tom sighed. "The sergeant is nice enough, I reckon. He's just following orders. And he gave me this copy of the Anderson *Intelligencier* newspaper. It's got a story on the front page about Manse."

Rebecca walked to the table, picked up the newspaper, and quickly read the story.

"Seems to me they only wrote what that Army captain had to say. Nothing about Manse finding out that those were the men who killed Larry," she sat at the table.

Her eyes pleaded with her brother.

"I want you to take me to Manse, Tom," she said. "I need to talk to him. I want to help him."

Tom fought to separate thought from emotion, and slowly shook his head.

"I doubt we could get past the soldiers here," he said. "And even if we could, we would probably just wind up leading them to Manse. Besides, I don't think there's much we could do to help him right now."

"But we've got to think of something," Rebecca raised her hands to the back of her neck, took off the locket and handed it to her brother.

"Manse gave me this at Christmas," she said.

"I know," Tom smiled at her. "Manse and I don't keep much from each other. He bought that for you when he went with me to buy Bonnie's wedding band."

Tom squeezed her hand.

"He was nervous as if he was buying *you* a wedding ring," he said.

"Then I guess he told you we were talking about our feelings – and our future."

"Some things Manse didn't have to tell me, Rebecca," Tom said. "We've lived closer than brothers most of our lives. So I've known for a long time that he loved you."

"And I love him, Tom – " Rebecca's tears flowed.

"I'm just so damned stubborn," she said. "I kept waiting for him to say all the things I needed to hear. I wanted him to be so sure of his love for me," she began to sob.

"I should have gone ahead and told him how much I love him," she dabbed at her tears with the washcloth.

"I should have given myself to him – or married him when you and Bonnie got married. At least then, when Texas Brown told him he had found Larry's killers, I would have been with him, close to him, and could have talked him into waiting for you to come home instead of going after them by himself," her tears began anew.

Tom stood and walked around the table and sat in the chair next to her and put her head on his shoulder and let her cry.

After a few minutes, her sobs subsided and she got up and walked to the water bucket. Again she wet the washcloth and wiped her eyes and face.

Then she came back to the table and sat.

"I want you to take me to Manse tonight," she said.

"But I told you – "

"Please – Don't argue with me, Tom. Just listen," she said. "If Manse stays around here, then sooner or later the yankees will kill him. But maybe I can talk him into going away. Far away. With me."

Again Tom shook his head.

"You don't know what you're saying, Rebecca. Manse is a wanted man. It will take all his military training and experience – all his courage and cunning – just to survive. If you are with him," Tom said, "Manse will place your safety above his own because he loves you – and then he will most certainly be captured or killed *protecting you..*"

Rebecca felt the pain of his words, and she knew he was right.

It was too late.

She and Manse had lost.

She held her tears inside, leaned over and kissed Tom on the cheek, turned and walked upstairs – to cry into her pillow and try again to sleep.

***

Tom was still at the kitchen table when Martin McCollum rapped on the back door, then came inside.

"Damned but it gets hot in South Carolina in the summer," he said.

"There's water in the pail. And a dipper hanging on its side," Tom said.

"Thank you," Martin said.

"Or, if you'd rather, help yourself to a drink from the jug," Tom said.

Martin said thank-you again, and drank from the dipper, and wondered if she had just drunk from it.

Then he poured whiskey from the jug and sat.

"Sergeant Jerlier said you wanted to see me," he said.

"Just wanted to know how long you reckon we're going to be confined to the house under armed guard?" Tom said. "We 've got crops coming in. The first we've had since The War. We need them to get us through the winter. And to be able to give the Army what they requisition. And to sell enough to try to pay the taxes that Samuel Heaton is bound to come collecting."

"I'll speak to Captain Phillips. He is difficult, but not totally unreasonable," Martin removed his hat.

"I'll appreciate anything you can do to help us," Tom said. "We have three mules, to pack things into town to sell, and pack-out supplies – until we get back our wagon that was stolen. Or can afford to buy a new one."

"I'll ask Captain Phillips for permission for you to make as many trips into town as you need."

Tom smiled thanks.

And smiled to himself.

With the Army's unwitting help, he could deliver meat from the smokehouse to Gerald McClure – for much needed money.

Then he could start trying to figure a way to bring more meat down from the mountains.

-11-

Martin McCollum walked out of the sweltering command tent he shared with Sgt. Alex Jerlier, into the liquid heat of a windless August afternoon.

Two young soldiers were sitting on a log in the shade a few yards from their guard post. Their rifles leaned side by side against a pine tree – too heavy to carry back and forth in this damn weather.

They stood when Martin emerged from the tent.

He returned their salute, and did not reprimand them for not walking their assigned posts in the sun. This summer was too hot for regulation army chicken shit. Besides, he wasn't sure what the hell they were supposed to be guarding anyhow. Not a damn thing ever happened here.

"I thought yesterday was the hottest it could get," Sgt. Jerlier slipped galluses over his shoulders as he walked from the path that led to the trench latrine. "But I'll be damned if today don't feel a hell of a lot hotter. Right, Lieutenant?"

"It's the humidity, Sergeant. And lack of wind. It was a day just like this, a year ago, when I arrived here. The people here call it dog-days – same as we call it in New York."

"Same as in Pennsylvania, sir," one of the young soldiers said. "But I never knew why – except that maybe because not even dogs stir around in this kind of weather."

"It's 'cause it's hot as a son-of-a-bitch, that's why," Sgt. Jerlier said.

The two young soldiers laughed.

Martin smiled.

"I am leaving command to you, Sergeant," he said. "I have to report to Captain Phillips at Headquarters before Retreat."

He put on his tunic and felt rivulets of sweat immediately form on his neck and flow from his armpits.

"I'll have one of the men bring your horse, sir," Sgt. Jerlier said.

"I'll go to the barn and saddle her myself," Martin said. "The exercise will do me good." He turned and walked across the road, toward the Jolly home.

Perhaps, if he were lucky, he would see her. Maybe even manage to speak to her.

***

Manse's finger rested on the trigger.

Even at this distance, he recognized that damn yankee lieutenant.

He held the back of Martin's head in the v-groove of his sights.

***

The farm was quiet.

On the porch, Maude Jolly rocked.

When Martin crossed the road and neared the house, he looked at her and touched the brim of his hat.

If she saw him, she did not acknowledge it.

***

Small pines blocked a clear shot.

Then Martin's blue uniform disappeared around the corner of the house.

Manse shifted his rifle's aim back to the soldiers on the log near the tent.

***

Tom Largent and Johnny Jolly were at the well, patching the wooden trough. They nodded when they saw Martin, but said nothing to him.

Martin nodded and kept his distance.

He entered the barn just as Robespierre was hoisting a bale of hay to the loft.

Four soldiers jumped up from the pile of feed sacks on which they were lying, snapped to attention, and saluted.

Martin did not return their salute, and spoke to Robespierre.

"Are you stacking that hay for Mister Largent?" he asked.

"No, sir, Mister Lieutenant, sir. This here is hay for the army horses," he said. "Them gentleman there," he motioned toward the soldiers, "they told me to stack it in the loft."

"Well, you can stop doing that right now," Martin smiled politely at Robespierre. "Army hay for army horses is army business. These men have no right to tell you to do anything."

Martin turned to the four soldiers, and raised his voice.

"Corporal, you and your men get off your asses and move that hay to the loft, right now. And if I ever hear of you ordering this man – or anyone on this farm – to do your work, I will have you summarily court-martialed, stripped of rank, and sentenced to the stockade for ninety days for disobeying this *direct order*. Is that clear?"

"Yes, sir. Perfectly clear, sir," the corporal said, and the soldiers immediately formed a chain and began passing bales up the ladder to the loft.

"I thank you for that, Lieutenant, sir," Robespierre said. "That was a awful lot of hay to take up there," he smiled. "Is there something I can be doing for you, suh?"

"Thank you for offering, Robespierre," Martin said. "As a matter of fact, you can saddle my mare for me. Then go help Mister Largent finish whatever he is doing at the horse trough."

Martin walked out of the barn and looked toward the house.

And wondered where she was.

***

From the upstairs window, Rebecca watched him come from the road, through the edge of the woods, past the house and into the barn. And she wondered how he could bear that uniform in this heat.

She turned when Bonnie roused from sleep and shifted on the bed.

Just being that pregnant must be terribly uncomfortable, Rebecca thought.

She turned and looked out the window again.

At the Lieutenant, standing there in the sun, as if he was waiting for something. Or someone.

And she was aware of what she had felt before whenever Lt. Martin McCollum was near – that he was definitely a very handsome man – for a yankee.

***

Sweat dripped into Manse's eye.

He lowered the Henry and wiped his forehead with his forearm, then once again lined up the sights on the soldier.

***

Sgt. Alex Jerlier wiped his forehead with his bandanna for what seemed to him the hundredth time today.

When he had re-enlisted after Appomattox, he never figured he would end up in this damnable place. He had requested to remain at the commissary supply depot in West Virginia, where he had been stationed during most of The War. It was a good war-time post. Most of the people there didn't know which side – north or south – they, or their neighbors, were on. And they didn't really give a damn.

So, for almost four years, Sgt. Jerlier had sold contraband supplies to both sides – and, in the process, gathered information that he used to insure silence from anyone who might consider reporting him to his superiors.

He cursed under his breath.

He should still be in West Virginia, where the profits were plentiful. But within months after The War ended, and he re-enlisted, Jerlier had lost control of his *business* to a captain who didn't want anyone as experienced as Jerlier in his organization. So he had put the sergeant on a list of *undesirables* to be transferred to this out-of-the-way hell-hole of Anderson-damned-South-damned-Carolina, where everybody was so poor there was virtually no profit in anything – information or contraband.

Now he rarely dealt in items of any real value.

Rather, he accepted small bribes from large planters in exchange for not requisitioning their full quota of provisions. Or, in lieu of money, he accepted incriminating information they could furnish him about other men of means – information he could then offer to withhold from the authorities for a price.

And, during the past few months, he had formed an alliance with Lt. Martin McCollum – furnishing the Intelligence Officer information in exchange for protection from the prying eyes of Captain Phillips.

And, unknown to McCollum, Jerlier had sold much of that same information to Texas Brown – who, through an intermediary, had paid him well for arranging the escape of a suspected Klansman from the stockade – so that Brown could kill the man before he had a chance to tell Captain Phillips everything he knew about Klan membership and activities.

That was how Sgt. Alex Jerlier had learned that Texas Brown was the leader of the Klan – information that, one day soon, he planned to sell to the Army – or to Texas Brown – depending on who offered to pay him the most.

***

Manse closed one eye and lined up the Henry rifle's barrel-tip-bead in the v-notch of the rear sight.

Then he exhaled slowly – held his breath – and steadily squeezed the trigger.

***

The bullet and the sound arrived at the same time.

Sergeant Alex Jerlier felt the impact knock him to his knees and pitch him face down into the dust – then he felt no more.

His body lurched and twitched, and was still.

A quarter of his head had been blown away.

At the sound and sight, the young Pennsylvania soldier who had been talking to Sgt. Jerlier froze for an instant – and that instant was all the time Manse needed to take aim, fire, and open a hole where the boy's heart had been.

***

"Holy mother of god," Martin said aloud, and drew his sidearm, and ran from the barn toward the road – toward the tent he shared with Sgt. Jerlier.

Robespierre knelt and prayed in the stall where he had been cinching the saddle on Martin's horse.

Tom flattened himself on the ground next to the water trough, and pulled Johnny down beside him.

Rebecca crouched beneath the window ledge – then raised her head and looked out, but could see nothing.

Bonnie awoke. Melinda cried and held tightly to her mother.

Maude Jolly continued to rock.

Soldiers ran out of the barn and positioned themselves behind trees. Others took cover at their picket posts.

Some yelled. Others pointed.

Then the farm was suddenly as quiet as it had been before the first shot was fired.

Martin arrived at his tent – and only by their uniforms did he recognize the corpses of Sergeant Alex Jerlier and the soldier-boy from Pennsylvania.

***

A smile crossed Manse's face as he watched the confusion.

Then he crawled a few yards behind the crest of the hill, stood, ran to his horse, slid the Henry in the saddle sling, mounted, and rode away.

They were the first two casualties of his war, but they would not be the last.

He would not go back to the mountains until more men died.

Soldiers. Bluebellies. Yankees.

***

***

For Manse, The War resumed that summer of 1866.

And once again he put his military skills to use.

Along roads to Pendleton, Antreville, Twiggs and Pickens – and on winding trails beside the Savannah and Seneca and Tugaloo Rivers – he executed ambushes, leaving Union soldiers dying in Southern dust.

He killed, and his emotions thrived on killing.

He rarely ate or slept – but when hunger or exhaustion forced him to stop, he knew which farms would take him in and hide him – which folks would share their food and whiskey – and who could be trusted to pass along any messages he left.

Like his dreams, his days and nights became blood and death.

Revenge and honor were his rationale for a commitment to irrational action.

He killed until he felt release.

Only then did he return to the cave.

***

In shadows near the Smith-McGee Crossing on the Savannah, Manse waited, listened and heard riders approaching from the other side of the river.

Then the hoof beats of ninety horses filled the covered bridge, and the apparition of ninety white-robed riders erupted from it.

Manse rode out of the woods. White hooded horsemen surrounded him.

The faceless armed men made Manse nervous.

His hand rested on his pistol.

Texas Brown removed his hood and smiled, as if he sensed the uneasiness Manse felt.

"Whit told me you wanted us to meet you here," he said. "So here we are," his smile broadened.

Manse relaxed, but knew this was not the time or place for conversation. He would say only what he needed to say.

"You still want that nigger Sed Jacobs?" he asked.

"Yeah. Sure we do," Texas said. "But the Army's got soldiers guarding his place."

"I'll take care of the bluebellies," Manse said. "You ride ten minutes behind me. When you get to Jacobs' place, there won't be any soldiers there."

Without waiting for Texas' reply, Manse turned his horse and rode fast for five miles, to the same woods from which he had watched Sed Jacobs' house the night he found Larry's killers there.

Four soldiers stood guard at the front. Six Cavalry horses meant two more were inside. Manse removed his rifle from the sling, nudged his horse clear of the trees, stood in the stirrups, tightened his legs against the stallion's flanks, raised the rifle, squeezed the trigger, and a soldier fell.

Without aiming, he fired three more shots in the general direction of the house, then galloped onto the road.

Five soldiers mounted and pursued.

Manse spurred his horse out of range, but not out of sight, and veered into the woods.

***

Ten minutes later, Klansmen surrounded the house, and Elk Marett shouted:

"Sed Jacobs, walk out or be burned out!"

The door opened and a young black man came out. Four Klansmen rode to him. Two dismounted and tied the man's wrists and ankles. A mule was led from the corral. The man was thrown across it on his stomach. They cinched his hands to his feet.

"Take everything inside that's worth having," Elk ordered.

Ten robed men entered the house. Two returned dragging a girl.

"What do you want us to do with this?"

"Tie her and throw her over my saddle," Texas said, and looked through hooded slits at the girl they hoisted across his lap.

She squirmed.

Texas brought his hand down hard on her buttocks.

"Lie still, nigger," he said, "or I'll kill you right here."

White robes came from the house carrying sacks.

"He had a lot of good stuff," Whit's voice was muffled by his hood.

"Pack it on his mules, and take all the livestock," Texas ordered, "then torch the place."

Within minutes the house and barn were aflame.

The Klansmen rode Southwest with their prisoners and booty.

Texas held reins with one hand and the girl with the other.

Six miles later, they dismounted in pine woods.

Whit untied the cinching bond and pushed Sed Jacobs off the mule.

Texas dropped the girl from his saddle to the ground, then dismounted.

Klansmen chopped down three trees.

They used two to build a cross.

They cut limbs from the third and largest tree, and hammered three iron wedges into the log.

The wood groaned as it split.

They piled brush around it, then poured lamp oil on the log.

Whit Whitfield walked to Texas.

"Everything's ready for him," he said. "What you want to do about her?"

"Leave her to me," he said. "And as soon as the cross is lit, order the men to scatter."

Texas walked to the man lying beside the log.

"Strip him," he said.

Klansmen tore off the man's clothes.

"Sed Jacobs, you have helped those who robbed and murdered white men," Texas said. "For that, the Knights of The Imperial Order of The Ku Klux Klan sentence you to death."

Sed Jacobs struggled to free himself from the men who held him. A rifle butt smashed his kidney. He stopped resisting.

Whit Whitfield raised his hand. Klansmen untied Sed Jacobs' ankles, picked him up and lowered him astride the log. A Klansmen used a piece of wood to push the man's genitals into the widest part of the split.

Whit Whitfield dropped his hand.

The wedges were knocked from the log.

The crack closed to the width of a hair.

Sed Jacobs tried to pull away from the pain.

He cried, then cursed, then screamed.

Texas nodded.

Torches ignited the brush pile.

A cheer rose from the Klansmen.

Elk Marett lit the cross.

On Whit's orders, Klansmen mounted and rode away.

Whit and Elk followed.

When they were gone, Texas Brown removed his robe and hood, and watched the burning brush ignite the log.

Then he looked from the man to the girl.

"You want me to cut him loose?" he asked her.

She nodded.

Texas drew a knife from his boot and tossed it on the ground within reach of Sed Jacobs.

The man glared at Texas, then looked at the girl, then back at the fire. Flames seared his hips and legs. He picked up the knife and plunged it into his groin, let out a guttural cry, and emasculated himself.

Blood gushing, Sed Jacobs stood, raised his arm, and threw the knife at Texas.

It fell short of its target.

Texas drew his pistol and fired twice, shattering Sed Jacobs' knees.

Unable even to crawl, he screamed curses at Texas.

"Please, mister, help him," the girl pleaded.

"Well, since you asked so nice, of course I'll help him," Texas smiled at her – and shot Sed Jacobs in the head.

He fell onto his pyre.

The girl screamed, then began to cry, and started crawling toward the burning corpse.

Texas planted his boot firmly on the back of her neck.

"Don't you move a damn hair, nigger," he said.

She did not move.

He holstered his pistol, walked to the log, retrieved his knife, walked back to the girl, knelt beside her, wiped the blade on her blouse, then tore it away – ripped off her skirt – rolled her on her back – looked at her body – and laughed.

"It's just like I told some friends of mine the other day," he said. "I never knowed no nigger wench to wear underpants."

He pinched the nipple of her breast between his finger and thumb until her tears came, then he released her and stirred the fire with his knife, and laid the blade on the coals.

"Please, mister, don't hurt me," she said, and spread her legs wide and raised her hips. "I'll do anything you want me to. Anything."

"I ain't interested in doing but one thing to you, nigger," he said, and held her throat with one hand, then he picked up the knife and pressed the flat of the white hot blade between her legs.

She screamed.

Texas sliced into her burning flesh, laughed again – and turned her onto her stomach.

***

In September, Bonnie's baby boy was born.

That night, Tom, Texas and Martin got drunk.

Upstairs, Rebecca held the newborn while Bonnie slept.

Melinda lay on the bed beside her mother.

Johnny sulked – too old to go into his mother's room, too young to get drunk on the porch.

And Maude Jolly sat by her bed – rocking and remembering.

***

October leaves blanketed the foothills as Martin drove the squeaking wagon along Lebanon Road toward the Jolly farm – and once again rehearsed in his mind what – given the chance – he planned to say to Rebecca.

He had learned that most of those who knew the Jolly and Largent families believed that someday Rebecca would marry Manse, even though there had never been an official announcement in the church by Preacher Eskew.

It was simply a given, they said, that once the Jolly farm was back in production, the announcement would come.

There were also rumors that since Rebecca and Manse were already living under the same roof – perhaps even in the same bedroom – marriage was not all that necessary.

Martin had laid those rumors to rest in his mind with the answers to carefully-asked questions in conversations about the family with Tom and Johnny – whose friendship he had nurtured since the first day he was assigned to the Jolly farm.

He had been so thorough in his investigation of the Jolly-Largent relationship, that he had even learned (from the jeweler who sold it) about the locket Manse had given Rebecca for Christmas.

When first he heard that Manson Jolly would inevitably wed Rebecca Largent, Martin had lost what little hope he had that he would ever be able to tell her how he felt.

Even after Manse became a wanted-man, Martin expected that almost any night she might slip away and join him, and they would leave South Carolina, and he would never see her again.

But Manson Jolly had obviously chosen to remain in South Carolina, on some kind of mad vendetta. And it was the increasing frequency and intensity of Manse's acts of violence – and the Army's increased determination to hang him – that had given Martin renewed hope.

Surely Rebecca must know that any feelings she had for Manse were as doomed as he was. The two of them could never share a life.

Perhaps Martin could convince Rebecca – if he got the chance to talk to her alone – as he was scheming to do today – that the best chance for her future was with him.

He drove the wagon off Lebanon Road, onto a trail that led to the clearing where he was to meet Texas Brown.

***

Texas had heard the squeaky wheel when the wagon was still almost a half mile away.

And Texas wished, above all else, that when Martin McCollum arrived, and delivered the gold, he could simply kill him on the spot.

Texas resented more than ever the fact that Martin was taking as much of the gold as he was. True, Martin had been the one who convinced Texas that the gold was in Anderson, and Martin had gotten Robespierre released from the stockade, but it was Texas Brown who had figured out what happened to the gold – or at least had determined that Robespierre was the man who held the key to the mystery. And it was him who had gotten Robespierre to tell him the names of the men who masterminded the theft.

True, it was Martin who had confronted the colonels and the judge, but, hell, Texas was sure he could have done that just as easily.

In Texas' mind, Martin was getting a share of the gold only because it was too dangerous for anyone, even Texas Brown, to murder a Union Army Intelligence Officer who (everyone knew) was looking for Confederate gold.

At least it was too risky to murder him here in Anderson, while he was still on duty.

But once Martin McCollum left South Carolina, as Texas knew he planned to do when his resignation took effect, then Texas would work out a plan to find him, wherever he went, and kill him, and take Martin's share of the gold – which Texas reckoned rightfully belonged him.

All Texas had to do was learn where Martin was taking his gold – and when.

***

Martin drove the wagon into the clearing and stopped.

"I could tell by that squeaking wheel that you finally got the Jolly's wagon back for them," Texas laughed and dismounted. "I heard you coming a half-mile away."

"Picked up their wagon and mules this morning," Martin said. "Which worked out well since I had some heavy hauling to do."

"Any problems with the colonels and the judge?"

"Delivery was completed without a hitch," Martin got down off the wagon, opened the trunk that was behind the seat, lifted out an oilskin packet, and handed it to Texas.

Texas almost dropped the unexpected weight.

Then he unwrapped the gold bar and rubbed it with his hand.

"I reckon this means we're rich," he said as he re-wrapped it.

"Indeed it does," Martin smiled. "And to make this day complete, Captain Phillips has approved my resignation and sent it to Washington."

"Well, now, that is fine news," Texas returned Martin's smile, and smiled to himself. "When's the Army turning you loose?"

"My discharge is effective November first."

" You going back to New York?"

"No, I have decided to go to your favorite part of America."

"Texas?" Texas could scarcely believe his good luck.

"Yes," Martin said, "I understand it's an ideal place for a man of sudden wealth."

"So I've heard," Texas said, and decided to press his luck. "Texas is a big state. Where you plan to settle down?"

"I'm not sure exactly where," Martin smiled again. "And, quite frankly, I'm not sure I would tell you if I knew."

"Hell, I'm just making palaver," Texas shrugged. "I don't really give a shit where you go."

He decided to let the subject rest. He would find a way, when the time was right, to find out everything he wanted to know.

One-at-a-time, Texas lifted the remaining oilskin-wrapped bars of gold from the trunk and put them inside two pairs of black saddle bags.

"I had these special made," he said. "Double-sewed to hold the weight."

Texas put the saddle bags on his horse.

"Where are yours?" he asked. "I don't see anything else in the trunk."

"You aren't supposed to see anything – the bottom is false," Martin said. "It's so well hidden, I wouldn't hesitate to let anyone examine it – even Captain Phillips."

"Plumb clever," Texas smiled. "Of course, every time I see that damn crazy Phillips nowadays, I have to laugh. I reckon he's gonna have a first-rate conniption fit if he don't catch Manse soon."

Martin did not return the smile.

"Manse Jolly's days are numbered, Texas," he said. "The captain accepted my resignation, and is expediting my discharge, only because more troops are being sent to the Anderson District. Two companies of The Fifteenth Maine Cavalry – commanded by Major Lowell Bartow. You've heard of him?"

"Can't say I have. Is he somebody special?"

"He is the man who ended the career of William Clarke Quantrill and his band of Confederate renegades."

Texas nodded, impressed.

"Does that mean Captain Phillips is being replaced?" he asked.

"No, the captain will continue to command the Anderson District garrison. Major Bartow's sole assignment will be to get Manse Jolly – dead or alive. He is causing more trouble for the Army than your entire Klan."

"I know," Texas grinned. "Folks around here call him the greatest Confederate hero since Robert E. Lee. They're even writing songs about him."

"They will likely change their tunes before long," Martin said. "Major Bartow has a reputation for being ruthless."

"I'll keep that in mind," Texas said, and mounted his horse. "I got a ways to go, so I reckon I best get started. Where you headed?"

"To the Jolly farm," Martin said.

Texas frowned.

"I thought the captain relieved you of duty out there," he said.

"He did. This visit is purely personal."

"And I'll wager my saddle bags her name is Rebecca," Texas said, and spat as he turned his horse north, toward the mountains.

***

***

Two guards came to attention and saluted when Martin stopped the wagon near the front porch of the Jolly farm.

"We heard you coming a long ways off," Johnny said as he and Tom came out of the house.

"Here's your mule and wagon, just as I promised, Mr. Largent," Martin said. "The Army wouldn't release them until witnesses vouched that they were yours. Even then, they didn't want to accept my word, or Texas Brown's, but they didn't dare argue with Mr. Gerald McClure – they need the meat he sells them," Martin smiled.

"This is mighty nice of you, Lieutenant," Tom said. "That squeaky wheel sounds like music to me."

"We can haul lots more with this than on all three of them mules," Johnny forced his way into their conversation. "We can use this to go into town, can't we, Lieutenant?"

"You have Captain Phillips' permission to continue to make one trip a week into Anderson," Martin said.

"Thank you for arranging that, too," Tom extended his hand to Martin. "You've been real good to us, Lieutenant, and as soon as we sell some more of the cured meat we got hanging in the smokehouse, I want to pay you something for all you've done."

"No, please, I would rather you consider this as a sort of going away present," Martin removed his right glove before shaking Tom's hand.

"You're leaving?" Tom looked concerned.

"Yes. I've resigned my commission," Martin looked around but didn't see her. "Which reminds me," he said. "There is a favor I would like to ask of you."

"Anything," Tom said, then hesitated. "What?"

"This trunk contains personal belongings. May I store it in your home until I leave?"

"Sure, you can," Tom exhaled audibly. "Johnny and I will give you a hand with it."

"No, it's rather heavy – " Martin said, and ordered two guards to carry the trunk into the house.

An hour later, he and Bonnie stood in the back yard and watched Tom, Johnny and Robespierre leave for town. Two soldiers rode behind them.

"It was real nice of you to get our wagon back," Bonnie said.

"I only wish it were more, Mrs. Largent," Martin said. "Is there anything I can do for you while Mr. Largent is in town?"

"I can't think of anything. I have to tend the baby. Melindy and Rebecca are going to collect eggs, then churn." She looked up as Rebecca came out the back door, "Where's Melindy?"

"Upstairs with Mama Jolly," Rebecca replied, but did not look at Martin.

"How is Mrs. Jolly?" Martin asked.

"No better, I'm afraid, Lieutenant," Bonnie said. "It's like she just doesn't care about anything anymore. It's mighty sad."

"But Melindy takes good care of her," Rebecca looked at Bonnie. "Maybe the Lieutenant can help me gather eggs," she said. "That way, Melindy can stay with Mama Jolly."

Bonnie hesitated.

"All right," she finally said. "If the Lieutenant doesn't mind?"

"It'll be my pleasure," Martin said, surprised – and unsure what to say next.

Silently, he and Rebecca walked to the barn. Inside she picked up four eggs from wooden boxes provided for nests, then searched crevices and corners for others – two behind sacks of corn; one on a shelf; one on an old buggy seat.

"I do believe chickens go out of their way to find places to hide eggs," Rebecca laughed nervously – unsure what to say next.

"It seems so," Martin stopped, then quickly ran his rehearsed speech through his mind one more time before touching her arm.

She turned to face him, but her eyes did not meet his.

"Miss Largent," Martin began. "Rather, Miss Rebecca, there is something I've been wanting to talk to you about for a long time – if you don't mind?"

"I don't rightly know if I mind or not, Lieutenant, until I know what it is you want to talk about."

"Won't you please call me Martin?" He wanted to get back to his rehearsed speech, but the way she looked made him forget everything else.

"I couldn't do that," she said. "It wouldn't be proper. But I could call you Mister McCollum, if you like." She kept her eyes downcast, as if looking for more eggs. His gaze seemed to look right through her, and she feared that if she raised hers to his, he might know what she was thinking.

"Well, that is better than Lieutenant," he smiled and calmed his nerves before continuing.

"I realize, Miss Rebecca," he began again, "that it's unseemly for me to be talking to you like this. Alone. Out in the barn. But sometimes circumstances keep us from abiding by all the social proprieties."

Rebecca picked up another egg.

"Yes. That is true," she said. "The War changed things a lot."

Martin waited a moment, then again found his rehearsed place.

"With your permission, Miss Rebecca," he said, "I would like to tell you some things about myself."

"I would be pleased for you to do that," she said, and meant it. "I don't really know much about you at all."

"I think I told you I am from New York," Martin said.

"I believe you told Tom that, and he told me," she corrected him.

"All of my family is now deceased," Martin pressed on, afraid he might forget his next line if he paused too long or digressed. "My father died a few months ago. He was my only living relative," the lie flowed easily. "I received word just this week that my inheritance from his estate is, if I may say so, rather substantial. And, to be honest, I am pleased to receive it because it will enable me to do many of the things I've always wanted to do."

Something in his voice made Rebecca raise her eyes to meet his. And his stare held her. She had never seen such intense eyes – so blue they were almost black. And suddenly, despite herself, she saw mirrored in them reflections of her own feelings – and fantasies she had been taught young ladies did not experience. But she did. And she suspected that others did, too.

"Frankly, Miss Rebecca, I had hoped one day to settle down in South Carolina," Martin said, "but I have come to realize that being a yankee makes it impossible for me ever to be accepted here. So I have decided to live in Texas." Now the words that were truly his dream rolled out effortlessly. "I understand that in many ways Texas is like the South once was – a place where a man can build a life and leave memories behind."

"That all sounds very nice, Mister McCollum," Rebecca said, and felt strangely uneasy about her next question. "Are you leaving soon?" she asked.

"The first week of next month."

"That's very soon."

Martin held her elbow tightly enough so she could not move.

"Rebecca," he said. "Forgive my bluntness but – will you go with me?"

Rebecca dropped the basket and pulled herself free of him.

"Now look what I've done," she said.

Martin picked up the basket and the sole unbroken egg.

"I am sorry I upset you," his eyes again met hers. "What are you thinking?"

"I'm not at all sure what I think or feel right now," she said, and knew that the truth was that she was afraid of what she was both thinking and feeling.

Martin moved closer to her.

"I've waited so long for this chance to talk to you. There is so much I want to say," he said. "I've rehearsed and rehearsed, to make sure I said all the right words. But now I guess the truth, said simply, is best –" He paused, then said: "I love you, Miss Rebecca Largent."

She backed away from him. Her face flushed. Her emotions churned. She was afraid of what she felt. Afraid of his words. And afraid not to listen and feel.

Martin held her shoulders.

Rebecca stared at her feet and waited.

"I know how you feel about yankees," he said. "But, please, believe me, regardless of where I was born, or which side I fought on in The War, I am, above all else, a man who loves you, and wants to marry you. In Texas I can give you the kind of life you deserve. Please allow me to do that."

She did not look up. Perhaps she should feel ashamed that she felt drawn to him. That his words, and the promise of the life he offered, appealed to her. That he aroused her, physically and emotionally. She shook her head to clear it. Then stared at him. And the uniform he wore. He was, after all, the enemy of all she held dear – of Manse Jolly, the man she thought she loved – of all the Jolly brothers – and, most of all, of her brother, Tom.

"What is bothering you, Miss Rebecca? Is it that I am not a Southern gentleman?"

"Not really," she said, and raised her eyes to his. "Tom says you're the only yankee he ever knew who acted like a gentleman."

"What, then?" Martin smiled. "Do you find me repulsive?"

"Oh, no," she flushed bright red. "I mean, I think you are quite the finest looking man I have ever seen."

Martin's smile broadened into a grin.

"Then tell me, please," he said. "What *is* bothering you?"

"The idea of going away from here – of leaving Tom and Bonnie and Mama Jolly and Melinda," she paused. "And Manse. He – they – would never understand. And the state of Texas is so far away. I know that if I went there with you, I would never see any of them again."

Her tears trickled.

Martin touched her cheek.

"I know it's not an easy decision," he said. "And I don't want to rush you. Please – take your time. Think carefully about what you feel – about whether you could ever love me enough to marry me. I will not leave South Carolina until you make your decision. I will wait, however long it takes, Rebecca, because I love you."

He drew her close and kissed her. She resisted for only a moment, then relaxed and put her arms around his neck and opened her kiss to his.

***

Texas Brown tied his horse near the cave entrance.

Manse came out from behind the rocks.

They shook hands.

"Brought you some supplies," Texas handed him two sacks, then took the saddle bags off his stallion.

They walked into the cave.

"Nice new bags," Manse said. "What's in them?"

"Explosives. Thought I'd leave them here until I needed them."

Manse unpacked the supplies in the shack.

Texas went to the back of the cave and put the saddlebags on a ledge.

"They'll be safe back there," Texas said when he came in the shack.

"What are you planning to use explosives for?" Manse poured whiskey into cups.

"I'm not sure yet," Texas said, and accepted the cup Manse handed him. "But the way I figure it, the Klan is gonna have to blow up something big real soon, just to attract a little attention."

He laughed.

"Everybody's about forgotten we exist," he said. "All they can talk about is that brave and fearless yankee-killer named Manse Jolly."

"That a fact – or just Texas-bull-shit?"

"A honest-to-god fact, Manse. You're a real hero," Texas smiled. "You're driving the whole damn Union Army crazy. Hell, the latest word is that they're sending two companies of blue-belly cavalry to Anderson just to chase you."

He took a folded reward poster from his coat pocket and handed it to Manse.

"They've even raised the reward on you to a thousand dollars," he said. "But you got nothing to worry about. They got no idea where to find you."

Manse looked at the poster, laid it aside, drained his cup, refilled it, drank and looked at Texas.

"You been by my house lately?"

"A few days back," Texas said.

"Is Mama okay?"

Texas chose words carefully.

"She's feeling kind-of poorly, Manse, but not sickly," he said. "Mostly she's still sad about Larry. And worried about you."

"You tell her I'm fine. Not to worry about me. You hear?"

"I'll tell her that," Texas opened a jug of whiskey and handed it to Manse. "Have a taste of this. It's store bought corn – Kentucky label."

Manse took the jug, took a long swig, then wiped his mouth on his sleeve.

"That's mighty smooth all right," he said, and handed the jug back to Texas.

Texas drank, and studied Manse's face.

"Just between us," he said, "are you really feeling all right?"

"Yeah, Texas, I really am," Manse said. "Fact is, except for missing home, I feel the best I have since The War."

-12-

Captain Ralph Phillips finished his mid-morning coffee laced with whiskey, and ordered another. He was sure that he was going to need several more to make tolerable the remainder of this day – November 1, 1866.

General Pickles and the Army High Command in Washington had let it be known, in no uncertain terms, that they were damned unhappy about recent events in the District of South Carolina under Captain Phillips' command. And now they had ordered Major Lowell Bartow and two companies of the highly decorated Fifteenth Maine Regiment, US Cavalry, to proceed with-all-due-haste to Anderson, to resolve the situation.

For three weeks Captain Phillips had been deluged with telegraphed and courier-delivered orders from Washington. He was to remain in command of the Union Army garrison, but henceforth Major Bartow's orders would take precedent.

The Major's mission was paramount. He was to have whatever he needed – or requested – to accomplish it.

Ten days ago, Bartow's senior aide, Captain Morris Holtzclaw, had arrived in Anderson by train. Within a few hours, he had commandeered the finest suite at the Benson House for the Major, and also arranged for the remainder of his staff – four first lieutenants and six second lieutenants – to be quartered there.

Captain Holtzclaw then delivered to the Anderson *Intelligencier* newspaper a complete biography of Lowell Bartow, which had subsequently been published in six special editions.

By now everyone in the district who could read, or find someone to read to them, knew that Major Lowell Bartow was a native of Bar Harbor, Maine, the son of an Admiral in the US Navy, and the grandson and great-grandson of admirals – and the first in his family to break tradition and choose a military career on land rather than sea.

Fortunately for Bartow's career, The War had erupted just months after he received his commission as a second lieutenant in the US Army. He was immediately assigned to the Fifteenth Maine Cavalry Regiment, and posted to the Central Command in Saint Louis.

The unit fought alongside several Cavalry and Infantry Brigades in battles near the Missouri and Mississippi Rivers.

But it was at the Battle of Vicksburg that Lowell Bartow emerged as a hero.

His hair was blond and curly. And he wore it long. Not just long enough to hang over his tunic collar, but long enough to cascade between his shoulder blades – except at formal military ceremonies when regulations required him to wrap it in a bandanna beneath his hat.

The newspaper stories reported – and Captain Phillips conceded that for the most part they were accurate – that at the Battle of Vicksburg, the Confederate Army had mounted a surprise offensive utilizing cavalry, artillery and infantry units that the Union Army was not aware were in the area – with the result that the US Cavalry was forced to retreat in disarray in the face of withering cannon fire and an onslaught of screaming Rebels.

Confederate victory had seemed inevitable – until Lieutenant Lowell Bartow removed his hat and unfurled his locks, and, sword raised, charged again and again into the enemy ranks.

The sight of the golden-haired young officer served as a rallying beacon for Union Cavalrymen. They closed ranks behind him and eventually routed the enemy in close quarters combat – during which Bartow repeatedly shouted orders that no prisoners be taken.

Confederate soldiers who managed to survive that battle gave unexaggerated reports of the screaming yellow-haired officer who exhorted his men to an orgy of blood-letting. Any Confederate soldier foolish enough to throw down his arms and raise his hands in surrender was summarily shot, run through, or decapitated.

Bartow's superiors concluded that he was clearly a born military leader. They needed officers like him. The fact that he took no prisoners was irrelevant. The smell of final victory over the Confederacy was strong in the nostrils of the Union High Command, so, within hours after the battle ended, they promoted him to First Lieutenant and gave him command of a company of cavalry, with orders to prevent any elements of the scattered Confederate forces from reuniting to form cohesive fighting units.

To help track down even the smallest groups of rebel combatants, Bartow enlisted Indians from the Mississippi Choctaw Nation to serve as his scouts.

The campaign was successful, and Bartow was promoted to Captain.

And when, after The War ended, the commander of Confederate guerrilla forces, William Clarke Quantrill – whose renegade bands had terrorized Missouri and Kansas throughout The War – moved his desperadoes into Kentucky and continued his campaign of murder, rape and pillage, the Union Army gave Captain Lowell Bartow and the two companies of the Fifteenth Maine under his command, free reign to do whatever was necessary to destroy them.

In the months that followed, more than four hundred of Quantrill's Raiders were killed. Some in running battles. Some by firing squad. Most by hanging.

Bartow's capture and execution of William Clarke Quantrill, near Taylorsville, Kentucky, ended the career of the most notorious Confederate renegade leader – and made Lowell Bartow the subject of journalistic adulation – and dime novels.

Members of Congress praised him.

He and his men, their horses, and their Choctaw scouts, were brought to Washington on a special train. And the President of the United States – "on behalf of a grateful nation" – decorated *Major* Lowell Bartow with the Army's highest military honor.

He was offered any command post he wanted.

He chose the Black Hills – the most volatile, dangerous, least militarily-accountable location in the Western Command – where he could fight and kill Indians any way he wanted.

But just days before he and his troops were to travel west, the High Command changed Major Bartow's orders.

His expertise was needed to deal with two vexing problems that confronted Union Occupation Forces in South Carolina.

In the small, otherwise inconsequential district of Anderson, there had suddenly emerged the most powerful and violent Klavern of the Ku Klux Klan in the Occupied South – and in the same district, an obviously maniacal renegade named Manson Sherrill Jolly was indiscriminately murdering Union soldiers.

Knowing Major Bartow's reputation, the Army High Command was confident he would capture and hang Jolly within a few weeks, and destroy the Klan shortly thereafter.

Captain Ralph Phillips had read all the newspaper articles, and the official reports – and heard all the stories, old and new, about Major Lowell Bartow – and he was angry as hell that the Fifteenth Maine was being sent to Anderson to do his job.

If the damned High Command in Washington had given him two companies of Cavalry to reinforce the Anderson garrison, as he had requested on nine separate occasions, then Ralph Phillips was confident that he could have effectively dealt with the problems of both Manse Jolly and the Klan. But no one at Union headquarters in Greenville, Charlotte or Washington had ever even acknowledged his requests.

Now, because the Army needed publicity in order to get more money appropriated by Congress for tighter military control over the Southern states, they had decided to send Bartow, who would no doubt capture Manse Jolly, hang him with great fanfare, then wipe out the Klan – and thereby perpetuate his reputation.

Captain Phillips admitted (to himself, at least) that he resented Major Bartow.

As a lieutenant in the Tenth Massachusetts Brigade, Ralph Phillips had also fought at the Battle of Vicksburg – and watched hundreds of his comrades die because of faulty intelligence about the size of the Confederate forces that awaited them on that Mississippi battlefield.

Ralph Phillips remembered the confidence he had felt when the engagement began – and the surprise of withering cross-fire that killed his horse, dropping it beneath him, throwing him to the rock-strewn ground with such force that he was knocked unconscious.

For how long, he wasn't sure.

At least one day. Perhaps two.

And he remembered awaking to find himself in a deep pit, surrounded by decomposing corpses – and covered by mangled bodies – and parts of bodies.

And the only sound he could hear was that of clods of dirt falling around him.

Presumed dead, Ralph Phillips was being buried.

With his last reserve of energy, he screamed.

And the pitiful sound that came from his mouth was barely loud enough to attract the attention of one of the prisoners on the burial detail.

They dragged him out of the pit, and sent him to a field hospital where the doctors said he was lucky to be alive, as opposed to buried alive.

But because he had suffered no serious physical wounds or injuries – and because of the shortage of able-bodied cavalrymen – he was ordered to return to duty after a short rest.

Two weeks later, he re-joined his unit which was then posted to the Western Territories.

And he would still be there were it not for the onset of his recurring nightmares – night after night of clawing his way through putrescent corpses in an effort to escape being buried with them.

The sheer terror of those dreams made sleep impossible – unless Ralph Phillips drank every night. Then every evening. Then every afternoon. And, eventually, every morning.

The commandant of the Western Command Unit in which he served decided that his drinking and lack of sleep adversely affected his judgment – specifically his ability to make what the Army called *rational military decisions.*

That was why they transferred him to the Anderson District of the South Carolina Division of the Occupation Army Of The South – where neither too much drinking, nor too little rationality, were of any real importance.

The Army High Command did not see Phillips' problem as medical. To them, he had simply become a drunk – a misfit – like most of the Union soldiers posted to Anderson.

And now it was obvious to Ralph Phillips that the High Command believed that the problems in this district were the direct result of the captain's continuing inability to make rational decisions and act upon them.

To the US Army High Command, Captain Phillips' inept command justified their decision to have the problems with the Klan and Manse Jolly resolved by Lowell Bartow, a true Hero Of The War who had experience in such matters – rather than by Ralph Phillips whom they quite frankly wished *had* been buried at the Battle of Vicksburg.

Phillips picked up the bottle from the bar, took a long swig from it, put it down, and looked in the mirror at the reflection of Martin McCollum staring back at him.

"By god, Lieutenant, you startled hell out of me," the Captain grinned. "I haven't had the pleasure of your company at breakfast – or lunch – for months. And I must admit, it gets damned lonely when only the occasional tax collector shows up for morning coffee," he laughed. "Surely you haven't given up drinking, Lieutenant. Or have you?"

"Almost, sir," Martin smiled. "I tend to drink in the mornings when things are not going very well for me. So I was drinking quite a lot for a while – when I could see no escape in sight from this hell hole – and the Army – and, if I may say so, from *you* , sir."

"Ah, I understand," Phillips said. "But now that your resignation has been accepted, and your discharge is effective next week, you have come here to tell me how much you've hated every minute you served under my command – "

"Not exactly, sir," Martin grinned. "Actually, I came here this morning to hand-deliver copies of the dossiers I furnished Major Bartow's aide, Captain Holtzclaw." Martin placed a sheaf of pages on the bar. "When he arrived last week, he ordered me to prepare Intelligence Reports on everyone connected with Manse Jolly – and the Klan – in addition to reports on prominent citizens – and the command staff here – including you, sir."

"And being a good soldier, you complied."

"I obeyed his orders to prepare the reports, sir – but by bringing these copies to you, I am disobeying his direct order that I not allow anyone else to see them."

"Then just why the hell, Lieutenant, are you giving them to me?"

"Because, sir, in the face of what I consider overwhelming problems – and with no support from your superiors – I believe you have performed well – no, amend that, sir – I believe you have performed *exceptionally well* with this command."

Martin stepped back, saluted, turned and walked from the Benson House Bar.

Ralph Phillips shook his head, glanced at the pages, took another drink straight from the bottle, stood erect, pulled down his tunic, looked at himself in the mirror, then took the bottle and the papers to a table and sat.

"Just enough time to learn everything Bartow knows about me and my command," he said to himself and began to read. "Then I'll go assemble *my* troops to greet the hero."

***

At mid-afternoon, Major Lowell Bartow, riding an Appaloosa stallion, led two companies of the Fifteenth Maine Regiment, US Cavalry – along with supply and support wagons, wranglers, farriers, and Choctaw Indian Scouts – down the Main Street of Anderson.

Four First Lieutenants rode at his quarter flanks; eight Second Lieutenants at theirs.

The special military train from Washington, via Charlotte and Greenville, had arrived at Belton Junction, ten miles east of Anderson, shortly before dawn, and could have easily been routed directly to the Anderson Depot. But Lowell Bartow knew that the sight of his men and equipment riding into town in parade formation was much more impressive than watching them clamber out of boxcars.

And he knew, too, that the town would be crowded. The newspaper articles printed in advance of his arrival assured that the streets would be lined with Unionists who came to cheer him, and local citizens who came out of curiosity.

For the occasion, as for all occasions where he appeared in public, he allowed his hair to fall down his back from beneath his hat. It identified, without doubt, The Hero of Vicksburg – The Man Who Killed Quantrill.

When the Fifteenth Maine Cavalry reached the Courthouse Square, Captain Morris Holtzclaw rode at full gallop from a side street.

Bartow raised his hand. The troop stopped. Captain Holtzclaw saluted the major. The major returned the salute. Then Holtzclaw reigned his horse beside Bartow's, and the major raised his hand and the troop moved forward, between the ranks of infantrymen and cavalrymen of the Anderson Garrison who lined the perimeter of the square.

Bugles and drums sounded and resounded.

Captain Ralph Phillips walked down the Courthouse steps – Lieutenants McCollum and Pearson at his flanks.

On the train ride south from Washington, Lowell Bartow had studied the intelligence reports sent to him by courier from Captain Holtzclaw. Now he put faces to the dossiers, including the one the captain had prepared on Martin McCollum who, because he was leaving within the week, was the least important.

Bartow was here under orders – that was the only reason he was here. He damned sure didn't need the publicity. And as far as he was concerned, catching and hanging one crazy bushwhacker, and wiping out a few dozen Klansmen, was a rather demeaning assignment for a man of his stature. But if that was what Washington wanted, he would produce the desired results, with the attendant fanfare, then resume his trek to the Dakotas.

Within a year, he fully expected to be a Colonel in command of the entire Western Division of the US Army. Within five years, he expected to be back in Washington – the youngest Army Chief Of Staff in American history.

Lowell Bartow dismounted and looked around the Courthouse square.

His first impression of Anderson was less than favorable.

But he had been informed that the Benson House Hotel was an exceptional hostelry. And he knew that his mess would be exceptional, too, because he had brought his own chef from Washington.

And Captain Holtzclaw had also reported that there was a fine gentlemen's gambling saloon and house of prostitution two miles south of town – with an above-average selection of young women – and boys.

He ordered Holtzclaw to see that the troops were billeted and the officers shown their quarters, then they were to be dismissed until reveille.

Captain Phillips and Lieutenants Pearson and McCollum approached the Major and saluted.

"Captain Ralph Phillips reporting, sir," Captain Phillips said. "I will be honored to show you to your quarters in the Benson House. But first, may I present my staff – "

Bartow flipped a casual salute.

"You may present your officers when I ask to meet them, Captain," he said. "And my aide, Captain Holtzclaw, will show me to my quarters when I wish to see them."

Bartow studied the man whose ineptness had required his presence here – and he could smell the whiskey on Phillips' breath from five feet away. No wonder the man was unable to handle simple problems. In Bartow's opinion, there was never any reason for a man to drink when he was on duty. Drinking was an off-duty pursuit – like whoring and gambling.

And Martin McCollum was, as Bartow had already decided, of such relative unimportance, that he had read neither Holtzclaw's nor Washington's dossier on the man. If McCollum weren't going to be around, why should Bartow waste his time reading about him.

As for this Lieutenant Pearson, he indeed did not look old enough to be in the US Army, much less an officer in command of a fighting unit. He had been sent to Anderson at the request of an uncle, or some relative, who was in the US Senate and did not want young Pearson exposed to any danger while serving his country during The War. Ironically, the young lieutenant was now in the middle of a nasty situation where a lunatic renegade was killing anyone wearing Union Blue.

Bartow smiled to himself and wondered how secure that made Pearson feel.

"Would the major care of freshen up, or have a drink or do anything in particular?" Captain Phillips asked.

"For your information, I bathed my entire body last night, Captain. It doesn't require any freshening. And if your question actually was whether I need to take a piss or a shit, the answer is *no*. If I do, I will let you know. And – I will say this only once – I do not drink while on duty. And I court-martial any trooper – or officer – who I find drinking on duty. As for what I want to do now, Captain – I want to talk to you and your officers."

"As you wish, sir," Ralph Phillips said, and thought, but did not say: *You pompous son of a bitch.*

Then he pulled his anger inside and led the way to his office.

Major Bartow removed his hat and gloves, and sat in Ralph Phillips' chair, behind Ralph Phillips' desk.

Captain Phillips, Lt. McCollum and Lt. Pearson stood.

"I find it unusual that there are only two officers here," he said.

"There are three other lieutenants under my command," Ralph Phillips said. "One is leading a patrol. One is handling requisitions since Supply Sergeant Jerlier was killed. The third is assigned to the Jolly farm where a squad of men is bivouacked," Ralph Phillips paused. "Lieutenant McCollum was in command of the squad at the Jolly farm, but he is leaving the service next week, so I have relieved him of his duties there."

"That seems a sensible decision," Bartow said, and looked at Martin. "I appreciated the information you furnished my aide, Captain Holtzclaw, and if I have any questions, I will have him contact you before you leave. Otherwise I see no reason why you should bother yourself with any further duties of any kind, Lieutenant McCollum. You are dismissed."

"Thank you, sir," Martin saluted.

Bartow returned his salute.

Martin did an abrupt-face and left the office.

Lowell Bartow took a pipe and tobacco pouch from beneath his tunic.

"The first objective of my assignment here is to rid this district of one Manson Sherrill Jolly," he said. "I have background report on the man, and a list of the charges against him – all of which raise in my mind one simple question, Captain Phillips: Why has your entire garrison been unable to capture or kill a lone gunman?"

Lieutenant Pearson answered before Phillips could speak.

"Jolly has lived here all his life, sir," he said. "He is harbored by residents – "

"Even though they know he is wanted?"

"Yes, sir. They consider him a hero. A Confederate soldier still fighting The War."

Bartow packed his pipe and nodded.

"One report I read stated that Jolly is aided by the Klan – " he said.

"That is an assumption, sir," Captain Phillips said, "based on a single incident when Jolly fired on troops guarding the house of a Freedman who was assisting us in an investigation. When my men gave chase, the Klan attacked the house, burned it, and abducted the two freedmen who lived there."

"If your men were pursuing Jolly, how can they be sure it was the Klan who attacked after they left?"

"The following morning we followed the tracks of about a hundred horsemen to a clearing where we found the remains of a cross beside the victims' corpses. It was definitely the Klan. The man had been emasculated and burned. The girl, who was only twelve or thirteen years old –" Captain Phillips saw images. His head swirled. He fell silent.

"Get on with it, Captain. Be specific. Only by hearing all the facts can I possibly know what I am up against."

"She had been sodomized. Tortured. And sexually mutilated, sir."

Bartow lit his pipe.

"We are obviously dealing with the same kind of violence and brutality exhibited by Quantrill's men," he clenched his teeth around the pipe stem.

"Being comprised primarily of former Confederate soldiers, the Klan is very well organized, sir," Captain Phillips said. "Just as I am sure Quantrill's Raiders were."

"Yes, indeed. Quantrill's men were indeed well organized," Major Bartow exhaled smoke and spoke to Ralph Philips with the modicum of consideration he accorded subordinates who showed proper respect for the Major and his achievements.

"Frankly, Captain Phillips," Bartow said, "I would prefer to place destruction of the Klan at the top of our-list, but my orders are clear. We are to give first priority to the capture of Jolly. Once we hang him," he smiled, "then you and I can devote our energies to destroying the Klan."

Lowell Bartow glanced at the pages on the desk in front of him.

"But, first things first, gentlemen. Tell me more about Jolly. These reports state he had five brothers killed in The War."

"Yes. And another murdered by bushwhackers," Ralph Phillips said.

"I think it is obvious, sir, that he kills for revenge," Lieutenant Pearson said.

Lowell Bartow shook his head slowly.

"Revenge? I might agree with you if he had killed four or five men, Lieutenant – " the major looked again at the papers before him. "Lieutenant Pearson? Isn't it?"

"Yes, sir," Lt. Pearson said, and braced himself to attention.

"Francis Marion Pearson –" Bartow nodded. "I find it very interesting, Lieutenant, to have in my command the namesake of one of America's most famous military leaders. If my memory of history as taught at The Academy is correct, I believe General Francis Marion was called *The Swamp Fox* – and he drove the British in South Carolina crazy during the Revolutionary War." Bartow smiled and studied Lt. Pearson's boyish face. "Was he a forebearer?"

"I would certainly be proud if he were, sir. But I was named for him because my grandfather served as his adjutant."

"And how is it, Lieutenant, that the grandson of the adjutant of The Swamp Fox ends up in the Union Army?"

"Following the Revolutionary War, sir, my grandfather and his family moved from South Carolina to Kentucky. He was a strongly Christian man who abhorred slavery. His views were unpopular. Two of his sons, my uncles, rode with the abolitionist, John Brown. When The War began, my family remained loyal to the Union."

"Admirable," Lowell Bartow nodded and smiled, then noticed that Ralph Phillips was shifting nervously from one foot to the other.

"By all means, be at ease, Captain Phillips. Take a chair. Have a cigar. I apologize for my digression, but I am unable to resist any opportunity to know more about the men in my command. More than is in military files. Personal things. But I am sure you have had the same experience."

"Yes, sir. Of course, sir," Ralph Phillips sat and accepted the cigar, and wished he could tell Bartow what he was really thinking at that moment.

"As I was saying before I interrupted myself, I do not agree with you, Lieutenant Pearson, that this Manson Jolly kills for revenge. I might agree if he had killed four or five men, but his continuing rampage reeks of an unbalanced mind. Possibly the result of severe head wounds. Or the *nostalgia*. Either can lead to excessive drinking and irrational acts. I noted it in more than one of Quantrill's men." Major Bartow studied his pipe. "Are you sure, Captain, that all the murders attributed to Jolly were committed by him?"

"He makes a point of letting us know he committed them."

"How does he do that?"

"Sometimes he kills two men out of three – leaving the third alive to identify him – or he shoots his victims in the stomach so they will live long enough to say who did it."

"And die a hellishly slow and painful death with a hole in the gut," Bartow frowned in disgust. "Jolly is clearly deranged."

Major Bartow slowly re-packed and lit his pipe.

"With only two companies of cavalry," he said, "I ended the terror of Quantrill and four hundred Confederate renegades. Because of that, the Army has granted me full, sole and absolute authority to do whatever I deem necessary to end the career of Manson Jolly," Bartow leaned across the desk. "Acting on that authority, Captain Phillips, I direct you to increase the reward on Jolly to five-thousand dollars – not in Union currency but in gold. Most people would sell their own mothers for that much gold," he smiled.

Ralph Phillips and Francis Marion Pearson nodded agreement.

"Lt. Pearson, I want you to have posters with the new reward on them printed immediately."

Bartow stood and walked to the window.

"And then, Lieutenant, I want you to find the local Tax Collector and tell him to bring me the records on Jolly's farm."

Lt. Pearson saluted and left.

"And I want you, Captain Phillips, to sign an order making it punishable by one year's imprisonment to harbor or give any aid to Manse Jolly."

"Begging the Major's pardon, but how do we prove the charges?"

"Don't be naive, Captain. We don't have to prove anything. We will simply arrest all suspects. Throw them in the military stockade. Then sort out the charges."

"But local and state laws – "

"Captain, the Confederacy is a defeated nation, occupied by the United States Army. In the south, all local and state laws are subordinate to Federal Military Law. And in this district, I alone interpret that law," Bartow said. "Now if I may return to the subject of this discussion. Who is Jolly's closest friend?"

"A man named Tom Largent. He and his sister have lived at the Jolly farm since their farm was foreclosed," Captain Phillips paused. "And a man named Texas Brown is a frequent visitor at the Jolly home."

"Texas Brown?" Major Bartow flipped through papers. "Ah, yes. I have a report on him. A rather vague report, I might add. Says he spends time with both Unionists and Southerners." Bartow looked up from the report. "I want to talk to him, Captain."

"If he is in town, he will be in the Benson House bar this time of day," Ralph Phillips said. "I'll send one of my men for him."

***

Fifteen minutes later, a sergeant escorted Texas Brown into Lowell Bartow's office.

The major stood when he walked in.

They shook hands.

"I don't want to waste a lot of your time, Mister Brown," Bartow said. "I am interested in what you might be able to tell me about Manse Jolly. I understand you know him and his family rather well."

The major motioned Texas to sit.

"I guess you could say that," Texas felt uncomfortable being in this office, sitting across a desk from the god-damn-yankee-son-of-a-bitch who killed William Clarke Quantrill – a man Texas Brown considered a greater hero than Lowell Bartow would ever be.

"When did you last see Jolly?" the major asked.

"I don't recall exactly," Texas took out a cigar, bit off the end and spat it on the floor.

"Your attitude – your lack of cooperation – could create serious problems for you, Mister Brown," Lowell Bartow said.

Texas Brown smiled.

"Major, I like to keep things simple," he said, "so let's you and me not waste a lot of time chewing words." He lit the cigar and blew smoke across the desk. "Sure, I know Manse Jolly. I know lots of people. Most of them welcome me in their homes. So I hear a lot of things. But I don't tell anybody what I hear – unless I've got good reason to." Texas leaned forward and met Bartow's stare. "And the day will most likely come, Major, when I'll decide to tell you something. And when that day comes, you'll be mighty glad you know Texas Brown. But if you think you can get any information from me by making threats, you're wrong – and the day I help you won't never come. Do you understand what I'm saying, Major?"

"I think we understand each other very well, Mr. Brown," Bartow nodded.

"Good," Texas stood. "Now, if that's all, I'll bid you a good-day."

Lowell Bartow stood and extended his hand.

"Good-day, Mr. Brown," he said. "Thank you for stopping by."

Texas Brown shook his hand – and knew that Lowell Bartow was a man he had to kill as soon as possible.

Texas walked from Bartow's office, into the outer office, now crowded with even more aides and their aides – and, across the room he saw Martin McCollum cleaning out his desk.

"How are you, Lieutenant?" Texas said.

"Fine, Mister Brown. I didn't see you come in. I must have been in the file room."

"I just came by to meet Major Bartow – at his request. Nice fellow," Texas smiled. "You look real busy."

"Just a few last minute details," Martin said.

"You'll have to let me buy you a drink before you go."

"I'll look forward to it."

Texas turned and walked to the front door as Samuel Heaton and Lt. Francis Marion Pearson entered.

Major Bartow came out of his office, followed by Captain Phillips.

"Major, this is Mr. Samuel Heaton, District Director of Tax Collections," Lt. Pearson said.

Bartow and Heaton shook hands and everyone in the office listened.

"The Lieutenant said you wanted the tax records on Manse Jolly's farm," Heaton removed his hat and handed papers to Bartow. "Taxes are current, as you can see."

Major Bartow looked at the papers and frowned.

"This is last year's receipt," he said.

"It was for a two-year period," Heaton wiped his brow.

"The truth, Mister Heaton, is that you haven't levied any taxes on Jolly's farm this year because you are afraid to do so. Correct?"

"Not exactly, sir. There are other considerations –"

"I have no interest in any other-considerations, Heaton," Bartow handed back the papers. "Levy another tax."

"But no taxes are due this time of year – "

"Call it a special *Fugitive Tax* – for two hundred dollars."

"But, Major – "

"No buts! Levy the damn tax, Heaton! Is that clear?"

"Yes, sir, perfectly clear, sir," Samuel Heaton said. "I'll go to the Jolly farm tomorrow," he hesitated. "You will provide an escort for me, won't you?"

"You will be protected, Mr. Heaton. I promise no harm will come to you."

***

Tom Largent was alone in the living room– everyone else had gone to bed – when he heard the horse coming up the drive.

He walked onto the front porch as Martin McCollum dismounted.

"Sorry to disturb you so late," Martin kept his voice low.

"That's all right, Lieutenant. I just hope you haven't brought bad news. They haven't caught Manse, have they?"

"No, nothing like that," Martin said. "I rode out to tell you that tomorrow morning Samuel Heaton will be here to serve you with a new tax levy. Two hundred dollars."

"Two hundred?"

"Yes. On orders from Major Bartow. Obviously the object is to get Mr. Jolly mad enough to go after Mr. Heaton – "

" – and the Army will be waiting for him," Tom sat on the porch swing. "Damn 'em," he said. "We've got some money put aside, but it has to go a long way."

"Take this," Martin handed him an envelope. "I just came into an inheritance."

"I can't take money from you, Lieutenant."

"Damn it, man, take it."

Tom hesitated, then accepted.

"I'm not sure what to say except, thank you," he said. "I'll pay it back, someday. I'll write you a note, if you want."

"That's not necessary. Just, please, don't ever tell anyone I gave it to you."

"I won't say a word. And thanks again – Martin."

"You're welcome – Tom."

They shook hands.

Martin walked from the porch, mounted his horse and rode away.

Tom put the envelope in his coat pocket and went upstairs.

***

Rebecca heard Tom walk by her room. She squirmed to get comfortable.

If only she could talk to Tom, but that was impossible. He could never understand, would never approve, no matter what. She sighed, pushed covers aside, got up, put on her dressing gown, and tip-toed to the door at the far end of the hallway.

She turned the knob and went inside.

"Who is it?" Maude Jolly's voice was a whisper.

"It's just Rebecca, Mama Jolly." She closed the door behind her, and saw Maude sitting in a chair beside the bed. "I wasn't sure you would be awake."

"I don't sleep much," Maude said. "I just sit here, wondering where Manson is – and praying that he's all right."

"He's somewhere real safe, I'm sure, Mama Jolly."

"Don't tell me stories, Rebecca. What Manson is doing is anything but safe – out there trying to pay back the yankees." She paused. "You don't sleep much these nights either, do you, Child?"

"How did you know?"

"I hear you up most every night, walking the floor. I reckon that's why you came in here tonight – to talk about what's troubling you."

"Yes, ma'am, you're right. I am upset," Rebecca said. "And I'm not sure how to explain it. Or that you'll understand."

"Only one thing makes a young woman talk like that – a man," Maude smiled, reached out and took Rebecca's hand. "Is it that young yankee officer?"

"How could you know that?"

"Don't be simple-minded, Rebecca. There haven't been any eligible men around here other than that Lieutenant. But then I don't reckon there are many young men left anywhere since The War," Maude paused. "Well, go on, child, tell me about him – and you."

"He's leaving the army, Mama Jolly. He inherited some money. Quite a lot, I think. And he wants me to go to Texas with him. He – Martin – that's his name," she paused. "Martin wants me to marry him."

"Gone as far as that, has it?" Maude shook her head and smiled again. "Not like it use to be. Mister Rufus Moorhead Jolly courted me for four years before he ever spoke of marriage. And I never called him anything but *Mister Jolly* until our wedding night. Yes, things have surely changed."

"You won't hold it against me if I marry a yankee, will you, Mama Jolly?"

"Once I would have felt it was a disgrace for any Southern girl to even think of such a thing. But now all the young men are gone away – like my Manson – or long since dead –" Maude's words trailed off to soft sobs.

"I'm sorry, Mama Jolly. I didn't mean to upset you." Rebecca leaned over and hugged her.

"It's not your fault, Rebecca. I cry easy," Maude Jolly said, and cradled Rebecca's face in her hands. "You go away with your handsome lieutenant, if your heart tells you to."

"I'm not real sure how much I love him, Mama Jolly," Rebecca said. "Not as much as I loved Manse – but now that just can't ever be," Rebecca's tears trickled.

"I understand," Maude nodded slowly. "The only question is, do you believe the lieutenant truly loves you?"

"Yes – I feel Martin's love for me. And I believe he will be good to me. And take good care of me. And, maybe, in time, I'll love him completely."

"Then marry him and try to love him well. And if God is merciful there won't be any wars to take your sons from you like mine have been taken away from me," Maude Jolly's tears mingled with Rebecca's. "But don't tell your brother, Tom, or anyone else, about your plans. I'll tell them for you after you've gone."

"Thank you," Rebecca said. "And pray for me, please, Mama Jolly."

"I do, child. Every night, when I pray for Manson – and for us all."

"And I pray, too, Mama Jolly. I pray that someday Manson will be able to come home again."

Maude shook her head.

"No, that won't ever be," she said. "They're all gone now – all my boys. Manson was the last."

***

The next morning, Tom and Melinda were on the front porch steps, soaking up what warmth they could from the November sun, when Texas rode up the drive.

Melinda ran to him.

Texas picked her up, gave her a kiss and put her down.

"Close your eyes," he said.

Melinda obeyed, and Texas took from his saddle bag a smaller version of his black hat.

She opened her eyes, squealed delight, put it on, hugged him, kissed his cheek, and ran into the house to show her mother.

Texas sat on the steps next to Tom.

"That was mighty nice of you," Tom said.

"Don't mention it. She's my favorite person in this world," Texas took out cigars. "How's the baby?"

"Doing real fine. You told Manse, didn't you?"

"Damn!" Texas shook his head. "I plumb forgot. We always got so much catch-up talking to do. But I'll try to remember."

"You going up there now?"

"On my way. Just wanted to stop by and see if that damn scalawag Heaton came out this morning like I heard he was planning to do."

"Yeah, Heaton and a whole platoon of soldiers were here just after dawn. He says we owe two hundred dollars more taxes. Gave me two weeks to pay it."

Texas took an envelope from his coat pocket.

"Here, take this," he said.

"What?"

"Dammit, take it. Don't argue with me."

"But, I've got – "

"Don't give me no crap that you-got-money. I know better."

Tom shrugged, smiled and took the envelope.

"Thanks, Texas," he said.

"Forget it. Just don't you never tell nobody – not Manse or nobody – that I ever gave you money. You hear?"

"Sure, Texas. I promise," Tom said, and put the envelope in his pocket. "Guess you noticed there aren't any soldiers around?"

"Yeah, I noticed," Texas said. "What happened?"

"A captain I'd never seen before was with Heaton this morning. He ordered the soldiers to leave. Said they weren't needed out here anymore."

"Don't you believe it – not for a flea-fart second, Tom. That Major Bartow is a sly son of a bitch. I'd bet my ass against a bowl of grits them soldiers ain't far from here," he looked across the road, toward the tree-lined hill top. "Probably up there watching us right now with field glasses. Bartow knows Manse ain't stupid enough to come here, but he figures that with the soldiers gone, you or Johnny might decide it was safe to go see him, and lead the soldiers to him. So for damn sure don't go up to the cave."

"What about you?"

"They've got their noses up my ass every time I leave Anderson, but they'll get tired and give up on me after a few hours in Pendleton."

***

After a long mid-day meal, Texas left the Blue Tavern, one mile north of Pendleton, and rode to Bennett's Inn, to dawdle upstairs with a woman until late afternoon when Elk Marett knocked on the door and told him that the three soldiers who were following him had returned to Anderson.

Then Texas rode north, doubling back three times to make sure he was still alone.

At the cave he and Manse unloaded supplies, then sat and drank and talked.

"This Major Bartow hasn't got but two things on his mind," Texas said. "To hang you, and destroy the Klan. And it seems like you're the main thing on his mind right now. It's pretty obvious he had Heaton levy new taxes so you'll come after him. But Tom says to tell you not to worry about the taxes. He's got enough money, so he plans to just wait a week, then go into town and pay Heaton."

"I been putting some thought to how to get that son-of-a-bitch Heaton," Manse drank. "Him being southern and still doing folks like he does makes him worse than if he was a bluebelly."

"There's truth to that," Texas said, "but it seems we both need to be putting our thoughts to doing something about this Major Bartow. He just ain't going to let up. He aims to get your ass, Manse, no matter what it costs." Texas reached in his coat pocket, took out several folded newspaper pages, and handed them to him. "I brought the *Intelligencier* story about him."

Manse focused on a quarter-page profile picture of Major Bartow.

"Looks kind of like a woman with all that long hair hanging out from under his hat," Manse said.

"Looks even more like one when he don't wear a hat, which is most of the time," Texas said. "Seems he likes for them blond curls of his to hang down."

"You've seen him?"

"Sure have. Seen him, and met him. He was in the Benson House Bar, so I went up to him and shook his hand and welcomed him to Anderson," Texas smiled the lie.

"Why the hell would you want to shake hands with a piece of yankee shit like him?" Manse asked.

"Like the Good-Book says, Manse – *know thy enemy*. And the more powerful my enemy is, the closer I want to get to him – for a real good look."

Manse nodded understanding.

"I know you're a good judge of men, Texas," he said. "In your business you have to be. So tell me about this Major Bartow?"

"I only talked to him a few minutes," Texas measured words. "But it don't take long to see he thinks real high of himself. And that wouldn't be a real problem, if he was just all-talk and blond curls. But when you read them newspaper stories, you'll see he's damn good at what he does – at what he done in The War – and what he done to Quantrill's Raiders."

"You're saying he's a man to be reckoned with – "

"I'm saying he's a man that needs killing as soon as possible – by me or you or the Klan – or all of us – before he has a chance to do to us what he says he's going to do to us," Texas removed another folded paper from his pocket and handed it to Manse.

"Sure seems he aims to get your ass quick as he can," Texas said.

Manse unfolded the poster.

"Five thousand?" Manse studied the poster. "I reckon you're right, Texas. I'd best get him and Heaton before they get me."

"I know how you feel about doing these kind of things alone, Manse," Texas said. "But maybe this time we best work together. Like I said, Bartow is just hoping you'll come after Heaton. There'll be a whole platoon of soldiers waiting for you." Texas finished his drink. "So don't do anything by yourself."

Manse did not reply.

"I figure we need to bide our time," Texas said. "Work out a real good plan."

"Yeah, maybe you're right, Texas," Manse said. "A plan to get Heaton – and Bartow – when they least expect it."

-13-

The door was half-open, so Texas Brown walked into Martin McCollum's room without knocking.

"I got a message that you wanted to see me right away," he said, then looked at the wide grin on Martin's face. "Are you in trouble — or just drunk?"

"I've had a few drinks," Martin's words slurred. "And there's no trouble — only good news. I asked Rebecca Largent to marry me, and she said *yes*. And I don't dare tell anyone except you, and I had to tell someone."

"Well, if that don't beat all," Texas took the glass of whiskey that Martin offered and felt jealousy, resentment and anger burn inside him. He had had plans for himself and Miss Rebecca Largent. He just hadn't had an opportunity to put them into action.

"Congratulations," he said, and drank. "You just better hope you get out of the state before Manse and Tom find out and hog-tie you and ram a Henry up your ass and pull the trigger twelve times."

"You aren't going to tell them, are you?" The fear in Martin's eyes was real.

"Me? Hell no. I got too much at stake. If Manse and Tom kill you, the Army will start looking into everything you did while you were here — and I sure wouldn't want that to happen," Texas smiled to himself, knowing that what he was saying was truly the only reason he hadn't already killed Martin for his share of the gold.

"Ah, the Texas Brown creed of loyalty," Martin said: "Never betray a man unless you are sure there is profit in it — and you won't get caught," he refilled their glasses. "Tell me, Texas — just between us — how long are you planning to wait before you sell-out Manse Jolly for the reward on his head?"

"What the hell do you mean?" Texas' tone was defensive. "I wouldn't do that."

"Then why are you staying in Anderson if you're not waiting for Manse's reward to go higher – so you can get even more gold when you turn him in?"

Texas glared at Martin, then took a deep breath.

"If you were sober and said that to me, I'd most likely bust your damn jaw right here, right now," Texas broke a grin. "But since you've trusted me enough to tell me that you're marrying Rebecca – and because you and me are partners, even if we ain't friends – and mostly because you're so goddamned drunk that when you wake up tomorrow you won't remember anything I say, I'll look-over your insults this time and tell you the honest-to-god true reason I'm staying here in Anderson," Texas' smile disappeared. "It's real simple, Martin – *I like my work*. I like doing whatever I want to do, to anybody I want to do it to, anytime I feel like doing it. Do you understand what I'm saying, Lieutenant?"

Martin felt uncomfortably sobered.

"Yes, I'm afraid that I do," he said. "And I guess that explains certain things – like the way that freedman, Sed Jacobs, and his sister died."

"That was a real nice night," Texas allowed his grin to return, and broaden.

"What about Manse Jolly? Does he enjoy his work as much as you do?"

"Manse kills for his own reasons. And I help him because he's valuable to me. So long as he's killing bluebellies, the Army chases after him and not the Klan."

"But once Major Bartow gets Manse Jolly – and he *will* get him – how long do you think it will take him to destroy the Klan and hang its leader – whoever he is?"

"I don't aim to wait around and find out," Texas said. "If they get Manse, I'm leaving. But meantime, I'll just keep on enjoying my work." He raised his glass. "Here's to Manse Jolly and the Ku Klux Klan – and to the bride and groom."

Texas and Martin drank, then Texas asked, "When are you and Missy Rebecca leaving?"

Martin hesitated, not sure he should answer, but then he shrugged his shoulders drunkenly and said, " I plan to pick up my trunk, and Rebecca, next Wednesday morning when Tom and

Johnny come to Anderson to buy supplies. I've purchased a horse and buggy and, by the time they return home, we will be married and across the state line. And the next day we will be on a train heading west."

"Well," Texas said, "if you're still planning on heading toward Texas, I might have a couple of ideas that will help you."

"Suggestions for my benefit?" Martin raised an eyebrow.

"Let's just say I'm interested in seeing to it you don't make some bad mistake like taking your bride to the wrong place – and creating problems for you – and for me," Texas said. "And since I've talked to lots of folks about living in Texas, you might be interested in some of what I've learned."

"Then, please, by all means, tell me," Martin said.

"Well, first of all, stay away from big places like Dallas and Houston and Austin."

"Why?" Martin asked. "I am rather partial to cities."

"And big towns are where there's most likely a Union Army Garrison," Texas said.

"I would feel much safer in Texas knowing that the Army was nearby," Martin said. "I would consider the presence of a military garrison a distinct advantage."

"And it's just that kind of thinking that makes me wonder how you yankees ever won The War. It just had to be dumb-luck," Texas said, and smiled, and refilled their glasses.

"I don't follow your logic," Martin said. "Precisely what do you mean?"

"Hell, Martin, if you settle down in some place like Houston or Dallas and start spending a lot of money – building a big house, or buying a big ranch – then you're bound to attract attention – and sooner or later a US Army Intelligence Officer – or somebody – is going to commence to wonder where you got all that money – and start poking around, asking questions – " Texas stopped talking and stared at Martin. "You following what I'm saying – ?"

"I think so," Martin said, and decided that perhaps, in this instance, Texas did indeed have Martin's best interest at heart – particularly since Texas's interests were the same as his own. Texas Brown didn't want Martin McCollum to be investigated in South Carolina or in Texas.

"I was hoping you might agree with my way of thinking," Texas said – pleased that he had Martin's attention and concern – both of which he needed if he was to direct Martin to a destination where Texas could find him when he wanted him.

"Presuming, then, that I do agree with your logic," Martin said. "Exactly what do you suggest that I do? Surely you've given that considerable thought."

"Not a lot," Texas said, "but some. And frankly I think you ought to head for a place in Texas I've heard about where a lot of ex-confederates have settled since The War – Milam and Robertson Counties."

"Are you seriously suggesting that I go live among ex-rebel soldiers?" Martin glared at Texas. "Is that some kind of joke? Or are you hoping that I'll be killed as soon as they hear my New York accent?"

"No, I'm not suggesting you go get yourself lynched by a bunch of rebels," Texas smiled.

"Then just what are you saying?" Martin asked.

"I'm saying that if I was you," Texas chose words carefully, "that if I was a ex-officer in the yankee army, I would go to a town called Cameron, Texas, and look up a man named Captain John Gray Smith, who was born here in Anderson District about forty years ago, and moved to Cameron about twenty years ago, and was a Confederate hero – "

"And he will welcome me with open arms – ?"

"Hell no," Texas said. "He won't want you settling anywhere near him, but he is bound to feel flattered that a yankee officer has heard of him, and come to him for advice. And because of that, he will most likely give you some advice that you can count on."

"Strange as it seems, that makes a lot of sense," Martin said. "I like it."

"Then, who knows, maybe you and me will meet up again out there," Texas smiled through his hate – and decided that he should plan to move to Cameron, Texas, sooner than he planned – and find Martin McCollum, wherever he settled – and kill him – and take his gold – and take Rebecca – whether she was willing or not.

***

***

When Tom and Johnny returned home the following Wednesday afternoon, Bonnie broke the news that Rebecca was gone.

Tom exploded.

"Dammit to hell, if I'd known, I could've stopped 'em. She must have told somebody what she was planning."

He looked at Bonnie.

"You swear she didn't tell you?"

"No. The only person she told was Mama Jolly. If you don't believe me, you go ask her yourself. She didn't breathe a word to me until after Rebecca and the lieutenant were gone. She says they went to Pendleton, to Preacher Edmunds, to get married."

Tom saddled his horse.

"You stay here, Johnny, and make sure some goddamnyankee don't run off with Melindy."

He galloped away.

When he knocked on the door of the parsonage in Pendleton, the white-fringed Rev. Albion Edmunds invited him inside and answered his questions. Yes, Rebecca and a young man had been there. Yes, he had married them. No, the young man wasn't in uniform. He was wearing civilian clothes. They were in a hurry. Left right after the ceremony. That was mid-morning. They were in a buggy. The preacher wasn't sure which way they went.

Tom nodded thanks and left.

They had almost a full day's head start. He couldn't catch them tonight even if he knew where they were headed, which he didn't.

He needed to talk to Manse.

Then it registered – he had left the farm thinking only of Rebecca – not of Union soldiers. Tom exhaled and held his breath, and heard the neigh from shadows beyond the church. They had followed him. If he wanted to go to Manse, he had to lose them.

He rode slowly north from Pendleton. One mile. Two. Three. Then he urged his horse to canter for a half-mile, until he reached a fork. There he left the road and entered thick woods where he stopped and waited.

Less than two minutes later, the Union Patrol that was following him arrived at the fork. A corporal dispatched three riders to the left. He and two others went to the right.

When he was sure they were gone, Tom rode deeper into the woods, toward the mountains.

***

Unsure of Manse's state of mind – and whiskey consumption – Tom approached the cave cautiously.

A fire was burning beside an empty bedroll at the entry to the shack.

"It's me, Tom," he said as he walked into the shack.

"You sure you weren't followed?" Manse said as he stepped from shadows at the back of the cave.

"Nobody trailed me," Tom tried to remain calm.

They sat by the fire.

Manse poured whiskey into cups.

"What's happened to bring you up here this time of night?" he asked.

"Rebecca has run off with that Lieutenant McCollum," Tom said.

"That bluebelly bastard!" Manse spat the words. "Any idea where he took her?"

"He hasn't took-her anywhere, Manse. Leastwise it doesn't appear he forced her."

Manse's head pounded. He didn't want to hear this.

"You sure?" he asked.

"Positive. I talked to preacher Edmunds. He married them in Pendleton this morning. And by now they've got a full day's head-start, going who knows where."

"Don't worry, Tom, I'll go after them. And when I catch 'em, I'll kill McCollum and bring Rebecca back home."

"I don't think – "

Manse held up his hand. Faint sound burned his ears. He blew out the lantern and grabbed his rifle.

Silence followed.

Then a voice from outside the cave said, "Manse? It's Texas."

Manse re-lit the lantern.

Texas walked inside.

"I thought I'd best bring you some supplies tonight. It's getting harder and harder to get away from them patrols in daylight – " he interrupted himself and stared at Tom. "What the hell are you doing here?" he asked.

"I had to come tell Manse that Rebecca ran off with that bluebelly lieutenant."

"McCollum? God-damn. When?" Texas was sure his voiced surprise was convincing.

"This morning. While Johnny and I were in Anderson."

"Tom's got to stay here, to look after Bonnie and their baby and Mama," Manse said. "So I'm going after them and bring Rebecca back," he spat in the fire.

"Do you know where they went?" Texas felt nerves stretch taut.

"No – but I'll find 'em," Manse said.

"Now, just hold your horses a minute, Manse," Texas said. "Let's us think this thing out." Texas had carefully rehearsed his argument. "You don't have any idea where to even start looking for them – but you know I got ways of finding out what's going on in Anderson. Remember, I'm the one that found Larry's killers." Texas paused for his words to take effect. " Yankees don't keep secrets too good, so McCollum most likely told somebody where he was going. I'll find out and we can go after them together. Give me a day or two."

"They'll have too much of a start on us by then."

"Being two or three days in-back of them – and knowing where they're headed – is a hell of a lot better than leaving now and wandering blind from Atlanta-to-New-York-to-hell-and-god-knows-where-else trying to pick up their trail."

"Texas is right, Manse," Tom said, and nodded. "Let him see what he can find out."

"Okay. But don't waste any time."

"I won't," Texas finished his drink.

"Instead of staying here tonight," he said, "I think I'll head straight back to Anderson, so I can start asking questions first thing in the morning," he stood. "You going home tonight, Tom?"

"Yeah, I reckon I better. I'll ride part ways with you."

***

It was an hour after dawn when Texas Brown entered Union Army headquarters.

Captain Morris Holtzclaw looked up from his desk.

"I want to see Bartow," Texas said.

"Major Bartow is busy."

Texas leaned over the captain's desk.

"Now you listen to me real careful, soldier-boy," he said. "I ain't in your goddamned army, so I don't give a sack of sow shit how many bars you got on your shoulder – I'm telling you to get off your ass and go tell Bartow that Texas Brown wants to see him. I don't think the Major will look too kindly on you if he finds out I was here asking to see him and you didn't tell him."

The captain went into Major Bartow's office.

Only seconds passed before he reappeared.

"The Major will see you at once, Mister Brown."

"Thank you, Captain," Texas said and walked into the major's office.

Bartow's face was covered with lather. A black man was shaving him.

"Good morning, Mister Brown. Sit down. I'll be with you in a minute."

"I don't have a minute."

Bartow eased the razor hand away.

"Very well, what is it?"

"Tell him to leave."

"Now see here, Brown, I'm – "

"Now you see-here, Bartow, goddammit, I got important things to tell you, so you get that nigger the hell out of here. I don't talk in front of niggers."

"Hand me that towel, and wait outside," Bartow said, and the black man left.

Bartow wiped away lather.

"All right, he's gone," he said. "Now, what the hell is so important?"

"I just thought you ought to know that Tom Largent left his farm last night and gave your patrol the slip near Pendleton and went to meet Manse Jolly."

"Where is Largent now?"

"He got home about three hours ago."

"And precisely what do you suggest I do with this important piece of information?"

Texas lowered his voice.

"If you arrest Tom Largent, then sooner or later one of three things will happen. Either he'll tell you where Manse is hiding. Or Manse will try to bust Tom out of the stockade and your soldiers can get him when he tries. Or Manse will leave South Carolina, hoping that when he's gone you will ease-up on his family. Whichever one of those things happens, you'll be rid of Manse Jolly."

"Very well thought out, Mister Brown. I can hold Largent for a year if I want to."

"Just one thing, Major – "

"Yes?"

"Don't mention my name. I had nothing to do with this. Is that clear?"

"Yes. That is very clear, Mister Brown."

"Good," Texas said and stood.

"But of course," he added, as he put on his hat, "if, as a result of what I've told you, you do capture Manse Jolly, I will damn sure expect the reward."

"You will be entitled to it, Mr. Brown," Bartow smiled. "And I will see that you receive it."

***

The gloved fist smashed into Tom Largent's face.

He struggled against the manacles that held his wrists behind his back.

"Once again," Lowell Bartow said. "Where did you go last night?"

"To look for my sister – "

Bartow's fists pounded Tom's stomach.

When he doubled over with pain, the soldiers on either side of him braced him upright.

Bartow smashed his knee into Tom's groin.

"I know all about your sister and McCollum," he said, "and I don't give a damn about them. What I want to know is where you went after you eluded our patrol."

Tom said nothing.

"Under Military Law, I can hold you for a year, Largent. I might even try you as Jolly's accomplice and hang you," Bartow paused. "Now, tell me – where is he?"

Tom spat out a bloody tooth.

"No matter what you do to me, I can't tell you something I don't know," he said.

"Perhaps your memory will improve with time."

Bartow turned from Tom to Captain Holtzclaw.

"Put him in the stockade. Interrogate him every morning and afternoon."

***

Inside the cave, Manse stared at the fire, took a long drink to ease his head, and listened to Texas Brown.

"You and me simply can't leave and go looking for Rebecca now, Manse," Texas said. "With Tom in the stockade, we need to think about what's best for your folks."

It was the fourth time in this conversation that Texas had made his point, and he was sure now that Manse would not leave.

Manse nodded.

He had heard the words, but his mind was on Tom.

"What are they doing to him, Texas?"

"I hear they beat him up pretty bad. Sometimes twice a day."

"Who does?"

"Bartow. Personal interrogation, he calls it."

Manse shook his head, trying to clear it.

"I got to get Tom out of there, Texas," he said.

"That's just what Bartow is hoping you'll try, Manse," Texas said – and decided he needed to say it all over again. "Bartow knows Tom is your best friend, that's why he arrested him. Now he figures you'll try to bust Tom out – or you'll give yourself up in exchange for the yankees letting Tom out – or you'll leave the state and run away."

Texas handed Manse a cigar, and repeated the argument yet again.

"But if you do any of those things, Manse, Bartow wins. If you try to bust Tom out, you'll be killed. If you give yourself up, Bartow will hang you – and most likely hang Tom, too. And if you leave, he can take credit for running you out of the state."

"Then what do you think I ought to do?"

It was the question Texas had been waiting for.

"Do exactly what Bartow don't expect you to do, Manse: Raise holy hell! Kill more yankees than you ever did before. Keep them bluebelly soldiers scared – and I'll stir up the Klan to keep the niggers scared. Between us, we'll drive Major Lowell Fart-ow plumb crazy."

Manse smiled, then stared at Texas.

"You think maybe Captain Phillips might turn Tom loose if Bartow wasn't around?"

"I'd wager he would," Texas said. "But Bartow's not going nowhere. He's gonna stay right here long as it takes to get you."

"You mean if I don't kill him first," Manse broke a laugh. "I never shot a yankee major before – "

Texas felt success draw closer.

"Well, I've been studying on it since the last time you talked about killing Bartow, and while I still favor the idea, it ain't gonna be easy to do, Manse," he said. "Bartow keeps a squad of his best men with him all the time. Sort of an *honor guard* assigned to protect him," Texas hesitated as if he were just now thinking of what he had already planned to say.

"But it would surely be a pure-jesus-blessing," he said, "if you could ever somehow figure a way to kill him."

Texas drank.

"While you been studying-on-it," Manse said, "I been getting a plan worked out in my mind." He paused to think. "Tell me, Texas: Do you know exactly how many men Samuel Heaton has got guarding him?"

"Whit says twenty men stay out at his plantation all the time. Heaton's scared shitless of you since he taxed your farm again."

Texas furrowed his brows.

"But I thought you were talking about a plan for killing Bartow," he said.

"I am," Manse smiled. "But first I want to make that yankee hero shit in his boots – so I'm going to kill Samuel Heaton – just to show the Major that not even twenty yankee soldiers can stop Manse Jolly – that I can blow his guts open anytime I take a notion to."

-14-

Samuel Heaton sat at a desk in the library of the Ezekiel Dickerson Plantation home which he had purchased, furnishings included, at tax auction.

And whether the damned Confederate die-hards of Anderson District liked it or not, his ownership was absolutely legal.

They were such a self-righteous bunch, these rebels, still refusing to accept defeat despite the fact that their pompous asses had been flayed by a superior Union Army. How dare they behave toward him as if he were some kind of traitor when, in fact, *they* were the traitors. He was Southern, just as they were, and he took pride in that heritage, but above all, he was a supporter of the Union of States that made America strong.

And Samuel Heaton knew that his attitude was not unique.

Thousands of other Southerners had pledged no allegiance to the Confederacy, and asserted no belief in what it represented.

In the minds of men like himself, The War, which had left 700,000 dead, was an abomination – an historical obscenity that had damned little to do with any great political differences between the North and the South. Those differences were a fiction created by rich Southron plantation owners who, before The War, constituted a mere five percent of the white population – yet owned more than seventy-five percent of all the land in the South.

The rest was owned by small farmers who had few if any slaves. And *they* had been far from unanimous in support of secession. True, in the referenda of 1861, sixty percent of them had favored leaving the Union, but that meant that forty per cent of white Southern landowners had opposed secession – a sizable segment of the population whose sentiments the Confederacy chose never to acknowledge.

As an example, in the election of 1863, candidates opposed to The War had actually won seats in the Confederate Congress, but were refused their elected places on the grounds that their opposition to The War had made them "traitors unfit to hold political office."

Samuel Heaton finished his fourth brandy of the evening, and snorted a laugh. How ironic, he thought, that the right of dissent – the right on which the Confederacy based its argument for secession from the Union – was held in such contempt by its leaders.

The War had been waged to protect the interests of large wealthy white plantation owners – but it was small white landowners who fought and died – most of them conscripted into the Confederate Army by Jefferson Davis because there weren't enough volunteers willing to fight to defend the rich-men's land. In fact, in a blatant display of disparity between rich-whites and less-affluent-whites, the Conscription Law exempted from Military Draft and Service one white male for every twenty-two slaves he or his family owned.

Samuel Heaton, and thousands of other educated, independent-thinking southerners, knew that the Southron-Planters had promoted The War to preserve their property and their way of life.

And it was their leaders who, even in defeat, were now writing *Gazetteer* articles praising "Confederate gallantry and heroism, and the honor of the great lost-cause" – articles written in comfortable homes, ownership of which they had retained solely because they had hidden away sufficient wealth to pay all levied taxes.

In Samuel Heaton's opinion, the post-war attitude of these ex-Confederates was outrageous.

He and his family – along with thousands of other Carolinians – had refused to swear allegiance to The Confederate States of America. And for their stance, they had been ostracized and persecuted – and worse. Three of his cousins had been arrested and charged with aiding the Union cause by helping freedmen find their way across the mountains to join the Union Army in Tennessee and West Virginia. One was hanged. The other two spent the rest of The War in prison making boots for rebel soldiers.

And during The War, Southern Union sympathizers like his family, were forced to provide meat and crops for the Confederate Army, and to pay exorbitant loyalty-affirmation-taxes to support the Confederate government.

Because of this, Samuel Heaton reasoned, it was only fair that the Union Army, which, after all, had won The War, should now take supplies in the same manner from Southern farmers, and tax Southerners for war reparations and all the administrative costs of governing the defeated Southern states.

He had no love for those Southerners who had persecuted him and his family. And now, because his allegiance had been to the victors, he had secured a position of responsibility and power to administer the laws under which the South must live.

They could call him a scalawag for working as a tax collector – but he was convinced that what he was doing was exactly what Southerners would be doing throughout America if *they* had won The War.

It was, he guessed, too much to expect that such men as Manse Jolly could understand his Unionist sympathy. The Jolly and the Largent families had lived for too many generations in the Piedmont shadow of plantation-owning, slave-owning Southrons – absorbing belief in their so-called codes of honor – and eventually following them into the madness of The War.

Samuel Heaton felt his bowels cramp.

He had suffered chronic dysentery ever since Major Bartow ordered him to re-impose taxes on the Jolly farm. He wasn't exactly sure how fear of Manse Jolly could cause loose bowels, but he was convinced there was a definite correlation.

Samuel Heaton stood.

Through the window, he could see the two soldiers standing guard on the verandah. He left the lamp burning on the desk. The Lieutenant in charge of the platoon of men assigned to protect the Heaton home had ordered that lamps in the downstairs rooms remain lit all night.

Samuel Heaton walked from the library into the foyer, nodded to the two soldiers guarding the front door, then went upstairs.

Only one lantern illuminated the second floor hallway.

He took out his watch. It was almost one in the morning. His family had been asleep for hours. He opened the door to the privacy-room, went in, lit a candle, opened another door, entered the toilet-cubicle, closed the door and raised the lid of the toilet, lowered his trousers and sat.

Not until he moved into this house had he ever used a toilet indoors, and apart from its convenience, there was nothing exceptional about the facility – just a pail beneath an oval opening in a wooden seat with a lid that closed tightly, to contain odors until servants (former slaves) emptied the bucket.

Samuel Heaton used imported cloth-paper to wipe himself, then stood, pulled up his trousers, opened the cubicle-door – and stared into the candle-lit eyes of Manson Sherrill Jolly.

Samuel Heaton's bowels moved again.

He opened his mouth – but before he could shout, Manse slid the bayonet blade into his throat, cutting off all but gurgling sounds.

Then Manse withdrew the bayonet and shoved it into Heaton's stomach, forcing it upward into his heart.

Samuel Heaton was dead before Manse lowered him to the floor beside the toilet.

Manse left the bayonet in his victim, blew out the candle, and retraced his steps from the privacy-room, along the empty upstairs hallway, down the servants' stairs, through the pantry, into the cellar, where he waited until he heard sentries pass the outside cellar-hatch, then he crept out, crawled behind bushes to the garden, and moved from shadows to trees, into the woods, for a mile, to his horse, and rode away.

***

Alone at a corner table in the Benson House Dining Room, Captain Ralph Phillips was finishing breakfast. He would have preferred to continue his practice of drinking his morning coffee, with whiskey, in the Benson House Bar, but since Major Lowell Bartow's arrival in Anderson, the bar was not allowed to serve Army Personnel until afternoon.

And that was just one of many major changes that Major Bartow had made. He had commandeered everything in the captain's office, including Phillips' large desk and comfortable chair. He had been relegated to use of a small table which had been brought from the outer office.

Though technically Ralph Phillips still commanded the Anderson District Army Garrison, Bartow obviously intended to make him ineffectual – even unnecessary – as soon as possible. His orders were routinely countermanded, and his authority was more eroded everyday.

All of this made Ralph Phillips angry – though not angry enough to confront Bartow, and certainly not stupid enough to try to file complaints with his superiors in Greenville, Charlotte and Washington – the ones who had sent him to this hell-hole, in the first place – and who seemed to delight in making his position as uncomfortable as possible.

But he was angry enough to spend much of his time during the day – and even more when drinking at night – devising means to rid himself of the plague of Lowell Bartow.

If he could retain his composure, perhaps the opportunity would arise to turn this entire damn situation to his advantage without actually resorting to his homicidal fantasies.

Captain Ralph Phillips drank the last of his fourth cup of coffee, which only increased his need for a cup of whiskey, and glanced across the dining room at the table occupied by Major Bartow and Captain Holtzclaw.

His thoughts were suddenly interrupted by two lieutenants who rushed into the dining room, braced themselves at attention in front of Bartow's table, and saluted.

Captain Holtzclaw returned the salute.

"What do you want, Lieutenant?" he asked.

"Sir, Manse Jolly killed Mister Samuel Heaton last night – sir."

"With twenty men on guard?" Lowell Bartow pushed away his breakfast plate. "Just how in the name of God did he manage that?"

"He slipped past sentries during evening mess, when the perimeter was thin," one of the lieutenants said. "We found evidence that he hid in the food-storage cellar of the house for several hours. Then he went up to the second floor by way of the servants' stairway after the family was asleep."

"And then – don't tell me, let me guess – he hid under Heaton's bed –" Bartow spat sarcasm.

"Not exactly, sir," the other officer said. "We think he waited in a linen closet in the upstairs hallway. The guards posted inside the house report that Mister Heaton worked in his study until almost one o'clock, then went upstairs to the privacy room to use the toilet before going to bed. Jolly murdered him there."

"You are sure it was Jolly?" Captain Holtzclaw said.

"Yes, sir. He obviously wanted us to know that he did it. He left a Confederate bayonet in the victim – and one of his Wanted Posters by the body. And another one in the cellar."

"I'll be a son-of-a-bitch," Bartow shook his head, then looked across the room at Ralph Phillips.

"Just what the hell are you smiling about, Captain?" Bartow said angrily. "You find murder amusing?"

"No, sir," Phillips said. "I just can't help smiling in amazement at the ability of this man, Jolly, to slip past even the tightest security."

Lowell Bartow was not amused.

"Perhaps, Captain," he said, "if you had been less amazed by Mister Jolly, you could have caught and hanged him months ago."

Ralph Phillips bristled, stood and walked to Bartow's table.

"With all due respect, Major, I directly attribute my inability to capture – or kill – Manse Jolly to an acute lack of manpower," he said. "I had barely two platoons to cover the entire district. But you, sir, command two companies of men who were able to defeat four hundred of Quantrill's Raiders – so, in all fairness to me, sir, may I ask, why haven't *you* been more effective against Jolly?"

Lowell Bartow glared at Ralph Phillips.

"The answer is quite simple, Captain," he said. "I do not yet know the area. And the men who have been here the longest – the men of the Anderson garrison – are under *your* command, and they spend most of their time at their desks – doing god knows what."

Major Bartow glared at Phillips.

"And while we're on this subject, Captain," he said, "I have yet to receive any worthwhile suggestions from you – based on your lengthy, if unsuccessful, experience with Jolly."

Ralph Phillips did not smile – except inwardly. This was the moment he had waited for.

"With the Major's permission, sir," he said, "I do have a few suggestion which may be worthy of your consideration."

"By all means, Captain. Let's hear them."

"I recommend, sir, that you allow me to relinquish my command of the Anderson garrison to you – formally transferring my troops to your field command – and integrating into your fighting units my men who know the district. I further suggest that you place squads or platoons of your cavalry under the command of my officers who know the areas where Jolly – and the Klan – are most likely to be found. And place your aides, and their aides, at those desks in the headquarters, to take care of the paper-work."

Ralph Phillips paused, awaiting reaction.

Lowell Bartow motioned him to sit at the table.

A waiter poured coffee for them.

Bartow lit his pipe.

"I have to admit I rather like those suggestions, Captain," he said. "I admire your willingness to forfeit formal command of the garrison, for the sake of accomplishing my mission here," he sipped coffee. "In all fairness, Phillips, I may have misjudged you. I have felt that you resented my coming here and taking charge. Usurping your authority. Taking over your office. And your desk."

Ralph Phillips did not say what he was thinking – that the word *resentment* no longer adequately described his feeling for Major Lowell Bartow – *hatred* came closer.

But now was not the time to express those feelings.

"We both have our missions here, Major," Phillips said.

"And if I formally relieve you of command, Captain, and follow your other suggestions, what then do you see as *your mission*?"

"In the absence of Lieutenant McCollum, whose reports you and I agree were valuable, I would like to consider myself your *de facto* Intelligence Officer. Thanks to information McCollum shared with me – and to my own sources, including Sergeant Jerlier, who was killed by Jolly – I believe I know more about this district, and the people who live here, than anyone else."

Ralph Phillips paused.

"And as my *de facto* Intelligence Officer, what precisely would be your duties?" Bartow asked.

"Specifically, sir," Captain Phillips said, "I would request a platoon of men to ride with me in pursuit of Jolly anywhere I choose within the Anderson District. We could follow leads wherever they take us – returning to headquarters only once a week, to report directly to you."

"An excellent tactical concept, Captain," Lowell Bartow said. "You have my permission to implement it immediately. You may disperse all of your garrison troops into my units, as you see fit. And you may have any of my men you want to serve in your special Intelligence Platoon – except, of course, Captain Holtzclaw and my personal staff."

"With all due respect, sir, I would like to have my garrison headquarters platoon serve with me. They know me well. And I know them all by name. Unless you have some objection, sir."

Lowell Bartow stood.

"Consider your request approved, Captain," he said. "As soon as I get to my office, I will issue general orders to create the changes. And I will designate Fridays for staff meetings. All troops will assemble here for briefings two hours prior to Retreat," Major Lowell Bartow smiled – almost grinned.

"By god, Captain Phillips," he said, "with this idea of yours, we may have Manse Jolly swinging on the gallows in a short time."

Captain Phillips returned Bartow's smile, saluted, then walked from the Benson House Dining Room.

Now that Major Bartow had accepted as valid the plan he had devised, Ralph Phillips could set up command posts for his special platoon in Pendleton or Pickens or other nearby towns, in pleasant inns or boarding houses where the food was excellent and the supply of good whiskey virtually inexhaustible.

As far as Ralph Phillips was concerned, from now on he could leave the battles against Manse Jolly and the Klan for Major Lowell Bartow to fight.

***

Manse opened his eyes and sat up.

The shack was dark and cold. Only a few embers of the fire remained.

He wrapped the blanket around his shoulders, stirred the fire, added splinters of fatty pine, and blew on the coals.

The kindling blazed timidly. He put two small pieces of wood on the flame and waited for them to catch. Within a few minutes they had created limited light and warmth.

He picked up a canteen of water. It was frozen.

He picked up an empty canteen and walked to the stream at the cave's entrance, but the stream was now ice. He looked up and saw the fire's feeble glow reflected in stalactites of the frozen waterfall.

He returned to the shack and looked inside the coffee pot. It was half filled – with frozen coffee. He placed it on the rock at the center of the fire, and guessed that it would take half an hour to thaw and come to a boil.

He uncorked a jug, picked it up, and drank.

The corn whiskey heated his throat and stomach.

At least it wasn't cold enough in the cave to freeze alcohol.

He took another drink, then added logs to the blaze. The fire and the whiskey's fire warmed and relaxed him.

He had arrived at the cave yesterday just before sundown, built a fire, made coffee, heated and eaten pone and dried beef.

Then he had slept deeply – more from exhaustion than from the whiskey he drank after his meal.

Manse took his daddy's watch from the inside pocket of his tunic. He had been asleep more than six hours – longer than he had slept at any one time since he was last here in the cave – almost a month ago – near the end of November.

That was the last time Texas had brought supplies.

And while they were together, Texas had informed Manse that Major Bartow had not only raised the reward on him to six-thousand-dollars in gold, but had also issued orders that anyone caught harboring Manse Jolly would be imprisoned in the army stockade for two years – without trial.

Rather than deterring Manse, that news had spurred him to action.

He had rested in the cave for only two days, rather than a week. Then he had ridden to Rogers Crossroads, midway between Anderson and Greenville, and watched and waited until a patrol of Union soldiers bivouacked in nearby woods. He attacked as they were finishing evening mess, first killing the perimeter guard, then killing four of the five remaining soldiers as they scrambled to return fire.

He shot the sixth member of the squad in the stomach.

It would take the man two days to die – sufficient time to report the identity of his killer.

Then Manse ranged north and south along the Seneca River, where heavily wooded terrain offered places to hide during the day.

At night, he set up ambushes at locations that provided easy escape routes. Sometimes he had to wait two or three nights before a patrol arrived. And he usually contented himself with killing only the lead rider – leaving the others firing wildly in disarray while he disappeared into the woods.

As patrols along the Seneca increased in size and frequency, he moved west, to the banks of the Tugaloo River – then north-east toward Pendleton and Pickens, and south toward Abbeville – killing whenever he could find a target.

And when he could no longer go without sleep, Manse relied on Whit Whitfield for a place to rest.

He always waited until after midnight, when Whit's wife and smaller children were asleep, then he left his horse in the barn with the older boy, Malachi, and went to the back door and rapped lightly.

Regardless of the hour, it was as if Whit had been sitting in the kitchen waiting for him.

Waiting with supper leftovers and a jug.

And Whit did most of the talking while Manse ate and drank.

"It's just that since folks heard what happened to Tom, they know that if they help you, Bartow will jail them, too – and leave their families to fend for theyselves."

"I understand, Whit," Manse said. "And I'm grateful to you for taking me in. I don't ever go to anybody's house anymore except yours. I can't take a chance they might try to collect that reward while I'm sleeping."

"Well, even if they're afraid to take you in, Manse, the folks around here still admire you as much as ever. Only people you got to worry about are them who ain't from around here." Whit filled their glasses. "You know I damn sure wouldn't turn you in for no amount of yankee gold, Manse. When you're up in my attic, you're safe as in your own bed."

Secure in the cave or relaxed on the bedroll in Whit's attic – Manse was warmed by the thought of comrades he could count on, and the knowledge that he was doing what he had set out to do – fighting His-War against the yankees – on His-Terms.

Then suddenly he felt a wave of sadness.

Bartow still hadn't released Tom, which meant that Bonnie and Johnny and Melinda – and his sweet Mama – were alone today, without him or Tom –

And they shouldn't ever be alone – especially not on Christmas Day.

***

Every Friday, Texas Brown visited Tom Largent at the stockade.

Every Saturday, he delivered food and supplies to the Jolly farm.

It was something he enjoyed doing.

The Jolly family had become his family. With both Tom and Manse away, they relied on him – and he liked that.

Until now, he had never felt that he really had a family to celebrate Christmas with.

And this year he could certainly afford to be generous.

His income from the Ku Klux Klan – whose two-hundred white robed members paid more dues, rode more often, and looted more than ever from their victims – had made Texas Brown a wealthy man.

He had not even touched the Confederate that gold that he and Martin McCollum had acquired.

And Texas was not only becoming wealthier and wealthier each month, he was having a hell of a good time doing it.

The night after Manse Jolly murdered Samuel Heaton, the Heaton family fled to Pickens, to stay with relatives until they could sell their home.

Two nights later, Texas and his Klansmen raided the unguarded mansion, looted it and burned it to the ground.

A week later, a freedwoman who had been seen in the company of a white soldier was abducted, tortured and flogged to death.

The following night, the soldier was ambushed and killed.

The incidents of flogging and torture were outnumbered only by lynchings.

And on his visits to the Jolly home, Texas found respite from his heavy schedule – assuring Bonnie that Tom was "holding-up-pretty-good" – and telling Melinda stories about cowboys and Indians – helping Johnny plan the week's work – and feeding lunch to Maude Jolly in her bedroom.

"Don't you fret, Mama Jolly," he told her. "Tom's gonna be turned loose soon. And them yankees won't never catch Manson."

"I wish I could believe that," Maude Jolly said.

"You can believe it, cause I promise you it's true," Texas said. "So you go ahead now and eat some more soup. Bonnie made it with okra, the way you and me like it."

"You're mighty sweet, Texas – trying to ease my woes like you do," she said. "You remind me so much of all my boys."

***

"As you requested last week, sir, I have compiled a report on this man Texas Brown," Lieutenant Francis Marion Pearson handed papers to Major Bartow.

"It is comprised mostly of rumors," he said. "Rumors alleging that Brown is involved with both the Klan and Jolly – but no specific evidence."

"No proof?" Major Bartow scanned the pages. "Do you have any idea why Lieutenant McCollum's intelligence files had so little on Brown?"

"No, sir. Except that he no doubt ran into the same problems I am having," Pearson said. "Getting people around here to talk about Texas Brown is about as difficult as getting them to talk about Manse Jolly."

"Is there any pattern to Brown's activities?"

"More than just a pattern, sir. A time-table. On Fridays he visits Largent at the stockade. Saturdays he buys supplies and takes them to the Jolly farm. He eats lunch there, and stays a couple of hours, then rides north – and disappears. No one sees him again until

Monday morning when he returns to Anderson. He manages to elude all the men I assign to follow him."

Major Bartow lit his pipe.

"In my unit I have four scouts I personally recruited – Choctaw Indians who can track a squirrel across granite. I will assign them to follow him next weekend – and we will find out precisely where the elusive Mister Brown goes."

***

Losing a yankee patrol was something Texas Brown did with ease – whether he was headed to a Klan meeting or to visit Manse.

But this Saturday afternoon, things were different.

Not until he had dismounted to lead his horse the last mile to the cave did he sense anyone trailing him.

The riders following him were better than any yankee army trackers.

Most likely they were Bartow's Indian scouts.

Whoever they were, they were close – very close.

If Texas eluded them now, they would return to Bartow and report where Texas had led him, and these mountains would be full of troops tomorrow.

And even if he and Manse managed to get away, Texas would become a wanted man.

Which was something he did not want.

Things were going too well.

Texas paused and thought about his alternatives – then made a decision and continued down the ravine toward the waterfall.

At the cave entrance, he and Manse shook hands.

"I just now discovered I'm being followed," Texas said. "Probably more than one. They'll most likely come in close to see for sure if it's you I'm meeting."

"I've thought about what to do if this ever happened," Manse said. "You build up the fire, put on a fresh pot of coffee, and keep talking like I'm still in here with you. And when you hear gunshots, you just start firing toward the entrance to the cave."

Texas nodded.

Manse picked up his rifle, went to the back of the cave, scrambled onto a ledge, then climbed up rocks to an opening at the top, squeezed through it and emerged on the ridge overlooking the ravine.

Three Union soldiers were making their way, tree-to-tree, toward the cave entrance.

Manse braced his rifle on a rock and put the lead-man's heart in his v-notch-sight, squeezed the trigger, and the man was dead.

Texas began firing from the cave.

The other two soldiers ducked behind rocks.

Manse smiled, aimed and fired twice. Two bullets split open the second soldier's head.

Manse aimed, fired again, and the battle was over.

He scrambled down to the ravine.

Texas came out of the cave.

"Damn good shooting," he said, and grinned.

"They never even knew I was up there," Manse examined the bodies.

"This one is close to my size. I'll take off his uniform. I've got an idea I'll need it for," he said.

Texas collected the soldiers' pistols and rifles.

"Ain't no telling what Bartow's liable to do when his Indian Scouts don't come back from trailing me," Texas said.

"I'll take care of that," Manse said. "Tonight I'll deliver their corpses to the yankees –"

He nodded to Texas.

"I reckon you ought to ride to Pendleton and spend the night there," he said. "That way, you can prove where you've been."

***

"Just what the hell did you have me arrested for, Major?" Texas Brown shouted.

"You are not under arrest, Brown. Merely detained for questioning."

"Well, this here goddamn lieutenant must have misunderstood you," Texas spat the words. "He and three soldiers knocked me down soon as I got off my horse. Then they took my pistols. Manacled me. And *said* I was under-arrest."

"Remove the manacles, Lieutenant Pearson," Major Bartow ordered.

"Yes, sir," Lt. Pearson said, and obeyed.

Texas rubbed his wrists.

"Sit down, Brown. And answer my questions, or I will put you in the stockade with Largent," Bartow said, and frowned and sat on the corner of his desk.

"Where did you go yesterday?" he asked.

"To the Jolly farm, like I do every Saturday," Texas sat.

"And after you left there?"

"To Pendleton. I stayed the night there."

"Can you prove that?"

"Matter of fact I can – Bartow – "

"*Major* Bartow to you."

"You want *Major* in front of *Bartow*, you put *Mister* in front of *Brown*," Texas said.

"Very well, Mister Brown. Can you prove you were in Pendleton last evening?"

"I sure can, Major. While I was there, I met up with the man whose job you took – Captain Phillips. We were both staying at Four Corners Inn. Fact is, we had a couple of drinks together after dinner. They have real good food there."

Bartow looked at Lieutenant Pearson.

"Do you know where Captain Phillips' platoon is operating?" he asked.

"When the captain left after Retreat on Friday, he said he would be in the Pendleton area last night," Lt. Pearson said. "And I believe he was proceeding to Pickens today, sir, for an indeterminate period."

"Take a squad to Pickens, Lieutenant. Find Captain Phillips and ask him if he can corroborate Mister Brown's account of his whereabouts last night. Report to me as soon as you return."

"Yes, sir," Lt. Pearson saluted and left the office.

Texas took out a cigar.

"Since it appears like I'm gonna be setting here quite a few hours waiting for that lieutenant to get back from Pickens," he said, "do you mind if I smoke, Major?"

"Go ahead" Bartow lit his pipe.

"I have a feeling, Mister Brown," he said, "that Captain Phillips will corroborate your story. If he does, then I am at a loss to understand what has happened."

"Tell me what it is that you don't understand, Major, and maybe I can help," Texas lit his cigar. "It ain't like I haven't showed you before that I'm willing to help out when I can."

"Yes, you were indeed of value to me in the matter of Mister Largent – though I'm still not sure *why* you chose to furnish me with that information."

"Like I just said, Major – I wanted to show you that I was willing to help out when you needed me."

Lowell Bartow raised his eyebrows, and stared at Texas Brown for several seconds before speaking.

"You know, of course, Mister Brown, that from time to time, I have you followed," he said.

"Yeah, I do," Texas smiled. "Frankly, it would be kind of hard *not* to notice a squad of Union cavalry trying to ride up my ass."

Lowell Bartow did not return the smile.

"But somehow, Mister Brown, you manage to elude my men whenever you want to," he said. "And that has made me damned curious about why you are so careful to prevent anyone knowing where you go and what you do."

"I told you the first time we met, Major, that I like my privacy – and that what I do and where I go is nobody's damn business but my own," Texas said, then paused and held Bartow's stare.

"I'm not violating any of your Occupation Army Laws, Major," he said. "So why are you so all-fired interested in what I was doing last night?"

Lowell Bartow hesitated, then decided to continue.

"Yesterday I sent three men to follow you," he said. "They were my best trackers. Choctaw Indians."

"They must be real good," Texas said. "I never noticed anybody at all behind me yesterday."

"Well, I assure you they were trailing you."

"Then they ought to be able to tell you that I went to Pendleton."

"Unfortunately, they can't tell me anything," Bartow said. "They were killed. All three of them."

"And you think I killed them? Your three best scouts? All by my lonesome? Is that what this is all about?"

"That was my reason for having you brought here for questioning – yes," Major Bartow looked perplexed.

"But your ability to account for your whereabouts – using one of my senior officers as your witness – has me genuinely confused," he said.

"Maybe we can figure it out, Major, if you'll just tell me everything that happened."

"All I know for certain, Mister Brown, is that about four o'clock this morning, near Old Forge on the Seneca River, one of our patrols met a rider who was leading three horses. When the patrol drew close, they saw a body tied across the saddle of each horse. When the rider was a few yards from the patrol, my men recognized him. It was Manse Jolly," Lowell Bartow paused.

"Go on, Major. What happened next?"

"My men opened fire. Jolly released the horses, drew his revolver, returned fire, and rode away."

"And the bodies on the horses were your three scouts?" Texas asked.

"Yes. The men I had sent to follow you."

Texas shook his head.

"Major, I swear to you, I wasn't nowhere near Old Forge last night," said.

Texas raised his right hand.

"I swear to you I was in Pendleton."

"As I said, Mister Brown, I am sure that Captain Phillips will confirm that you were where you claim you were. You would be a fool to tell me so blatant a story if it were a lie. So I will not hold you," Major Bartow said.

"I sure appreciate that, Major," Texas said.

"But I must admit yet again," Lowell Bartow exhaled a long sigh, "that I am dumbfounded by what occurred. Obviously my three finest scouts lost you, and while they were trying to pick up your trail, Manse Jolly ambushed them."

"From what you say, it sure seems like that must've been what happened," Texas bit his lip to stop the smile.

"But that still leaves unanswered, Mister Brown, the question of how a squad of seasoned US Cavalrymen could fire more than fifty rounds at Manse Jolly at close range and not hit him," Major Bartow took a bottle and two glasses from his desk drawer.

"I simply do not know what to make of all this," he said, and poured drinks.

"Me neither, Major," Texas blew a thick cloud of smoke. "It surely is a mystery."

-15-

Texas Brown sat across the table from Tom Largent in the windowless guard room of the military stockade.

"Sorry I couldn't visit last Friday," he said. "I had to ride to Atlanta for a couple of days." He opened a hamper and handed Tom a jar. "I brought a basket of home cooked food, and a newspaper. And some lemonade Bonnie made special for you." He smiled. "I added a little corn-flavoring."

"Thanks," Tom said, and took a long drink. "That's mighty good," he said and wiped his mouth with the back of his hand. "It's sure been hot as hell in here."

"Hot-as-hell everywhere," Texas said. "The *Intelligencier* says that this June is the hottest in more than twenty years."

"I can believe it," Tom took another drink. "How's Bonnie? And the baby? And everybody?"

"All right, I reckon, considering they're all natural-worried about you. I still go out every Saturday, to take supplies and eat dinner," Texas said. "I sent all the regular supplies out by Whit Whitfield and Elk Marett last weekend when I was away. But I'll be going out tomorrow – back on my regular schedule."

Texas took a box of cigars from the hamper, removed two, and handed one to Tom.

"I try never to miss a visit with Mama Jolly, if I can help it," he said, and struck a match.

"You're a mighty good friend, Texas Brown," Tom bit off the end of the cigar. "I thank you for everything you do. I don't know how we could get along without you."

"Your folks are my family, Tom," Texas smiled. "I couldn't hardly do anything less than what I do." He held the match for Tom, then lit his cigar. "How are you doing?"

"Nobody's beat on me for a while, but it's still rough as hell being locked up in here," Tom lowered his voice. "How's Manse?"

"Still driving Bartow crazy."

"I mean, how does he look. Is he okay?"

"Well, to be real honest, he don't exactly look too healthy."

"You tell him I said for him to take care, you hear," Tom frowned. "And you be careful, too, Texas. Wouldn't want nothing to happen to you. You're the only contact I got with my folks, and the only contact Manse has got with anybody he can trust."

***

"Is Bartow still having you followed?" Manse asked.

"No. He stopped doing that after his three best scouts got killed by that southern hero, Manse Jolly," Texas said.

"He don't have any time to think about me," Texas laughed. "He's got too damn many other problems. On top of all the soldiers you been killing, and all the niggers the Klan flogs and lynches, there's been a whole mess of violent crimes – most of it by Lowdowners. The worst was last week. A whole gang broke into the Burgess sisters' house, down near Flat Rock Church and raped them two old ladies – both of 'em more than seventy-years-old. One doctor reckons they was raped maybe twenty times."

Texas shook his head.

"I tell you, Manse," he said, "it's plumb terrible what some men will do. But you can rest assured the Klan is gonna find out who done it and take care of them real good," he stretched out on his bedroll. "Of course this ain't the only part of the South where the yankees have got problems. Things are so bad, Congress has passed whole new bunch of laws called The Reconstruction Acts."

Texas frowned.

"*De-Struction-Acts* is more like it," he said. "Hell, they've even done away with state governments. Divided the ten Confederate states into five Military Regions. North and South Carolina is one, with a bluebelly general name of David Sickles as the dictator. Rumor is that Martial Law is next."

"You always did say things was going to get a lot worse before they ever got better," Manse took a drink. "Guess that's what accounts for all the yankee patrols I see, no matter which way I ride.

I don't dare bivouac in any one place for very long. And what with the bigger reward, I can't chance staying the night at anybody's house – unless I can get to Whit's place, which I'm not near all that often. Sometimes, I have to go two or three days without sleeping," Manse said. "Bartow sure is making things rougher than they were a while back. I reckon he's more hell-bent than ever to get me."

"You thought any more about getting him first?"

"Yeah, I keep thinking about lining his curly blond hair in my rifle sights when I see him on patrol one night."

"That ain't at all likely to happen," Texas said. "The Major quit riding anywhere at night after you killed Heaton. Spends three or four evenings a week at that fancy new gentlemen's club and whore house, either playing cards downstairs, or playing with the ladies upstairs. He's taken a room there, so he can stay all night."

Manse watched cigar smoke curl and looked for answers in memories of The War.

"Is there ever a time when Bartow assembles all the troops?" he asked. "All of them – with none out on patrol?"

"Yeah, there is," Texas said. "Once a week. At Friday's Retreat Ceremony on the courthouse square. That's when Captain Holtzclaw makes announcements about all the new laws, and how they're gonna hang you and destroy the Klan –and all that same old shit. Then Bartow gives the troops a talk. But if you're thinking you can kill him at Retreat, forget it – he's right smack in the middle of his Honor Guard and his officers. You wouldn't stand a chance of getting him in your sights."

"You're probably right," Manse refilled his cup. "That reminds me – I been meaning to ask you: Have you still got those explosives?"

"What explosives?"

"The ones you brought here in your saddle bags, and put in the back of the cave."

"Oh, those?" Texas felt uncomfortable. "No," he said, I took them to Elk Marett's place. All I got in them bags now is some money and personal things."

"Can you get me some explosives?" he asked.

"I reckon I can do that," Texas hesitated. "You got something special in mind?"

"Yeah," Manse smiled. "I got a plan for the yankee soldiers that patrol the Seneca River north of Three-And-Twenty Creek. "

***

Lowell Bartow looked up from the reports on his desk.
Francis Marion Pearson was standing in the doorway.
"What is it, Lieutenant?" the major asked. "You look ill."
"I feel ill, sir," Lt. Pearson walked into the office. "Early this morning, my patrol found five freedmen and two white men hanging by their heels from trees near Antreville. They were naked. They had been castrated – and their stomachs slit open. Their intestines were hanging down to the ground. But they were still alive. Barely." He sighed audibly. "We put them in a supply wagon and headed directly to the field clinic in Abbeville, but they died on the way."
"The Klan?"
"Yes, sir. Two crosses."
Lowell Bartow stood.
"Have my clerk telegraph an urgent request directly to General Sickles, asking him to grant me emergency powers to impose Martial Law in this district immediately."

***

Manse reined in his horse near the entrance to Three-And-Twenty Bridge on the Seneca River, dismounted and carried a bag of explosives to the span's mid-point and wedged it between a primary beam and an upright. Then he sat on the beam, lit a cigar, smoked and waited.

He had reconnoitered this crossing point regularly.

Every evening a union patrol – one sergeant, one corporal, and six troopers – came from the western side of the river, crossed the bridge and rode toward Pendleton.

This evening, they would not make it.

Manse exhaled a cloud of smoke and, despite summer's heat that had continued into September, he shivered – as if his throbbing head had exploded and sent slivers of ice through his body.

Manse reached inside his tunic and took a small flask from the pocket.

He opened it and drank.

The yankee posters said they wanted him dead-or-alive – but dead was the only way they would ever get him. And he had proven to them, over and over, that killing him wasn't going to be easy.

He had killed dozens of soldiers on patrol, and their comrades had fired hundreds of rounds at him, but he had never suffered a scratch.

Texas Brown said that folks called him "The One Man Army – Yankee Killer – Avenger of Southern Honor – The Man That Bullets Can't Touch."

And Manse knew that the Army called him by different names – "Renegade Killer – Outlaw – Murderer – Bushwhacker."

But to Manse it didn't matter what anyone called him – killing was what he had to do.

It was his only salvation –

The sound of hoof beats stirred him from thought.

He stood, touched the glowing tip of his cigar to the fuse, then ran from the bridge to his horse – mounted and rode two hundred yards – stopped and turned and watched.

The patrol reached the bridge and thundered across.

The explosion blew timbers and horses and men into the air, and dropped them onto rocks in the shallows below.

Manse slowly nodded, threw away his cigar stub, and rode east.

Before dawn, near Powdersville, he led his horse into a thicket, brought water from a creek, spread his bedroll, ate dried beef, and tried to sleep, but could not. Daylight was his enemy.

When darkness came, it brought rain.

Manse put on his cavalry oilskin and rode south, then west – inscribing a wide arc around Anderson.

All day Wednesday he hid in a root cellar, ate more dried meat, and drank a canteen of whiskey – but still could not sleep.

Night wiped clouds from the sky, and an almost-full moon emerged.

He left the Abbeville road south of Anderson and waited in the woods.

Half-hour later, on schedule, a Union patrol rode toward him. Manse lodged the lead rider in the v-notch of his rifle sight and squeezed the trigger.

The shot echoed.

The rider fell.

The others broke formation.

Manse fired twice more without aiming, then rode away, through woods, across fields, toward the road between Twiggs and Dean's Station – to Whit Whitfield's farm.

Whit opened the back door.

"Come on in," he said.

Manse ached with fatigue.

"Can I rest here a while?"

"Any time," Whit said, and took Manse's bed roll and led the way.

Manse followed him into the kitchen, then up a ladder, through a trap door, into the crawl-space between ceiling and roof.

Manse took off his gun-belt and tunic, and spread his bedroll.

In a few minutes, Whit brought him a plate of food and a jug of whiskey.

Manse looked down into the kitchen.

Whit's wife, Sara Jane, smiled up at him.

Manse nodded thanks.

"You look plumb tuckered out," Whit said.

"I am that," Manse said. "No sleep since Monday. If it's all right, I'd like to stay here until tomorrow."

"Stay long as you like. I'm going to a Klan meeting tonight. Any message for Texas?"

"Just tell him I'll see him next week at the usual place."

***

***

Manse awoke shivering and sweating – not sure how long he had slept – and, for a moment, not at all sure where he was.

No sound reached him.

He crawled to the trapdoor, slowly raised it, and looked down at Sara Jane Whitfield, seated at the kitchen table.

When the trapdoor opened, she stood and moved the ladder to it.

Manse picked up his gun-belt, slung it over his shoulder, and climbed down.

The kitchen was hot with supper smells.

"I'll fix you a plate," Sara Jane smiled. "Whit ate afore he left. I just fed the little kids and got them to bed," she nodded toward the closed door to the bedroom. "I fixed vegetable soup with ham-hock, cornbread and buttermilk. Hope it's to your liking."

"Sure smells good," Manse smiled. "But first I got to go wash up."

He walked out the back door into the welcomed cool of autumn night, to the outhouse where he hung his gun-belt on a peg, stripped, and emptied his bowels and bladder. Then he carried his clothes and gun-belt to the barn trough, laid them on the ground close by, pumped water and bathed, and put his clothes back on.

When he returned to the kitchen, Sara Jane Whitfield handed him a tray.

"Whit said he thinks you had best stay in the attic when you're here – even to eat. We got some real nosy neighbors not more than a mile away. They're all the time coming over here just to see what we're doing," she started up the ladder. "Hand me the tray when I get to the top."

When Manse lifted the tray up to her, he could not avoid looking up her skirt.

She wore nothing beneath it.

He followed her up the ladder, laid his gun-belt beside the bedroll, then sat.

She sat beside him and lit a candle.

"You sleep okay?" she asked.

"Yeah. Best I've slept in a while," Manse said, and looked at her. In the candlelight her freckles glowed orange.

"I hope the young'uns didn't bother you none." Her face flushed the color of her freckles. "I tried to keep 'em quiet as I could," she said.

"Didn't hear a sound," Manse began to eat.

"I've met your oldest boy," he said. "What's his name – Malachi?"

"That's right – Malachi," she smiled. "He spends most of his time out at the barn. Even sleeps out there. He's kind-of slow. Got the stutters real bad. Him and Whit don't get along too good."

Manse decided to change the subject.

"Don't recollect I've ever seen your littler ones," he said.

"They're usually asleep by the time you get here at night. And you usually leave afore they wake up. You don't usually sleep all day, like you done today," she said.

Manse smiled. "How old are they?"

"Robert E. Lee is three. Rebel-Elise is two." She smiled back at him. "Whit and me didn't want them to know that you was up there in the attic. They would want to come see. You know how chilluns are. But someday when they're older, I know me and Whit will just bust our buttons bragging about how Manse Jolly use to come here and sleep in our attic."

Manse smiled again, and continued to eat.

When he finished, Sara Jane climbed down the ladder. He handed the tray down to her, and she handed up a pot of coffee and a cup.

Manse mixed whiskey and coffee, took out a cigar and lit it.

Sara Jane returned to the attic and sat next to him.

"I suspect you get real lonely hiding out all the time," she said.

"Yeah, I do."

"You don't have no regular lady friend that you go visit?"

"No, I don't."

"Then what do you do? I mean, a man has to have a woman, ever once in a while, don't he?"

Manse felt uncomfortable.

He drained his cup, refilled it.

"A man can learn to live without almost everything, when he has to," he finally said.

Silence filled the attic.

"You mind if I ask you something?" Sara Jane moved closer to him.

"Go right ahead," Manse said.

"How does it feel to kill somebody?"

Manse did not answer.

She put her hand on his thigh. He felt the heat of her palm through homespun.

"Please don't think I'm one of them bad women. I'm not. I swear it. I just cain't help what I feel ever time you come here. It's something about you that's different from other men. Something exciting."

Manse tried to move away.

"That Texas Brown who comes to see Whit, he's got it, too — but not near so strong as you." Suddenly Sara Jane Whitfield turned and put her arms around him. Her fingernails dug into the back of his neck. Her lips covered his. Her tongue opened his mouth.

Then, just as suddenly, she pulled away, rolled over and lay on her side, her back to him, and was quiet.

The throbbing in Manse's head echoed unspoken words: Honor. Sanctity of marriage. Loyalty of friendship.

Then he noticed that one of his pistols was missing from its holster.

He looked at Sara Jane.

"Did you take my revolver?"

"Yes," she sat up and pointed it at him. The front of her dress was unbuttoned from top to bottom.

"Come here," she said.

"I don't think, Sara Jane — "

"I said, come here," she grabbed his hair and pulled him to her breast.

And throbbing words gave way to the pounding in his groin. Manse took the pistol from her hand, laid it aside and surrendered to feelings long suppressed.

She took off her dress.

He touched her and she moved against his hand.

He kissed her and she moved against his lips.

She opened his trousers and took him in her hand and drew him inside her. They lingered, bonded, as if no movement were necessary.

When it ended – when he withdrew – they kissed, touched, and said nothing.

Then she was gone, and the trapdoor closed behind her.

Manse lay in attic darkness filled with the smells of her – and knew there could be no repetition.

He finished the rest of his whiskey, then slept again.

Just before sunrise, Whit awakened him.

In the kitchen, Sara Jane cooked and served breakfast without meeting Manse's eyes.

Daylight broke orange as he rode from the Whitfield farm.

At mid-morning he stopped in a secluded clearing beside the Savannah River eight miles southwest of Anderson. There he stripped, bathed, and took the Union scout's uniform from his saddle bags and washed it along with his clothes. Then he lay naked under the mid-day sun while they dried.

Late in the afternoon, he put on the Union Army uniform and rode into Anderson, past sidewalks crowded with people who didn't bother to look at his face once they saw his uniform.

They had come to town to watch the Retreat Ceremony, and to hear the latest news about the Army's War against Manse Jolly and the Ku Klux Klan.

He stopped at the entrance to the alley behind McClure's General Store and looked toward the courthouse square thirty yards away.

He did not dismount.

Hundreds of cavalrymen and infantrymen converged on the square, assembled with their units, and were called to attention.

A twelve-man Honor Guard surrounding five officers, with the unmistakable blond curls of Major Lowell Bartow at the center, marched out of the courthouse, to the review area in front of the flagpole.

Manse removed his rifle from its saddle sling.

From his position on Major Lowell Bartow's right, Capt. Ralph Phillips stepped forward two paces.

"All leaves have been canceled," he announced. "No off-duty passes will be issued. All troops not assigned to patrol will remain on reserve-duty in town."

Captain Phillips turned to Major Bartow and saluted.

Major Bartow returned the salute but did not step outside the protective ring of his Honor Guard.

"I have received authority from General Sickles to place this District under Martial Law effective immediately. I am ordering a sundown to sunup curfew until further notice. Anyone found out of his home during curfew will be jailed."

There was a murmur from the crowd lining the sidewalks.

Major Bartow raised his voice.

"Further," he said, "the reward for Manson Sherrill Jolly has been raised to seven-thousand-five-hundred dollars in gold. And a reward of one thousand dollars will be paid for the apprehension and conviction of any member of the Klan," Major Bartow paused. "I know that you men under my command have just returned from a week of day-and-night patrols," he said. "And each of you deserves a rest. But there will be no rest for any of us until Manse Jolly is hanged and the Ku Klux Klan destroyed."

Major Lowell Bartow turned to face the flag, and saluted.

The bugle sounded.

Soldiers brought rifles to present-arms.

Officers saluted.

The flag was lowered.

When it reached half-staff, Manse brought his rifle to his shoulder.

The circle of Honor Guard and officers continued to shield Bartow.

Manse chose a secondary target – and fired.

The bullet smashed into Ralph Phillips left temple.

The impact lifted him off his feet.

The left posterior portion of his brain was torn from his skull.

Numbness flowed downward through his body.

By the time it reached his legs, Ralph Phillips was dead.

Manse re-cocked, aimed, picked new targets at random, fired – and fired again – and again –

Soldiers fell – dead and wounded.

Some returned fire.
Others broke ranks and fled.
Civilians scattered.
Manse spurred his horse onto Main Street and rode out of town.
Standing in The Benson House doorway, Texas Brown smiled and shook his head in disbelief.

-16-

In an effort to remove themselves from the line of fire as quickly as possible, Lowell Bartow, his guards and his officers retreated at double-time into the courthouse – leaving the body of Captain Ralph Phillips where he fell.

Once safely inside, Major Bartow sent Captain Holtzclaw back into the street, to locate platoon leaders and have troops blockade all roads leading out of town.

He ordered Lt. Pearson to compile a casualty report.

Then Major Bartow went into his office, took a bottle of brandy from a desk drawer, poured a drink, and drank. Poured another. And drank it.

He was still sitting at his desk drinking twenty minutes later when Captain Morris Holtzclaw entered his office, followed by Lieutenant Pearson.

"Well, don't just stand there," Lowell Barrow said. "Give me a report."

"Fourteen military personnel killed, sir," Lt. Pearson said. "One officer, Captain Phillips, and thirteen troopers. Eighteen wounded, including seven civilians."

Major Bartow's nerves were now steadier. He offered glasses to Holzclaw and Pearson, and poured drinks for them.

"What size force launched the attack?" he asked.

"All reports indicate one man, sir – Manse Jolly," Holtzclaw said.

"Impossible! One man couldn't possibly kill and wound that many that quickly." Major Barrow poured himself another drink.

"Several witnesses saw and identified Jolly," Lt. Pearson contradicted the major. "He was alone. Wearing a Union Army uniform. On horseback. He fired from the entry to the alleyway behind McClure's Store. I presume Captain Phillips was his primary target – "

"Don't be naive, Lieutenant," Barrow interrupted, "Phillips was the mad-man's target-of-opportunity because he could not get a clear shot at the officer in command – "

"Correct, sir," Captain Holtzclaw said. "You were obviously his target of choice and Captain Phillips was his target of opportunity."

"In any event, sir, it was Captain Phillips who was killed first," Lieutenant Pearson said. "Then, before anyone could react, two of your guards were also shot and killed. And, in rapid succession, the two troopers who were lowering the flag – then the bugler." Pearson emptied his glass and put it on the desk. "The witnesses who were nearest to him agree that Jolly fired six shots, then rode north on Main Street and turned into another alleyway. There are no reports on his movements after that."

"That accounts for only six casualties," Barrow said. "What about the others?"

"There was panic, sir," Capt. Holtzclaw said. "I fear that some of our troops responded to the attack by firing rather wildly. Their volleys struck other soldiers – and some civilians."

"And no one saw Manse Jolly ride out of Anderson?"

"No confirmed reports to that effect, sir."

"And you've blocked off the town?"

"All roads in and out, sir."

"That's not good enough," Lowell Barrow said. "Encircle the town. I want the entire perimeter so goddamn tight not even a snake can slip through. Is that clear?"

"Yes, sir," Captain Holtzclaw saluted and turned to leave.

"Also –" Lowell Barrow raised his voice, and the captain turned to listen to him. "Confine all civilians to their homes. Then begin a top-to-bottom building-by-building search of the entire downtown. Followed by a basement-to-attic house-by-house search. Once a home is searched and cleared, the occupants will be given a pass allowing them to go downtown once a day to buy food. Otherwise, no one goes out. We will post notices of the hours when shops may open."

"With all due respect, sir," Lt. Pearson said, "we simply don't have the manpower, to surround the town, maintain order, and conduct building-by-building and house-by-house searches."

"We will have the manpower, Lieutenant. I am immediately requesting that General Pickles send reinforcements here – additional companies of cavalry and infantry – and, by god, he *will* send them."

***

A week later, Texas Brown sat alone at a table in the Benson House Bar – the same table at which he had sat alone every day for seven days.

For all intents and purposes the Benson House might as well have been boarded up. The bar and dining room were open only to hotel residents – all of whom, except for Texas, were Army Officers who were either camped on the perimeter of the town, or in the streets maintaining order.

Because all Andersonians were confined to their homes, none patronized the Benson House.

In fact, under the newly imposed Act of Martial Law, a military pass was required for anyone to be on the streets. Shops and banks were open only three hours a day. Residents had to present Army permits before being allowed to buy any provisions.

Texas was confined to the Benson House.

He had been allowed to go to the courthouse, one time – to complain to Major Barrow about the unfairness of his Benson-House-arrest. But the Major had stood firm. He would permit no one to leave or enter Anderson until the Army found Manson Jolly.

Lowell Barrow was convinced that Manse was hiding somewhere in the town – and it was just a matter of time until soldiers found and arrested him.

Texas didn't argue with Major Barrow – didn't tell the major that he was full of shit – that Manse Jolly had ridden out of Anderson immediately after the shooting – using back-alleys for his exit.

Rather than try to change Bartow's mind, Texas had waited until late one night and attempted to leave town on foot.

But he was quickly spotted, surrounded, arrested and taken to Major Barrow who confined him to the Benson House without even a pass allowing him to walk on Main Street.

And – Lowell Barrow warned – if Texas Brown was caught trying to leave town again, the major would have no alternative but to order him executed by a firing squad.

Texas knew that, under Martial Law, the major could – and probably would – do precisely that.

For that reason, Texas sat quietly at a table in the Benson House Bar and bided his time.

For five days, Major Barrow had had almost a battalion of soldiers under his command. They had ransacked every building in Anderson, and now they were searching every room of every house. But Texas knew that Barrow would not find Manse in Anderson, and eventually he would call off the search — so it wasn't just his current Benson-House-Arrest that upset Texas – it was the conclusion he had reached while sitting alone, that eventually Barrow was going to win the war that he was waging against Manse and the Klan. There was no way they could prevail – and they would be damned lucky to survive.

Two things had convinced Texas.

First – and most important – it was *necessary* that Barrow succeed. His reputation had been built on his accomplishments as a wartime hero. His future in the US Army was dependent on his ability to continue to succeed at every assignment he was given.

Second – because of his previous successes, the Major had the unlimited and unconditional backing of the whole damned US Army. And simply because of its sheer power, the Army could not be defeated.

The only way the Klan and Manse stood even the slightest chance of surviving, Texas decided, was to get rid of Barrow.

So while he waited in the Benson House Bar, Texas spent a lot of time thinking about what he could say to Manse Jolly to make Manse angry enough to attempt, *again*, to kill Barrow – and do it successfully this time.

Texas despised Lowell Barrow and all that he stood for.

If Barrow was dead, perhaps his replacement would be more like Captain Phillips – ineffective at command, and ignored by his superiors..

The more Texas thought about Lowell Barrow, the more his hatred of the man increased.

He wished he had had the major as a prisoner when he was a guard at Andersonville Prison. He would have taught that cocky long haired piece of yankee shit a lesson or two.

There was a section at Andersonville called The Hospital where they kept Confederate Soldiers who had gone crazy during combat. They were men who couldn't even remember their names – or that they were human. Men who were no more than animals – violent beyond belief.

Whenever Texas and the other guards decided that a certain yankee prisoner thought he was something special – better than other men – they chained him in an underground room beneath The Hospital and turned the *animals* loose on him – and watched as they used their teeth and nails, and hands and feet to rip and crush and tear the yankee prisoner apart.

Texas Brown would like to feed Lowell Barrow to those animals, but since he couldn't have that pleasure, he would try instead to instill enough anger in Manse Jolly to accomplish something close to the same thing.

Just as soon as he got out of this damnably nice hotel.

***

Manse stayed in the cave for a week.

October arrived – but not Texas Brown.

The silence made Manse uneasy.

On the ninth day, he left the mountains and rode slowly south – stopping often to listen for sounds of horsemen.

South of Twiggs, he heard a patrol approaching and rode off the road into pine woods, and waited.

After two squads of Union cavalry passed, he decided to stay off the main route and follow instead a trail running alongside a creek that wound its way west-southwest. Eventually, he knew, it had to lead to the Savannah River.

After about a mile, the creek made a sharp bend, then widened into a beaver pond, and Manse saw a figure lying on the bank, a cane fishing pole propped beside him, and a Confederate infantryman's dress-cap covering his face.

Before Manse could turn his horse away, the figure – a boy, maybe fifteen or sixteen years old – sat up and removed his cap and held it above his forehead to shield his eyes from the sun.

He stared at Manse for a moment, then smiled recognition.

"Afternoon to you, Mister Jolly," he said.

Manse's hand moved instinctively to his holster.

"How do you know me?" he asked.

"Everybody knows you, Mister Jolly," the boy said. "Your picture is on posters on the front of just about every building in Twiggs. And when me and my folks went to Anderson last month, your picture was all over the place there, too," his smile was unbroken. "I reckon you're the most famous man in these parts."

The boy put on his cap, laid his fishing pole on the ground, and walked toward Manse.

Manse raised his hand.

"You hold it right there, young fellow," Manse said.

The boy stopped.

Manse looked around.

"What are you doing out here?" he asked.

"Fishing, Mister Jolly."

"You alone?"

"Yes, sir. Though if my daddy had known I was going to meet up with you, he surely would have come with me. He's a mighty big admirer of yours."

Manse relaxed.

The boy turned and walked back to his fishing pole, knelt and unrolled an oilskin packet.

Manse's hand returned to his holster.

The boy unwrapped two sandwiches.

"I usually don't have any trouble eating two of these," he said, "but I'd be pleased to share one with you, sir," he held it up for Manse to see. "It's pork-roast. With a special hot-sauce that my mama makes. I'll wager they're the best you ever tasted."

"I got to say it does look mighty good," Manse took his hand away from his holster, dismounted, led his horse to the creek, let him drink, then took the sandwich from the boy.

"I thank you," he said, and bit into it.

The boy watched him chew.

"You're right, that is fine roast pork – and the best sauce I ever tasted," Manse said, and realized how long it had been since he had eaten.

"I'll tell Mama you said that," the boy's smile became a grin, then he leaned over and laid his sandwich on the oilskin, raised up, wiped his hand on his shirt, extended his hand.

"If you'll allow me, I'd be proud to shake your hand, Mister Jolly," he said.

Manse shifted the sandwich to his left hand, wiped his right hand on his shirt, and they shook hands.

"I'm Thomas Dean Hall," the boy said.

"I'm pleased to meet you, Thomas," Manse said.

The boy picked up his sandwich and they both returned to eating.

"I reckon you must live right near, or you wouldn't know about this good fishing hole," Manse said between bites.

"Yes, sir," Thomas said. "About a mile from here. My Daddy is A. Jackson Hall. He's a planter. We owned a good sized farm before The War. But we've lost most of it to taxes in the last year or so." The boy finished his sandwich, knelt and washed his face and hands in the creek, then drank. "But I reckon lots of folks have lost *all* their land, so we're thankful we still got some acres left."

"Too many good folks have lost land," Manse swallowed the final chew of his sandwich, knelt, washed pork grease and sauce from his face, then stood, walked to his horse, took a canteen of whiskey from a saddle bag, opened it and drank, then looked at the boy.

"This here is corn liquor, Thomas" he said. "And I reckon you're a mite young, so I won't offer you any."

"I don't imbibe, Mister Jolly," the boy said. "My Mama asked me to take the pledge, and I did. But there was lots of men my age in my unit who did their share of drinking."

"You were in the Army?" Manse said. "I figured that Infantry cap must've belonged to your daddy or somebody else in your family."

"No, sir, Mister Jolly – this here is *my* cap, sir," Thomas said.

"But, to be real truthful, I didn't actually go fight in The War," he added. "My daddy did. And so did my uncles. And cousins. But for most of The War, I was too young. But I finally got to join the First SC Volunteers when I was fourteen – six months before Appomattox. The Volunteers went to Anderson and marched in the parades at memorial services for the men who had been killed," he bowed his head. "I wasn't really anything but a Private-Drum-Boy, Mister Jolly – but if The War had held on for another year, I would've gone and fought the yankees."

"Don't you ever apologize for what you did, Thomas," Manse said. "It was real important to honor our fallen men. And by doing your part at memorial services, you freed up a soldier for combat – so you *did* fight for the South," Manse put his hand on the boy's shoulder. "And all your life you should be real proud of that."

"Yes, sir, I always will be," Thomas said. "And I'll be even prouder that this day came when I met you and shook your hand and had this talk with you."

"It's been a proud meeting for me, too," Manse smiled and shook the boy's hand again.

"But now I reckon I best be on my way," he said. "I have to see somebody before sundown."

He walked to his horse and mounted.

"You take care of yourself, Thomas Dean Hall, you hear?" Manse said.

"The good lord watch over you, Mister Manse Jolly," the boy said. "You ride real careful, sir. And remember – you're in all our prayers."

***

The sun was setting when he reached Whit Whitfield's farm.
Sara Jane waved to him from the back porch.
Manse touched the brim of his hat, nodded and rode to the barn.
At the barn door, Malachi Whitfield swung to the ground on a rope attached to the loft hoist beam.

"Af-f-ter-n-noon M-M-Mister Jolly," he said, and held the stallion's halter while Manse dismounted. "I'll w-w-water y-y-your horse. If'en y-y-you w-w-want."

"Thank you, Malachi," Manse smiled. "I'll be much obliged if you'll do that."

The boy's eyes smiled in reply.

"Where's your paw?" Manse asked.

"In here!" Whit Whitfield's voice boomed from inside the barn.

Malachi led the horse to the trough and wiped him down while he drank.

Manse walked into the barn.

Whit was cinching his horse's saddle.

"I was just leaving. We've got a meeting," he said.

"Mind if I ride with you?" Manse asked.

"Mind? I'd be damn honored." Whit led his horse outside.

"Malachi! Bring Mister Jolly's horse here. Right now," he yelled.

"That boy is slower than winter molasses," he said to Manse.

"Can't rush a drinking horse," Manse said and offered Whit a cigar, and nodded a wink toward Malachi.

The horse continued drinking, and Malachi kept on wiping him down.

And by the time Whit had lit and inhaled a few times, Malachi had led the horse to Manse, and he mounted.

With Whit in the lead, they rode a narrow road west, toward the Savannah River, then took a trail through a pine forest, emerging in a field of dried corn stalks. Then they followed a game trail through denser woods along the river.

Suddenly four hooded figures stepped from the underbrush, rifles leveled.

"It's me, Whit," Whit said. "With Manse Jolly."

The men led them to a large clearing filled with more than a hundred white-robed men – their horses hitched to lines in the surrounding woods.

In the center of the clearing, Texas Brown sat on a log.

"It's Whit," the man leading the horses said. "And Manse Jolly."

Manse felt their eyes on him as he dismounted.

Texas walked to him. They shook hands.

"Glad to see you – and surprised," Texas said, and picked up a jug and handed it to Manse.

Manse took the jug, drank, paused and stared at Texas.

"Just where the hell you been? I thought you would have showed up at our usual-place by now."

Texas felt Manse's tension, and knew that every man in the clearing and the woods was listening to their conversation.

"Hell, Manse, no-damn-body was allowed to leave Anderson after you shot all them soldier boys at Retreat," Texas raised his voice. "I tell you, old friend, that was one fine piece of marksmanship – "

"Sure was," Whit said.

"Took a lot of guts," a voice came from the crowd.

"Only Manse Jolly could do that," another said.

Texas smiled.

Manse did not.

"You got the look of a man full of bother, Manse," Texas said.

"I reckon I'm a man more full of wondering," Manse said. "Wondering why anybody would call that bastard Bartow a hero. Far as I could see, he's a pig-shit-yankee-coward – hiding behind a whole squad of guards even when he's saluting the flag. No way I could draw a bead on him. Had to settle for that bluebelly captain."

Manse spat disgust.

"Did I kill him?"

"You damn sure did – Captain Ralph Phillips is dead'ern hell," Texas said, and laughed – and decided that now was the time to continue talking. "Hell, Manse, Bartow was so sure you were hiding somewhere in Anderson, that he put guards on all the roads. Circled the whole damn town with soldiers. Wouldn't let nobody in or out. Then his soldiers searched every building and house in town. And the son-of-a-bitch had me confined to the Benson House. Threatened to have me shot by a firing squad if I so much as stuck my head outside," Texas took a drink and again passed the jug.

"They even searched my room," he said. "One of them lieutenants even got down on his hands and knees and looked under my bed." Texas smiled, and there was laughter from the men.

"This morning was the first time in a week anybody was allowed to leave Anderson." Texas said. "And I went straight-away to your farm with a wagon-load of supplies. I figured taking your family the things they needed – and news about Tom and you – was the most important thing I could do."

Manse heard the Klansmen murmur their approval.

Texas Brown always took care of families.

"Yeah, you did right, Texas, and I thank you," Manse said, and felt more at ease.

"Are my folks all right?" he asked.

"They're doing pretty good, I guess – everything considered. Mind you, your Mama is still awful worried about you and Tom. And upset that I couldn't stay to dinner this afternoon. But I had to get the word out – to call a meeting. If the Klan don't ride regular, these here men of action get real restless," he looked around and grinned.

Klansmen smiled agreement.

Manse remained silent, unsmiling.

"What's gnawing at you, Manse?" Texas said.

"You didn't say anything about Tom," Manse said. "You heard from him? Seen him?"

"Major Bartow wouldn't let me visit him last week. I asked, but he said hell-no," Texas watched Manse's face and knew his lie was getting the desired reaction. "But I got ways of getting information from inside the stockade – "

Texas stopped in mid-sentence.

"Dammit, Texas, go on and tell me!" Manse glared at him.

"They say Bartow has started personally questioning Tom again. About where you might be hiding."

"Beating him again, like he did before?" Manse looked concerned.

"I hate to tell you this, Manse, but I think Bartow's gone way past that. They tell me he burned Tom with a branding iron. And he took his leg away from him and makes him stand for hours on one leg, and when he falls, they prod him with swords, and use a horsewhip on him – "

"God-damn-him," Manse's anger came in short breaths. He raised the jug and took a long swig.

"I've got to get Tom out of there, Texas," he said.

Texas shook his head.

"No way you can do that, Manse," he said.

"Not even with all your Klansmen?"

"I've got a hundred men here now," Texas said. "And another hundred will be here inside an hour. But Bartow has more than four times that many under his command in Anderson. "If we attack the stockade, they'll trap us and cut us to pieces."

"You're saying there's no way we can get Tom out?"

"I'm saying that attacking the stockade won't help Tom," Texas said. "But killing Bartow will."

"I tried that," Manse said.

"Right, and what you and me both learned from your attack is that Bartow is damn well protected – when he's in Anderson," Texas paused. "So it stands to reason that if you can't kill Bartow in Anderson, you got to kill him somewhere else."

"Where?" Manse said.

"I think the best place to get him would be at that gambling-club whore-house where he spends most evenings," Texas said. "The Major fancies himself quite a ladies man."

"I wouldn't even call them females at that place women, much less, ladies," Whit smiled. "Course I reckon Texas knows lots more about them than I do."

Klansmen laughed.

Texas smiled at the men, glared at Whit, then turned to Manse.

"It's a socializing place for bluebelly officers and scalawags and carpetbaggers," Texas said. "I go there time and again to have a drink and listen to what's being said. Yankees all run off a lot at the mouth when they've had a few drinks – Bartow included."

"You reckon he's there tonight?"

"Being it's Saturday night, most likely he is," Texas said. "I can ride there and find out for sure. You stay here with Whit and Elk and the men. If I'm not back in an hour, that means Bartow is there, and I'll meet you in about two hours. Whit knows where."

***

***

Three hours later, Manse and the Klansmen met Texas at a church cemetery two miles west of the whore-house.

"We're in luck," Texas said as he reined in beside Manse. "Bartow's there. I had a drink with him. But like always, he's got his guards protecting him – two men at the front of the house, two out back, and six more inside. Three of them followed him to the upstairs parlor just before I left."

"Whit and I worked out a plan while we were waiting," Manse said.

"Good," Texas said. "You can tell me about it while we're riding to the whore-house."

He dismounted and put on a robe and hood. A klansman rider brought him a bay mare and led away his white stallion.

They walked their horses along a creek bed for thirty minutes, then dismounted and tied them.

White robes moved quietly through woods and thickets until they reached a road. On the other side was a two-story house. A covered porch ran the width of the front. Two soldiers with rifles stood at the door. A dozen horses were tied at the hitching rail. Ten more were on a cavalry-line at the side of the house.

Texas raised his hand. Manse looked right, then left, and saw Klansmen run across the road and crouch in a ditch.

"We'll cover you and Whit," Texas said, and crossed the road.

"You okay, Whit?" Manse asked.

"Long as I'm with you – hell yes."

Manse and Whit stood, and each used a short length of rope to tie together two whiskey jugs and drape them over their shoulders.

Then, laughing and talking loudly, the two men staggered from the woods onto the road toward the house.

"Halt – " one of the front-door guards shouted. Then a corporal and a private walked from the porch to the road.

"Where are you two going?" the corporal asked.

"Home, General, to my wife, if 'en she'll still have me," Whit slurred.

The soldiers came closer.

Manse turned away and bent over.

"What's wrong with him?" the corporal asked.

"Pears like he's vomiting, don't it?" Whit said.

Before the soldiers could react, Manse straightened up, and he and Whit shoved pistols into the soldiers' stomachs.

"Don't make a sound," Manse said.

Whit took their rifles.

The Corporal stared at Manse. "You're – "

"Corporal, what's going on out there?" a lieutenant shouted from the front doorway.

"Tell him it's just a couple of drunks," Manse said.

"Corporal – " the lieutenant's voice was louder.

"It's just two drunks, sir. That's all," the corporal shouted.

"Very well." The lieutenant's voice went back inside the house.

"Thank you, Corporal," Manse said, and he and Whit used the butts of their pistols to knock the two soldiers unconscious – then they dragged them into the underbrush and bound them.

Jugs swinging, they then ran to the side of the house.

Voices and laughter and the sounds of a piano came through an open window.

Manse and Whit uncorked the jugs and poured lamp oil along the base of the house's weathered wooden siding.

When all four jugs were empty, they set the timbers on fire.

Flames crackled and spread.

Manse and Whit ran to the ditch at the edge of the road to join Texas Brown and the main contingent of Klansmen.

Flames lapped wood. Smoke billowed.

Shouts rose from inside the house.

The front door opened, and men and women ran onto the front porch.

Klansmen opened fire.

Three men and two women dropped. The others retreated inside.

Klansmen surrounded the house, firing into it from all sides.

Occasional shots were returned.

A woman clutching her dressing gown started to climb out a window. A volley hurled her back into the flames.

A soldier appeared at the window, fired into the night, was punctured with bullets, and fell forward, draped over the window sill.

The front door opened again. Two men ran out – their pistols blazing.

Manse, Whit and Texas fired, and the men fell.

Horses reared and galloped away, dragging hitching rail posts behind them.

Three men came out the back door into crossfire.

A woman being lowered from a second story window screamed as bullets struck her. Two others appeared at the window. One was shot. The other one jumped, hit the ground and lay still. Shots rolled her body over.

Through a second story front window, three soldiers climbed onto the porch-roof, knelt and lay down rapid fire toward the ditch. They were followed by four more soldiers who were surrounding and protecting a man and woman.

The man had long blond hair.

"There's Bartow!" Texas shouted and pointed.

But Manse and a dozen Klansmen had already seen the blond curls. They laid down a barrage at the targets crawling along the edge of the porch-roof.

Four of the soldiers were killed before they could jump.

Bartow had only a few feet to go when three shots hit him.

He rolled off the roof, dropped to the ground and began to crawl away from the house.

Manse stood.

Shots ricocheted around him.

Texas grabbed his boot and tried to pull him down, but Manse shook him loose and, a pistol in each hand, calmly walked through the battle toward his prey.

When he reached Bartow, he put the toe of his boot under the Major's shoulder, and rolled him over.

Bartow's look was recognition, not surprise. He tried to raise his sidearm.

Manse stared at Bartow.

The officer was bleeding from the shoulder, leg and abdomen.

"For Tom Largent, you son of a bitch," Manse squeezed the triggers of both pistols and opened a hole the size of his fist where Major Lowell Bartow's eyes had been.

The inferno that had been a house collapsed.

Texas and Whit began a chain of hand signals.

White robes crossed the road.

Manse joined them.

"Wait a minute," Whit said, and ran to the two bound guards lying in the underbrush – and shot each of them in the head.

"Might be all right that they recognized you, Manse," he said, "but I cain't afford to have nobody remembering my face. I got a family."

Manse nodded, walked into the woods, to his horse, mounted, turned and looked back at the inferno, then rode away.

-17-

Tom Largent held Melinda on his lap. Bonnie held their son. Maude sat across from him. Johnny poured coffee.

"You want more pancakes?" Maude Jolly asked.

"There's still plenty of batter," Johnny said.

"No, thank you, I reckon I'm as full as a man ever ought to be," Tom smiled at Melinda. "Were you a good little girl while I was away?" he asked.

"As good as a little girl ever ought to be," she said, and giggled.

Tom's laugh was cut short by the sound of hoof beats.

Johnny looked out the window.

"It's Texas Brown," he said.

Tom put Melinda down and walked to the back door.

Texas swung from the saddle.

"Heard in town that they let you out," Texas came into the kitchen. He and Tom shook hands, hesitated, then embraced and laughed.

"I'm sure pleased to see you loose," Texas walked to the table and hugged Maude Jolly, then leaned over and kissed Melinda on the cheek, leaned over and kissed Bonnie Jolly on the forehead, and the baby on the head, then shook hands with Johnny.

"Pull up a chair. Have some pancakes. Visit a spell," Maude Jolly said.

"Wish I could, Mama Jolly, but I rode out just to talk to Tom about a couple of things, then I got to head on up to visit a friend of mine in the mountains," Texas grinned, and everyone knew, but no one asked.

"You give your friend my love," Maude Jolly said, and smiled.

Texas smiled again, then he and Tom walked outside.

"The yankees give you any reason for setting you free all of a sudden?" Texas asked.

"All I know is that Lieutenant Pearson came to the stockade and told me that Manse had killed Bartow, and that Captain Holtzclaw was now acting commander of the Anderson garrison, and he had decided that keeping me locked up was more trouble than it was worth."

"Might be something to that," Texas laughed. "Of course I'm just a simple man who don't know anything much about the Klan or Manse Jolly, but the talk that I hear around Anderson is that Manse Jolly went to the Klan – which he hadn't ever done before – and asked them to ride with him to get Bartow – because of what Bartow had done to Manse's friend, Tom Largent."

"Well, killing Bartow sure got me set free," Tom said, then paused. "But actually it was kind of strange – "

"How's that?"

"Except for being locked up, those last three months in the stockade weren't all that bad. Bartow hadn't had me beat up for a while. And last time I saw the major at the stockade, he didn't even question me about Manse. He just frowned like he was real unhappy, and said he was going to turn me loose as soon as my year was up."

Texas smiled to himself, and decided to change the subject.

"I passed by a whole platoon of soldiers camped down the road," he said, and handed Tom a cigar.

They bit, spat and lit.

"They're the ones that escorted me home," Tom said. "Guess they'll be bivouacked there permanently."

"Yankee patrols are all over Anderson district," Texas exhaled smoke. "I haven't seen so much Union cavalry in one place since Manassas. And I hear that more are coming. The yankees are hell-bent on getting Manse now."

"When was the last time you saw him?" Tom asked.

"The night Bartow was killed. I've been up to the cave three times since then, but it don't appear like Manse has been there at all," Texas said. "I figure he most likely rode up to someplace higher in the mountains – which I reckon is a good idea."

"I think it would be an even better idea if Manse left South Carolina completely," Tom said. "When you see him, try to convince him to do that, will you? Tell him how many troops are being sent here to get him – how damn-dead-set the yankees are on hanging him. Maybe he'll listen to you."

"I been thinking the same thing – that it's time Manse got the hell out of the state," Texas paused. "Maybe me, too."

"I'd call that real wise – for both of you," Tom said.

"I'll talk to him," Texas said, and stood and put on his hat. "Now that you're out of the stockade, you can look after the family, so Manse ought to be willing to leave."

***

When Texas arrived at the cave, there was still no sign that anyone had been there.

He tethered his horse, carried whiskey, food and coffee into the shack, spread his bedroll and built a fire. Then he walked to the rear of the cave, took his saddlebags down from the rock ledge, wiped off dust, and opened them. The gold bars were there, just like he left them. He smiled, closed the saddle-bags, carried them to his bedroll, and put them underneath it.

He made coffee, added whiskey, drank, and stretched out – his hands behind his head – his hat over his eyes.

He had been doing a lot of thinking since that night at the whore house. Now he needed to make some decisions.

Lowell Bartow was dead. That was what Texas wanted. And it was good. But the public outcry over his death was greater than Texas had expected. The Union Army – and the nation – had lost a hero. The Major's body was being sent to Washington for burial with highest military honors.

Speakers in the United States Congress – as well as prominent preachers and newspapers and journals – were demanding that the killers of Major Bartow be caught and hanged – and that the Klan in South Carolina be destroyed, once and for all.

The President had personally ordered The Army High Command to give the problems in Anderson top priority. He wanted results. Immediate results.

And the Army had not left its campaign against Manse and the Klan in the hands of the Anderson Garrison.

Cavalry and Infantry from Greenville, Charlotte, Columbia and Charleston were pouring into the district, and rumor had it that these forces were only the beginning.

Texas wasn't sure that all the rumors were reliable, but he considered them valid warnings that he should leave South Carolina – and the South.

If he stayed in Anderson, eventually someone in the Klan would sell him out for the reward money.

Or he and his nightriders would all be hunted down and killed by Union Cavalry.

He had a fortune in gold in his saddle-bags. More money than he could ever spend. He should go somewhere and enjoy it.

But he hadn't dared tell anyone he was thinking of leaving. Not even Whit and Elk.

What he should do, he decided, was simply disappear.

And he also decided that he wanted Manse Jolly to go with him.

They both knew how to survive. They could cover each others' flanks – and, together, they would survive.

All he had to do was convince Manse that now was the time to go. And he had an idea how to do that.

Texas closed his eyes and dozed.

The fire had died to embers when Manse's voice woke him.

"Don't touch the rifle," he said. "Get up, real slow."

"Please, don't shoot me, Mister Jolly," Texas laughed and stood.

Manse entered the shack.

"I thought it was you," he said. "But I had to make sure."

"I don't blame you," Texas smiled – and stared at Manse. His clothes were clean, his hair and beard trimmed.

"Goddamn, you look like a new man," Texas said.

"I feel good," Manse said. "Reckon I ought to – I haven't done anything but eat and sleep for weeks," he took the cup of coffee Texas offered. "After that night at the whorehouse, I figured the bluebellies would be out in force, so I rode up to the North Georgia mountains." He added whiskey to the coffee. "At first I was fearful of going anywhere to ask for food or a place to sleep. But then one afternoon I rode through a pass and saw this farmhouse in a valley all by itself – and I decided to chance stopping there. And damned if the farmer there didn't call me by name. Recognized me from the wanted posters. So did his wife and two boys." Manse paused to drink. "At first I wasn't sure I could trust them. An awful lot of

Unionists live up in them parts. But these folks let me know right away that they were Confederates – with no use for yankees. They had a boy killed at Second Manassas. And Sherman burned 'em out over near Jonesboro, Georgia. That's why they moved up to the mountains." Manse sat. "They've got a real nice farm. And they acted like I was some kind of hero or something. They even had one of my posters in the parlor alongside tin-types of Lee and Beauregard. The way they treated me was so respectful it was embarrassing. And that lady is about the best cook in the world next to Mama. And talk about good corn liquor –" Manse took a jar from a supply sack. "Try that."

Texas unscrewed the lid and drank.

"Smooth as I ever tasted," he said, and looked at Manse and laughed aloud.

"What's funny?"

"Me, that's what. Here I been worried shitless thinking you was hiding out in the woods somewhere, sleeping in the rain with nothing to eat, much less to drink – I mean, hell Manse, the first week of November gets damn cold in these mountains – and all this time, you been living like a king."

Manse joined the laugh, drank from the jar and lit a cigar.

"They turned Tom loose," Texas said.

"Thank God," Manse said. "You seen him? How is he? And my folks?"

"Fine. Saw him and them yesterday."

"And what are the yankees doing now that they got no Major Bartow?"

"Looking for you harder than ever. The reward's gone to ten-thousand in gold."

Manse nodded.

"They arrest any of your boys?" he asked.

"Pearson and Holtzclaw arrested near-about everybody in Anderson – including me," Texas spat in the flames. "I tell you, them bluebellies are awful mad and upset, what with twenty-two soldiers shot dead at the whore-house – plus five civilian men and eight women killed – and a whole lot more wounded – and burned in the fire."

"They arrested you?" Manse half-smiled.

"They sure as hell did. The very next day. But I told 'em I couldn't have been with them Klansmen outside the whore house shooting soldiers and starting fires, because I was inside the whorehouse – and had been there all evening," Texas grinned. "Three yankee officers vouched they had seen me having a drink with Bartow. And I swore I was upstairs with a lady when the shooting started – and that I ran down to the cellar and escaped out the back way, and high-tailed it to Anderson, to the Benson House."

"What about your other men?"

"They questioned 'em but had to turn 'em loose because most all of them could prove they was at revival services at Old Stone Church that night," Texas laughed.

Manse smiled.

"The yankees can't prove who is underneath our robes and hoods – that's why we wear them," Texas said. "But they sure got plenty of witnesses who identified you."

Manse exhaled, slowly, calmly.

"You and the Klan been riding much since that night?" he asked.

"Hell, no. We're laying real low," Texas said. "You never seen so many soldiers as they've sent to Anderson to get you – and the Klan," he took another drink. "I swear to you, Manse, it looks like the fields around Mannasas right before the second battle."

"Don't them bluebellies know by now that I can't be caught – or shot –" Manse laughed.

"I'm afraid that what's happening ain't really very funny, Manse," Texas said. "They've already sent another battalion of cavalry and infantry into the Anderson District, with more coming," Texas shook his head slowly. "And there's a rumor that General Canby, and another whole regiment, will be here in ten days."

Texas' expression and words registered, and suddenly Manse was no longer smiling.

Texas stared at him.

"You've run up one hell of a total, Manse," he said. "A story in the Anderson *Intelligencier* says you've killed more than a hundred soldiers. And that don't include civilians like Heaton and Tompins. So now the yankees have got to hang you – or corner you and kill you – even if it takes the whole Union Army to do it."

"Let 'em try," Manse leaned toward Texas. "Even if they bring every goddamn soldier in their bluebelly Army to Anderson, they won't get me. There's still folks who are willing to hide me."

"Not many," Texas said. "The Army has put out new Martial Laws to make riding with you – or sheltering you – a hanging-offense, Manse. With that, and the reward up to ten thousand in gold, it's plain not gonna be safe for you anywhere in these parts."

Manse silently studied the glow of his cigar.

"They're hell-bent on destroying the Klan, too, Manse," Texas said. "A thousand-dollars reward for any Klansman. Three thousand for the leader."

"Then I reckon you need to be extra-special-careful, Texas," Manse said. "I hide out alone and ride alone, but you got a lot of Klansmen. And one of them is just liable to turn you in for that kind of money."

"I know," Texas said. "That's why I'm planning to get the hell away from here." He paused. "And I think you ought to come with me."

Manse was silent for a few moments, then he looked at Texas.

"Where to?" he asked.

"To the only place I ever wanted to go to live – the state of Texas," Texas said.

Manse squinted at the fire's coals, and said nothing.

Texas decided to push harder.

"What I hear from some yankee officers who knew him, is that Lieutenant McCollum took Rebecca to a town called Cameron. In Milam County. In east Texas," he said. "We could look for them out there."

"Yeah. I reckon we could do that," Manse said. "You know it's kind of strange – I had almost forgot about them," Manse looked at Texas. "When are you thinking about leaving?"

"Real quick. Before the whole district gets covered over with more yankee soldiers than leaves," he said. "I'll just need a couple of days to finish up some business – "

"Exactly when, then?"

" I reckon first thing Friday would be good," Texas said.

"This Friday?" Manse squeezed his eyes closed.

"Yeah. I was thinking this Friday," Texas paused, and stared at Manse. "Something's bothering you," he said. "What is it?"

"Just that I sure would like to see Mama and Tom and Bonnie and Johnny and Melinda before we go. Might be a long time before I see them again. If ever," Manse looked sad.

"Let's think on it," Texas said. "The main problem is that there's a whole platoon of soldiers camped a quarter mile from your farm. "

"A whole platoon? That's a pretty damn big problem – "

"Yeah, it is, unless – "

"What?"

"There are about ten of my boys I would stake my life on. I could get them to go with me, and we could attack the niggers who live on the farm next to yours – and burn them out."

"What have *they* done?"

"They ain't *done* anything," Texas said. "But they live so close that the soldiers are sure to hear the shooting and see the fire, and come to investigate. And when they get close, we'll ride northeast and lose them in the hills. And while they're chasing us, you'll have time for a visit with your folks."

"Don't you reckon we've done that diversion tactic so many times they are wise to it by now?"

"Hell, Manse, you know that yankees don't think that way. When they hear shots, all they know to do is shoot back. And when they see white robes, they chase them."

"If you feel sure about that – and if you've got ten men you're sure you can trust to ride with you –"

"Hell, the ones I'm talking about would rather ride with me than eat," Texas threw his cigar into the fire. "We'll do it Thursday night, and you can see your folks then."

"And we leave Friday?"

"Friday at dawn," Texas stood.

"I had planned to sleep here tonight," he said, "but I guess I better ride back to Anderson. I've got lots to do," he picked up his hat. "I'll leave my bedroll and saddle-bags here."

***

***

Manse was not hungry. He watched the fire, smoked and drank. When the jar of corn whiskey was empty, he stretched out and pulled a blanket over himself – a pistol in each hand.

The fire died.

Unfocused images of Larry, Maude, and Tom drifted through twilight sleep.

Melinda, covered by flowers, floated above him.

Rebecca and Martin entered his dream in a shadow of blues and grays.

Texas Brown rode through, white robe flowing.

Around him, faces on blue bodies grimaced and dropped into flames.

Manse, at their center, sank in a pool of red.

Finally he slept.

A figure entered the cave, slipped through shadows into the shack, knelt astride him, grabbed his forearms and pinned him.

Manse awoke too late.

Struggle against the shadow's strength was futile.

"Please, Mister Manse, it's just me, Robespierre – " the shadow said.

"Robespierre? What the hell are you doing? Dammit, turn me loose."

"Please, Mister Manse, I don't mean no harm. I just needs to talk to you. Promise you won't shoot me and I'll turn loose."

"Why the hell would I shoot you, Robespierre?"

Robespierre released his grip.

Manse sat up, tucked his pistols in his belt, rubbed his wrists and rekindled the fire.

Robespierre sat and waited.

"How'd you find this place, Robespierre?"

"I followed that Mister Texas Brown. I been waiting out in the woods for the longest time. I was afeared you'd shoot me if I come in afore you was good asleep. I'm sorry I scared you."

"You scared me all right," Manse took a long drink. "Now tell me what's so damn important you'd risk your ass sneaking up on me like this?"

"It's this way, Mister Manse – you done me a big favor, letting me live at your place. And you and Mister Tom always treated me real good. And you know I knowed Mister Tom's Daddy and your Daddy and all your brothers – "

"Dammit, Robespierre, get to the point! What are you doing here?"

Robespierre was quiet for a minute, then said, "I come about that Mister Brown."

"Texas? What about him?"

"He's up to no-good, Mister Manse. He's just plain mean. He don't feel for nobody but hisself. And he's fixing to do you dirt."

"What do you mean he's fixing to do me dirt?"

"I ain't sure exactly what it is he's up to – I just know that him and that yankee lieutenant what ran off with Miss Rebecca was in cahoots."

"And what makes you think Texas and McCollum were in *cahoots*?"

"After you was gone from your farm, and that lieutenant was staying out there with them soldiers, I seen and heared him and Mister Brown talking together lots – arguing mostly about money and – " Robespierre stopped talking.

"Go on, Robespierre – and what?"

"Mister Texas Brown is planning to help them soldiers catch you, Mister Manse."

"Now hold on, Robespierre. I know that Texas sometimes acts friendly with yankees, but he's got his own reasons for that – and that doesn't mean he is planning to do anything against me – "

"But he was helping that Major Bartow, Mister Manse. I knows that for sure."

"You know? How?"

"Because this good friend to me use to shave the major ever-morning. And he told me that one morning a captain come in and said 'Texas Brown is outside and says he needs to talk to you real bad.' And the Major say, 'Tell him to come in.' And sure enough Mister Brown he come busting in and say, 'I got to talk to you alone.' And the Major say, 'Talk while I'm getting shaved.' And Mister Brown yelled, 'If'en you want me to help you to catch Manse Jolly, you get that *boy* outta here cause I don't talk in front of niggers.' So my friend went to that waiting-room office and waited, and in a few minutes Mister Brown and Major Bartow come out of the major's office real fast, like their britches was on fire, and the Major told the captain to get a squad of men and go arrest Mister Tom Largent."

Manse squinted.

"But why would Texas want Bartow to arrest Tom?" he said.

"I ain't sure, Mister Manse, except that that was the day after that Lieutenant McCollum and Miss Rebecca run off. And I reckon Mister Brown might've done it to keep Mister Tom from going after them."

"Robespierre – " Manse was becoming exasperated. "Just why would Texas care if Tom went after Rebecca and McCollum?"

"Don't you see, Mister Manse, if Mister Tom had brought Miss Rebecca and Lieutenant McCollum back – then Mister Tom – or you – or the Army – or somebody – might've found out about all the gold that Mister Brown and the Lieutenant got that made them so rich."

Manse shook his head, to try to clear it.

"Robespierre, you've got me confused," he said. "I've got no idea what you're talking about. Texas may have some money, but he's not exactly *rich*. Lieutenant McCollum neither, far as I know," Manse paused to find the right words. "I'm afraid you've just been listening to too many colored-folks stories, Robespierre," Manse touched the man's shoulder. "Now don't think I don't appreciate you coming all the way up here to tell me all this," he said. "I know you believe what you're saying is important, and you wanted to warn me. And you did the right thing. And I thank you for that. But right now the biggest favor you can do for me, Robespierre, is to go back to my farm and stay there and help Mister Tom take good care of my folks. Promise me you'll do that – please."

Robespierre started to speak, but only sighed resignation – then sighed again and said, "Yes, sir, Mister Manse, I promise."

"And don't you worry about Texas Brown," Manse smiled. "In a couple of days he'll be gone from here. And so will I."

Robespierre's eyes questioned Manse.

"I plan to come by the farm to tell Mama and everybody goodbye," Manse said. "But don't you say anything to anybody about seeing me. Or tell them that I'm coming by."

"I won't say nothing," Robespierre said. "But is you sure it's a good idea you coming to your house, Mister Manse? They's a whole lot of soldiers camped right down the road."

"I know about them," Manse said. "But Texas and I have a plan to take care of them – "

Robespierre frowned.

"But Mister Manse," he said, "I done just told you that that Mister Brown is – "

Manse smiled.

"Robespierre, for god sakes stop worrying," he said. "Things are going to be all right. Take my word for that." He stood. "Now, let's you and me collect some things I won't be needing, and you can carry them back to the farm with you," Manse picked up pots and pans, an ax and butchering knives, and put them into a supply sack.

Then he picked up an old saddle and handed it to Robespierre.

"You might as well have this for your mule," he said. "I reckon you're a mite sore from riding bare-back."

Robespierre nodded thanks and they walked out of the cave.

Robespierre cinched the saddle on the mule, then mounted.

Manse tied the supply sack to the horn.

"Be careful between here and the road," Manse said. "Wouldn't want a patrol to catch you."

Robespierre smiled.

"Them soldiers don't see colored folks too good in the dark," he said. "But I'll still be careful."

Robespierre's eyes met Manse's and clouded.

"And you be careful, too, please, sir, Mister Manse," he said. "Special careful of ever-thing – and ever-body."

-18-

"Lots of shots," Johnny said when he walked from the porch into the parlor. "And there's a sky-glow, like a big fire over towards that freedman's farm. The soldiers all rode in that direction." He hesitated. "Wish I could go see."

"You stay right here," Bonnie said. "No sense in looking for trouble."

"Your mother is right," Tom backed her.

Johnny shrugged, then turned at the sound of someone behind him.

Manse grabbed Johnny and hugged him.

"My God – " Tom and Bonnie rushed to Manse.

"I can't stay long," he said, and embraced them. "Texas and I are heading west in the morning. But I had to come home and see you all before I left."

"What was all the shooting about?" Tom looked concerned.

"Just some of Texas' boys drawing the yankee soldiers away," Manse smiled. "Must've worked. I didn't see any."

"You sure look a lot better than I expected," Tom said.

"You, too," Manse said, and stared at Tom as if looking for scars.

The room filled with silence. There was so much to say – so much to ask – that Manse didn't know where to begin.

"How's Melinda?" he finally said.

"She's asleep," Bonnie said. "I'll wake her."

"No, don't. I'll go by her room before I leave," Manse said, then touched Bonnie's arm. "And how's that new baby?"

"Manson Sherrill Largent is just fine," Bonnie smiled.

"And I'm wagering he grows up worthy of his name," Tom said.

"I'm mighty honored you named him after me," Manse smiled.

"You want to see him?" Bonnie asked.

"I sure do."

"I'll get him," Bonnie started upstairs.

"Is Mama asleep?" Manse asked, and followed her.

"I don't know."

"Please go tell her I'm here," he said. "I don't want to frighten her by just walking in."

Manse waited outside his mother's door.

When Bonnie came out, she said, "Mama Jolly is awake – and waiting for you."

Manse went in.

His mother was sitting in a chair by the bed.

"Manson," she reached for him.

He kissed her and knelt by her chair. They held each other in long silence.

Then she took her arms from around his neck, put her hands on his shoulders and pushed him to arm's length.

"Let me look at you," she said, and squinted in the lamplight. "Why, you look fine, Manson – you look just fine," she touched his cheek. "Now you tell me the truth, son. Why are you here? Must be something awful important happening for you to risk coming home – especially right now."

Manse smiled sadly beneath her touch.

"I had to come see you tonight, Mama, because I'm going away tomorrow with Texas Brown," he said. "I'll write you. I promise. And before too long maybe I can settle down somewhere and you all can come join me."

"I've been praying all these months that you would walk through that door like you've done tonight, Manson – so I could lay eyes on you one more time," Maude Jolly tried to smile through tears. "Now that that prayer has been answered, I only pray that the Lord will watch over you and protect you wherever you go."

Manse hugged her and kissed her.

"I love you, Mama," he said, then stood, and, without looking back at her, walked out of the room.

Maude watched the door close behind him.

"Good-bye, Manson," she said.

He went to the room where Melinda was sleeping, bent over her bed, and kissed her cheek.

She stirred and opened her eyes.

"Uncle Manse? Is that really you? Or are you a dream?"

"I'm a dream, Melinda," he said, and smiled and sat on the bed.

"Then I hope I don't wake up right now," she reached up and touched his beard.

"Then you just keep on sleeping and dreaming," he said. "I'll see you again soon."

"When, Uncle Manse? When?"

"Look for me when our flowers bloom, Melinda," he put his hand over her eyes, and they closed beneath his touch.

Manse left the room and walked downstairs.

In the parlor Bonnie handed him her sleeping son.

Manse drew the baby to him and kissed its forehead, and smiled at Bonnie.

"You take good care of this Manson Sherrill Largent," he said. "And when he's older, try to explain to him the truth about all that's happened."

"I will," Bonnie began to sob, kissed Manse's cheek, took her son and went upstairs.

"You're a lucky man, Tom Largent," Manse said, and accepted the drink Tom handed him.

"That I am," Tom said. "I'm blessed by both my family and my friend." They drank and Tom lowered his voice. "Robespierre told me he followed Texas up to the cave. Said it was because he needed to tell you something important, but he wouldn't tell me what it was – and I didn't press him about it. He's a good old soul, but he's plumb scared of his own shadow these days."

"Wasn't anything – not really. Just colored-folks talk, far as I could tell," Manse smiled. "Mostly rambling on about Texas and McCollum being in-cahoots – something about the two of them having a lot of money. Lots of gold, Robespierre said."

"Well, I don't know about any gold," Tom said, "but when Heaton came out here last time to collect more taxes – right before Bartow had me arrested – Texas and Martin both brought me money to pay the taxes, and insisted I take it – and not tell anybody."

Manse frowned. "How much?"

"Texas gave me nine hundred dollars," Tom said. "And Martin, over two thousand."

"That's a hell of a lot of money," Manse said.

"It was blood-money, Uncle Manse," Johnny said. "Them two was always putting their heads together and whispering about things out by the barn."

Tom glared Johnny into silence.

"We got too little time together to spend it talking about the likes of that damn yankee, McCollum," Tom said. "But hearing his name does remind me – this letter came from Rebecca a while back," he handed an envelope to Manse. "The return address is Cameron, Texas. Her letter says it's a town in Milam County. She said they were thinking about buying land and settling somewhere in those parts," Tom nodded solemnly as he spoke. "I know he didn't *force* Rebecca to go with him – but there was something awful suspicious about all that – and I'm hoping you're still aiming to go after her."

Manse looked at the envelope.

"Cameron –" he said aloud. "Texas told me he had heard that was where they went," Manse said and put the letter in his pocket. "At least it's a place to start looking."

"I don't reckon there's any way I can write to you?" Tom asked.

"I don't know why not," Manse said. "Just write to the return address that Rebecca put in her letter. I know we'll be going there, to pick up her and McCollum's trail. You got the address written down?"

"Sure do. I kept it 'cause I plan to write Rebecca one day," Tom paused. "But I don't figure it'll be real smart for me to address a letter to Manse Jolly, even if it goes to some little town in Texas. Too many eyes see letters – and your wanted poster is in just about every post office."

"Then send it to another name. Send it to – let's see – send it to *Mr. Red Horse*. How's that?"

Tom and Johnny laughed.

Suddenly the kitchen door opened so forcefully Manse thought it was coming off its hinges.

Robespierre filled the frame.

"Horses coming," he said. "Soldiers! Hurry, Mister Manse," he held the door open. "I told you that man was gonna do you dirt, Mister Manse. I told you."

Manse hugged Tom and Johnny and hurried through the kitchen, out the door, swung into the saddle and galloped past the smokehouse and barn, toward the woods – just as Union Cavalry charged up the drive and rounded the corner of the house – less than a hundred yards behind him.

A barrage of shots whined past him and ricocheted off trees.

Then the back of his right thigh felt as if it had been struck by a hammer. The impact was followed by intense pain and a sensation of liquid warmth.

Manse rode faster – along the creek bed – up an embankment – down into a gully.

These were his woods – every tree, every rock. Within minutes he had out-distanced his pursuers, and the shooting soon stopped. They had lost him in the half-moon's light.

He reined into a ravine, waited and listened, removed a length of rope from his saddle bag, tied it around his upper thigh to stop the blood flow, then urged his horse north.

An hour before dawn he arrived at the cave.

When he dismounted, pain shot the length of his leg, groin to ankle. He limped into the shack, sat on his bedroll, re-kindled the fire, loosened the rope around his thigh and let the blood flow for a full minute.

It did not gush or spurt. He sighed relief – the bullet had not torn an artery. He retied the rope and added wood to the fire.

While it blazed, he took several drinks of corn whiskey.

Then he slid his knife from its sheath and laid its blade on the coals.

He removed the rope, and allowed the blood to flow again. He took off his boots, unbuckled his belt and removed his trousers, cut away one leg of his underwear and examined the wound.

The bullet had entered the back of his thigh and traveled through flesh for several inches along his thigh-bone before lodging against it. He sighed relief again – it had not struck with sufficient force to break the bone. And it had stopped before reaching his knee – which it could have shattered and left him crippled.

But despite feelings of good luck, Manse knew what every soldier knew – that no gun-shot wound is minor, and that he must do two things – remove the bullet, to prevent lead poisoning – and cauterize the wound to stop the bleeding.

He poured whiskey on a bandanna and wiped the wound.

The whiskey burned raw flesh.

He drank, and the whiskey burned his stomach.

He picked up the knife.

The blade was hot.

Clenching his teeth, Manse forced the tip into the wound and slid it along the bone.

Pain raced through him. He felt dizzy. He took a cartridge from his belt and bit it.

He pushed the blade deeper. Sweat drenched him.

Then he felt the knife's point touch and move the bullet. He slid the tip around it and slowly worked it back along the bone and out of the wound opening.

The bullet did not emerge whole.

It had fragmented, and that would mean trouble later. But there was nothing he could do about it now. Locating and removing lead fragments required surgery he was neither qualified nor equipped to perform.

He used his bandanna to wipe the blood from his knife and his hands.

His task was half-completed.

Manse put the blade back on the coals, loosened the rope, let the wound bleed freely, then tightened it again.

He took a drink, and waited for the blade to get hotter.

He took another drink, waited a few more minutes, and poured the rest of the whiskey into the wound.

Then, in one determined movement, he picked up the knife and pressed the flat of the blade against the wound.

His flesh steamed, then fried.

Nearly unconscious, he held the blade in place until it cooled.

He removed the rope. No blood oozed.

He used the bandanna as a bandage and exhaled a long sigh. He had done all he could do.

He put on his trousers.

He needed to empty his bladder and his bowels.

But most of all, he needed a drink.

Manse threw aside jars, bottles and jugs – all empty. Then he remembered that Texas always carried a bottle or jug.

Manse crawled to Texas' bedroll, pulled aside the blankets, and opened the saddle bags.

***

An hour after dawn, Texas Brown arrived.

Manse was lying by the dying fire, his eyes closed. Texas looked at the empty jars, smiled and walked to his bedroll, knelt and lifted the blanket.

"Lose something?" Manse sat up – a pistol in each hand. "Don't move, Texas," he said.

"What the hell's the matter, Manse?" Texas asked.

"I asked you a question," Manse said. "Did you lose something?"

"Yeah. My saddlebags were here. Did you move 'em?"

"I sure did. And they were mighty heavy."

"I was gonna tell you about what's in 'em, Manse," Texas started to stand.

"You just keep kneeling right there."

"What the hell is this, Manse? Why the gun? I thought – "

"I've got a real good idea what you *thought*, Texas," Manse said. "You *thought* I wouldn't be here this morning. You thought I'd either be in jail waiting to be hanged, or already dead. That's what you *thought*."

Texas stared at Manse's bloody trousers. "What happened to your leg?"

"What the hell you think happened? I got shot by your yankee soldier-friends."

"There were soldiers at your place last night?"

"You ought to know."

"Now, hold on, Manse, I swear to you, I didn't know," Texas stared at Manse's pistols. "I did just what I promised. Me and my boys burned out them niggers, and the yankees come after us."

"Except the ones that came after me."

"So that's what happened," Texas kept staring at Manse's pistols – and tried to remain calm. "I noticed there wasn't an awful lot of soldiers chasing us, but I figured the rest was helping them niggers fight the fire. I reckon the yankees must have guessed that we was staging another diversion – so you could go to your house," Texas smiled. "Guess we didn't fool them too good this time."

"I don't think the yankees had to figure out anything this time," Manse said.

"Wait a damn minute. You think I told the bluebellies?"

"Didn't you?"

"Hell, no, I didn't!"

"Then how do you explain what's in these?" Manse lifted the blanket off the saddlebags.

"I was going to tell you about that, Manse. I swear I was," Texas sweated. "I got that gold for – "

" – for promising to deliver Manse Jolly – dead or alive – that's what-for," Manse spat the words. "This is blood-money!"

"No, Manse. I swear to you – that's part of the Confederate gold that was stole – "

"Confederate gold?" Manse's head pounded. His nostrils flared. "What kind of goddamn fool you take me for, Texas?"

"But it is, Manse. I swear it to God. Martin McCollum and I – "

"So you were in-cahoots with him," Manse's voice rose. "And I reckon you knew about him and Rebecca planning to run away a long time before it happened – but you came up here and pretended to be surprised when Tom told you," Manse felt anger turn to rage.

"You bastard! You knew, didn't you?" he yelled the words.

"Well, yeah, Manse, I did know, but – "

"And it's all true – isn't it? You went to Bartow – and you got him to arrest Tom, didn't you?"

"Manse, please, listen, it's not the way it sounds – "

"God damn-you, you got Tom put in that yankee stockade – " Manse cocked both pistols.

"Yeah, but only because – " Texas searched for words – then suddenly knew that this time words would not work.

He slid his hand inside his coat and wrapped it around the two-shot pistol he wore inside his waistcoat.

Manse tightened his fingers on the triggers.

"Just what the hell were you hoping for next, Texas – to see my shot-to-shit body on display in front of the Anderson Courthouse? Or did you just plan to watch me hang?"

Manse squeezed triggers.

Texas drew the pistol from his waistcoat.

Shots sounded far away.

Texas grabbed his stomach with his left hand, and fired his small pistol into the floor.

"You're crazy – Manse – god-damned-crazy –"

Manse fired again and watched Texas' eyes bulge.

The pistols felt soft in Manse's hands. The cave filled with fog.

"You're – wrong – Manse – you damn crazy drunk – I'm the only friend – " Texas' pistol dropped from his hand.

Manse squeezed triggers again.

Texas crumpled, doubled up, and was silent.

Manse shot again. And again.

Texas' body rolled over and was still.

Manse got to his knees, then slowly stood and holstered his pistols.

The cave was silent. Its floor was cotton, dry and soft beneath his feet.

He walked to Texas Brown, leaned over, removed the cigar case from his coat pocket, took one out, bit off the tip and lit it. Then he removed from Texas' waistcoat pocket his watch and a small leather pouch containing a few silver and gold coins.

Manse felt warmth cover him.

Another battle had ended.

He picked up the two pairs of saddlebags filled with gold bars and limped out of the shack.

Texas had tethered his white stallion just outside the cave. A supply sack was tied behind its saddle. Manse put one pair of saddlebags on Texas' horse, and one on his horse.

Then he lifted off Texas' supply sack.

It was heavy.

Very heavy.

Inside it he found two jugs of whiskey and large leather bag of silver coins – and another filled with gold coins – and a record book of dues paid by Klansmen.

Goddamned son of a bitch!

Manse spat.

It wasn't enough that Texas Brown had collected the reward money for Manse Jolly, he was also taking the Klan's treasury with him.

Now Manse was convinced – absolutely – that wherever Texas planned to go, he had come to the cave this morning only to get his gold – not expecting Manse to be there – not expecting ever again to see Manse Jolly alive.

The fact that he didn't have any supplies in his supply sack proved he didn't plan to travel with a wanted man.

Hell no – not Texas Brown. He was rich – and he planned to live well, in fancy hotels – on Manse Jolly's blood-money.

Manse tied the supply sack to the horn of the white stallion's saddle, tied its reins to the saddle sling of his horse, then went back into the shack.

He picked up his Henry rifle and bedroll, then knelt and took off Texas' gun belt and pistols, and stood and looked at Texas.

Manse heard and felt nothing.

Cotton deadened sound and emotion.

"I wish you hadn't done it, Texas," he finally said aloud.

"I was really looking forward to us going west together," he tossed his cigar into the fire's ashes.

"Now I reckon I only got one more score to settle – Martin McCollum."

-19-

His pace west was slowed as much by fear of capture as by the pain in his wounded leg.

He avoided towns – camping instead in remote areas – seldom daring to stop at farms to ask for food and shelter.

Infection's fever increased by the end of his first week of riding.

His thigh swelled and ached down into his ankle and up into his groin. He knew that the remaining shrapnel should be removed, but any town large enough for a doctor presented the risk of a garrison of Union soldiers ready to be summoned for the price on his head.

So again he heated his knife's blade in campfire coals and cut into his thigh. And with whiskey's assistance, he endured the pain and opened a channel for the flow of the greenish putrid smelling liquid that battlefield surgeons called "noble pus".

After the ordeal, he slept fitfully, locked in fever's delirium. But his nightmares were not of multi-color monsters. Rather he relived in detail his most frightening memories of The War.

Within twenty-four hours of releasing pus from the wound, the swelling eased and his fever subsided, and he rode again. But after a few days, the symptoms recurred, and he was forced to repeat the process.

Soon he had lost count of the number of times he cut into his thigh to let infection flow. Each hour's riding forged itself into the next. Days became weeks – and nights came too often.

He remained instinctively cautious, even when he drank more than usual to kill the pain. He never opened and drained and dressed his wound while spending the night at a farm. It was not a good idea, he thought, to allow himself to be seen as wounded and weak.

And he never stayed any place more than one night.

As he traveled southwest, the change of seasons was barely perceptible.

At a store near a crossing point on the Mississippi River, he stopped to buy supplies, and wrote a letter to his family:

"I travel slow and careful. Most folks are real nice. If they recognize me from posters, they never let on. Today I am at a place where there's a barge that will ferry me across to Louisiana. I asked if there are any Union soldiers around, and the storekeeper says they are only at the bigger towns. And farther west, he says, there are even fewer yankees. That is welcome news. I've asked him to mail this letter to you. I hope it finds you all well. You are in my thoughts and heart. Please write to me when you can. I'll be pleased to have news of you all. God keep you." (signed) *Red Horse.*

***

Time and place and the pace of his trek eluded him.

He learned that Christmas was only two days away when he stopped at a farm owned by a Freedman named Abraham Isaac Jacob.

"I couldn't decide which name I wanted most," he said, "so I took 'em all," he smiled and introduced his wife, Emma, and their six children.

He also told Manse that the swamp whose banks he had ridden for the past two days was half in Louisiana, half in Texas.

Manse felt safe in the home of Abraham and Emma.

He relaxed and soaked in a wooden tub of hot water, slept on clean blankets spread over fresh hay in the barn, and shared their celebration of Christmas – Bible stories mixed with those told to Abraham and Emma by parents only one generation from Africa – and a feast of wild turkey and roast pork, yams, rice and gravy, and dried apple cobbler.

On Christmas morning, they gave Manse a shirt Emma had made. She had sewn it to fit Abraham, that was obvious, but he was only slightly heavier than Manse, so it fit fine.

The children shared with him the candied fruit that was their treat, and showed off the shoes and clothes Abraham and Emma had bought for them on their last trip into the nearest town, thirty-five miles away.

Manse regretted that he had no gifts for them – then he remembered the pouch of Klan money that he had dipped into only a few times along the way.

He gave each of the children silver coins, and to Abraham and Emma, he gave five gold dollars each.

Abraham protested that it was too much, that they didn't expect payment for sharing their Christmas with him, but Manse insisted that they take the money, not as any kind of payment, but as "a gift from me – and a man who used to be my friend." (He was tempted to draw a comparison to Judas Iscariot, but decided that would be too difficult to explain.)

He left them two days after Christmas, with kisses from the children, and hugs from Abraham and Emma – and a supply sack that bulged with food. And four jugs of Abraham's best homemade whiskey, thonged to hang over the horses' haunches.

***

Five days later he camped in a stand of piney woods on the sheltered side of what passed for a hill in east Texas. His fever had returned and lancing the wound was necessary.

He drank heavily – in preparation for the pain of self-surgery and the turmoil of nightmares that inevitably followed.

In the chill of the next morning's sunrise, he was awakened by the neighing and rearing of his horses straining at their hitching line.

And from over the rise he heard the unmistakable hoofbeats of at least a platoon – perhaps even a company – of cavalry.

Despite pain, he crawled the fifty yards to the crest of the hill, expecting to see a field of Union Blue.

But all he saw was open grassland and a herd of wild horses.

He stood and slowly made his way back to his camp, to his horses, and removed the saddle bags, supply sack and saddle from Texas' white stallion – took off its bit and halter, slapped it on the rump and watched as the horse reared, whinnied loudly, and galloped toward the herd – ready to take on its leader and lure away the best mares.

Manse had to struggle to hold the reins of his small rust stallion.

"Can't let you have your head, old friend. Leastwise not yet," he said. "You and me have still got a ways to go."

He put Texas' saddle, saddlebags and supply sack on his horse.

"Sorry about all the extra weight," Manse patted the horse's neck. "I promise I'll buy you a pack-mule first chance I get."

***

On January 5, 1868, Manse Jolly rode onto the Main Street of the town of Cameron, Texas.

He saw no Union soldiers when he dismounted at the building bearing the sign "General Merchandise & Post Office."

Inside he saw no wanted posters, and no customers, so he walked to the counter and asked for his mail.

"Red-Horse, you say?" The old man thumbed through a stack of letters.

"Yep, here's one," he said and handed an envelope to Manse.

"Thanks," Manse took the letter.

"Do you know if a man named Martin McCollum lives around here?" he asked.

"McCollum? Can't say I ever heard the name."

"You sure?" Manse persisted. "I was told that him and his wife came here about a year or more back."

"If they was living hereabouts, I'd know," the man said. "'Of course we do get lots of folks just passing through, looking for places to settle. Most of 'em end up calling on Captain Jack Smith. He knows more about these parts than just about anybody."

"You're speaking of Captain John Gray Smith – Lightning Jack Smith?" Manse said.

"One and the same," the man said. "Hero of Vicksburg – Devil's Run – Black Swamp."

Manse felt confused. Of-course he had heard of John Gray Smith – Anderson District's most famous Confederate son.

Born not far from the Lebanon Community where the Jolly and Largent families lived, Smith had left South Carolina and moved to Texas almost twenty years ago. He had become a successful rancher, and when The War began, he raised, trained and led a famous Brigade of Cavalry.

How, Manse wondered, had Martin McCollum's trail led him to Lightning Jack Smith's home town? It had to be more than mere coincidence.

"If this fellow you're looking for came through Cameron, he most likely talked to Captain Smith," the man behind the counter said.

"Where can I find Captain Smith?" Manse asked.

"Big spread on Little River, north of here. Just across the river, in Robertson County. Take the only road north out of Cameron. It forks a few miles out of town, but the way to Captain Smith's place is marked real plain."

Manse thanked the man, bought some cigars, left the store, mounted and rode out of Cameron.

When he was safely away from the town, he stopped and opened the envelope from Tom:

"Your words have been happily received," the letter began, "Mama Jolly rests more easy knowing you are safe. We all pray for you, especially Melinda. Your namesake is well. There's not much to report. For a while after your visit we had lots of yankees coming out here asking questions, but now they tend to leave us alone.

"On a trip into Anderson, Johnny and I saw a newspaper with a story quoting a yankee colonel saying that since nobody had seen you or Texas Brown lately, the Army figured that you both had probably left the state, separately or together. You didn't mention him in your letter. Give him our best. He was a good friend to us. Melinda asks about him almost as much as she does about you.

"As for politics, things here are still a mess. The yankees had an election. Over eighty thousand Freedmen voted – and only forty thousand whites. So now seventy-six Freedmen are running the state government. There will soon be nothing left of South Carolina. Reconstruction is destroying the South – and southerners won't ever forget or forgive what's being done to them.

"In the midst of this, the Klan has gotten even more active, and more violent, than ever. It is giving the Army and the scalawags and carpetbaggers pure-hell. Rumor has it that their new leader is a double-w. And I reckon that in our hearts all us confederates are cheering them on, even if we don't ride with them.

"Well, I reckon that's about all that's worth writing about from here. Please, write to us when you can. Accept our love, and our prayers for your protection.

"God be with you, my Brother." *(signed)* Tom.

Manse put the letter back in his pocket – and heard Texas Brown's laugh echo above the sound of wind brush-stroking pines.

Manse's head ached. He felt dizzy. His groin hurt. The infection was festering. His fever was increasing.

He urged his horse faster, but trotting was painful, so he slowed to a walk. Almost an hour later, he came to a drive leading off the road to a westernized version of an ante-bellum home. Smaller houses and trees lined the drive. Behind them were pastures and crop-land. And dozens of men, white and black, were working around the out-buildings.

When Manse reached the front of the house, a black man – dressed better than the field hands but not liveried like servants at plantations before The War – took the reins of his horse and tied it to a hitching post.

Manse dismounted and grimaced in pain.

Before he could tell the servant who he was, a voice reached him from above.

"Welcome, sir. Join me, please – up here on the verandah."

Manse walked up the stairs.

The man who greeted him was tall and thin, and leaned heavily on a cane. His blue eyes were younger than his deeply-lined face, long white hair and beard.

"John Gray Smith, Captain, Army of The Confederacy, at your service, sir," the man said, and did not wait for a reply, as if he did not expect his visitor to give his name

They shook hands, and the man's grip was strong – unexpected from such a scrawny hand, on such a downright skinny man.

"Please, sit and have a drink with me," he limped to a table laden with pitchers and glasses and bottles.

"What's your pleasure, sir?" he asked. "Whiskey, gin, lemonade, water?"

"Whiskey, please," Manse said, and sat.

The captain sat across from him and slid a glass and a bottle across the table.

"I think a man is his own best judge of how much and how fast he needs to drink," the captain said.

Manse poured, and was about to drink, when he saw the stack of wanted posters on the chair next to him.

His hand went to his holster. He started to get up.

"Sit back down, please," the captain said. "If I intended you harm, sir, I would hardly leave those posters in plain view," he half-smiled. "I keep them there for a purpose. From a man's reaction, I can tell whether or not he is among them. But then I had already recognized you, Mister Jolly. I have read many stories about you – and watched with interest as the reward for you has risen dramatically."

Manse's hand again rested on his pistol.

"Relax, Mister Jolly. I assure you that no one here will turn you in, regardless of the size of the reward. To do so would dishonor us all, and bring swift and violent retribution. Every man who works here is a veteran of the Confederate Army," he sipped his drink. "A few even have rewards on their heads – though, I must admit, none nearly so impressively large as yours," he smiled more broadly. "And, in case you are wondering, there are no yankee soldiers in Robertson or Milam Counties. The Union Army doesn't seem to feel that occupying East Texas is worth the manpower. So, please, finish your drink. I'll have your horse tended, and your saddle-bags taken to a guest room, and a hot bath prepared."

"I thank you for your offer of hospitality, Captain Smith," Manse said. "It's a privilege and honor to drink with a true Confederate hero like Lightning Jack Smith," Manse smiled, raised his glass, and drank, "but I came here just to ask a few questions about a man you might have talked to when he came through Cameron a year or so back," Manse finished his drink. "If you can give me any information about him, I'll appreciate it – and be on my way."

Captain Smith reached across the table, picked up the bottle, and poured Manse another drink.

"Mister Jolly," he said, "I lost half of my right foot to the green-rot a few months after Vicksburg, so I reckon I'm more observant than most of the way men limp, and the stains on their trouser-legs, and the sweet-smell a festering wound carries," his eyes locked onto

Manse's. "I would say you're in considerable pain, sir – and feverish – and I'd wager you're drawing the noble-pus yourself. But you can treat yourself only so long before you'll likely lose that leg – and maybe your life. The stain is high up on your thigh – an especially bad spot. And since whoever it is you're looking for is, as you yourself said, already a year or more ahead of you, I suggest you have a hot bath and a few drinks – and draw the noble pus again, to ease your pain and fever – then rest. We'll talk at dinner. If I can help you find whoever it is you're looking for, I will. But first of all, you had best pay attention to that leg."

***

The hotter the water, the better, the captain said, and the servants prepared a tub of water so hot Manse thought his skin would blister.

And the captain sent a servant with liniment to draw out the noble pus when Manse lanced his leg – and ointment to spread on the wound, so it would remain open – and a liquid in which the servant soaked strips of muslin to wrap the wound and absorb pus and blood.

After he finished his bath and bound his wound, Manse slept for almost two hours, then a servant awakened him, and he dressed and went downstairs to dinner.

He felt much better.

But it was not the reduced fever in his leg that lifted Manse's spirits that evening – rather it was the sight of the young woman Captain Smith introduced him to.

"This is my daughter, Elizabeth-Mildred," the captain said. "Most everybody calls her Lizabeth, but I call her Millie. That was her Mama's name, god-rest-her. She died three years back."

"I'm pleased to meet you, Miss Smith," Manse tried to smile and say more but managed only to stammer something about the weather – and stare at her.

Manse guessed her age at maybe twenty.

She was as thin as her Daddy, almost as tall, and had his sharp features.

(Manse's Mama would have called her raw-boned.)

Her hair was auburn, more red than his.

And her eyes were the greenest he had ever seen – no doubt inherited from her mother.

Her face was sun-leathered.

And, by-god, she was pleasing to look at.

She wore a long skirt unlike any he had ever seen – not frilled and full like most Southern women preferred. In fact, Manse finally realized, it wasn't really a skirt but rather a pair of trousers with legs flared so wide they gave the illusion of a skirt.

It was designed, he decided, to enable her to ride straddle-saddle.

Her boots were heeled and pointed, and her blouse was identical, except for color, to the shirt her father wore.

She was, Manse felt sure, more comfortable on a horse than in a parlor.

"Please, call me Millie, like Papa does," she smiled, and reached out and shook Manse's hand, and her grip was as strong as her father's.

Then she took his arm and escorted him to the dining table.

A servant held her chair, and Manse sat across from her.

Millie sipped wine. Manse drank whiskey.

"Papa says you have a wound you're tending yourself, but he thinks it probably should be seen by a surgeon," she said. "So tomorrow I'll ride with you over to Major Sanders' spread and we'll let him take a look at it. At sun-up I have to get our drovers organized and on their way. They're driving two-hundred head up to Fort Worth. But right after breakfast we can go over to the Major's place."

Manse continued to stare silently at Millie Smith. It wasn't that she was beautiful – she wasn't. But there was something special about her – he just wasn't sure what.

"Major Sanders was a surgeon in The War," Captain Smith said. "Everybody around here calls him Major – or Surgeon-Major – instead of Doctor. He took care of me when I was wounded. Still takes care of us. He gave me the ointment I sent to your room – "

Manse felt embarrassed when he suddenly realized that the Captain was talking to him but he wasn't listening.

"Of course you will go with Millie to see Major Sanders first thing tomorrow," Captain Smith said.

"I appreciate the offer, Captain," Manse said, forcing himself to return to the conversation, "but I'm planning on leaving before sunup. Provided you can help me decide where I'm going."

"But I told you, Mister Jolly, you need to get that leg looked at before you do anything else –" the Captain's tone was an order.

"Papa, I think Mister Jolly has to make that decision for himself," Millie said. "You're always saying a man is his own best judge of the things he needs to do."

"She always hoists me on my own petard, Mister Jolly," Captain Smith shrugged and smiled. "And, of course, Millie is right – only you can decide what you must do."

"Will you please stop calling me *Mister Jolly*," Manse smiled from father to daughter. "Call me Manse. Or Manson," he said, then drank to clear his throat and organize his thoughts.

"Very well, Manse," Captain Smith said. "I won't try further to persuade you to see Major Sanders," he leaned forward. "So now I guess it's time you told me about this person you're looking for."

"There are two of them – Martin McCollum – and Rebecca," Manse said.

"They are obviously very important to you," the Captain said. "I presume they are husband and wife?"

Manse had not thought of Rebecca and Martin like that, and he didn't like the image it conjured.

He fumbled for words – then they came out in a torrent:

"Martin was a yankee lieutenant. When he got out of the Army, he ran off with Rebecca, the sister of my best friend, Tom," Manse paused, to make sure they were following his explanation. "Tom was wounded in The War. Lost his leg. So he can't ride like he use to. That's why he asked me to try to find Rebecca and make sure she is all right – and talk to Martin about some things."

Manse stopped and hoped there wouldn't be too many questions.

"And what did you say Martin's last name was?" the captain asked.

"McCollum. Martin McCollum."

"McCollum?" Captain Smith nodded. "Yes, indeed – now that you have said his name again, I do remember him. Nice looking young man. Very polite – for a yankee. Unfortunately, his accent was undeniably New York. He came through here a year or so ago. Stayed at The Cameron Inn and, quite properly, sent a note asking leave for himself and his wife to call on us." Captain Smith paused. "I never dine with yankees, of course, but I did invite them out for afternoon drinks on the verandah. We talked for a couple of hours. He told me he had been stationed in Anderson District, South Carolina, which I know is your home, Manse, – and where, I am sure you know, I was born and lived until I moved to Texas twenty-four years ago," Captain Smith paused. "To be quite candid, at first I was quite suspicious of McCollum, and how he had managed to find his way from Anderson, South Carolina, to Cameron, Texas – but in the course of our conversation, he explained that while in Anderson he had developed a close friendship with a southerner named Brown, who had suggested that he come to Cameron and seek my advice about living in Texas."

"Brown?" Manse half-mumbled the word.

"Yes, I'm pretty sure that was the name," Captain Smith said. "McCollum wanted to buy some ranch land, and had already talked to a number of landowners in this area before he called on me. But no one around here would sell land to him, which I told him I thought was just as well. I didn't think he would be happy here – an ex-Union officer living amongst so many ex-Rebels."

"Did his wife seem to be all right?" Manse asked.

"She appeared fine," Captain Smith said. "I remember that she was a very pretty young woman, but I don't recall that she said much of anything. He did all the talking. Specifically, he wanted my advice about land in Texas. I suggested he look south of San Antonio. That is where Texas begins to become less-Southern and more-Mexican. Land is cheap. It's also sparsely settled – and people who live farther apart tend to leave each other alone."

"And that's where they went?" Manse asked.

"Indeed they did. I received a letter from McCollum several months later. A very gracious letter – that is why I remember it so well. He thanked me for my advice and said they had purchased land about a day's ride from the Fria River. The nearest town is

Yancey. That was the mail address. And they had named their spread The Double-M-Ranch."

"You have a mighty fine memory, Captain," Manse said.

"Papa never forgets anything," Millie said. "And likewise he never keeps anything from me."

She looked from her father to Manse.

"When I arrived home this evening," she said, "Papa came to my room and told me a lot of what he knew – what he had read and heard – about our house-guest, *Manson Jolly*. And now that you've explained why you have come to Texas, I feel obliged to ask you a rather impertinent question: Are you truly looking for this man, Martin McCollum, so you can report back to your friend Tom that his sister is safe? – Or are you planning to add yet another yankee to your list – and make Rebecca a widow?"

Manse tried to avoid her eyes but could not.

"Sooner or later, Manson Jolly," Millie said, "The War has got to come to an end for everybody – including you," she reached across the table. "Why don't you stay here a while and let Major Sanders fix your leg. Rest and sleep." She touched his hand. "Talk to me and Papa while you heal. Who knows – you might even decide that one more yankee isn't worth killing."

"As for the future," Captain Smith said, "when your leg heals I can offer you work. My men know your name. Word has already spread that you are here. They would welcome ranching with you."

Millie squeezed his hand.

Manse held her eyes – and slowly shook his head.

"I appreciate everything you're saying, and I know you mean well," he spoke slowly and chose his words carefully. He did not want to offend them. "But there's just no way you can understand everything that's happened." He paused. "And there's just not enough time for me to try to explain it all."

He paused again.

"Simply put," he said, "I can't let go of what's not finished. I've come too far to stop now."

The dining room was silent.

"But I would be obliged to you, Captain," Manse said, "if you would sell me a good pack mule. Me and all my things are a mighty big load for my little stallion."

-20-

A half-day's ride from the Fria River, an arrow on a sign pointed off the road:

To The Double-M-Ranch.

An hour later, Manse arrived at a gate beneath an arch. The beginning of a rock fence stretched a few yards in either direction. He opened the gate, closed it behind him, and rode two miles on a wagon trail that ended at a hedged carriage drive leading to an adobe house still under construction. More than twenty workmen were filling walls, tamping them, erecting poles-and-beams, and laying slate and tiles.

The completed section of the house was larger than most plantation homes, and Manse wondered just how big it would be when finished.

"You looking for something?"

A gaunt man with sandy hair walked around the corner of the house.

"This where Martin McCollum lives?" Manse asked.

"Is – but he ain't here."

"When will he be back?"

"Him and the missus went to San Antone for a week. Due back this evening," he studied Manse. "You looking for work?"

"Work? No," Manse said. "I'm – a relative – of his wife."

"All the way from Carolina? Why didn't you say so?" He took the reins of Manse's stallion. "My name's Donald," he said. "I'm Mister McCollum's foreman. Hope you'll forgive me not being polite, but I had no way of knowing who you was."

Manse dismounted.

"I'll get one of the servants to take your bags and bedroll – and fix you a bath and something to drink," Donald lifted saddle bags from the pack mule and set them down.

"Mister McCollum and his missus don't eat dinner at night," he said. "They eat Mexican style – you know: big *comida* in the middle of the day, then just a little something before bed-time."

He spoke fast, as if trying to give Manse as much information as he could, in the shortest possible time.

"But I'll get the servants to fix you something to eat right now," he said. "They're all Mexicans, and don't speak English, so I'll have to tell 'em what you want – unless you speak Mexican?"

"No, I don't," Manse said.

Donald shouted a string of words and the ornately carved front door opened. An older man, dressed in white shirt and pants and sandals came out, picked up Manse's two saddle bags, staggered under their weight, and yelled something at someone in the house. Immediately two young men came out and carried the bags, supply sack and bedroll.

The older man smiled at Manse and led the way through large, sparsely furnished rooms with white stucco walls and massive wooden beams, down a long hallway to a bedroom of tile and stone.

Servants appeared from nowhere, and soon Manse was out of his clothes and soaking in hot water.

He examined his wound.

Green pus oozed. His groin ached and his thigh burned. His fever was getting higher. It was past time for another lancing – but he decided not to do it with all the servants watching. It would have to wait until later tonight – or tomorrow morning.

A Mexican boy brought him a glass of alcoholic fruit punch.

Manse sipped and soaked.

A man who grinned and talked non-stop – and seemed sure Manse understood every word –clipped his hair and beard.

By the time Manse got out of the tub, dried off, and put on clean clothes, it was almost sundown.

The servant who had escorted him to this room, appeared and motioned him to follow.

Manse tucked his pistols in his belt and walked behind the man to a room where food and wine awaited him on a long dining table.

Manse sat, ate and drank, and when he had finished, the same servant led him to another room – this one with floor to ceiling bookshelves and a massive stone fireplace.

A desk and straight chair were on one side of the room.

In front of the fireplace were two sofas and three overstuffed chairs.

The servant pointed to one of the chairs with a table beside it and a footstool in front of it. On the table were a decanter, a glass, a humidor and an ashtray.

Manse sat and poured himself drink.

Bourbon.

Honest-to-god *aged bourbon*, the likes of which he had not tasted since before The War – and damn few times then.

This was the drink of Southrons, not planters.

Manse rolled the taste of burnt oak around in his mouth, swallowed, poured another, lit a cigar and waited.

An hour later he heard them arrive.

Manse walked to the window and looked out. An enclosed coach pulled by two horses stood at the entry. There was not enough light to see the passengers.

He heard Donald's voice as the front door opened.

"He told me he was some kin of Missus McCollum," Donald said. "He's in the library. Hope I done the right thing."

Manse turned and waited.

"Manson," Rebecca ran to him, hugged him and kissed his cheek.

She was as beautiful as he remembered her. And her dress was more expensive than any he had ever seen her wear.

"Welcome to our home, Mister Jolly," Martin McCollum, held out his hand.

Manse did not shake it.

"How are you?" Martin said.

"I'm fine, Lieutenant," Manse nodded. "Just fine."

"Please – call me *Martin*, not *Lieutenant*," he said. "I'm no longer a yankee-soldier."

"To me, you'll always be a yankee soldier – *Martin*," Manse said. "But then I don't reckon I would've recognized you in that fancy western suit."

He turned to Rebecca.

"But I would've recognized you anywhere," he said.

An uncomfortable silence descended.

"You look well, Mister Jolly – "

"I reckon I ought to feel good – Martin. I just had a hot bath. And half a bottle of your fine bourbon."

The silence became heavier.

Rebecca looked sad.

"I wrote to Tom and Mama Jolly and Bonnie and Johnny," she said. "But I never got an answer."

"You didn't really expect one, did you?" Manse's tone was sharp.

"No, I guess not," Rebecca said, and turned away, but not before Manse saw her tears.

"Sit down, Mister Jolly. Let me pour you another drink," Martin filled glasses.

Manse sat in an easy chair.

Martin sat beside Rebecca on the couch.

The awkward silence remained.

"When did you leave South Carolina?" Martin asked.

"About three months ago, I guess," Manse said. "I don't rightly recall the day. I had to travel the long way around. Stay out of towns. Too many posters up."

"I assure you, Mister Jolly, that there are no Union Forces in this part of Texas," Martin finished his drink and stood.

"Now, if you will excuse me," he said, "I feel rather dusty after our trip. I think I'll wash up. I understand you've had dinner. I hope it was to your liking."

"It was good," Manse said. "Real good, thank you."

"I had best go freshen up, too," Rebecca said. "We'll be back down in about a half-hour, Manson."

When they left him alone, he drank and went over in his mind what he had to do.

First, he would explain everything to Rebecca –

Then – there just wasn't any way around it – he had to kill Martin McCollum.

Manse was finishing another drink when Martin and Rebecca came downstairs.

A servant brought a bottle of wine and served them, then refilled Manse's glass with bourbon.

Rebecca broke the silence with questions about the family.

Manse answered with words halting, disjointed, and hoarse.

Rebecca became visibly distressed when he told her about Tom's arrest.

"The only reason they did it was because he was my friend," Manse's anger flashed.

"That goddamn Major Bartow kept him locked up in the stockade for almost a year," he said. "And from what I heard, they treated him bad. Of course, I didn't actually see Tom or any of my folks until the night before I left South Carolina. And even then I only saw 'em for a few minutes."

Manse paused to drink.

"Poor old Mama – we both cried when I told her good-bye," he said. "But I did get a chance to hold Tom and Bonnie's baby boy – my namesake – Manson Sherrill Largent – for a minute or two."

Once again the room became quiet.

"Of course Melinda was asleep, so I told her that it was all a dream," Manse felt unsure what to say.

"And Johnny – I tell you, Rebecca, that boy Johnny is getting to look more like Larry every day."

He heard his words echo, as in the cave.

"Damn yankees finally turned Tom loose. Said there was more trouble with Tom in jail than before," Manse smiled and nodded. "I made sure of that."

He stood and walked to the fireplace. A servant brought coffee.

Martin stood by the couch, lit a cigar and gauged his words.

"Mister Jolly – Manse – Rebecca and I were talking while we were upstairs," he said. "And we decided to invite you to stay here with us for as long as you want. I'm just getting started ranching, and I don't know much about farming and cattle and all. You could be a great help to me. We could work together. I assure you, you will be safe here."

"I wish you would consider it, Manson," Rebecca smiled at him. "I know you probably don't plan to make your visit permanent – but won't you please stay for a while?"

Manse glared at her.

"You think I rode all the way here just to *visit* you and Martin?" He snapped the words.

The smile in Rebecca's eyes turned to fear.

"Then – why are you here, Manson?"

"I came to kill Lieutenant McCollum," Manse's voice was calm. "But don't worry, Martin, I won't do it in front of Rebecca."

Martin's left hand rested on the derringer tucked in his waistcoat pocket.

Manse's right hand went to his pistol.

Rebecca stood and stepped between them.

"Sit down, Martin, please," she said, and waited until he sat.

Then she turned to Manse.

"Please tell me, Manson – why do you want to kill Martin?"

Manse put his glass on the mantle, and spoke into the fire.

"It cost a lot of money to build a house like this," he said, and turned to face her. "It's sure a lot nicer place than you and I could've ever had in South Carolina."

Rebecca took two steps and stood close to him.

"I think I know what you are thinking, Manson," she said. "But I didn't deceive you when I told you what I felt for you. What I felt for you then – and what I feel for you now – is a love that will never change. Martin knows that. And he has been patient and understanding with me," she spoke softly to Manse.

"And in the time Martin and I have been together," she said, "I've felt my love for him grow. And now I'm happy with him. He's a good man, Manson – even if he is a yankee."

"The fact he's a yankee don't particularly bother me, Rebecca," Manse said. "But he just plain can't be a *good man* – not and do what he's done."

"I swear to you, Manson, that Martin didn't drag me out here against my will. I came because – because, after you were gone, the only future I could see for me was with Martin," Rebecca paused. "So you can't kill him just because I ran off with him," she said. "Or because I've fallen in love with him."

"I'm not talking about you and him running off – or falling in love," Manse said. "What I *am* talking about is where Martin got the money to buy all this land and build this big house."

"So that's it," Martin said. "You found out."

"Yeah, damn you, I found out," Manse spat the words. "Now tell your wife where you got all your *gold*, Lieutenant."

Rebecca looked at Manse.

"I know where he got it, Manson –" she said.

"You know?" Manse frowned.

"Please, Manson, let me explain," she touched his arm.

Manse jerked away from her.

"Go on," he said, "I'm listening."

"I didn't know about the gold when we got married. But when we got here and bought this land, Martin told me."

"How could you stay with him, knowing that?"

"What difference does it make if Martin stole Confederate gold? It was already stolen, anyhow. All Martin did was take some of it from the real thieves."

"Confederate gold?" Manse looked past her to Martin. "You goddamn yankee liar! Why didn't you tell her the truth? Or don't you have the truth in you?"

"But that is the truth," Martin said. "Admittedly, I lied to Rebecca at the beginning, when I told her I had inherited money. But later, I told her that Texas Brown and I – "

"You admit you were in it with Texas?"

"Of course. Why should I deny that?"

"Then as long as you're not denying anything, Lieutenant, go on and tell Rebecca the whole truth. If you don't – I will."

"Then by-God, Mister Jolly, by all means, go ahead and tell her whatever the hell it is you're talking about. Obviously you know things that I don't."

Rebecca picked up the decanter, filled a glass and handed it to Manse.

"Please, Manson, tell me what you know," her voice remained soft. "I want to hear everything you have to say."

Manse drank and felt calmer. The pounding in his head eased.

"It's real simple," he said. "This good man you love – this husband of yours – this Martin McCollum – and my *friend,* Texas Brown – made a deal with that Major Bartow. He gave them the reward money in gold, in advance, in exchange for Texas' promise to deliver Manse Jolly – dead or alive."

Martin looked at Rebecca, then looked at Manse, and shook his head.

"Who the hell told you that?" Martin asked.

"Nobody had to tell me," Manse said. "I figured it out for myself."

"You're stark-raving-mad," Martin said.

"Wait, Martin, let him finish," Rebecca said, then turned back to Manse. "Go on, Manson, tell us what you figured out."

"Well, first of all, I know for a fact that Texas and Martin suddenly had lots of money. I know because they both gave Tom money to pay taxes."

"Did you, Martin?" Rebecca asked.

"Yes," Martin said. "But I didn't know that Texas did."

"Then, a few days later you and Martin ran away," Manse said. "Tom wanted to follow you. So did I. But before we could leave, Texas Brown got Bartow to arrest Tom and put him in jail, so he couldn't follow you. And he knew that if Tom was in jail, I wouldn't leave and go after you."

Rebecca shook her head.

"It's true, Rebecca," Manse said. "Before you and Martin left, he and Texas had already made their deal with Bartow. But if Tom and I went after you, then Texas couldn't deliver me."

"This is damned preposterous," Martin said. "Everything you've figured-out is not only incorrect, it is totally illogical. First of all, you are here, so obviously Texas Brown didn't deliver you to Major Bartow when I left."

"He decided to wait."

"For what? If, as you say, we had been paid in advance, why would he wait?"

"Because, after Bartow jailed Tom, I told Texas I was going to kill Bartow. And since you and Texas had made a deal with Bartow that nobody else knew anything about – Texas figured he would wait until I killed Bartow, then deliver me and collect the reward all over again."

Manse poured another bourbon.

Martin took a deep breath, sighed, and handed Manse a cigar, then spoke slowly.

"Manse," he said, "Major Bartow arrived in Anderson just a few days before Rebecca and I left. There was hardly time for me to make any kind of deal with him."

"Deals don't take a lot of time," Manse said.

Martin turned to Rebecca and shrugged his exasperation.

"Please tell Manse where my gold was hidden before we left South Carolina," he said.

"In the false bottom of a trunk," Rebecca said.

"And where was that trunk stored?"

"At Mama Jolly's house. In the living room."

"For how long?"

"A little over three weeks."

Martin turned back to Manse.

"Think about what Rebecca is saying, Manse. My trunk, containing my gold, was at your mother's house for more than three weeks before Rebecca and I left. And Bartow came to Anderson less than two weeks before we left. Obviously, he didn't give it to me," Martin's eyes locked on Manse's. "I swear to you, the gold I have is Confederate gold. Would you like for me to prove that to you?"

"Sure," Manse said. "Prove it. But don't tell me to go ask Major Bartow – he's dead."

"I figured that was the case," Martin said, and walked to the library door and locked it, then closed the drapes, went to the fireplace, knelt and reached up the chimney. A click sounded and one of the stones swung ajar on a hinge. Martin unlocked and opened the cast-iron door behind the stone, and took out two wooden boxes.

"When we came here, Manse, these boxes each contained eight gold bars," he said. "I melted down two and cast the gold into small ingots that I used to buy land and livestock, and to build this house." Martin looked up. "Manse, do you have any idea of the value of these gold bars?"

Manse shook his head.

"I never owned any gold," he said.

"These boxes each contained a hundred thousand dollars worth of gold," Martin picked up a bar and stood. "The reward on you hasn't reached two hundred thousand dollars, has it?"

"No – " Manse's head hurt.

"This gold's value is only part of my proof that I didn't get it as reward money for turning you in. The rest of my proof is this – " Martin handed him the bar.

Manse stared at the seal and the letters *CSA*.

"US Army gold does not bear The Seal of The Confederacy," Martin said.

Manse squinted and felt the chill of the cave – and remembered that last morning.

Why hadn't he listened to what Texas Brown said? Why hadn't he looked at the bars? And the CSA Seal on them?

Manse handed the gold bar back to Martin.

His own voice was an echo in the cavern.

"You and Texas and Bartow weren't in cahoots," he said.

"Manse, I swear to you that Texas and I got this gold from the three men who stole it from the Confederate Holding Bank. As for Texas, he and I were never *friends*. Except for our scheme to get this gold, I never had anything to do with him. If he made any kind of arrangement to sell you to Bartow for the reward, I knew nothing about it. You'll have to ask Texas – "

"I can't – " tears burned Manse's eyes.

Rebecca touched his cheek.

"I don't care about the others I killed," Manse said.

"I don't give a damn about Bartow and Heaton and Phillips – or even the ones with names I didn't know – I don't give a damn about any of them, but Texas mattered. He was my friend."

Manse shivered and began to sob.

"I thought long and hard about it – and I never would've shot him if I hadn't felt real sure he had done everything just the way I figured he had. But I was wrong," Manse said. "As damned wrong as I was sure I was damned right."

He sat and held his head and let tears flow.

Martin was silent.

"Why don't you try to get a good night's sleep, Manson?" Rebecca finally said. "Things will look different in the morning."

"Rebecca is right," Martin said. "We can talk more about this tomorrow – when you feel better."

"Yeah, in the morning," Manse nodded. "I don't feel too good. I've got a hurt leg. I didn't tell you that, did I?"

Fog filled the room.

Rebecca helped him stand, and walked with him to the bedroom. She kissed him and wiped away his tears – and left him sitting on the side of the bed.

When she closed the door, Manse mumbled something, fell across the bed and sobbed until the images that brought his tears sank inside him.

***

When Manse awoke, the only light in his room came from the lamp on the desk.

Beside it were a decanter and a glass.

Pain burned his thigh and pierced his groin.

The cold sweat of rising fever drenched his clothes.

The throbbing in his head was more intense than ever. More intense even than it had been on that day in Virginia.

He stood and walked to the desk, picked up the decanter of bourbon and drank from it.

Unbidden spectres filled the room.

And from outside he heard Texas Brown's laugh on the wind.

He did not want to sleep.

He found paper, ink and a pen in the desk drawer and began to write.

***

When Martin and Rebecca came down to the patio for morning coffee, Donald was waiting for them.

"That man who come here yesterday from Carolina, come down to the bunk-house afore sun-up and shook me awake and said for me to give you this," he handed Martin an envelope. "And he said to tell you he left something for you in the dining room."

On the dining table, Martin and Rebecca found two oilskin packets.

Martin unrolled them and looked at the two gold bars, then gave the envelope to Rebecca, and said, "It's addressed to you."

Her hands and voice shook as she read aloud:

"Dear Rebecca —

"I have decided it's best I go away. I need to find a place that's warm. I've been alone and cold too long. I'm leaving two of the gold bars for you. A late wedding present, I guess."

Tears blurred Rebecca's eyesight. She wiped them away, then continued.

"I plan on sending the rest of the gold to Tom and my family. I know somebody who will make sure it gets to them. And with this much gold, the Jolly and Largent families won't ever have to worry about money again.

"As for me, I'm not sure where I'm going. I don't reckon it really matters. All the Jolly brothers are gone now.

"Please, don't ever forget me — and that I love you. I always have." — (signed) *Manson*.

***

That last day of January, 1868, the south Texas sun burned him and fever chilled him.

That night he camped in a small blind canyon, out of the prairie wind, and built a fire. He heated the blade of his knife in the fire's coals — drank half a bottle of bourbon — did not eat — and passed out before he could open and drain the festering wound.

By sunrise his fever was the highest it had ever been.

He was awakened by sounds of horsemen. Union cavalry. He had heard the rattle of those sabers too many times before.

And this time they had him boxed in. There was no escape from the canyon. He would have to stand and fight.

It might be the end for him, he decided, but he wouldn't give the yankees the satisfaction of taking the gold.

He lifted the saddle bags and struggled through the brush, looking for a place to hide them.

He had gone only a few yards when he saw the entrance to an animal's lair — a small opening low in the canyon wall, between two boulders. He didn't have time to move rocks and crawl inside, so he pushed the saddle bags past the boulders, into the space behind them. Then he gathered the largest stones he could handle and used them to conceal the opening – and he looked around for landmarks he could remember, so that one-day he might return here and get the saddlebags and take them to Captain Smith, and ask him to make sure they were delivered to Tom Largent.

But first he had to survive the yankee cavalry that was now riding into the canyon.

Manse drew his pistols, stood and limped unsteadily toward the canyon entrance to meet his destiny.

But when he emerged from the canyon, he saw nothing – and heard only the sound of the chilling northwesterly wind.

Delirious, he struggled back to his campsite.

He rekindled the coals of last night's fire.

But the pain in his leg was so intense he could not wait to heat the knife.

He plunged the cold blade into his thigh.

Pus and blood spewed.

He wrapped the draining stab-wound, and finished the bottle of bourbon.

His fever raged.

He needed a doctor – the poison was spreading.

He drew on all his energy to mount his horse.

But he could not ride back to the Double-M-Ranch.

Rebecca rekindled memories of love and family and a life forever lost.

Martin evoked the hatred, violence and terrors of The War that never ended.

And together they had forced him to face the truth of the only *murder* he had ever committed – the killing of Texas Brown.

Manse wanted, more than anything, to talk to Tom – to ask him to lead the way out of this labyrinth, as he had done so often during The War – to help him climb from the mire.

But Tom was far away, and Manse knew they would never meet again.

What he decided that morning, as the Texas blue-norther swept its frozen wind through him, was to go where there was a surgeon who might be able to save his life – and hopefully his leg.

And if he lived, perhaps the people there would not be afraid of him – especially her – and they might even accept him and become his friends – and the pain and wounds of his mind and soul might someday be made whole – along with his body.

Manse pulled the poncho from his supply sack, put it on over his tunic, wrapped it tightly about him, lowered his head against the norther's rain and ice, and rode toward Robertson County Texas.

***

Martin McCollum spent that morning with his foreman, Donald.

They started out early to check the boundaries of the last section of land he had bought, but the storm forced them to take refuge in a line shack, to wait out the wind and hail.

Which suited Martin just fine.

His mind was not on ranching.

Truth be known, he had decided several months ago that living in the middle of Texas – in the midst of nothing but endless miles of open land – was not to his liking. He had been raised in a big city, and he missed crowded sidewalks and the myriad advantages that a city offered.

He had made a choice to come to Texas because he had told Rebecca that he planned to live there, and if he changed his mind, she would never consent to living up-north.

With his wealth, however, he could live very well in any city in the world – and he regretted the day he had ever told her they would live in Texas.

He had not, however, been able to find any excuse to discuss with Rebecca the idea of abandoning the Double-M Ranch and the investment he had made in land and livestock. Nor did he think it possible that he could convince her to give up building and furnishing her dream-house.

But now suddenly Manse Jolly had come into their lives.

In Martin's mind, Manse was crazy as hell. As crazy as Ralph Phillips. Perhaps even crazier.

Captain Phillips had been irrational, and a drunk – a bad combination. But Jolly was obsessed with killing, and a drunk – a more lethal combination.

Martin was sure that he had not seen the last of Manse Jolly. True, he had left – ridden away – destination unknown. But he could easily reappear next week – or next month – or next year.

And when he did, he might make good on his promise to kill Martin McCollum.

That was the argument Martin had decided to make to Rebecca.

He would convince her that their staying in Texas was dangerous – that Manse was certain to come back to kill him and take Rebecca back to South Carolina.

Martin would feign fear far greater than what he felt – in order to frighten Rebecca into fleeing Texas with him – as she had fled South Carolina with him.

He would convince her that they should go to San Antonio as soon as possible and sell their land to the Mexican *padrone* from whom they had purchased it.

Even if they took a great loss on their investment in the ranch and house, the two bars of gold that Manse had left them as a gift would more than offset the loss.

After the ranch was sold, they would go to New Orleans – and from there, to Europe.

It would be easy to talk Rebecca into going to those romantic cities she so enjoyed reading about – London, Paris, Rome, Athens.

Perhaps they would settle in that part of the world.

They could certainly afford to take their time deciding.

And if she expressed concern about Tom, he would remind her that Manse Jolly was sending the Jolly and Largent families the rest of the gold he had taken from Texas Brown.

With that much money, they would be one among the wealthiest families in South Carolina.

And he would promise her that if she ever wanted to return to America and see her family, he would arrange that for her.

He never intended, however, for that to happen.

Martin would make sure that any letters she wrote to Tom, or anyone in South Carolina, were never mailed.

And he would bribe someone at the post-office in Yancey to destroy any letters for her that arrived after they left. None would be forwarded to her. None would be returned.

Martin McCollum smiled to himself.

What wonderful irony – that Manse Jolly had not only made it possible for Martin to possess Rebecca – he now provided the excuse Martin needed to take her away to lead the kind of life he had always wanted.

-21-

Nightmare's soldiers subdued him, stripped him, impaled him on swords, pumped hot water into him, sliced open his thigh, spread the gash and pushed a bayonet, white-hot, to the bone. He smelled his flesh fry – and through colors that glowed and swirled, he saw Millie's face and heard Captain Smith's voice.

Then the burning and scalding began anew, and he saw his torturer, fat and bald.

Manse struggled but could not move.

He begged the Captain and Millie to help him, but they disappeared into darkness so thick it smothered him. He screamed for Rebecca and his Mama, and shouted for his brothers and Tom and his father.

But all he heard in the darkness was Texas Brown's laughter rising from the cave's floor.

Then, after a period of time he could not measure, Manse awoke to the familiar odors of war and death – noble-pus, green-rot, ether, urine and feces.

Pain resonated through him, and his sight returned, appearing as colored light filtering into the room.

He saw Millie and tried to reach for her, but his wrists were tied to the bedposts.

He raised his head and saw that his right leg was strapped to a board, and his left ankle was roped to the foot-rail.

He was naked.

A black man was changing the bed linens.

Millie was wiping his body with a damp cloth.

"Manson?" she said and stopped bathing him.

"Untie me, please," he said.

His voice was a dry whisper.

His throat hurt.

Millie hesitated, then began untying him.

"We had to tie you. You were delirious, lashing out at everybody," she said. "You broke a ranch-hand's jaw," she removed the ropes, then spoke to the black man. "Asa," she said, "go tell Captain Smith that Mister Jolly is awake. And ask him to bring the doctor up here as soon as he arrives. "

The servant nodded, gathered soiled linen and left.

Millie unfolded a clean sheet, covered Manse's nakedness from chest to toes, and tucked it around him.

"Water," Manse said.

Millie took a joint of ribbon cane from a glass on the bedside table and put the end in Manse's mouth. He tasted childhood memories of sugar and watered whiskey to ease a fevered throat.

Millie poured medicine into a glass, took the cane from his mouth, lifted his head from the pillow and said, "Drink this."

Manse swallowed bitterness. Millie refilled the glass with water and he drank it. His throat felt better.

"How long –?" he struggled to push words out.

"Eleven days," Millie replied. "Two riders found you over near Walker's Creek shoals. They never would have seen you lying there in the tall grass if they hadn't spotted your horse and that old mule Papa sold you. They said that the mule kept trying to pull away – to come home, I guess – but its reins were tied to your saddle horn, and your horse wouldn't leave you – like it was standing guard, waiting for you to get up," she smiled at him.

"They told us that all you said, over and over, was, *Captain Smith – Miss Millie*. And as soon as Papa saw you he sent for Major Sanders – who came here right away to tend your wound. And he has come every morning since. And stayed as long as need be. All night, some nights."

Manse tried to keep his eyes open. He wanted to stay awake – to look at her. He wanted her to continue talking – needed her voice to soothe the throbbing.

But the power of darkness reasserted itself.

She smiled and leaned over and kissed him.

And the taste of her lips lingered even after he returned to sleep.

***

***

The needle probing his open wound awakened him.

Captain Smith and Millie were standing at the foot of the bed, and the face Manse recognized as nightmare's rotund torturer, looked up from the wound he was tending.

"By-God, sir, it's good to see your eyes open," Surgeon Major Sanders pushed his wad of tobacco to one side of his mouth to accommodate a steady flow of words.

"You were carrying a lot of yankee shrapnel in that leg," he said. "I had to slice away almost half-a-pound of good-flesh to get all the splinters. That doesn't include the green rot I cut out. It had spread quite a ways."

He stopped talking only long enough to spit into the chamber-pot beside the bed.

"For a while there I wasn't taking any wagers that you would survive," he said. "Green rot likes to hide in corners. That's why we had to keep you flushed out with emetics and hot enemas, and fill the wound with maggots."

He spat again and wiped his mouth on his sleeve.

"Wonder-worms, that's what I call them. Eat away only the rot and leave the healthy flesh. During The War, they saved thousands of lives, and tens of thousands of limbs. Of course, Indian Medicine Men have been using maggots to fight green-rot for several thousand years."

Major Sanders picked the bloated crawlers from Manse's thigh.

"When they start coming out of the wound, they are starving because their diet of green rot is disappearing," he said, and put the worms in a bottle. "When five or six crawled out of your thigh, I knew the danger of the rot killing you would pass without me having to take off your leg – which was good because amputation so close to the torso is rarely successful. With your leg still on, and the dry-rot gone, I knew you stood a good chance of living – if you woke up at all."

He spat again into the chamber pot.

"Often as not, when the fever gets as high as yours, the patient never wakes up. Last night was your crisis. And, thanks be to the Lord, this morning you're alive and awake."

"I'm beholden to you and the Captain and Miss Millie," Manse said.

"The most important thing is that you've been spared," Surgeon Major Sanders said. "Now just rest and eat and heal."

"I'll see to his diet," Millie said. "Just tell me what."

"He's empty, so start him off with just broth and dry bread for two days," the doctor said. "Then add grits and eggs and soup. In a week, he can have whatever he wants in the morning. Just make sure he eats a big meal at mid-day – two meats, three vegetables, two breads. But no sweets until he is more active. He should eat a light supper right after sundown."

He turned to Manse.

"I'm giving you laudanum," he said. "It's the best pain-killer I know, but it's an opiate, and some men get addicted to it. If that happens, it can destroy your mind and your body. To wean you away from it, I want you to drink whiskey to ease the discomfort and help you relax. Of course you may still need laudanum, too, when the pain is real bad – which it's likely to be for a while," Major Sanders spat again.

"I had to scrape your femur – the big bone in your thigh – to get out all the shrapnel and infection," he said. "That's going to take a fairly long and painful healing-time."

With his forefinger and thumb, Major Sanders then pulled the tobacco wad from his mouth, tossed it in the chamber pot, spat and put in a new wad.

"I'll keep a maggot or two on stand-by duty," he smiled. "You still have some fever. Until it breaks completely, we need to keep a close eye on things, to make sure there are no complications. Any questions?"

"How long –?" Manse hesitated, unsure how to ask in Millie's presence.

Surgeon Major Sanders anticipated the question.

"With Asa's help," he said, "you'll be able to take care of your bodily functions in the jar and pot."

"How long before I can get up?" Manse asked.

"You can sit up in a chair in a day or two," the doctor said. "When the fever goes away, probably within a week, you can hobble about with some help. Just don't get impatient and think you know more than I do."

"I'll see to it he follows your orders," Captain Smith said.

"So will I," Millie smiled at Manse.

***

He slept the sleep of laudanum and whiskey and flight from pain, waking only when Millie fed him – or to cry out for more medication – or when Asa helped him use the urine jar or sit astride the chamber pot.

In that twilight of half-conscious sleep, he dreamed Millie's body lay close to his, separated from him only by the sheet. Awake he could not remember what was real, and did not know when day turned to dusk to dawn to day.

Then one morning he opened his eyes and the room came into focus, and he knew the fever was gone. And he realized that Millie was asleep beside him, her head on his shoulder.

He wanted to remain motionless, but could not because of the pain in his leg and the fullness of his bladder.

He kissed her forehead.

Millie's eyes opened and stared and, for a moment, questioned, then she touched his cheek.

"I really hate to wake you, ma'am," Manse said, and smiled feebly, "but I need some laudanum – and Asa. And I reckon I need Asa most."

Millie looked at the empty chair by the door.

"He's probably down the hall," she said, "I'll get him." She stood and put on a peignoir. "Is it your bladder or – ?"

"My bladder. It's about to explode."

"Let me help you sit up and give you the jar, then I'll go get Asa while you use it," she lifted his legs and turned him until he was sitting on the edge of the bed, then she reached down to get the jar – and dragged the sheet off him.

He quickly covered his erection.

She handed him the jar and left the room.

When Asa arrived, it was several minutes before Manse could urinate. When he finished, Asa helped him lie down and covered him.

Millie returned, gave him laudanum, and handed him a drink – half-bourbon, half-coffee.

"I can't tell you how happy I am your fever broke," she spoke nervously, fluffed pillows, and avoided his eyes. "However, I must say it did surprise me that it happened so suddenly – though I do recall Major Sanders said it might happen like that."

Manse was not sure what to say. Opiate and whiskey and pervasive pain didn't add up to clear thinking.

"I guess I should have asked Asa for a nightshirt to sleep in," he said.

"Taking proper care of you is a lot more important than your modesty – or mine – "

"But you really should always get Asa to – "

"Now don't you start telling me what I should and shouldn't do, Manson Jolly. Just because you're embarrassed – "

Millie stopped in mid-sentence, sat on the bed, took his hand, sighed deeply and looked at him.

"I have been beside myself with worry over you," she said. "I knew Major Sanders would do everything he could for you, and the servants would clean up after you – but I wanted to be close to you, so I bathed you with cool towels when you sweated – and I covered you when you had chills – and I held you when you were delirious. And though I know you didn't really need for me to do any of those things in order for you to survive, I needed to do them – for me," Millie's tears began.

Manse squeezed her hand.

"I thank you, Millie Smith, for caring that much about me," he said.

"Since you've been here with me," Millie said, "I've come to the realization that I've cared about you ever since that evening when I saw you for the first time. Even though you were hell-bent on leaving right away to find that yankee lieutenant and his wife, I knew you'd come back to me – just like I knew, all the time you were lying here full of dark-fever and green-rot, that you wouldn't die and leave me. I knew it because I believe in God – and I know

He brought you here to me – for your sake and mine," she smiled through tears. "You are someone very special to me, Manson Jolly."

They looked at each other and were silent.

Then Millie kissed his lips.

"You are too much a Southern gentleman to ask me," she smiled, "so I will go ahead and answer the question that I know is on your mind. *Yes*, every night you've been here, I've slept on this bed beside you. And it didn't matter whether you were aware I was here or not. All that matters is the reason that I did it – because I love you."

She lay down beside him and put her head on his chest.

"And until you're well, and strong enough to talk to me about the future – or push me out the door and send me back to my own bedroom – I plan to stay right here."

**

Manse finished the letter to Tom, sealed the envelope, then looked out the parlor window at Millie who had just dismounted from her palomino mare and was, Manse judged by her gestures, giving two ranch-hands hell about something.

She had a fiery temper with a streak of rudeness born of privilege – but, thank god, neither was often directed at him.

Manse smiled to himself.

He liked looking at her, no matter what her mood. Her thin body made her seem taller than she was, and her face, despite the hawkish nose and sharp chin, had its own beauty. There was no doubt, in looks and temperament, she was her father's daughter.

Every morning for almost a week, Millie and Asa had helped Manse limp down the stairs to the parlor where he sat either at the desk or in an easy chair, his leg propped on pillows on a footstool. Then, once he was settled, Millie kissed him and left to oversee the ranch's operation.

Despite morning visits from Captain Smith and Major Sanders, Manse missed her, from the moment she left until she returned at noon.

Following the mid-day meal, they sat in the parlor and talked, or if the weather warmed, they sat on the verandah and talked. Then they would go to the sun room and talk until they were interrupted by Captain Smith who joined them for a late afternoon drink.

After supper, they went to Manse's room where Asa helped him out of his clothes and into the nightshirt and robe Millie had bought for him at the General Store in Cameron.

Then, following Major Sanders' orders, they walked the length of the upstairs hallway twenty times, to help Manse regain strength. (Millie did not need the exercise. She was, Manse was convinced, stronger than he had ever been – even before he was shot.)

After their nightly walk, Millie changed the dressing on his wound, gave him his medication, and held him until they slept.

His life with Millie made Manse the happiest he ever remembered being.

He smiled as he watched her walk across the verandah, knowing that within minutes she would enter the parlor and they would embrace and kiss, and begin to talk anew – though they had, it seemed, talked about almost everything.

Almost everything.

Millie had told him about growing up on a Texas ranch, about her Mama, about life while her Papa was away during The War, about her Mama's illness and death, about the men who had been her suitors, and about traveling with her Papa to Fort Worth and Dallas and San Antonio and New Orleans.

Manse had told her about growing up on a farm in South Carolina with six brothers and three sisters, about his Mama and Daddy and his friend Tom. He told her about The War – not all the memories, but all that he could – and he told her about Larry's death and how Manse Jolly had become a wanted man – a criminal in the eyes of Yankee Law – and how he lived as an outlaw and eluded capture – and how he justified killing.

And he told her about Texas Brown and Martin McCollum and Rebecca. Not everything, but all that he could, as best he could.

And during hours of talking, he tried to recall everything that happened when he visited Rebecca and Martin at the Double-M Ranch – and what he had done with the saddle bags of gold. He thought he could find them again. He remembered some of the landmarks around the blind canyon where he hid them. But he wasn't sure. And Millie said that he shouldn't worry. She and the ranch hands would help him find them when the time was right.

And during those hours and days and nights of talk, Manse and Millie often held each other and shared tears and pain and anger and frustration and understanding – and just as often, they laughed.

The two of them, Manse reminded himself again, had talked about almost everything *except* the subject that loomed largest between them – their future.

"I missed you," Millie came into the parlor, leaned across the writing table and kissed him. "What have you been doing?"

"I finally wrote my folks," Manse said. "I told them I had seen Rebecca and Martin and that Rebecca is fine and seems happy. I gave them her address, and asked them to write to her. But I didn't tell them I was sending them the gold. I want to wait until we find it, then I'll let them know it's coming." He paused. "Of course I told them where I am – about how nice you and the Captain have been to me. But I didn't say anything about my wound. No sense worrying Mama."

Manse picked up the envelope.

"I asked your Papa the date, to put on my letter," he said, "and he told me that today is February fifteenth. So I've been sitting here trying to make sense of what happened to the time. I seem to have lost track of a lot of it."

He looked at her.

"Do you remember dates?" he asked.

"If they're important, I do," Millie said and smiled. "And every day since I met you has been important to me, so I remember each one very well. The first evening that we had supper was January fifth. You left for Yancey on the sixth. Exactly fifteen days went by before they found you near Little River. That was January twenty-first. You were in the dark-sleep eleven days, until the fever broke and you fully woke up on February second. Lord knows I remember that those were the longest eleven days and nights of my life. Your first trip downstairs was on February tenth. And ever since you woke up, you and I have been talking every waking minute – except for the few hours every morning when I try to convince my ranch-hands they have to take orders from me even if I am a woman," she sighed. "I had to fire the second-section foreman a few minutes ago –" Millie interrupted herself. "But you had a reason for asking me about dates, didn't you?"

"I was just thinking," Manse paused to find words. "About us and how much time we've spent together. With all our talking, I guess we've come to know each other real well, and – "

"And –?"

Manse hesitated. Perhaps, he thought, he still wasn't ready to talk about *everything*.

"It's almost meal-time," he said. "Maybe this should wait."

Millie sat on the edge of the desk.

"You're not eating anything or going anywhere, Manson Jolly," she said, "until you tell me exactly what is going on in your mind."

"I'm not trying to keep anything from you, Millie," he said. "Just the opposite. I'm trying to tell you what I'm thinking – and feeling – about the future – about us – you and me."

"And exactly what are you thinking and feeling about the future? Us? You and me?"

"It's hard for me to explain," Manse said. "I told you before that I've always had trouble knowing what I truly feel. Sometimes I think I'm real sure about something – but then suddenly it turns out I'm wrong. Like about Martin and Rebecca – " he paused. "And about the gold – and Texas Brown –"

Manse's choked on words and was silent.

Millie put her hand on his shoulder and waited.

"I've come to have very strong feelings about you, Millie Smith," he finally said. "I care for you. And I want more than anything to believe – that I truly love you – "

"Oh, Manson," Millie knelt by his chair and put her arms around him. "I love you. And I've wanted so much to hear you say that."

"And I've wanted to say those words to you, because I truly do believe I love you, Millie," Manse said. "But tell me, please – how can I be sure?"

"Believing in love is all there is to love, Manson."

"Are you positive?" he asked. "Is what I feel really enough?"

"It's enough for me," Millie said.

"Then I reckon you need to help me walk to the dining room," Manse nodded solemnly, "so I can ask your Papa to let me marry you."

-22-

Manson Sherrill Jolly and Elizabeth Mildred Smith were married at noon on March 3, 1868, in the parlor of the Smith home in Robertson County, Texas.

Millie, who had neither the patience nor the inclination to wait for a wedding dress to be made, wore the pale green gown she had worn as a bridesmaid at her cousin Ella's wedding two years before.

Manse wore Confederate dress grays with the Cavalry insignia of Captain Smith's East Texas Brigade.

In South Carolina's First Cavalry, only high ranking officers wore such fine uniforms. The best that Sergeant Manson Jolly had ever worn was chestnut home-spun, patched and re-patched.

Captain Smith gave Manse the uniform, and had a tailor from Cameron come to the house to fit it, and when Manse asked whose uniform it was, the captain explained that at the outset of The War all officers and enlisted men in his Brigade had been issued one dress uniform and two battle uniforms. After their Departure Parade, most of the men stored their dress uniforms at home – planning to wear them in the Victory Parade on their triumphant return from The War.

Because less than half the men who went to war came home, there were plenty of uniforms available in all sizes.

Captain Smith wanted the wedding to take place at the Little River Baptist Church, but Surgeon Major Sanders decided the ceremony should be held at the Smith home.

"Manse is just not quite fit enough to be out yet," he said. "Besides, a man who is getting married needs to save his strength."

Having the wedding at home suited Millie and Manse just fine, however it presented a problem for the Captain: The foyer and parlor could accommodate no more than fifty chairs, but every soldier who had served in Captain Smith's East Texas Brigade – as well as every Confederate veteran in Milam and Robertson

Counties – expected an invitation, and planned to attend (with his wife, if he were married) not only because Millie was Captain Smith's daughter, but because she was marrying a man they considered a hero.

Captain Smith agonized over who to seat in the house, and who would be relegated to standing on the verandah. He wanted to offend no one, but, clearly, choices had to be made.

While discussing the matter one evening during dinner, the Captain mentioned that he was active in the San Andres Masonic Lodge in Cameron, and that his fellow Masons all expected to attend the wedding, which presented yet another problem.

And, he added, he hoped that when Manse was able, he would attend a meeting of the Masons with him – and eventually consider joining the order.

Manse replied that he was already a Mason, as was his father, and Tom's father. And that all the Jolly brothers had been inducted into the Masonic Lodge before The War, except Larry, who had been too young.

This news pleased Captain Smith, as he was sure it would please the members of the San Andres Lodge – and it provided a solution to the problem of seating the wedding guests.

The Captain reserved chairs inside the house for those former Confederate Cavalrymen who were also members of the San Andres Masonic Lodge. Chairs for all other guests would be provided on the verandah where a reception would be held following the ceremony.

And all veterans were asked to wear their uniforms.

***

At the wedding, Captain Smith wore his dress-grays, with nine medals of combat, and seven decorations for bravery – and the Confederate Sash of Valor that had been presented to him by General Robert E. Lee.

But it was obvious to all that Captain Smith's greatest pride was the daughter who held his arm as they came down the stairs, across the foyer and into the parlor.

Surgeon Major Sanders was Manse's best-man.

They stood beside the small writing table that served as an altar, and Manse smiled as he watched Millie and her father approach him through a sea of Confederate Gray dotted with the myriad colors of the finest gowns the wives owned.

Millie's cousin, Ellen Terrell, was her maid of honor.

Ellen's husband, Feaster Terrell, attorney, justice of the peace, and fighting-chaplain in Captain Smith's Brigade, performed the ceremony. It was short and simple, as Millie had requested.

Then she and Manse kissed and walked to the front door.

The verandah was a wall of Confederate uniforms and bright dresses.

The aroma of early spring flowers mixed with smells of pork, mutton, and beef roasting over fire pits.

Ranch-hands and their families waiting for a glimpse of the bride and groom gathered around tables and benches near the cooking fires.

Millie and Surgeon Major Sanders led Manse to a chair.

He sat and propped his leg on a stool.

Drinks were poured, and Captain Smith spoke loudly enough to command attention.

"On this special day," he said, "I propose a toast to the fairest bride in this great state of Texas, Mildred Elizabeth Smith Jolly, and to her husband, Manson Sherrill Jolly, hero of The War, and Avenger of Southern Honor. May God grant the two of you a long and happy life."

He raised his glass – and his voice:

"And to the memory of our fallen comrades – and our beloved Confederacy. May their glory live forever."

He drank.

The toast was followed by a ripple of words of congratulations and polite applause.

Then from across the verandah came a blood-curdling scream – the sound that during four years of warfare had sent fear through enemy hearts from Vicksburg to Richmond –

The Rebel Yell!

The Battle Cry that gave no quarter – granted no mercy – took no prisoners.

A second voice joined the first and soon the high-pitched howl of more than a hundred men resonated like a thousand.

Millie cringed at the force of the clamor that grew into a roar – then a wail. It engulfed her, and its intensity was frightening – particularly the ferocity with which it came from Manse, who stood up, oblivious to the pain in his leg, and helped sustain the Rebel-Yell for several minutes.

It might have gone on longer had Captain Smith not summoned a servant to bring him a pistol which he fired into the air to command a return to the normal level of conversation.

Before he sat down, Manse hugged Millie.

"I love you, Mrs. Jolly," he said. "This is the happiest day of my life. I thank you for it."

***

By nine o'clock the guests had left – at Captain Smith's suggestion, and the ranch hands had returned to their cabins and quarters – on Captain Smith's orders, and Manse and Millie had gone upstairs – not to his room, but to her room.

"From now on," she said, "this is *our* room."

Manse sat in a chair by the bed. Millie poured him a glass of brandy, and while he drank it, she went into the privacy alcove. When she came out, she was wearing a white silk peignoir and sleeping gown. She helped Manse undress and lie down, covered him with a sheet, and extinguished the two lanterns, leaving only the light from the candle on her boudoir table. Its mirror reflected the candle flame, casting a soft glow across the bed. Millie unfastened the three buttons at her bodice and removed her peignoir, untied the bows on the shoulders of her gown, let it fall to the floor, and stood motionless in amber candlelight, watching Manse raise his eyes slowly from her legs to the auburn covered junction of her thighs, across her abdomen, over her small breasts, to her hair. Released from the confines of combs and braids, it cascaded over her shoulders, glistening red in the candlelight.

Their eyes met and they both smiled.

Millie removed the sheet and lay down beside him. Manse turned on his side and drew her to him. They kissed, touched, explored. And after what seemed to Manse, an interminable time, she took him in her hand and drew him to her, and he moved to lie on top of her – but the pain in his leg stopped him.

"Dammit," the word erupted.

Millie touched his lips, and kissed his lips, and eased him onto his back and crouched on her knees, then straddled him. He felt her grip him tightly and lower herself onto him – felt her direct him into her – felt her engulf him.

But whenever he tried to use his hips to respond, pain shot from his thigh into his groin, counteracting arousal.

Millie smiled through his embarrassment.

"You just lie real still, Manson," she whispered in his ear. "Let me do everything. Then, when your wound has healed, I promise I'll lie real still and let you do everything for me," she kissed him and moved in a slow crescendo that soon reached implosion.

Then they lay still, exploring resolution.

Twice Millie visited the privacy alcove.

Three times Manse went.

Millie sipped champagne during moments of respite.

Manse drank two glasses of brandy, then went back to bourbon.

When it was obvious to Millie that, despite his passive role, Manse was experiencing pain, she suggested he take laudanum, but Manse refused, saying that he wanted to sleep without medication, without sedation – to feel her close beside him all through the night.

And when at last sleep became their primary desire, Manse slept deeply.

Then, toward dawn, a cadre of demons rode out of their cavern hidden deep in his mind's darkness.

He shouted at them, ordered them to leave, but they prodded his leg with burning bayonets and tortured his soul with memories of The War.

He awoke abruptly.

Millie was astride him –trying to restrain his twisting, kicking and flailing.

Once awake, Manse was immediately calm – and apologetic.

Millie kissed his cheek, stood, put on her peignoir, lit two lanterns, inspected the blood-soaked bandage on his leg and removed it.

"You've completely torn loose a suture – and after all my efforts to keep you lying still," she said, and smiled at him, and wrapped his thigh with a strip of fresh linen to staunch the blood.

"Were you having one of those nightmares from The War, like you told me about?" she asked when the wound was dressed.

"Yes," he nodded. "I haven't had one in so long I thought they had gone away for good. I should have known that laudanum was the reason."

Millie stood and poured laudanum into a glass.

"Drink this," she said.

Manse downed it in a gulp.

"I agree with Surgeon Major Sanders," Millie said. "There's no sense in you suffering from night-pains or night-mares. You should continue to take laudanum every night."

Millie then filled the glass with bourbon.

"But," she quickly added, "only after we have made love."

-23-

At the end of March, Surgeon Major Sanders pronounced Manse physically fit to ride in a buckboard – but not yet ready to handle the reins, which required the left foot to brake and the right leg to brace for control.

So Millie drove.

Their first day out, they rode a half mile along a tree-lined lane behind the main house to a large garden with log cabins built around it.

"This is where the servants live," Millie said. "They were all slaves Papa brought with him and his young wife when he sold the land he inherited in South Carolina and moved to Texas."

Millie stopped the buckboard.

"Actually, slavery didn't fit into Papa's plans," she said. "He didn't want to grow field crops like tobacco and cotton like the Southrons did. He wanted to raise cattle and horses from the fine breeding stock he brought with him. So what he needed was wranglers and *vaqueros* – and since Texas was full of such men, the only slaves he brought with him were house servants who could read and write – house niggers to do accountings and inventories and, of course, teach their children to do the same."

Millie waited while Manse lit a cigar and drank from his canteen of white-water, then she started the buckboard rolling.

"Soon after he got to Texas, Papa set his slaves free. They could leave anytime they wanted, or stay and work for him. And would you believe it, Manson, not a single one of them left. They, and their children, run the house and everything connected with it – the cooking, cleaning and maintenance, and the smoke-house and the dairy – all under the watchful eye of Asa who is the patriarch, and his wife Auntie Robin who runs the kitchen exactly the way my Mama taught her, and my Grand-Mama taught her Mama. Asa's brother is a carpenter and does all the woodworking and repairing inside the main house, and supervises new construction for Papa. They all share in the garden work, and get a share of what grows there and what's put up for winter. And Papa gives them a part of the poultry and eggs – and the mutton, pork and beef. And he also pays them. Each man gets two dollars a month. The women get one. I tell Papa that's not fair – that the women work just as hard as the men do, but I haven't talked him into changing that – not yet, anyway," Millie stopped talking and smiled at Manse.

"I do hope I'm not boring you," she said.

"You know better," Manse leaned over and kissed her cheek. "I want you to show me everything, the whole ranch – I don't care if it takes all day."

Millie laughed.

"Manson, it would take three days just to ride from one side of the ranch to the other in this old buckboard," she said. "And the way the land lies, it would take a week to ride the perimeter."

Manse shook his head.

"Just how many acres are there?" he asked.

"In Texas we don't measure land in acres," Millie said. "It's too much trouble. We measure it in squares. A square is one mile square, and there are six-hundred-forty acres in a square. Our ranch – which is not really very big by Texas standards – is eighteen squares."

Millie drove the buckboard along the lane, through pine woods to a clearing with three houses painted white, each with a garden and small barn and outbuildings.

"The married foremen live here with their families," she said. "Every one of them served in Papa's Brigade in The War."

"That reminds me," Manse said. "I've been wanting to ask your Papa a question but I haven't found exactly the right time to do it, so I'll ask you, if that's all right?"

"Of course," she said. "I only hope I know the answer. It sounds serious."

"It's not, really. I'm just curious," Manse shifted on the hard buckboard seat. "In the part of the South where I come from, a landowner who formed his own Brigade paid for just about everything his men needed, and in return, the Confederacy usually commissioned him a Colonel. But your Papa was only a Captain.

Not that Captain isn't a high rank, but Lightning Jack Smith was one of the most decorated men in the Confederate Army, so naturally I wonder why he wasn't a Colonel – or even a General?"

Millie's smile was broad.

"I think I can answer that," she said. "I've been close to two men in my life – Captain Smith and Sergeant Jolly – both heroes of The War – both men of honor and courage. And neither is the kind of man who sought adulation and fame."

Millie stopped the buckboard and turned to look at Manse.

"You have told me about you and your brothers and Tom serving in the Confederate Army. Now let me tell you about Papa. When The War came, he could have remained safely out of it, selling cattle and horses to one side or the other – or both. But his heritage would not allow him to remain aloof. He felt compelled to serve the cause he believed in. So he formed his own brigade which was not a battalion or regiment – just a company of men. But it was a unique company." Millie's pride was in her voice. "Papa is an admirer and student of the strategies and tactics of that great South Carolina hero of the Revolutionary War, General Francis Marion, *The Swamp Fox,* who drove the British crazy with his raids where and when they were least expected. So Papa trained his Brigade to do the same – to ride great distances, and strike without warning, then disappear. That's how he got the name Lightning-Jack-Smith. He and his men lived off the land, and traveled with minimum supplies – a spare horse, rifle, pistol and ammunition. They fought more skirmishes than any unit in the Confederate Army." Her smile broadened. "But because his Brigade was never larger than company strength, Papa never elevated himself above the rank of Captain." She paused. "I'm sure that one day you and Papa will talk about The War. He says that it's still too fresh in his mind to make easy conversation. And I think you feel the same."

"Yes, I do," Manse said.

Millie started the buckboard moving again.

And Manse was once again aware of the terrain.

They were now headed back in the general direction of the main house, then the lane suddenly emerged from woods onto open land where herds of horses were separated from other herds by fenced runs connected to cutting pens and corrals adjacent to stables and barns.

Near the stables were four buildings, long and narrow.

The first one, Millie explained, was the bunk-house for white ranch-hands. Their number changed with the needs for round-up and cattle drives. Most of the men were drifters who rarely stayed longer than a few months. But a few had worked for Captain Smith since before The War.

The second building housed *vaqueros*, the Mexican drovers. Only a few lived there permanently, but the building was large enough to accommodate the influx of migrant families of *braceros* who arrived by foot and wagon each spring to plant the hundreds of acres of corn, wheat, barley, and oats that were the staples for a cattle and horse ranch. And the *braceros* returned for two months at harvest time.

The third building was made of logs.

Next to it was a smithy.

Here lived black cowboys. Without exception, they were ex-slaves – runaways who had arrived here before The War and been given work by Captain Smith. Several had served in Captain Smith's Brigade, and later married into the families of servants.

As they came closer, Manse saw that the fourth building was actually six adobe huts connected by covered walkways.

Indian families lived here.

Indian wranglers, Millie said, were the only men Captain Smith trusted to break and teach his fine horses.

Millie turned the buckboard toward the main house and announced that now they were going home so Manse could rest before lunch.

He agreed, on condition that she rest with him.

***

During the remainder of that week, they ventured only as far as they could go in a morning, then stopped and ate the lunch that had been prepared and packed by Auntie-Robin.

Millie spread a blanket and laid out the food, then helped Manse down from the buckboard, poured him a glass of bourbon, poured herself a glass of wine, and they ate and talked.

Millie told him that when he was stronger and able to ride horseback again, she would show him the rest of the ranch.

"It's just too much land to try to cover in this slow buckboard," she said.

"Maybe, when I can ride farther in a day, we can go toward the Fria River and try to find that blind canyon I told you about – the place where I hid the saddle bags," Manse said.

"If you rode the route Papa drew on the map for you," Millie said, "then it shouldn't be any trouble retracing your path."

"I don't think I strayed," Manse said. "And even though I don't recollect exactly where I camped that night, I know it was one day's ride from where I crossed the Fria."

"Then I'm sure we can find it," Millie said. "And just to make sure, we'll take along a couple of the Indians – though I'm not at all sure why you're so dead-set on finding those saddle bags."

"I told you, the bags have gold in them," Manse said, and reminded himself that he still hadn't told her *everything*.

"But you have got plenty of gold already," Millie smiled at him. "The riders who found you brought Papa the supply sack that was tied to the saddle horn of your pack mule, and it was so full of gold and silver coins, it was a wonder that old mule could carry it."

"The gold in my saddle bags is in bars, and it's worth a lot more than what was in the supply sack," Manse said. "Your Papa and I have talked about it, and he's agreed that if I can find it, he will have two of his best men deliver it to my family in South Carolina – which is what I want."

"Then, I promise, we'll look for it – as soon as you're able," Millie said. "But right now, I've got to give some thought to running this ranch. I've taken off a whole week, and, much as I've loved every minute of it, I've got to get back to work."

Manse said he hoped that didn't mean he had to go back to the confines of the house.

"You don't think I would ever again leave you alone in the mornings, do you?" Millie kissed him. "I plan to put you to work – ranch-work, I mean," she laughed. "Papa and I both want you to get to know every inch of this land – to know every hand by name, and every horse and steer by sight and brand – even the coyotes and snakes and prairie dogs – because Papa and I both are looking forward to the day when you will be running this whole spread."

***

By the first of May, Manse was back on his horse, riding beside Millie.

With the recovery of his strength, and the absence of pain, their love-making took on new vigor and frequency, and though Millie repeatedly offered to relinquish her position of leadership, that rarely happened.

Nor, despite the return of his strength and the absence of pain, was there appreciable change in Manse's pattern of drinking and use of laudanum. He drank bourbon with his morning coffee and regularly during the day. And he took ever-increasing doses of laudanum at bedtime to ensure sleep without dreams.

With Millie's daily applications of pine-oil liniment and oil of arnica to keep the tissue supple, the fiery scar that ran the length of his thigh gradually turned to a reddish gray. By the time such ministrations were no longer needed, mutual massage had become a part of their evening ritual.

It was during such a quiet moment in mid-May, as Manse was rubbing Millie's back, that she sat up, kissed his cheek, took the bottle of oil from him and put it aside.

"I think we need to talk about something," she said, and her eyes were serious.

Manse nodded and waited.

"I don't know whether you've noticed or not, but since we've been married, I haven't once had my time-of-the-month," Millie held his hand.

"To be honest, I reckon I hadn't noticed. Maybe once or twice I wondered if you might leave our bed when it did happen – which is what I understand most southern ladies do during that time – like they do when they are near term with child. But since I never have lived with a lady before, I'm not always exactly sure what to expect."

"You are such a dear man," Millie kissed his cheek. "Most men would have pretended to know all-about-everything, whether they did or not – "

Manse smiled self-consciously.

"My time is always mid-month, sure as the moon rises," Millie's eyes teased him. "So when my time didn't arrive two weeks after we were married, I had a hint that something was happening inside me. And when the middle of April came and went, and then mid-May came closer, and still my-time hadn't arrived, I went to Auntie Robin, who is a mid-wife, and let her examine me and read my signs. And she says she is absolutely sure I am more than two months with-child. You, Manson Sherrill Jolly, are going to be a father."

Manse could not speak. His arms enveloped her. They lay down and held each other for a long time.

Then Manse trembled.

"What is it, Manson?"

"You won't – I mean – things won't change – between us – will they?"

"If you mean, will I withdraw from our bed, the answer to that is, *no, not-ever*. I want to sleep close to you even when I am so heavy with child I can scarcely move. Of course, we will soon have to forego your filling me with love – which I will miss as much as you – but we can still touch each other. In fact, Auntie Robin tells me that there are several oils I need to have rubbed into my body every day, to keep my muscles strong and my abdomen supple as the baby grows. I told her I felt sure you would do that for me."

"I will do anything you ask," Manse held her close. "Just so long as you don't leave me alone. I never ever want to be without you."

"I don't think you ever will be," Millie kissed him then sat up on the edge of the bed. "As for right now, there is one subject I never mentioned before because there was no reason to, but now I think you need to know."

Manse sat beside her, poured a drink, and waited.

"My mother had a very difficult time when I was born," Millie said. "I was a breech-baby, and the mid-wives had trouble getting me to emerge. It was too late for cesarean surgery, and for a while it seemed both Mama and I might die. But Auntie Robin sent for help – a Mexican *partera* and an Indian *comadrona*. According to Auntie Robin, it took all their effort and knowledge to save us – plus a lot of praying to God and to Jesus and to Nuestra Señora and to the Spirit of Earth and Sky and, I suspect, to more than one spirit in the African pantheon. And when, finally, I came out, and my Mama and I were both fine, each of the midwives took the credit, and each of their religions took the credit, and so they *all* consider that I belong to them, and they are all going to want to catch my baby – excuse me, I mean, *our baby*."

"But under the circumstances, I mean because of what happened to your Mama, you are going to let Surgeon Major Sanders take care of you, aren't you?"

Millie smiled.

"Manson," she said, "doctors do a lot of good when it comes to tending wounds and injuries and curing some ailments – but when it comes to birthing and babies and the care of mamas, I place my faith in midwives. They understand things about women and birth that medical doctors cannot comprehend because medicine is the domain of men, and birth is the domain of women," Millie touched his cheek. "Now don't frown like that," she said. "Auntie Robin will tell Surgeon Major Sanders if she thinks I have a problem. And if there is anything he thinks I should do, he will tell Auntie Robin and she will tell me. I feel sure, however, that when my birth time arrives, Papa will see to it that Surgeon Major Sanders is in the parlor downstairs in case he is needed – though his presence will more likely be needed to help you and Papa get through the ordeal."

"You have to promise me you will take care of yourself, and tell me everything that Auntie Robin tells you, so I can help you every way I can," Manse touched her abdomen.

"Soon you will feel the baby there," Millie said, "but not quite yet." She held Manse's hand. "Auntie Robin will soon have the *partera* and the *comadrona* come here to examine me, but that will be mostly just to keep peace among the mid-wives. At this stage, they will all suggest the same thing – that I drink lots of herbal teas – mostly raspberries and cohosh roots and squaw vine leaves – to strengthen my womb. It's later that they will disagree about everything."

***

Millie was furious when Surgeon Major Sanders and Auntie Robin told her in mid-June that she could no longer ride horseback – neither straddle-saddle nor side-saddle.

Millie loudly protested that she would not spend the next six months sitting on the verandah doing needle-point and reading. She had a ranch to run – or, as she quickly amended it – *she and Manse* had a ranch to run.

To bolster their arguments, Major Sanders and Auntie Robin brought in reinforcements.

Lupita, *la partera*, said that with each passing week the front passage of Millie's body was becoming more delicate and La Señora Jolly (she pronounced it *holy*) must protect that entry from pounding against the saddle.

Nai-Se-Kashrah, the *comadrona* (whose Choctaw name translated "Feather of Great Power") explained that the totem of life within Millie's womb was held in place by slender threads connected to Millie's body to give the baby traits that would render it identifiable throughout its life as having come from her, and to provide nourishment for the baby's growth while it was within her, just as Millie would nurture the child with her milk after its birth. And equally important, the *comadrona* said, there were spiritual threads stretching from the baby to Manse, to provide traits of the totem father, so that all who saw the child would recognize its sire. And these threads might easily be broken if not properly cared for – which did not mean the mother should be coddled but rather that Millie must do everything possible to reduce to a minimum the breaking of any of those threads.

The *comadrona* then presented deer-skin moccasins to Millie and Manse, with instructions that they wear them as they walked together two miles before breakfast each morning, and two miles before dinner each evening. The boots and shoes of the white race, she said, separated the soles of the feet from the earth, which was not good because it was through the feet that the earth transmitted its wisdom to those who trod its paths.

Thin moccasins made from the skin of the deer allowed the soles to feel the land and absorb all it transmitted. And while walking together, Manse and Millie would not only feel their minds and bodies strengthened, but the bond between them would grow ever stronger.

Millie and Manse acquiesced to the demands of the midwives and Surgeon Major Sanders, though the prospect of Manse leaving her every morning made Millie unhappy.

Remembering his long and lonely mornings without her, Manse understood her unhappiness, and he looked for a way to make the next six months easier for her.

Then an idea came to him.

He and Asa's brother built a cushioned seat for the buggy – a seat upholstered and comfortable like a sofa, and after breakfast on the following Monday, he asked Millie to walk with him to the front gate, as if to leave her for the morning, but instead helped her to board the strange-looking contraption.

At first she was skeptical, but when Manse sat beside her and she realized that this weird wagon would give them months of mornings together rather than separated, she became so ecstatic that Manse had to insist that she not express her appreciation by making love to him on their new rolling-couch – at least not until they could drive it into a patch of woods near Little River several miles from the main house.

-24-

Manse stepped out of the tub of tepid water, dried himself with a towel of homespun, and put on a clean nightshirt.

In her sixth month, Millie had become increasingly sensitive to odors. Now even the smell of horses nauseated her. She could no longer tolerate riding in the upholstered buggy, which Auntie Robin said was just as well because she didn't need all that jostling during her final three months.

Besides, Auntie Robin said, if the baby didn't soon begin to make a normal turn, the birth was going to be breech.

Manse walked from the privacy alcove into their bedroom.

Cool September air billowed curtains at the open windows. Millie had covered herself with a sheet that followed the outline of her enlarged breasts and the protruding mound that was their baby.

Manse's smile became a grin.

"Are you laughing at my poor misshapen body?" Millie said.

"You have never been more beautiful – " Manse walked to the bed and pulled aside the sheet. "Or more desirable," he said, and leaned over and kissed her, then sat on the edge of the bed and lowered his head to her abdomen.

He could remember nothing in his life that had brought him the joy he felt when he listened to the heartbeat within Millie's womb.

Then he put his head on her breast and listened to her heartbeat.

Her love had brought him back from the edge of death, from the depths of nightmare, through madness, to this time of absolute ecstasy.

"I feel very guilty, making you wash off the smell of horses every night before you come to bed," Millie said. "It's really so silly for me to be nauseated by horse smells, of all things. I've loved horses all my life –"

"Now don't start that again," Manse said. "Remember what Auntie Robin told you: It's not unusual for a woman with-child to get sick at her stomach over the most familiar things – even things she loves. I'm just thankful I don't make you sick," Manse smiled again, stood and walked to the other side of the bed. "I'll happily wash off the smell of horses, or do anything else it takes for you to let me sleep close to you, Miz Millie Jolly," he picked up the bottle of laudanum and drank, then chased it with a glass of bourbon.

"I'm awful happy you feel that way, Mister Manson Jolly," Millie said. "It's bad enough that I had to stop riding with you a month earlier than I planned. I don't know what I would do if we didn't have our nights together."

She reached for him.

Manse lay down beside her. She rested her head on his shoulder. They were silent in the candlelight. No words were needed – only closeness and sleep.

***

He rode slowly along the ridge. Through the mist of mountain morning he could see the river below. He thought it was the Rapidan, but perhaps that was only a name, not a place he had ever been.

Then he heard the waterfall, and knew he was near the cave. He dismounted, hitched his horse to a sapling, removed his rifle from the saddle sling, loosened the short sword in its scabbard and walked through woods that became more dense with each step.

He emerged in a clearing, crossed it and squeezed through a narrow entrance that led into a cave he did not know – a mammoth room, dimly lit, with dozens of openings through which he heard gunshots and cannon fire.

He turned to leave, but the entrance was no longer there. He looked for a way out, but at every opening men waited in shadows, their shapes barely discernible.

Then Texas Brown's laugh resonated and he looked to his right and saw him – with large holes in his brocade waistcoat – his guts spilling down his black trousers and across his finely tooled boots – guts trailing along the cave's floor as he walked toward Manse, raised his pistols and fired.

Manse dived behind a rock formation – and landed between two corpses. Heaton and Red Tompin reached for him. He pulled away from them and ran past Texas, toward a fissure in the cave's wall – and emerged onto a battlefield.

Artillery concussion deafened. Bugles sounded. Men screamed and were blown apart. Pieces of flesh filled the air and landed around him.

Manse slipped and fell into a crater with five bodies, mangled and covered with maggots – and he recognized his brothers.

He scrambled out of the crater, back onto the battlefield.

Blue uniforms, splattered red, attacked him. He fired his rifle until it was empty. He fired his pistols until they were empty. Then he drew his short sword and stabbed and sliced and dismembered and eviscerated and decapitated, until he stood waist-deep in the gore he had created – and felt himself sinking in blood and excrement – surrounded by faces – recognized, remembered and unknown.

He struggled to free himself from the mire, looked up and saw Millie and a small child beckoning to him from a ledge. He redoubled his efforts, broke free and ran through an opening – into a room where men fell on him and beat him, until he managed to crawl under an overhanging rock, into a space no larger than a sepulcher.

Then the quiet and darkness of the tomb enveloped him.

***

The light of false dawn filtered through the window of the bedroom where, only a few months before, he had awakened from the dark sleep – the room where they slept before he and Millie married.

Manse recognized it even from his position underneath the bed.

His head ached. His face hurt. His body felt like he had been in one hell of a fight. He struggled to slide from beneath the bed and stared up at Captain Smith and Surgeon Major Sanders. Behind them, in the doorway, were Asa and two ranch foremen.

"Millie?"

It was the only word that was important.

"She has some nasty bruises, but she is all right," Major Sanders said, then he and one of the foremen helped Manse to stand.

He tried to focus thoughts but could catch only glimpses through the mist of last night's memories. He wanted to ask questions, but his attention was on the pain cramping his bladder.

Manse shrugged away the hands that tried to help him, and unsteadily walked to the alcove, removed his torn nightshirt, and urinated for a long time. Then he poured water from the pitcher into the bowl, splashed it on his face – examined in the mirror his split lip and blackened eye – put on underwear and trousers, and walked back into the bedroom and sat on the bed.

"Drink this," Major Sanders handed Manse a glass of liquid – half-bourbon, half a bitter taste he did not recognize.

Manse rubbed the back of his head.

"Manson," Millie came into the room, hurried to him, sat beside him.

At the sight of her, his fears emerged as tears –

One of her eyes was swollen closed – her face was blackened by bruises – her lip was cut.

"Oh, God – my God – Millie – what did I do?"

He hugged her.

Captain Smith – his countenance dark – ushered the foremen and servants out of the room, closed the door behind them, sat in a chair by the window, stared out, and was silent.

Major Sanders stood near the bed.

"I have a pretty good idea what happened here last night," the doctor said, "but I don't want to rush to conclusions."

He paused.

"Tell me everything you remember, Manse," he said.

Manse's eyes would not leave Millie's face.

He touched her swollen lip. She winced.

Tears choked his voice.

Eventually he answered.

"I bathed in the alcove," he said. "Then came into the bedroom. Took my laudanum. And drank a glass of bourbon while I talked to

Millie. Then we went to sleep. I don't remember anything else until I woke up in this room this morning – lying under the bed."

His words trailed into silence.

Major Sanders looked at Millie.

"And what do you recall?" he asked her.

"I woke up in the middle of the night," she said. "Manse was crouched by the side of the bed, calling to someone. I spoke to him, but he didn't answer me," Millie wrapped her arms around Manse's neck, held onto him until her tears eased. "Then he got down on the floor and started crawling toward the alcove, so I got out of bed and walked to him and knelt beside him and touched his shoulder and said, *Manson, wake up* – and he turned and hit me on the side of my head with his fist and knocked me sprawling to the floor. Then he struck me three or four more times," Millie sighed.

"All I could think of was the baby," she said. "So I lay on my side and grabbed my knees, so my chest and shoulders would shield my abdomen," Millie's voice trembled. "Then suddenly, Manson stood up and ran toward the door – and slipped on the scatter rug and fell. He seemed stunned. At any rate, he didn't move, so I got up and ran to the door, opened it and hurried down the hall, screaming for Papa all the way – "

Millie stopped talking and looked at her father who continued to stare out the window.

"It was some time after three o'clock," Captain Smith said. "I had gotten up to relieve myself when I heard Millie. Auntie Robin's granddaughter was on night-call, and she came up the back stairs into the hallway as I opened my door. I yelled at her to sound the fire bell – and to summon Asa and Auntie Robin – and my foremen – and to send a rider for Major Sanders. I wasn't sure what was going on, but I knew Millie wouldn't scream for help unless it was one hell of an emergency."

He turned and looked at Millie.

"Then I helped Millie into my room," he said, "and came back out into the hallway and saw Manse rush out of their bedroom and dive to the floor in a manner that reminded me of a man taking cover in the heat of battle."

Captain Smith stood, walked to the bed and looked Manse in the eye.

"When the fire bell sounded, you seemed to hear it, Manse," he said. "You paused, motionless, as if listening for something or someone – then you crawled a few feet, waited again, came up into a crouch, moved farther down the hall, dropped to the floor again and crawled through the open door into the front bedroom." Captain Smith looked at Major Sanders. "I decided not to venture after him. Rather I returned to my room to care for Millie. I remained there until help arrived, then I left Millie in Auntie Robin's care, and I led Asa and my two foremen to the room Manse was in. He had climbed atop the armoire, and when we entered he leapt on us – attacked us like a man possessed. Despite all our efforts, we could not subdue him –"

The captain paused.

"I shouted to Asa to go get more men to help us," he said. "Then suddenly Manse dropped to the floor, crawled away, and slid under the bed and lay very still. When he did not move for several minutes, I had a lantern brought close and looked under the bed and, to my surprise, he was sleeping peacefully. I called his name but he did not answer. So we let him sleep."

Major Sanders nodded.

"And that is where I found you, Manse, when I came to the room after tending Millie's injuries," Major Sanders said.

Manse shook his head, hoping to shake pain from it, but the throbbing only intensified.

He heard what they were saying, but it was as if they were talking about someone else.

"Manson has had nightmares before," Millie said. "Surely you recall, Major, that shortly after we were married he asked you about continuing to take laudanum so he could sleep without having bad dreams – and you prescribed an ounce before bedtime."

"I remember," Major Sanders said. "That much laudanum should keep a man asleep for about seven hours. Does it do that for you, Manse?"

"It did for a while," Manse replied. "But recently I've been waking up earlier and earlier. When that happens I usually have a drink or two, and take some more laudanum – then go right back to sleep. But sometimes I wake up in a cold sweat, and I know I've been dreaming because I remember parts of the dreams and I'm afraid to go back to sleep," Manse searched Millie's eyes. "Millie seems to sense when I am dreaming. She wakes up and holds me and talks to me until I relax," he said.

Major Sanders waited until Manse looked from Millie to him.

"Do you remember," he asked, "when you started having nightmares?"

"I remember having scary dreams about the devil and ghosts and things like that when I was a little boy – like I reckon most children do," Manse said. "But the kind of nightmares I have now started during The War."

Captain Smith interrupted.

"I am sure that every man who ever experienced combat has had bad dreams about it later on in life," he said. "I know I do. Some nights I relive the loss of my foot – and the loss of comrades – the kinds of horrors we all witnessed," Captain Smith said. "I recall that you once told me, Major Sanders, that it was your observation that the more violence a man experienced during The War, the more vivid his nightmares are – and the more often they recur." He hesitated, choosing words carefully. "But, thanks be to God, I've heard of damned few men who – how shall I say it? – go *berserk* – and attack those they love and –"

The captain stopped in mid-sentence.

"You are right, my friend," the doctor said. "Fortunately it doesn't happen to many men. But nonetheless, it *does* happen."

Major Sanders returned his attention to Manse.

"Were you having nightmares last night?" he asked.

"Now that you mention it," Manse said, "I do seem to recall some pieces of dreams that were in my mind when I woke up. But after a few minutes they went away."

"And while we have been talking here," the major asked, "have some of those same pieces-of-dreams returned again?"

"Some strong flashes of them – yes, sir. Like lightning in my mind – "

" – or like flashes of artillery fire – lighting a smoke-darkened battlefield – " Major Sanders finished the sentence.

"That's exactly it!" Manse stood, but Millie pulled him back to sit beside her.

Major Sanders nodded slowly.

"It is called The Nostalgia, Manse," he said. "I've seen a lot of it since The War. It seems to have its greatest effect on men who experienced a lot of hand-to-hand combat – close-quarters-killing – and those who were wounded more than once – particularly men rendered unconscious by artillery concussion."

Major Sanders took a plug of tobacco from his pocket, then decided not to chew, and put it back.

"No one – not doctors or anyone else – fully understands The Nostalgia," he said. "All we know is it is much more serious than having nightmares and waking up screaming and bathed in sweat. Men who suffer The Nostalgia arise from their nightmares and relive memories as though they were actually occurring again. Anyone who sees them thinks they are awake. Indeed, the men believe they are awake. They believe that what they see is real. To them a piece of furniture may become a cannon. Someone who walks by them or speaks to them or touches them may be perceived as an attacking enemy – and they defend themselves as violently as if they were in combat," Major Sanders nodded solemnly. "The results can be devastating," he said.

Millie squeezed Manse's hand.

"What you're saying, Major Sanders, is that last night Manson thought he was back in The War," she said.

"He didn't *think* he was back in The War, Millie. As far as he was concerned, he *was* back in The War."

"I knew it," Millie smiled. "I just knew you wouldn't hurt me, Manson," she was almost jubilant. "You were striking out at something or someone who exists in one of your nightmares."

"But it was *you* he hit," Captain Smith said. "And it was my men he attacked. I don't even want to contemplate what would have happened if he had been armed with a pistol – or knife – "

"Oh, Papa, Manson wouldn't have –" Millie looked at Manse. "You wouldn't have – killed anyone? Would you?"

In silence they waited for his reply.

When words came to him, Manse directed them to Millie.

"What Surgeon Major Sanders says is true," he said. "Last night I was reliving part of The War in my mind," he held her eyes with his. "But what you said is also right – I wasn't hitting you, Millie. I didn't see you, I saw someone else – and I attacked that someone else. The only problem is that your Papa is right, too – it was *you* I struck and hurt. And if I'd had a weapon, I most likely would have killed everyone here – including you – and our baby," Manse held his breath to stifle tears.

Millie shook her head.

"I'll never believe that," she said.

Then she looked from Manse to Major Sanders.

"Isn't there anything you can do?" she asked.

"If there is a cure for The Nostalgia, Millie, I am not aware of it," Major Sanders said. "I have read, however, that with the passage of time, episodes of The Nostalgia tend to decrease in frequency – though that is not always the case."

"Even if there is no cure, surely there must be something you can prescribe that will help," Millie said.

"Only laudanum – and other forms of opium – to ensure sleep. And even with increased medication, I suggest that you and Manse still take certain precautions."

"What do you mean by precautions?" Millie asked.

"Night-time separation – "

"I will not be separated from Manson at night, or any other time," Millie glared at Major Sanders. "He is my husband, and we will share the same bedroom, no matter what. I will take care of him as I cared for him when he was in the dark sleep. And he will be healed just as he was healed then."

"That is wishful thinking, Millie," Captain Smith raised his voice. "Damned dangerous – stubborn – wishful thinking – "

"Don't shout at me, Papa!" Millie's voice rose louder than her father's. "Manson and I will decide what Manson and I will do – not you and Major Sanders – "

Manse touched Millie's lips with his index finger, then he kissed her swollen lips with his swollen lips.

"I don't think we ought to take any chances, Millie," he said. "In three months our baby will be born. Until then, let's follow Major Sanders' advice."

He turned to the Major.

"Will it be all right for me to stay in Millie's room with her until she goes to sleep?"

"As long as you remain awake, there shouldn't be a problem," the doctor said.

Manse managed to smile at her.

"I will stay with you every night until I am sure you are sleeping," he said. "Then I will go to the front bedroom and take my medication and sleep. And first thing in the morning, I will come back to you. The only time we will be apart is when you are asleep."

"And after our baby comes?"

"We'll see how I'm doing – then decide about that."

Millie was silent for a minute.

"All right, Manson, I'll agree," she said, and forced a smile. "But you must promise never to leave me at night until after I have gone to sleep."

-25-

Manse was careful not to deviate from the precautions mandated by Surgeon Major Sanders, but his fear remained that the Nostalgia would return, and somehow he might hurt Millie.

To assure himself that he would sleep through the night, Manse doubled his night-time dose of laudanum — without asking Major Sanders' approval — with the result that, when he went to bed, he passed into unconsciousness rather than mere sleep — and suffered intense headaches when he awoke.

Never sure what had happened during the night, each morning he went directly to Captain Smith's room to ask if there had been problems. And only after the Captain assured him that all was well, did he go to Millie's room to have breakfast with her — to renew their closeness — and to discuss with her his plans for the day.

Manse used Millie's knowledge of the ranch's operation as an excuse to linger at the main house after breakfast — and to return there early for lunch — to consult with her about problems and solutions.

After their mid-day meal, they took a walk, then went to Millie's bedroom for a quiet hour together before Manse returned to his responsibilities as a rancher.

While he was away from the house, Millie reviewed ranch accounts and wrote letters — then took a nap before she bathed and dressed and came downstairs to the study where Manse found her at day's end.

Weather permitting, they sat on the verandah until dinner. Manse drank bourbon. Millie drank herbal tea. And again they talked — never shying away from discussion of nightmares and The Nostalgia. It was as if their willingness to confront the subject made it less threatening.

But the very best part of each day for Manse was the intimate few hours he spent with Millie before he went to his bedroom to sleep.

Neither of them liked spending their nights apart, but they both accepted the need for caution.

Millie was convinced, however, that time would cure The Nostalgia.

Manse wanted to believe she was right.

Together they reinforced each other's faith in themselves and their love.

***

As days grew shorter and nights longer, the Nostalgia did not recur, and their life settled into a tranquil routine.

By the beginning of her eighth month, the protrusion of Millie's normally slim waist appeared disproportionately large.

Three times each week during that November, Auntie Robin and Lupita spent the afternoon massaging her back and thighs, and teaching her exercises that they believed would turn the baby from feet-first to head-first. But their efforts brought no changes – and served only to spark loud and belligerent midwifery debates between the women.

Indeed, their confrontations became so intense that Millie forbade their visiting her at the same time.

Nai-Se-Kashrah refused to enter into the arguments. It was her contention that when the baby was ready to meet the world, it would decide which way to emerge and would turn itself accordingly.

And when the time for birthing finally arrived, Manse, Captain Smith and Major Sanders drank bourbon and brandy in the parlor while Millie endured more than seven hours of labor in her room upstairs.

As Nai-Se had predicted, the baby began to turn with Millie's first contractions. At that point, the *comadrona* assumed command. Auntie Robin and Lupita did whatever she said, and Millie became so actively involved in following Nai-Se's directions that she had little time to think about pain.

The three midwives helped Millie to alternate positions during each contraction – lying on her back during one – then standing during the next – squatting during the next – then crouching on all-fours for the next two – breathing on command, then relaxing.

And in each position, Nai-Se slid her slender hands inside Millie, to help the baby alter its position.

And so it was that, at 3:39 a.m. on December 15, 1868, Ella Manson Jolly was born.

Out of deference to her seniority, Auntie Robin was allowed to catch the baby, who weighed just over seven pounds. Lupita tied off the cord, and Nai-Se cut it. Lupita caught the placenta. It was, according to Auntie Robin, "as easy as breech birthing ever gets."

Then Millie picked up her tiny daughter and looked at her for the first time.

Ella Manson Jolly was definitely her mother's child. Red hair, narrow face, sharp nose and long slender body.

The midwives immediately knelt by the bed and prayed, each to her own savior, then they bathed Millie, used cotton to staunch the ooze of blood, and covered her and her newborn with a sheet and blanket.

Lupita left to take soiled linens downstairs – and to bury the muslin wrapped placenta.

"Go fetch Mister Manson to come see his daughter," Millie said to Auntie Robin.

When Auntie Robin left the room, Nai-Se brought Millie a cup of herbal tea.

"Drink this," she said. "It will renew your strength, and make healthy milk for the baby."

Millie drank the bitter-sweet brew.

And when Nai-Se took the empty cup from her, Millie smiled at her.

"From the very beginning," she said, "your voice and your touch made me know that everything would be all right."

She reached up and embraced the *comadrona*.

"Great faith and power dwell within you, Señora," Nai-Se said. "That is why your seed takes the form of a woman-child. The spirits bless a mother by giving to her a woman-child – for we are the creators, the givers, the holders of life."

She took Millie's hands and drew them to her face, smiled and let tears fall on Millie's palms.

"Your daughter is whole and beautiful," she said. "And she will be your greatest comfort throughout the rigors that lie ahead in your life. Now close your eyes, Señora, and rest."

Nai-Se folded Millie's arms around her infant, and they slept.

***

Millie awoke to the exquisite feeling of her daughter nursing at her breast.

Manse was standing by the bed, watching, beaming. He leaned over and kissed Millie's lips, then kissed his baby girl's cheek.

He and Millie grinned and said, in unison, "she is beautiful, isn't she?"

Captain Smith and Major Sanders maintained a respectful distance across the room.

"Come here, Papa, and look at your grand-daughter," Millie pulled aside the rebozo and let Captain Smith and Major Sanders see the naked baby at her breast.

"Ella Manson Jolly," she said, "this is your Grand-Papa."

The Captain took a step toward the bed, then hesitated.

"Now don't be silly, Papa," Millie said. "There is nothing here that you haven't seen before," Millie stretched out her hand.

The Captain came closer, leaned over and kissed her forehead, then accepted her hug – and kissed the top of his grand-daughter's head.

At Millie's invitation, Major Sanders came to the bedside and looked at mother and child and nodded that all was well.

When the Major and the Captain had left the room, Manse sat on the edge of the bed and held his daughter, and Millie touched his cheek, and their tears of happiness flowed.

-26-

Manse loaded two cartons onto the back of the buckboard, then went back inside the General-Store-Postoffice and brought out a larger box, wedged it between the cartons, and used a length of rope to tie everything securely in place.

This morning's errands in Cameron should have taken less than an hour, but the town was crowded with holiday shoppers, and they all recognized and spoke to him, and he exchanged pleasantries with each of them, in order not to be thought impolite. So it was now nearly noon, and he had been in town almost three hours, and had just now completed the last of the items on his list.

As Manse climbed up onto the buckboard, Sheriff A.D. Cooper rode by on his black mare, and touched the brim of his hat in silent salute. It was a friendly greeting, and it came from a man who was a close friend of Captain Smith, so Manse responded with a respectful nod, and a tip of his hat.

But he couldn't shake his nervousness at the sight of the man.

Manse had been on the run, living outside the law, for too long.

And Sheriff Cooper was the highest law enforcement officer in Milam County, and he no doubt had copies of Manse's Wanted Poster in his office – and had discussed Manse's presence in their jurisdiction with the sheriff of Robertson County – and the Texas Rangers stationed at Waco.

Though Captain Smith had repeatedly assured Manse that he was absolutely safe living and working in the midst of ex-confederates – and Manse didn't doubt that in Milam and Robertson Counties the Captain's protection was above any law – still he worried.

Too many people knew who he was, and where he lived – and the size of the reward on his head – which was precisely the reason he rarely ever came into Cameron.

His dread of strangers persisted, and the nearest and largest concentration of people he did not know was in the town of Cameron.

His fears had increased when Captain Smith wrote to the Masonic Lodge in Anderson District, asking that Manse's records be transferred to the San Andres Lodge in Cameron.

When, however, the records eventually did arrive without incident, Manse was forced to conclude that his Masonic brothers in South Carolina were guarding the secrecy of his whereabouts just as Captain Smith said they would.

But Manse remained cautious – to the extent that, though his Masonic credentials were all in order, he had not yet come into Cameron to be formally inducted into the San Andres Lodge.

And his mail still came to *Red Horse* in care of the General Store, and was picked up and brought to him by Asa.

In his most recent letter, Tom had written that the Union army had neither lowered the reward for Manse Jolly – nor lessened its interest in finding him.

Troops were still camped near the Jolly farm in case Manse came home for another visit.

Rumors were rampant that Manse had returned to the Anderson area along with Texas Brown – and that the two of them lived in the mountains from where they commanded the stronger, bolder Klan, in confrontations with occupation troops, carpetbaggers, freedmen and scalawags.

That rumor pleased Manse.

As long as the Union Army believed he was in South Carolina, they wouldn't be looking for him in Texas.

Texas.

The name brought guilt's cold bile to the back of Manse's throat.

He pushed the taste down into his stomach, took a bottle of bourbon from beneath the buckboard seat, drank, swallowed, and felt warmth displace chilling.

Then he forced a smile, to himself as well as to others who greeted him, and started the buckboard moving along Cameron's main street – and out of town.

He was determined that nothing was going to spoil this day.

It was Christmas Eve, and he had come into Cameron to pick up gifts he had ordered for Millie and Ella – the two ladies who were the center of his life – and the center of his happiness.

***

Christmas morning, Manse awoke early – lying on his stomach beneath the dining room table.

He smelled and tasted blood before his eyes focused and he saw it pooled on the floor beside his face.

He touched his beard and traced the trail of crusting red to his nostrils.

He raised his head and saw Major Sanders, Captain Smith and Asa standing by the doors leading to the verandah.

Near them were two foremen and four ranch hands – pistols drawn – arms hanging loose by their sides.

The drums in Manse's head throbbed so loudly he could barely hear Major Sanders' voice.

"Just stay where you are, Manse," the Major said. "And slowly slide your rifle and sword out from under the table."

Only then did Manse realize the weapons were beside him.

And with that realization came fear.

He pushed his rifle and short sword toward a foreman who reached under the table to take them.

The ranch hands holstered their weapons.

Manse crawled from beneath the table on a floor covered with splinters of glass.

He stood and looked around.

The dining room was a shambles. Mirrors were shattered, chinaware and crystal broken, windows shot out.

Though he remembered nothing, Manse was sure he knew what had happened.

"Millie?" he said, and looked helplessly at Captain Smith.

"She is fine," Major Sanders said. "You went to her room, but the night-servant had locked her door as I ordered her to do," the

Major's voice was matter-of-fact. "I don't think I need tell you that you must have forgotten to lock your own door."

"But I did lock it, Major," Manse said. "I lock it every night just before I take my medicine. And I always put the key in the table drawer before I lie down."

Manse tried in vain to remember.

"Usually I'm asleep in a matter of minutes," he said. "And I don't have dreams or The Nostalgia and don't wake up until dawn."

Major Sanders spat in the brass spittoon.

"I am afraid," he said, "that you've been taking laudanum for so long, you've built up a tolerance. And when you rose up in The Nostalgia last night, you somehow knew where that key was. I don't know exactly where you thought you were but I venture to guess you went down the hallway, to that other bedroom, looking for a place to hide. And when you couldn't get in, you made your way downstairs and found your rifle and close-quarters sword – then saw your reflection in the dining room mirror and thought it was the enemy and opened fire."

The Major spat again.

"You sure shot hell out of the place," he said. "Thank god everybody inside and outside the house had enough sense to stay away. I'm not sure what caused your nosebleed. That is all that it appears to be – just a nosebleed – no sign that you wounded yourself in your attack."

"Why don't you go upstairs and wash up," Captain Smith said. "Then go see Millie. The Major and I have prevailed on her not to come downstairs. We convinced her you were sleeping-off the Nostalgia, and that you have not shot anyone, nor have you been shot. She is, of course, anxious to see you."

Manse looked at the Captain.

"I am sorry about what happened, sir," he said. "And I insist that you let me pay for the damage. I have money in a pouch in my supply sack, as you know."

"We'll talk about that later," Captain Smith said. "Right now, go see your wife and daughter. After all, it is Christmas. And I assure you that, with the efforts of Asa and his brother and their families, we will have this room in condition for dining by mid-afternoon."

Manse hesitated, unsure what to say.

Then, one at a time he met and held the gaze of each man in the room and said, "thank you – and Merry Christmas."

***

They were upset by what occurred Christmas Eve.

Manse more so than Millie.

She insisted that it was all part of the healing process – that Manse was working the demons out of his head and heart and soul – and that eventually everything would be all right.

Manse was not so sure he would ever be free of them.

Every evening after dinner they went upstairs where Manse held the baby (before and after she nursed) until Auntie Robin took her to bed. Then he and Millie held each other and talked.

And the subject they could neither avoid nor resolve was The Nostalgia.

During those discussions, Manse drank coffee with his brandy or bourbon, to help him stay awake – and he remained in the room with Millie until she was asleep.

Then he went downstairs to the study where Captain Smith and a ranch hand waited for him. He and the captain talked for a while. Then the captain went to his room.

Manse usually read or just sat in front of the fire drinking for another half hour before he walked upstairs with the ranch hand.

He had agreed to follow whatever new precautions Surgeon Major Sanders and Captain Smith thought necessary – including their decision to lock him each night in a small upstairs bedroom.

In addition to a bed, the room had a privacy screen, an armoire with the mirror removed, a desk and chair, and a hanging lantern.

Its single window was slat-boarded from the outside with one-by-tens spaced two inches apart to allow morning sun to enter, but nothing – and no one – to leave.

A ranch-hand sat outside the door. His instructions were to stop Manse if he somehow got through the locked door. Otherwise, regardless of what noises he heard coming from inside the room, he was to do nothing.

***

***

In mid-January Manse broke through laudanum's sleep barrier and arose from nightmare's war to do battle with himself in his locked bedroom.

He smashed the privacy screen and chair to kindling.

His nose bled profusely, saturating his night-shirt.

He pulled drawers from the desk and bureau and threw them against the window, breaking every pane of glass.

Then he crawled under the bed and went to sleep.

The next day, Captain Smith ordered all furniture removed except the bed – then the window was boarded from the inside with solid planking.

***

In February his medication failed again.

Manse tore apart the bed, saturated the bedding with lamp oil and set it ablaze.

Smoke alerted the guards who opened the door and found him curled up in the corner, semi-conscious. They dragged him from the room.

Before the fire could be extinguished, it did enough damage to cause Captain Smith to have the lantern and lamp oil removed and a double-bunk built and anchored to the wall.

When Millie saw the room, she felt angry and sad.

It was, she said, no more than a prison cell. She would not tolerate such treatment of her husband.

Manse put his arm around her and told her that while the room was small and dark –and certainly not as nice as sleeping with her on a feather mattress – it was a hell of a lot more comfortable than a lot of places he had slept during The War.

It would suit him fine, he said.

"Well, if you say so," Millie said, and left – and never returned to that room.

***

***

Intertwined after love-making, Manse lay on his back – Millie on top of him. The odor of their ardor filled them with peace. Manse wanted more than anything else to close his eyes and sleep close to her – but he dared not.

His bladder was full, and her weight on top of him added urgency to his need to relieve himself. He put his arms around her shoulders and slowly turned on his side, disengaging himself from her as he eased her onto the bed beside him.

She stirred softly, sleepily, and spoke his name.

He kissed her and sat on the edge of the bed, then stood and walked to the privacy alcove, urinated, put on his clothes, returned to the bed, and stared at her body glistening in the candlelight.

Millie sat up, then got out of bed, smiled at him through half-closed eyes, put on her robe and walked with him to the door.

They kissed, embraced without words, then Manse opened the door, entered the upstairs hallway, closed the door behind him, and waited until he heard her lock it.

The two ranch hands assigned to guard him that night were waiting. They nodded without speaking, and walked with him to his room where they waited while he undressed and put on a nightshirt, then took his medication and drank a half-glass of bourbon. After that, they locked him in the darkened room for the night.

***

In the darkness of her room, Millie began to cry, as she cried every night after he left her – tears of frustration that she could do nothing to help the man she loved defeat the malady that caused them both so much pain.

She knew that their reassurances to each other were facades, behind which they hid their true feelings.

She implored Surgeon Major Sanders to find a solution – a cure.

But the only solution he was able to offer was increased doses of laudanum.

***

***

During April The Nostalgia returned twice, but there was little damage he could do to himself or the room.

Indeed, were it not for waking up on the floor, his beard and night-shirt soaked with blood from his nose, Manse would not have known that anything had happened during the night.

Only Asa, who brought him water, a washing bowl and clean clothes every morning, saw the evidence.

**

In May The Nostalgia began recurring weekly.

And tonight – the second night of June – as Manse Jolly lay in the dark, sweating in his windowless cell, he realized that now there was something very different between him and Millie – something he felt whenever he embraced her.

It was the same response he often sensed in people – but never so powerfully and intimately as he felt it with this woman he loved more than life itself –

– Millie was afraid of him.

-27-

The summer's normal fare of thunderstorms began to roll out of west and northwest Texas in mid-June. But it was soon apparent that the weather pattern of 1869 was going to be different. Rather than the afternoon storms abating, and skies clearing by sunset, the rain and lightning persisted.

At night the winds became southerly and brought thunderheads and more rain.

Downpours continued into the next morning, then the winds shifted again, bringing more rain in the afternoon.

Soon the soil could absorb no more.

Streams and rivers overflowed their banks.

Manse and the top drover-foreman led ranch-hands, migrant workers and house servants to the northern-most boundaries of the ranch in a desperate effort to find and round up cattle and horses stampeded from their normal grazing land by lightning and thunder, and stranded by rising waters.

Despite all their efforts, dozens of animals drowned daily in normally dry creek beds and arroyos filled to overflowing by the deluge.

The work was exhausting, and seemingly endless.

At the end of each day, the men collapsed in line shacks for a few hours sleep before starting out again in pre-dawn darkness.

They lived on hard-tack and jerky and whiskey.

Manse filled three canteens with a mixture of syrup-thick cold coffee and whiskey — and drank the brew day and night.

When he could no longer fight fatigue, he gave his rifle, pistols, knife and short-sword to the foreman, then tied a rope from his ankle to a bunk-post, took a large dose of laudanum, and slept.

Under the circumstances, it was the most secure precaution he could devise.

And it appeared to work.

The Nostalgia did not manifest itself during even a single night of the days and weeks that he directed the search of gullies and streams, rises and woodlands.

***

On the eighth morning of July, Manse awakened to the eerie sound of silence.

The rain and thunder had stopped

He untied the rope from his ankle, rolled out of the line-shack bunk, stood, and walked outside.

The sun was attempting to break through leaden skies, turning them the color of tarnished silver.

It was time, he decided, to return home – to Millie and Ella.

This was the longest he had been away from them – and they were constantly on his mind.

He reclaimed his rifle, pistols, knife and short-sword – and left the remaining rescue efforts in the experienced hands of the foreman, who warned him to ride slowly and carefully on the sodden trails – and specifically to ride the ranch's western boundary, well away from the flood-stage Little River and its swollen tributaries and arroyos.

***

The morning sky lightened as he rode south.

At mid-day Manse was more than half way home.

But then the sky began to darken.

Black clouds stretched upward from the northwestern horizon to the heavens and closed behind him.

And when they had surrounded him, they unleashed furies of lightning, thunder, wind, hail and rain.

Manse put on his poncho.

Despite the heat, he felt cold.

He took out his canteen and drank, lowered his hat, and wrapped the poncho tightly around him.

A few miles farther, the trail branched off toward Walker's Creek and the Little River – the shortest route home.

But Manse remembered and heeded the foreman's warnings, and took the boundary trail along higher ground leading toward a stand of pines.

Suddenly, through the rain and thunder, he heard muted neighs and saw horsemen waiting in the woods ahead of him.

He estimated their number at a hundred or more.

He reined-in his stallion – watched and waited.

Then they charged out of the woods toward him.

Blue uniformed cavalrymen fired Henry rifles.

Officers raised their swords.

Shots kicked up mud around his horse's hooves.

A bullet penetrated his poncho and burned into his shoulder.

He drew his rifle from its sling, raised it, and fired three times – and knew that battle was hopeless against such odds.

Then he recognized the white stallion and rider closing the distance between them.

He recognized, too, the blond mane flowing from beneath the hat of the Union Cavalry officer charging his flank.

And he recognized other faces – faces long ago forced into his underground cave.

Manse turned his horse and retreated from the barrage of fire laid down by the attacking horde.

More riders appeared –on his left and right – corralling him toward Walker's Creek and Little River.

Then the sun broke brightly through clouds and rain, spinning hot ice around him.

Frozen tears and bright light blurred his vision.

Rifle shots ricocheted behind him as he rode into the woods.

He skirted an arroyo and urged his horse faster.

Soon they were racing along the edge of Walker's Creek.

Then the rain-weakened earth gave way.

Manse and his horse plunged down the embankment.

He struggled to stay in the saddle, but the rushing flood waters lifted him off his stallion and tore the reins from his hands.

He tried to swim, but sank.

He took off his sword and knife and canteens and boots – and his pistols – and managed to get back to the surface – but his efforts to reach shore were to no avail against the raging current.

It swept him along, wherever it wanted to carry him.

Then it smashed his head against an outcropping of rocks – and he felt the impact, and heard a cracking sound – and numbness spread through his body.

He tried to scream into the swirling stream – tried to call out to them – to Millie and Ella – and his Mama – and Rebecca – and Tom – and Melinda.

But the water that slowly filled his lungs drowned all sound and suffocated him with silence –

And Walker's Creek drew him under.

Here, at last, it ended.

EPILOGUE

Manson Sherrill Jolly was born in 1841 in the Lebanon section of Anderson District, South Carolina.

On July 8, 1869, he drowned, along with his horse, in the flood-swollen waters of Walker's Creek, a tributary of Little River near the boundary of Robertson and Milam Counties, Texas.

He was 29-years old.

He is buried in The Little River Baptist Church Cemetery.

His pallbearers were Masons of the San Andres Lodge of Cameron.

The Escort Of Honor at his funeral was comprised of Veterans of the Army of The Confederate States of America.

According to the San Andres Book of Records, a special meeting of that Masonic Lodge was held on August 22, 1869, at which "Brother Manson Sherrill Jolly, a faithful laborer, is hereby deemed worthy to receive the rites of death and burial accorded a Master Mason."

***

Mildred (Millie) Elizabeth Smith Jolly was born in 1847 in Robertson County, Texas.

She married Manson Sherrill Jolly in 1868.

They had one daughter, Ella Manson Jolly.

Following the death of her father, Millie moved to Fort Worth, Texas, where she married Philip Stonemetz of Colorado City, Texas. They had two daughters, Laura and Belle.

Millie died in 1924 at the age of 77, and is buried at Fort Worth.

***

***

Ella Manson Jolly, daughter of Manson Sherrill Jolly and Mildred Elizabeth Smith Jolly, was born in Robertson County, Texas, in 1869.

In 1892, she married Thomas Beekman Van Tuyl, a Fort Worth, Texas, banker.

They had four children: Thomas, III; Andrew, Elizabeth and Laura.

She died July 17, 1930, at the age of 61.

She is buried at Fort Worth.

***

Captain John Gray "Lightning Jack" Smith was born in Anderson District, South Carolina, on Feb. 8, 1825.

As a young man, he moved to Robertson County, Texas, where he became a successful rancher and horse breeder.

During the Civil War, he was a highly decorated hero of the Confederacy.

General Robert E. Lee personally presented him The Confederate Sash Of Valor.

He died September 1, 1880, at the age of fifty-five.

***

In 1874, Maude Jolly died in her sleep – in her rocking chair.

***

In 1875, Tom and Bonnie Largent moved to North Carolina with their son, Manson Sherrill Largent, and Bonnie's daughter, Melinda Jolly.

They later moved to Alabama – then to Texas.

They had four more sons.

***

***

Martin and Rebecca McCollum sold their Texas ranch in 1868 and moved to New Orleans.

In 1870, Rebecca Largent McCollum died in childbirth.

The baby was stillborn.

Following Rebecca's death, Martin McCollum moved to Europe.

He lived for two years in London, and three years in Paris.

In 1876, he emigrated to Rio de Janeiro where he became a successful arms merchant.

In 1881, he married one of the daughters of the President of Brazil.

***

Whit Whitfield and Elk Marett were never unmasked as leaders of the Ku Klux Klan.

Whit served as an Exalted Grand Dragon of one of the South Carolina Klaverns until his death (of natural causes) in 1917. He is buried in Abbeville County, South Carolina.

Elk left South Carolina in 1886, and reportedly lived in several mid-western states before moving to California, then Alaska.

***

Soon after the troops of the US Army of Occupation left South Carolina, Robespierre McGukin was arrested and charged with the rape and murder of a young white girl.

Following a perfunctory trial, he was hanged on the courthouse square in Anderson.

His was the last "legal execution by hanging" in Anderson District.

***

***

In 1912, four professors from Clemson Agricultural College (located 18-miles north of Anderson) surveyed the mountainous area between the Chattooga River and the town of Walhalla, South Carolina, in search of caves whose conditions might prove conducive to the aging and storage of blue cheese.

In a cave behind a waterfall in a remote cove, they found the skeletal remains of a man – along with a silver cigar case and silver buttons bearing the engraved monogram "B" – and the remnants of finely-tooled black boots.

The professors reported their find to the authorities, and the remains were taken to a hospital for examination.

No identification was made.

The skeleton was buried in a potters' field.

The cave proved unsuitable for aging and storing cheese.

***

The reward for Manson Sherrill Jolly "Dead or Alive" was the largest ever offered by the US Government to that date.

It was never paid.

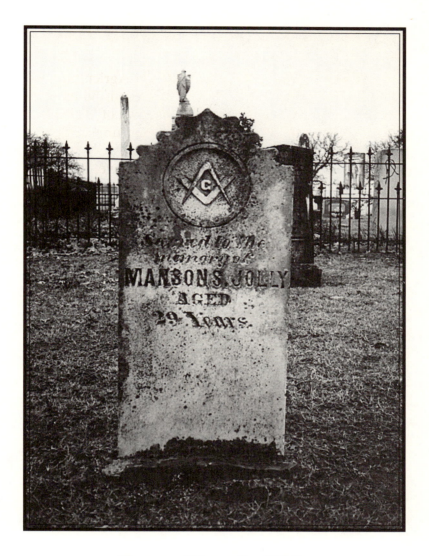

The grave of Manson Sherrill Jolly
The Little River Baptist Church Cemetery
Milam County, Texas.

Sacred To The Memory Of
MANSON S. JOLLY
Aged 29 years

(Photo By Jim Wilson, Pine Bluff, Arkansas, Descendant of Manse Jolly)

The grave of John Gray Smith, Little River Baptist Church Cemetery, Milam County, Texas. The Inscription reads:

Sacred To The Memory Of
CAPTAIN JACK SMITH
Born Anderson District, SC Feb. 8, 1825
Died Robertson County, Texas, Sept. 1, 1880
Aged 55 years, 6 mos, 22 days

ABOUT THE AUTHOR

WILTON EARLE was born in South Carolina and graduated from The University of Georgia.

For twelve years he worked in Latin America as a newspaper, radio and television journalist.

Since 1976, he has been a script-consultant to film directors and producers in Europe, the United States, and Latin America.

MANSE is his fourteenth book.

ALSO BY WILTON EARLE:

FINAL TRUTH: THE AUTOBIOGRAPHY OF A SERIAL KILLER
             (WITH DONALD 'PEE WEE' GASKINS)
CAL: THE WALL
THE COMING
GULLAH
MANSE JOLLY
TANTRA
HANG-UP
TANTRIK CIRCLE
KALI: THE DREAM (VASHIKARANA)
*TERILYNN (PUBLICATION: FALL 1996)

PLAYS
AUTHORIZED ADAPTATION:
GEORGE ORWELL'S 1984   (DRAMATIC PUBLISHING CO)

AUTHORIZED ADAPTATION:
JOHN HOWARD GRIFFIN'S   THE DEVIL RIDES OUTSIDE

IN SEARCH OF FINAL TRUTH   (PRODUCTION PENDING)

Alprazolam

Utopia Limited